Praise for Marina Adair

"With a beautifully layered plot, a unique
cast of characters, laughter, and tears . . .
Marina Adair just keeps getting better!"
—Jill Shalvis, *New York Times* bestselling
author on *RomeAntically Challenged*

"Marina Adair's books always make me sigh
with happiness. She writes warm, funny, wonderful
stories about lovable characters in genuine
situations. I can't wait for every new release!"
—RaeAnne Thayne, *New York Times* bestselling author

"Marina Adair is a breath of fresh air. Her delicious
characters come alive on the page to steal our hearts
and warm our souls, and her stories are the stuff
we dream about when we close our eyes at night.
Don't miss a word from this magnificent author!"
—Darynda Jones, *New York Times* bestselling author

"Complex family relationships ground Adair's second
When in Rome romance, which manages to be lighthearted
and humorous without sacrificing depth of feeling. . . .
Adair masterfully balances their cute developing
relationship with their stressful professional and personal
lives. The result is a sweet, satisfying romance."
—*Publishers Weekly* on *Hopeless Romantic*

"If Marina Adair is not on your literary radar,
she needs to be . . . insightful and witty, steamy,
and hilarious. It has it all. *RomeAntically Challenged*
will be your next guilty pleasure."
—*Fresh Fiction* on *RomeAntically Challenged*

BOOKS BY MARINA ADAIR

Romcom Novels
Situationship
RomeAntically Challenged
Hopeless Romantic
Romance on Tap (novella)

Sweet Plains, Texas series
Tucker's Crossing
Blame It on the Mistletoe (novella)

Nashville Heights series
Promise Me You

Sequoia Lake series
It Started with a Kiss
Every Little Kiss

The Eastons
Chasing I Do
Definitely Maybe Dating
Summer Affair
Single Girl in the City
Four Dates and a Forever

Heroes of St. Helena series
Need You for Keeps
Need You for Always
Need You for Mine

St. Helena Vineyard series
Kissing Under the Mistletoe
Summer in Napa
Autumn in the Vineyard
Be Mine Forever
From the Moment We Met

Sugar, Georgia series
Sugar's Twice as Sweet
Sugar on Top
A Taste of Sugar

Situationship

MARINA ADAIR

KENSINGTON
PUBLISHING CORP.

www.kensingtonbooks.com

To Hannah Jayne,
the Sofia to my Dorothy

Thank you for being a friend.
Travel down the road and back again.
Your heart is true, you're a pal and a confidant.
And if you threw a party,
invited everyone you knew.
You would see the biggest gift would be from me
and the card attached would say,
thank you for being a friend.

—Andrew Gold

Dear reader,

It's been a while since I've written a little girl in my books, mainly because it's been a while since I've had a little girl. Over the years, I've had the honor and privilege to watch my daughter grow up, graduate from high school, and go off to college to begin her next chapter. After all, that's the role of a mom, right? To prepare our kids to leave the nest. Lately, my nest has started to feel a little empty.

I know the appropriate thing for a mom to say is that the present age of their kid is her favorite age. But in all honesty, my favorite age is between four and five. Old enough to manage potty time by themselves but still young enough to curl up in your arms while you read them a bedtime story.

I was looking over family photos when I had my aha moment. What's better that one tiny tyke? Two. Just like that, Lily and Poppy were born. Two halves to represent the fearless four-year-old juxtaposed by quiet spirit, both inspired by the memories and photographs (a lot of photographs) of my daughter during that precious time in her life.

While I can't go back in time, I did use some fun antics and warm memories from my daughter and my fun adventures. I hope you love Teagan and Colin's story as much as I loved writing their journey. Most of all, I hope you get a tiny taste of just how lucky I was to be a part of my daughter's life.

Warmly,

Marina Adair

Chapter 1

If life gives you lemons, it's only fair that a
guy with vodka isn't far behind.

—Unknown

Teagan Bianchi was at the crossroads of Forgiveness and Letting Go when her GPS crapped out—a problem of living life on autopilot for too long. In the past she would have relied on her intuition. But intuition was one finicky prick.

"Are we there yet?" a tiny voice asked from the back seat. It was the fifth time since their last potty stop. One of thousands on their trip from Seattle to California.

Teagan always encouraged curiosity in her daughters, so it wasn't the question that bothered her. It was the feelings it evoked. It made her feel like a fraud. Even worse, a failure.

"What does your tablet say?" she asked Poppy, her elder daughter by seven minutes. After thirty-three weeks of sharing thirty-six centimeters, the twins had come out of the womb inseparable.

"Da blue dot is by da red dot," Poppy said, her Ts sounding more like Ds.

"What number does it show?" She glanced over her shoulder at her daughter, and all four years of her smiled back, filling Teagan with a sense of purpose. With the disillusionment of her marriage in the rearview mirror, she was moving away from her immediate past and toward a happier and simpler time.

"Five," she said, holding up the coordinating number of fingers. "One, two fwee. Four. Five."

"That's right. Good job," she said, and a bark of agreement came from the back seat as a wet nose nudged her shoulder.

Their horse-sized puppy, who'd broken free from his crate—with help from his two partners in crime—wedged his head between the two front seats.

"GD, back seat only."

Garbage Disposal barked excitedly at the mention of his name, then took a flying leap, and 120 pounds of dog landed on the passenger seat with a thud. Teagan leaned right, pressing herself against the window to avoid being smacked in the face by a wagging tire iron.

"You want me to pull over and put you in the cage?" she threatened but he panted happily and stuck his head out the open window so he could drool on the cars behind them. Part Portuguese water dog and part Great Dane, Garbage Disposal looked like a buffalo with two left feet fathered by Mr. Snuffle-upagus. While he more than lived up to his name, he had a heart the size of his stomach.

Teagan pulled through the quaint downtown, noticing gas-lamped streets, brick sidewalks, and awninged storefronts, then turned down Lighthouse Way, where the landscape opened, revealing the crystal blue waters of the Pacific Ocean. Coiling with intensity, the waves gathered speed before crashing against the cliffs ahead. On her left sat rolling hills dotted with cypress trees and rows of bright-colored Victorians. To her right was the road to fresh starts, childhood memories . . . and heartache.

It was the last part that had panic knotting in her chest and activating her internal countdown. She was *one, two, fwee, four minutes* away from the place she'd called home for most of her childhood—well, the happy parts anyway.

Pacific Cove was a sleepy beach town nestled between Monterey and Carmel. Settled by Episcopalians, it was a sea of steeples on a stunning horizon. It was later home to many military families during World War II, thanks to its location close to three military bases: Army, Navy, and Coast Guard. Teagan's grandmother had been one of those Navy wives whose last missive from her husband had been a *Just in Case* letter with his wedding ring enclosed.

Grandma Rose had reinvented herself in this very town, and Teagan could too. Or at least that was the hope.

"Are we there yet?"

At a stop sign, Teagan turned back around to look at Poppy. "You just asked that question."

"Lily wants to know. You said we'd be there at *fwee-oh-oh.* And it's *four-oh-oh.*" Hushed negotiations ensued. "Lily say that four comes after fwee."

Teagan's ETA hadn't accounted for the wind drag of towing a twelve-foot trailer or the volume of potty breaks. "We're about four minutes out from Nonna's." Even though Nonna had passed and willed the beach cottage to Teagan, she always thought of it as Nonna Rose's house.

"We're about four minutes out from Nonna's." Word for word, Poppy repeated their ETA to Lily and then, doing their twin thing, her too-big-to-be-toddlers and too-small-to-be-schoolkids had a complete conversation without saying a word. "She's gotta go number one."

Better than number two. "Sweetie, can you hold it for just another few minutes?"

Lily, who was having a silent conversation with the tops of her shoes, shook her head, then gave a thumbs-down to her sister.

"She said no," Poppy translated, and Garbage Disposal barked in solidarity.

Teagan had known that last juice box was a bad idea. Almost as bad as adopting a rescue puppy three months before moving two states away. A clumsy, untrained, former outside dog who loved to be inside and eat Teagan's shoes, handbag, tampons— the list went on.

"Five minutes, that's all I'm asking for."

After an intense exchange of looks, Poppy said, "Fwee works but not four."

Teagan gunned it. She knew better than to tempt fate. Especially when Lily's Go Time was about as accurate as a nuclear countdown clock. T-minus fwee was Go Time—toilet optional.

She blew through the stop sign and took a hard right onto

Seashell Circle. An ocean-soaked breeze filled the car—reducing the stench from Lily's bout of car sickness, which had kicked in her twin's sympathetic reflex.

Winding her way down the hill, she made the final turn into her old neighborhood and a sense of rightness, a sense of home, swept through her body. Because there it was, the purple and white Victorian where she'd spent the first half of her life making memories.

They'd arrived, intact, if not a little wrinkled around the edges, to begin their fresh start, leaving behind a history of pain and disappointment.

Complete with clapboard siding, massive stained-glass windows, and widow's walk, Nonna Rose's house—now Teagan's house—butted up to pristine beach, which was shared by the neighbors on Seashell Circle. At one time, this house had meant everything to her but as she pulled up to the empty drive, she was reminded that Nonna was gone, and Teagan's earlier excitement was painted with a coat of sorrow.

Another thing she intended to change.

With nine seconds to spare, Teagan pulled into the drive and pushed the button to open the side door. Her daughters freed themselves from their boosters and a flurry of arms and legs exploded out of the car. Garbage Disposal sailed through the window as if it was a fence and he was a thoroughbred at the Royal Cup.

Lily ran behind the big magnolia tree in the front yard, lifted her sundress, and squatted—a recently acquired skill. Adhering to the *where one goes, the other follows* philosophy, Poppy did the potty-squat even though she didn't have to go. Garbage Disposal barked and ran circles around them.

Teagan dropped her head against the steering wheel, accidently honking the horn and dislodging a cheesy poof from her hair. Yup, that pretty much summed up the past year.

She looked at the dog hair stuck to every surface, including but not limited to the passenger seat, the dash, and interior roof of the car. Then there were the grape juice stains on her armrest and clothes.

"Why couldn't you have packed lemonade?" That was the one chore she'd left for the morning: packing the kid's snack bags. Somehow in her exhaustion, she'd packed cheesy poofs and grape juice. It was almost as if karma was doing it on purpose.

She thunked her head to the wheel again, wondering about her next move.

"Careful, you might knock something loose." The voice startled her—in more ways than one.

She must be hearing things. Her sleep-free, peace-free, caffeine-free state was to blame. Surely when she looked up, no one would be standing outside the window smiling. The voice definitely had a smile to it. And brought a feeling of nostalgia that had her heart racing.

Don't stroke out.

Teagan closed her eyes for a moment to compose herself. Hard to do when she smelled like vomit and looked like roadkill.

With the bright smile of someone in control of their world, she looked up and—*yup*. She was definitely hallucinating. Because standing outside her window was a blast from her past, who did *not* look like roadkill. No, her unexpected visitor looked cool, calm, and incredibly handsome.

How was it she'd forgotten his family owned the vacation house next door to Nonna Rose? And how was it that the first time she'd seen him since her divorce she looked as if a convenience store bomb had gone off around her?

Colin West, in nothing but bare feet, wet jeans, and bare chest, still damp from washing his truck, looked like the sexy-dad-next-door.

He twirled his hand in the universal gesture for *roll down the window* and, even though her heart wasn't in it—it was lodged in her throat—she complied.

"Excuse that." Teagan looked at her daughters racing around the yard with their sundresses repurposed into superhero capes, leaving them naked. "I'm sorry, they're . . . it's been a day."

"Been there."

At the foreign voice, Garbage Disposal's head poked out from beneath a shrub. Covered in leaves, with one ear flopping topsy-turvy, he chewed on a garden hose—the neighbor's garden hose.

"Um, I think my dog . . ." *Oh boy.*

Garbage Disposal lurched. Hard and fast, galloping across the lawn in record time with all the grace of a flamingo in a snowbank. He was infamous for licking toes, knocking spill-able things off tabletops with his tail, and knowing the precise latitude and longitude to give the ultimate doggie-high-fives to the crotch.

"Watch out, he's bigger than he looks. . . ."

With a single hand motion, Colin said, "Down," and Garbage Disposal lay down, resting his head on his big paws, look-ing up at Colin as if he were his new master.

"Good boy." He crouched down and gave the dog a good rub, which ended with Garbage Disposal rolling over on his back, proudly showing off his doggie bits.

"How did you do that?"

"Magic," he said, sitting back on his heels. That was it. No "Hello" or "Good to see you" or even "Why the hell are you here?" Just a single evocative word.

"Magic."

"He's still got some puppy left. How old is he?" he asked, his attention still on the dog.

"Oh, I have no idea. He isn't mine," she lied.

"Funny, he thinks you're his pack."

"Pack, smack. He looks all cute and innocent and, okay, he's kind of mine. The girls and I went to the shelter and he followed us home."

Colin chuckled.

"And before you tell me what a good dog he is, he's a dog training school flunk-out." Not that anyone could tell, since Garbage Disposal was giving a good-boy wagging of the tail as if he'd earned a gold star in obedience school, when in reality he'd flunked out three times. "Probably why he kept following us when we told him to stay."

"There aren't bad animals, only bad teachers." Colin looked up, his gaze tinged by amusement.

"Are you saying I'm the problem?"

At that exact moment, Poppy jumped up on the porch step. Hands raised to the heavens as if she were some Amazon warrior ready to wreak havoc on the mere mortals, she tied her dress around her neck and pumped a single hand in the air. Lily followed suit until there were two nearly naked tots chasing a dog around the magnolia tree.

"It *is* me," she admitted.

In a very Colin-like move, he rested his arms on the car door frame above her head, leaning in and getting up close and personal. It took everything she had not to stare at his chest, which—with his forearms on top of the door—was at direct gawking level. Looking at his face wasn't any better. He was near enough that she could ascertain he hadn't shaved recently and that his eyes were glimmering with amusement.

"Are you laughing at me?"

"Wouldn't think of it." He didn't bother to hide his grin. "First rule in long trips, superheroes aren't just for boys. Pack dress-up capes, coordinating flags, and plenty of tiaras or they'll get creative." He chuckled. "Just wait until they're teens."

"Is it worse than the terrible twos?" she asked.

"I thought they were older than that."

"They're four, but still going through the terrible twos. I'm afraid it's a permanent condition. You're a doctor. Tell me it gets easier."

"Vet," he clarified. "And I wish I could. Maddie hasn't been easy in seventeen years."

Right about now, Teagan would give anything to go back and be a bright-eyed, naive, and trusting teenager again.

When had everything become so difficult?

"Maddison's a teenager?"

"Unfortunately," he said. "In fact, you just missed her stomping off and slamming the door because I looked at her wrong."

"How did we get so old?"

His eyes slowly slid down her body. "You don't look a day older than you did that summer before sophomore year, when I first saw you."

She smiled with the same mischievous smile she'd worn when she snuck out her bedroom window and met him at the cove. It had been her first time sneaking out, her first time skinny-dipping—oh, she'd had a lot of firsts that night. She could tell by the smile on his face, his thoughts weren't far from hers.

"Just be grateful yours don't talk back yet."

"Only one talks." It hadn't always been that way. Lily had always been the quieter of the two, more cerebral, but after her dad moved out, Lily stopped talking. To anyone who wasn't her twin.

"Even better."

"Oh, Poppy talks enough for everyone in the family. In fact, there wasn't a silent moment on the entire trip from Seattle."

He looked at the small trailer behind her. "Movers coming tomorrow?"

"Nope. This is it." She swallowed because *this was it*. This was the moment every recent divorcée dreaded. The *where's your other half* question.

Surprisingly, he didn't say a word about Frank's absence, but his gaze did shift to the empty passenger seat, and she thought she'd be sick.

Her ex. Her lying, selfish, bonehead of an ex, who'd cost her family nearly everything. The writing was still wet on the dotted line of the divorce papers, but they'd separated a year ago, when things took a turn for the worse.

She knew all too well how confusing it could be for kids when their parents reenacted *The War of the Roses* on a regular basis. By the time Teagan's parents divorced, things had become so bitter, she'd promised herself if she ever had kids, she would never put them through that, so she'd stayed in her marriage as long as she could.

She'd tried so hard to make it work. Frank wasn't a bad man; in fact he was an incredibly sweet man and a good father. But he lived with his head in the clouds and his money on a poker table.

For a long time, she'd obsessed over what she could have changed. Done differently.

"You okay, Bianchi?" His voice was quiet, and she knew he'd figured it out. He only used her nickname when he was razzing her or concerned for her. This time it was a little of both.

She waved a dismissive hand. "Oh, just tired from the drive." Her pants were going to burst into flames for that lie. But the last thing she wanted to do was talk about her last ex with her first ex.

He studied her and then thankfully let it go without any further questions. "If you need help unloading the trailer, I'm right next door." She was tempted to take him up on the offer. She was exhausted, her back was killing her from the long drive, and she still had to empty the boxes in the U-Haul trailer, which was due back tomorrow before ten. But his voice held a cool distant tone.

Maybe the past wasn't buried in the past. Not that she blamed him.

"I've got it," she said, even though she totally didn't have it.

"If you change your mind." He jabbed a thumb over his shoulder.

"Noted."

His face went carefully blank, and he stepped back from the car. "I forgot. You're good at notes."

Well played but *ouch*.

"If you change your mind, let me know. Oh, and for the record, lemonade is overrated, unless it has something stronger in it."

Chapter 2

Sisters never quite forgive each other for
what happened when they were five.

—Pam Brown

Harley Ashford was a lioness.

A big, fat, cowardly lioness who also lacked a brain and a heart. Otherwise, she'd be back in Los Angeles living her dream life, at her dream job, with her dream boyfriend. Instead, she was sitting on the back patio in a pair of pajamas and Nonna Rose's quilted robe, eating chocolate-chocolate-chunk ice cream straight from the carton.

In fairness, chocolate-chocolate-chunk ice cream was a dinner Nonna Rose would have approved of. There was a lot about Harley her nonna had approved of—even the parts of Harley that usually turned people off.

"Love you, Nonna." Harley toasted her grandma in heaven with an ice cream scooper.

As she sat on the edge of the two-story patio, her legs dangling over, she watched the gold and blue landscape, white capped waves joining sand and sky together. Her life was forever buoyed up by this town. Her nonna's house grounded her; it was the place where security and love allowed her to dream of all the things she could become and the woman she could aspire to be.

She was scooping up more ice cream when her cell rang, sending her heart plummeting to her stomach.

Shit. It was Bryan. Sweet, sexy, understanding Bryan, who'd told her he was falling for her. The exact reason she capped things at six months. Always. Any longer and she felt agitated, cooped up. With Bryan none of those feelings arose, until he wanted to take it to the next level.

Harley didn't do next levels. She suffered from an acute case of Dating Vertigo. Even whispers of taking things to the next level made her woozy. Which was why her feet were planted solidly on the ground floor. Things were simpler down there. No room for misunderstandings or unrequited feelings, and absolutely, positively no room for heartache.

Until there was.

Harley was the master of the situationship. Random, shallow, situation-based dating that never allowed real feelings to solidify. If the situation began to smell like a budding relationship, Harley ran screaming for the nearest exit.

Even from the start, things with Bryan had felt different. Around him, she was different. Calmer, peaceful—happy. He inspired things inside her that she'd never felt. Scary things. Which was why she'd waited until he'd left for the work before fleeing Los Angeles under the cover of night.

Subconsciously, she'd headed north, surprised when she pulled into Nonna's driveway. Maybe the universe was telling her she needed a safe place to work through her emotions. And Nonna's house had always been her safe place.

She'd found the spare key in the hidey-hole—another affirmation that she was making a sound and mature decision. Which was why, not wanting Bryan to think she'd been murdered or kidnapped, she called him . . . when she knew it would go to voice mail.

"*Hi, Babe,*" she'd begun. "*Sorry I won't be here when you get home. My nonna, she's . . . uh. Well, she . . . passed on so I need to go home. To, uh, help my sister. Help her look after the house. Not sure how long I'll be gone.*" She'd almost hung up, then decided to add, "*Don't wait for me. Okay, gotta go.*"

She should have made it into the *Guinness World Records* for telling a lie without actually lying. Her nonna had passed a year ago, and while Harley was looking after the house, especially the kitchen portion, the house didn't need looking after. Pacific Cove was the kind of place people left their doors unlocked and their car keys under the driver's seat. As for handling the service, because her sister was a control freak with borderline OCD, Teagan had handled everything—so efficiently she'd handled Harley right out of any meaningful contribution. Lastly, Harley knew exactly when she would be back.

She'd return to LA the moment after Bryan realized there were other, more emotionally experienced fish in the sea and he was better off without her. Or when Harley got her hormones under control and banished the ridiculous notion that she, a four-time romance flunky, could go the distance. Until then, Pacific Cove was her place of peace and harmony.

She considered, for a split second, answering but sent him to voice mail instead. She let out a long breath and dipped the scooper into the carton.

"You're one mean mother clucker, Harley Ashford," she said around a spoonful of melting ice cream.

She was reaching for the dish towel to wipe her mouth when she heard a rustling. No, more like a rattling followed by a series of thumps, loud and determined thumps, which were startling in the empty house. And they were coming from the front door.

She went still and, *shit,* someone was fiddling with the door lock. Unsettling because no one knew she was there. No one! Not even her boss.

Grabbing "The Slugger," a 1965 Louisville Slugger, which Nonna kept in the umbrella stand, Harley tiptoed toward the door. Growing up with a roadie for a father, Harley knew how to handle herself. She might be afraid of commitments, but an amateur intruder didn't rank on her list of things to run screaming from.

Choking up on the bat, she waited until the door opened and leapt out of the shadows.

"Yippie-ki-yay, motherfucker!"

"What the hell?" the intruder screamed as an elephant-sized

attack dog raced into the house barking and growling. "Take whatever you want. Just leave."

"She said a bad word," Pocket-Person One said, while another pocket-person jumped between the adults. "And so did you, Mommy."

One hand out like a crossing guard, the other on her hip, her cape flapping in the wind, Pocket-Person Two shook her head—just once, but Harley immediately lowered the bat.

"Lily says to get back or else," Pocket-Person One informed her and that's when a sinking feeling churned in her stomach. Those two pocket-people were her nieces. And standing behind them was the one person in Pacific Cove Harley had gone to great lengths to avoid.

Her sister.

"Jesus, Harley. Why are you attacking me and my kids?"

Yup. It was Teagan, her—same parents, different last name—older sister who thought she ruled the world.

"Why are you sneaking up on me?" She rested the bat against the wall.

"Hard to sneak when it's my house. Wait." Teagan paused. "Why are *you* here?"

"Um, because Nonna said I was always welcome." And she was hiding out.

"Nonna Rose is in heaven," Pocket-Person One, aka Poppy, informed her.

"Well, an invite now requires some advanced notice or a courtesy call." Teagan entered, and the girls shot into the house, running in circles around the adults, who were also circling.

Harley pulled her phone from the robe's pocket, dialed her sister, and Teagan's phone rang.

"Cute." Teagan sent her to voice mail. "Why are you here, Har?"

Part of Harley, the part who missed her big sister, ached at her childhood nickname. The other part of her went into combat mode. Teagan might technically own the house, but it was Harley's home too. Or at least it used to be for a month every summer and rotating Christmas breaks. Harley had a lot of memories of growing up, but her favorite ones were made right here in this house, with Nonna and her mom—and yes, Teagan too.

"Why are *you* here?" she countered. "You don't come until July and—" Harley glanced at her nieces. "Why are your kids naked?"

"Self-expression," Poppy said, likely repeating a phrase that was one hundred percent Teagan.

Then the toddler raced into the house, her hands out like Superman. Her mirror image followed—her hands dug firmly into her hips, lips pursed as if suffering from chronic constipation.

"You know how I feel about answering a question with another question," Teagan said and—*huh*—her sister suffered from the same affliction.

"I'm here for a long weekend," she said, which wasn't a complete lie. It had started out as a long weekend—that had been five weeks ago. "And you?"

Teagan stepped back and, with a sweeping gesture that encompassed the big trailer in the drive, said, "We're moving in."

"Moving in? Here? Like permanently?" This did not bode well for Harley's grand plan to get her shit together. "Why?"

"It's my house and if you'd returned even one of my calls, you'd know the answer."

Not wanting to touch *that* with a yardstick, Harley turned her attention to her nieces—who were still naked. Pigtails askew and cheesy goo on her cheek, Poppy marched with a stick in hand; Lily followed as if they were the stars in their own parade.

"You been reading them *Lord of the Flies?*"

"Just Peppa Pig," Poppy announced.

"You talk?" she asked Lily.

They both stopped, faces grim. "Families stick together and embrace each other's differences," Poppy explained.

Teagan sighed. "It's just been a long trip."

Harley eyeballed her sister and froze. What the actual fuck was happening? Her perfect sister, who always dressed as if she were brunching at the White House, looked as if brunch had exploded all over her. Her usual soft waves were more corkscrews than curls, her makeup consisted of grape-juice-stained lips, her jeans had tiny cheesy goo handprints on them, and she smelled like—

Harley took a huge step back. "Is that vomit?"

"Maybe," Teagan said. "Probably. Oh, and it's mixed with dog drool."

"That was a dog? You hate dogs." Harley shook her head in disbelief. "Who are you and what have you done with my sister?"

Poppy stopped marching. "Who are you?" she asked like the Cheshire cat.

"Auntie Harley," she said, wondering how long it had been since her last visit. Wow, it had been two years ago, when she'd made a huge mistake—committed a wrong she wasn't sure she could ever right.

"Who's Auntie Harley?"

"Uh, well . . ." *Auntie Harley* volleyed that question to Mommy Teagan. Only Mommy Teagan volleyed back by simply raising one eyebrow. "That's me!"

"Yay!" Poppy shouted and both girls jumped up and down in unison. One minute they were spinning with joy; the next they rushed her, sliding all up in her personal space bubble before shrink-wrapping themselves to her legs like little koalas clinging to trees.

Harley froze, stress hives forming down her arms and neck. She didn't know what to do. Pick them up? Were they too old to be picked up? Maybe hug them and kiss their cheeks? How? They were so squirmy.

Squirmy made her nervous. Made her sweat in uncomfortable places.

Think, Harley. Think. What would a cool aunt do?

"Can we get a high-five? Up high, Popcorn." Delighted by her nickname, Poppy squealed and jumped high to smack Harley's hand. "How about you, Lily Bear?"

Crickets.

Harley looked at Teagan, who shrugged, then back to the girls. As if communicating through the ether, Poppy said, "She wants Lily Cakes, so we're bof snacks."

"It's a twin thing," Teagan explained.

"Right. Up high, Lily Cakes." She held up her hand and, with a sweet, heart-melting smile, Lily gently slapped palms.

Poppy picked up The Slugger and Teagan grabbed it right as the kid pulled up on the bat, ready to swing and take someone out at the knees. Unfazed, Poppy ran into the living room, dropping her last remaining article of clothing—her Wonder Twins Underoos. Lily followed her sister's lead.

"Um, is that normal?" Harley asked.

"Just pretend it isn't happening and they'll put their clothes back on."

"Will she sit on the couch or chair like that?"

"No, we have a strict 'no clothes, no couch' policy."

"As we all do."

"When you have twins, we'll revisit this conversation. Until then I'd prefer it if you didn't pass judgment on matters of which you know nothing."

"Poppy's a little hellion."

Harley meant it as a compliment, but she could see the mama bear flare up in Teagan's eyes. "Really?" Teagan snapped. "Is it like looking in a mirror?"

"Whoa. Why are you coming at me?"

"Look at her. She's naked, screaming like a banshee, and wearing blue lipstick. Blue lipstick!"

"You used to have pink hair."

"That was a rebellious phase, and it was only pink for a week before I went back to blond."

"All I'm saying is that freaking out over lipstick sounds funny coming from a woman in house slippers."

Teagan did that fast-blink thing she always did when trying not to cry, and Harley felt like a jerk. "I just drove twenty-one hours over two days. By myself. With Bigfoot's dumber brother. And twin toddlers. Well, technically the toddler stage ends at three and they're four, but just barely. When it comes to number one, Lily is a sure thing. If the toilet is there, we're good. But Poppy, she's hit or miss, which made the trip super fun. It also causes Mrs. Lancaster serious concern."

"Who's Mrs. Lancaster?"

"Their preschool teacher in Seattle," Teagan said as if it was obvious. "But it's not just her. Frank's mom has serious concerns as well. One being that she thinks I'm the reason the girls don't want to spend time at her house. It has nothing to do with the creepy dolls she collects. I swear some of them are possessed. Oh, and Frank lost the house, which was the last straw. So we're officially D. I. V. O. R. C. E. D." She held up her bare finger as proof. "Which is why I drove down the western seaboard in a car I hate that Frank said I'd love. I hate it. I really do. It looks like a tampon, Har. A giant white tampon on wheels. And these past eleven hours have confirmed a lot of things I hate: like kale, exercise, kids' books that make sounds, dogs of all shapes and sizes, and shoes that pinch my toes." She took in a shuddery breath. "So forgive me if big girl shoes don't rank high on my Mommy Do List."

That was a lot to take in, but Harley had stopped listening after the divorce mic drop. "You and Frank are—"

"Over? Yup." Her sister popped that P with all the fires of hell.

"When?" she asked.

"Three months now."

And wow, that hurt. Teagan had been in the throes of a failing marriage when they'd last spoken, and she hadn't said a word. Divorce was a huge life event. Then again, when it came to huge life events, they were more a "miss" than "hit" kind of sisters. The last they'd spoken had been Christmas, when Teagan called to say thanks for the presents Harley had sent the girls. Books that made noise.

That had been it. Thanks, a few pleasantries, and "See ya." No, "B dubs, Frank and I are toast" or "Things are really hard right now, and I could use my sister." Not even a quick call to say that the girls were now diaper free.

"What happened?"

Harley loved her brother-in-law. He was fun and spontaneous and a lot like Harley. Despite all of his screwups, Teagan
had loved and supported him, never losing hope that he'd eventually turn things around. Her sister's unwavering loyalty had
always made Harley believe that Teagan would never give up on
her either and that, one day, her sister would forgive Harley for
her part in Frank's relapse.

But if Teagan had turned her back on the husband she'd loved
so steadfastly, what hope did a hell-raising sister have?

"Divorce?" she asked again, just to clarify that this wasn't
some Frank-inspired joke where he'd pop out of the closet and
scream, "Surprise!" Because that was a total Frank thing to do.

"Yes. And I don't want to talk about it. Not in front of the
G. I. R. L. S."

"We're da G. I. R. L. S.," Poppy screamed from the front
room, and Harley thought she heard Teagan whimper.

"Okay, you have a point."

"Speaking of points, why are you playing Goldilocks in my
house?" And just like that entitled Teagan was back.

"You mean, Nonna Rose's house?"

"Grow up, Har. Nonna's gone, and she left me the house."

A year ago, a statement like that would have felt like a swift
kick to the gut. Now it felt more like a light punch to the shoulder. It didn't matter what that piece of paper said—there was
no way Nonna was in her right mind when she'd left the house
solely to Teagan. Nonna Rose would never hurt Harley that
way.

As far as she was concerned, this was her house as much as
it was Teagan's and, according to www.LegalEgal.com, owner-
ship was nine-tenths of the law. And she wasn't about to give up
her nine percent . . . or was it ninety? She wasn't sure.

She'd only skimmed the page on contesting wills.

"This will always be Nonna's house. It even says it on the
sign above the front door." She pointed to it as proof.

Teagan walked to the front door, yanked the sign down, and
handed it back to Harley.

"Are you serious?" Harley asked. "This is the sign I made

her for Christmas when I was eight." The sign she'd spent two whole days making perfect. And to maintain focus for two days was a feat even for grown-up Harley.

"How long have you been here?" Teagan asked.

Harley went up on her toes and rehung the sign. "Just a few weeks."

"Then what's up with the remodel?"

Harley put on a bright smile, then did a Vanna White move, complete with the graceful hand whoosh. "Doesn't it modernize the place?"

"It looks like bohemian meets shaman yoga studio."

Harley clapped. "That's exactly the look I was going for."

"Yeah, well, it's not really me. I want it back the way it was."

Harley rolled her eyes. When it came to change, her sister was like a sloth. "I'll get on that right after I get back."

"I give it twenty minutes before Garbage Disposal disposes of your swing."

"It's a free-hanging chair, and the dog would have a hard time chewing through the solid wood bottom."

"You'd be surprised. Last month he chewed through Poppy's mattress. Five thousand dollars later he's still alive. So about the chair . . ."

"I'll take my chances. Like I said, I have a beach yoga class."

"I think you can miss a class, because this"—Teagan did her own, ironic, Vanna White gesture to encompass the entire front room—"isn't happening. You staying isn't happening."

All the amusement was sucked from the room in one breath as Harley had to face the hurtful truth. She'd been the only one playing.

While Harley and Teagan came from the same parents, they couldn't be more opposite. Teagan had been raised by their mom and Nonna, two strong, loving, independent women who held her hand through the hard times and offered her guidance during the big moments. The only hand Harley ever held was her own.

She remembered the time she'd arrived early for her summer visit and Teagan had to take Harley with her everywhere she went. The mall, the movies, her friend's beach party. Teagan had groaned the entire time, but it had been one of Harley's favorite memories—tagging along with her sister as if it was an everyday occurrence.

It was the only time she could remember them both staying at the beach house at the same time.

To call her parents' divorce hostile didn't even come close to describing the disaster. Her dad, Dale, had a Peter Pan complex times three, and when it came to women, he made Tiger Woods look like Husband of the Year.

The look on her mom's face when she'd found out about his philandering ways would forever be etched in Harley's brain.

Holding a laundry basket, her mom stormed out of the house into the garage, where Dale was packing up for a concert. She snagged a roadie glove from his hands and said, "Did you know that California state law says I get half of everything?" She held up the right glove. "And you can bet your cheating ass I'm going to take half your amplifiers, half your drumsticks, half the strings in your guitar, half your boxers. The new ones." She dumped the basket upside down and a pile of material landed at her feet. "Don't worry about your concert tee collection, I've already taken my half."

"I've been collecting those for years!" A hundred shirts, his entire collection, cut right down the middle.

"How long have you been collecting women?" her mom screamed.

"What the hell?" Dale yelled.

"Next I'm taking my half of your La-Z-Boy."

"You're crazy. How are you going to take half of a La-Z-Boy?"

"When I take one of your chainsaws."

Her mom took that fifty-fifty rule seriously—splitting everything right down the middle, including their kids. She kicked Dale out and moved in with Nonna Rose. Since Harley and Dale both suffered from severe wanderlust, Dale got custody of Harley and Teagan lived with Mom and Nonna full-time in Pacific Cove—where Harley always felt like a visitor.

She knew in her heart that her mom would be horrified to know just how deeply the divorce arrangements had hurt her. It wouldn't have been so bad if both sisters had been sent to live with Dale, but her mom had fought for one daughter and let the other go without a second thought.

"Don't get all ruffled. I'll be leaving soon. I have a job in LA that starts next week," she lied—kind of. She did have a job in LA, but she was on vacation for another few weeks and was planning on extending it.

"That might be for the best," Teagan said.

"Right." She picked up her yoga mat by the door, amused at the recurring constipated look on her sister's face. "Can't miss class—I'm teaching it."

"I thought you said you were just passing through. How are you teaching yoga classes on the beach?"

"Oh, it's not normally on the beach. But since it's your first day home, I'll give you the garage."

Chapter 3

When I see you, I admit I start to lose my
grip and all of my cool.

—Unknown

There was still a chill in the air when Teagan woke up the next morning. The sun struggled to break through the early morning marine layer, violet and orange streaks glistening off the whitecapped waves, which were eating up the shoreline as the tide came in.

In the distance, sailboats swayed on the swells, brightly colored windboards caught speeding air, and surfers bobbed up and down, waiting for the perfect wave. Teagan drank in the moment.

"I've been waiting for you my whole life," she said, stepping into the shallow surf.

The rolling tail of the wave soaked the cuff of her jeans, but she didn't care. This was nirvana. Watching the sun come to life while, wiggling her toes in the brisk water as the Pacific danced around her, the sound of the ocean was the only thing that could be heard.

Oh, and barking. Lots of barking. Barking at seagulls. Barking at seaweed. Barking at waves, which constituted nonstop barking.

Teagan had come out to let Garbage Disposal do his morning thing and burn off some of that puppy energy. Twenty minutes in and his energy hadn't dwindled.

Arf! Arf! He dropped the tennis ball at her feet, which bobbed in the water.

"Last time."

She'd said that ten throws back but he was kind of cute when he jumped on the lapping waves, trying to defend his human from the big, bad water. Had the surf been anything higher than ankle-deep, she would have appreciated his protective instinct.

While Teagan loved the beach, she was terrified of the ocean.

Grabbing the ball with the launcher, she pitched it down beach, giving herself a high five when it covered a good hundred yards. Her high school softball team hadn't named her Bazooka Bianchi for nothing.

Garbage Disposal shot off like a bullet, racing down the beach to pounce on the ball after only one bounce. Shoving it in his cheek, he gave a few Marlon Brando barks, with simultaneous leaps from side to side, then was off.

Belly low to the ground, legs moving like a gazelle playing tag with a cheetah, he ate up the beach, getting dangerously close to tackling speed. Speed that would launch her into undertow territory.

With no time to move aside, she prepared for the worst—the worst being landing ass-first in the water. Eyes squeezed tight, arms crossed protectively over her chest, and lifting her right leg to protect her core, Teagan braced herself for impact—a one hundred-and-twenty-pound impact.

In hindsight, the leg had been a mistake, because when Garbage Disposal made contact, she went flying backward, plunging into the frigid Pacific waters. The seventh wave in the set, which surfers claim is the biggest and most powerful, began to curl at the shoreline—taunting her with its whitecapped speed. Teagan had just enough time to block her face when it crashed down on her.

Not prepared for a saltwater neti pot cleansing, or the abject terror it triggered, Teagan held her breath until her lungs burned. She clawed at the sea floor, but the sand slipped through her fingers, giving her little traction.

When she figured out up from down, she was able to stand and stagger closer to shore until another wave hit, this one smaller, but still carrying enough kick to knock her forward.

Better than backward. She was distracted by a face full of water and found herself on the losing end of some undertow, which caused her to lose serious ground.

Garbage Disposal, mistaking drowning for playtime, leapt, his big paws on her chest, his tongue licking her from chin to hairline.

"Stop." He didn't stop. "Down." He lay down on her. "Off."

That seemed to be a command he remembered because he backed away. Teagan got to her feet, only to find herself wading in hip-deep water, struggling for balance as the surf continued to roll in. She was preparing herself to be dragged out to sea, where she'd die the horrible death of her recurring nightmare, when two large hands gripped her arms and pulled her to safety.

"You okay?" her rescuer asked.

She held up a finger. "I need a minute."

Bent at the waist, she coughed and trembled as her savior held her steady. The water swirled around their feet, barely touching their calves.

After she caught her breath, she glanced around. "My dog!"

"I thought he didn't belong to you."

Teagan went still. Beside her, emitting testosterone and Prince Charming vibes, stood Colin. His sun-soaked brown hair was a little wild, the ends blowing in the wind.

He was sporting mirrored sunglasses, navy-blue board shorts, and bare feet—all of which were dripping wet. Besides his dry hoodie, he looked as if he'd just come in from windsurfing. Something he'd done every summer morning when they'd dated.

Teagan met his gaze, soft with concern, and felt herself still trembling from the near miss with the rumbling tide. The past mixed with the present and she found herself wanting to hug him and run home and hide under the covers all at the same time. Embarrassingly, she started to cry. No sounds or actual tears, just a few sniffles.

But she was okay. She looked around to find herself on blessedly dry ground. Her hair was plastered to her face, her pajamas soaked, and her flip-flops were somewhere between Carmel and Mexico but she hadn't died. She wasn't at the bottom of some oceanic trench choking on seaweed and saltwater.

It had been a long time since she'd gone into the ocean. And, if it were up to her, it would be the last.

She looked at Garbage Disposal, who was staring up at her as if she were his favorite toy ever. "I've come to terms with it. The whole lost puppy thing wore me down."

"You have a knack for attracting devoted strays," he said, looking like a safe, calm buoy in the middle of the tsunami of troubles that had become her life. He might have been one of those strays when they were younger, but there was no mistaking the fact that these days, Dr. West was a competent, capable—unflappable—man who'd made himself a happy home.

She was still desperately trying to make her house a real home. For her girls and herself.

"My sister would disagree with your assessment."

It wasn't that Teagan didn't want to spend time with Harley. She loved her sister with the fierceness of a thousand suns. At one point in their childhood, very early on, they were each all the other had—they'd been each other's entire world—then the divorce happened and they'd been ripped apart. That was a long time ago—one time in her life that didn't remind Teagan of failed promises and heart-shattering disappointments.

Harley was sweet and genuine—she didn't have a judgy bone in her body. Her heart was too big for that. Trusting her to follow through, though? That was like playing Trust Me If You Can Roulette, and Teagan wasn't willing to bet her kids' happiness on what was, at best, a total and complete crapshoot. She didn't want to open her home and her girls' hearts to someone who had a hard time sticking.

Harley wouldn't mean to hurt anyone, and she'd be genuinely sorry, but in the end she'd wind up making promises she couldn't keep. Teagan knew what abandonment could do to a person. She didn't want that for her girls. Which was why she was gun-shy about allowing Harley, or their dad, into their lives for any extended period of time.

The occasional Christmas card or birthday call was enough for Teagan to keep tabs on her sister without setting herself up for a hurricane of heartache.

Wanting some attention, Garbage Disposal shoved his big head between her and Colin. Once he'd put enough space between them, he shook. Droplets of water and sand flung all over the two humans. The dog looked proud of his accomplishment.

"Come on, GD," she said. "At least apologize."

Arf! Arf!

"GD?" Colin asked.

"He came with the name Garbage Disposal—I'm assuming because he'll eat anything. But GD is more kid appropriate than me yelling 'God Dammit' every time he does a nosedive into the garbage can or decides my wooden rolling pin is a new delicacy."

"You're shivering. Here." Before she could decline his gentlemanly offer, he pulled the sweatshirt over his head—one-handed in a very masculine way—leaving him bare chested and her speechless.

Good Lord, he was built. The kind of built that came from fighting the waves for sport. He still had a good foot on her, but he'd filled out—everywhere. Defined pecs, rippling abs, trim hips, which barely held up his indecently low board shorts, and the kind of legs that were made for tangling in post-sex sheets.

Maybe it was the sexy tattoo on his calf, his very muscular calf—a nautical knot intertwined with a coat of arms. Maybe it was the way his lips curled up into that *Gotcha* grin. Or maybe it was the way he carried himself, as if saying the world could try its best, but in the end he'd still be standing. Whatever it was, she couldn't look away.

"I see you haven't gotten over your peeking habit," he said laughing, loud and husky.

Her belly warmed, the same way it used to when she'd wake up early, just to sit on the shoreline and pretend to read the latest bestseller, when in actuality she'd been watching him. Board shorts, wetsuit unzipped and hanging from his hips—she couldn't get enough. One day, he'd caught her gawking.

"So you do know I exist?" he'd teased and she'd felt herself blush.

"Just watching the sea otters."

He wasn't having it. "You can either sneak peeks all summer or agree to that date I keep asking you about," he'd said with enough teen-boy swagger to leave her speechless.

"I have to work at the bread shop today." And every day. Side by side with the other Bianchi women. Most times that was exactly where she wanted to be, tucked safely at her nonna's side. But there were times, like this, when she wished the summer was hers, to read, watch the otters, or flirt with cute boys. But her nonna had rescued Teagan from a chaotic and uncertain situation, so Teagan spent her life trying to repay Nonna, even it meant working through the summer and after school.

"Then I guess I'll be coming by to pick up my mom's order." He winked. "And Tee, be ready for me to ask you out again. We could go windsurfing."

"The answer will still be no."

"Until it's yes."

She swallowed hard and began sweating in uncomfortable places. There was a reason she was staring down sixteen and had never been kissed. Well, two reasons. First, Teagan was about as smooth as a bed of nails when it came to the opposite sex. She was shy and awkward, often disappearing behind the covers of a book rather than make eye contact.

And second, "My nonna said I'm not allowed to date until I'm sixteen." She closed her eyes and groaned at how lame that sounded.

"Then I guess I'll have to just keep asking until you turn sixteen."

No boy had ever been that persistent, and she'd never felt the thrill of a crush. But she had a crush all right—a Romeo-meets-Juliet kind of crush that had flutters tickling her stomach every time he stopped by the shop or went out of his way to say hi to her around town.

He was turning to walk off when she found herself leaping to her feet and walking toward him. "Wait," she called out because, with him, she wanted to be bold. To pretend, just for the summer, that she was the kind of girl who said yes to dates with the boy next door. "You should ask me again."

He lifted a brow. *"About the windsurfing or the date?"*

"Neither. I mean the second one." She closed her eyes. *"Actually, I can't say yes to the second one either."*

"I'm getting mixed signals here," he teased.

She groaned with embarrassment. *"I guess I don't know what I want."*

"Good thing that I do."

"And what's that?" she whispered.

"You." He sounded so sincere that her heart melted into a puddle of goo. *"So I guess the question is, what do you want, Tee?"*

"To say yes to the date, but I can't."

He approached her, eating up the distance between them until he was so close she could smell the sunshine in his hair and the salt on his skin. *"Then what can you say yes to?"*

"Hanging out with a new friend."

He reached out and tucked a piece of windblown hair behind her ear. *"And where will we go on this non-date?"*

"Maybe for a walk. On the beach." She closed her eyes, because here came the hard part. *"At midnight."*

That surprised him, which was okay because she'd surprised herself. Teagan liked rules and guidelines—they made the world easier to navigate. She'd never lied to her nonna, never broken a rule, and certainly never snuck out. At midnight. To meet a boy.

"You going to climb down that trellis?"

"You going to be waiting on the beach for me?"

"Hell, yes."

Trying to play it cool, she shrugged. *"Then, I guess I'll see you at midnight."*

A zing shot through her body at the memory. That night with Colin was the first of many firsts. Her first date, first kiss, and the first of many midnight walks along the shoreline holding hands with Colin and talking about their futures. Until, one night, their futures began to intersect and realign, sharing the same direction and destination.

There were still moments, over the past twenty years, when

she'd thought back on that night and that kiss and how magical it had seemed at the time.

"What? I wasn't peeking." She pointed to her eyes. "Just having a little tunnel vision from nearly dying." She snatched the sweatshirt and yanked it on, hoping he wouldn't notice her blushing.

She zipped it up and her heart did a little tap dance. The hoodie was still warm from his body and smelled like surfboard wax and the kind of confidence that came from being at the top of the food chain.

"You still—" he began.

"Think the open ocean is a shark-infested, seaweed-strangling death trap?" A hard lesson she'd learned when her dad tried to teach her how to boogie-board, then got distracted chatting up a group of female surfers. Had it not been for the lifeguard, Teagan would have likely drowned. It was her first realization of how dangerous broken promises could be. "Absolutely."

They were quiet for a moment, as if neither knew what to say next. Then he looked awkwardly over his shoulder. Oh, he was looking for an out.

"Thanks again," she said at the same time he said, "You sure you're okay?"

Again in unison, "Fine." "You're welcome." Followed by an even longer, more uncomfortable silence.

"Your sweatshirt." She started to unzip it and he held out the same hand signal as when he'd told Garbage Disposal to stop. And wouldn't you know it, she stopped.

His lips twitched. "Keep it."

She didn't argue for fear that he'd give another command she'd feel compelled to follow. "Thanks."

He gave a short nod. "Well, I'd better . . ." He jabbed a thumb over his shoulder and, taking his surfboard under his arm, headed back toward his house.

Teagan watched him go. When he was out of sight, she pressed the collar of the sweatshirt to her nose and breathed deeply. He might be bigger than when they were teens, but he smelled exactly the same.

Chapter 4

Having a sister is like having a best friend
you can't get rid of.

—Amy Li

If the universe only doled out what one could handle, it clearly thought Teagan was a badass.

The morning had started out . . . well, like every other morning since she'd been thrust into single parenthood. Frank might have failed her in a lot of ways, but he'd always been great with the girls. He made every day feel like a trip to Disney World. There wasn't a lot of structure or continuity to the girls' schedule, but he managed to get the basics covered.

Teagan was barely coping. She was surrounded by bowls, dirty utensils, and multiple batches of dough in different states of rising. That was just her kitchen. She was still in her pajamas, covered in a mountain of flour, and her abandoned coffee had reached Pacific Ocean temperatures. It was the last part that was the most upsetting.

Eyes stinging from a serious lack of sleep, she stood at the kitchen island, flipping through her grandma's recipe binder. Teagan liked binders, organizational dividers, and colored pens. The only part of her world where she went by feel was baking. While science was the foundation of baking, perfecting a recipe came down to feel. This batch of dough felt like rubber.

"Dammit." She'd over kneaded it.

"That's a bad word," Poppy informed her with delight.

While Lily was sitting on her princess stool with her legs

crossed, reading her favorite book in a calm zen state, Poppy was in a constant state of motion. Her energy level registered a blaring ten. She sat on the floor, using wooden spoons for drumsticks, a large pot for bass, a whisk as a microphone, as she pretended to be a rock star. Garbage Disposal was her backup, howling the entire time.

Teagan's state could be described as sheer panic. Balancing mommy duties while preparing for her first day as a vendor at the farmer's market had her confidence about resurrecting Nonna's bread business a little shaky.

Running into Colin had left her a whole lot shaky. She knew he spent time at his parents' summer home, all the family did, but she hadn't expected their second run-in to be when she was looking like unbaked bread. Then there was Harley. Her *life is one big party* of a sister, who was still squatting in Teagan's house. Scratch that, Harley wasn't just squatting. She'd turned what used to be a peaceful place of solace into an eclectic bohemian burrow complete with a hanging chair that had ER Visit tattooed on every macraméd inch.

"Can you turn it down a little?" she asked. "Just until I get this batch in."

"Oh-tay," Poppy said solemnly while Garbage Disposal lay down in silent protest. "But I was just getting to da drum solo."

"I'm sorry, sweetie. Mommy just needs a little quiet this morning." As she turned to grab the carton of eggs, she stubbed her cold bare toe on a pair of boots that were two sizes too small to be hers.

Hopping on one foot while holding the other, she silently cursed Harley's name.

Either her sister hadn't understood the meaning of "move out" or she didn't care about Teagan's ultimatum, because although a stack of moving boxes had appeared at the bottom of the stairs three days ago, that was as far as they'd made it. If it took a five a.m. drum solo to get her message across, then so be it.

"Actually, you know what, sweet pea? Turn it up."

"Really?"

She looked down at her baby, eyes bright with excitement, and her heart melted. She and Frank may have had a lot of problems, but they'd made two perfect little people who owned Teagan's heart.

She got down to eye level and kissed Poppy's forehead. "Absolutely." Poppy flung herself at Teagan, wrapping her arms fiercely around Teagan's neck. "Love you, kiddo."

In a blink, Poppy was back at her drum set, banging out a beautiful, bold, and migraine-inducing drum solo. And Teagan couldn't help but smile at her little dreamer.

Not a moment later, Harley strolled into the kitchen. Given the evidence of her silky ponytail, wrinkle-free top, and micro-mini yoga shorts, she'd had a blissful night's sleep, a hot shower, and time to give herself a blowout.

The last blowout Teagan had experienced was her back tire, twenty miles north of the California border.

"Morning, Auntie Harley!" Poppy squealed, and jumped up.

"Hey, Popcorn." Harley ruffled Poppy's hair. "Lily Cakes." She gave Lily a kiss on the cheek.

"Did we wake you?" Teagan asked, flashing a pleased smile.

"Nope, the universe woke me." Harley walked toward the back door and reached for the handle.

"No, don't open the . . ."

Too late. The door lock clicked and Garbage Disposal was off, galloping across the kitchen like a horse out of the gate, barking in delight and picking up as much speed as his feet could manage on the slick hardwood floors. His tail nearly took Teagan out at the ankle, instead making a home run with a cup of milk—which crashed to the floor, splattering white droplets everywhere.

"Sorry, little dude. Not today," Harley said, and Garbage Disposal skidded to a stop. No jumping, no licking, none of the unruly puppy behavior he exhibited with Teagan, nothing but perfect obedience.

Traitor.

"What's the big deal? He's a dog. Dogs go outside from time to time."

"This dog can run like a cheetah and eats everything. Hair ties, Christmas ornaments, he even ate a roll of toilet paper. The entire roll. Have you not heard his name?"

"What's outside that he could eat?"

"Besides your yoga mat, flip-flops or the barbecue knobs? Anything on, near, or around the beach? Someone's deck railing or, Lord help me, another one of my patio chair cushions. Do you know how much money I've spent on vet bills? He's barely a year and I'm terrified for the girls' college fund." Teagan lowered her voice and mouthed, "He's a dick."

"Or he's a dog doing doggie things." Harley lowered her voice as if about to impart secrets of national security. "Maybe he just has to do his thing."

"He already did his thing," Poppy informed her. "Two times. One time he did number one and two. One time it was just number one."

"You guys talk a lot about bathroom habits."

"Have you ever potty-trained a toddler?" Teagan asked. "No? Well, I did. Two of them, actually. At the same time. Conversations are necessary for survival."

Harley looked at her like she was crazy. And maybe she was, but wasn't any single parent?

"If he isn't on a leash or closely supervised, can we keep the door shut?"

"Your house." Harley strode to the coffeepot and poured herself the last mug of coffee. Teagan waited until her sister doctored it with cream and sugar—two things Teagan rarely allowed herself—then snatched the mug right out of Harley's perfectly manicured fingers.

"Rude much?" Harley asked.

"Make your own pot," she heard herself say. "You should be thanking me. Caffeine makes you gassy."

"Apparently, it makes you grumpy." She turned to Poppy. "How about you start banging out that solo."

Poppy got one smack to a pan before Teagan grabbed the spoon. "Can you go play with your sister while Mommy and your auntie talk?"

Poppy looked at Harley as if she were a source of authority.

"Seriously?" Harley gave an innocent hands-up, to which Teagan replied with a *don't test me* look moms around the world held sacred.

"Sorry, kiddo. I was dying to be the Anna to your Elsa, but you got to take it up with your mom. She is the keeper of all the rules," she said and Poppy groaned. "I feel your pain, Popcorn."

"Keeper of all the rules?" Teagan repeated. Harley made her sound like some uptight, helicopter mom with nothing better to do than inflict protocols and busybody rules on fun-seeking children.

"You're the one holding the spoon." Harley lifted Lily off the chair and set her on the floor. "Why don't you two go play on my free-hanging hammock."

Two sets of blue eyes looked hopefully up at Teagan. Tired of being the bad cop—she'd had four years of that in her marriage—she ignored her inner safety guard. "Why not. Just be careful."

Both girls jumped up and down in unison before running over to thank—*yup*—Harley. They hugged Harley's legs, Lily on one side, squeezing so hard she scrunched up her face until her eyes closed. Poppy on the other, holding on with one arm, the other tiny fist pumping the air like a bull rider on a bronco. "Aunt-tie Har-ley! Aunt-tie Har-ley! Aunt-tie Har-ley!"

She eyed Aunt-ie Har-ley who gave a *What?* shrug. But her smug grin said she knew exactly what she'd done.

The girls bolted, tearing through the kitchen—but not before giving Aunt-tie Har-ley butterfly kisses.

Teagan's heart gave a painful bump in her chest. Butterfly kisses were *their* thing. Frank didn't even get butterfly kisses and he was the OGC—Original Good Cop.

"Be safe and don't spin too fast," she hollered after them.

Harley hopped up on the counter. "What are you going to say next? You'll shoot your eye out?"

Growing up, everything in Teagan's life had been out of her control. Which explained a lot. Her parents met young, married young, and their relationship never outgrew the drama of young love.

Her mom was a small-town girl with small-town dreams. Her dad was a bigger-than-life guy with a bigger-than-life existence. He wanted to tour the world. Her mom's world was a tidy five square miles. She once said marrying Dale was the craziest and stupidest thing she'd ever done.

Which was why Teagan avoided crazy. Because it usually led to stupid. And she might be a lot of things, but stupid wasn't one.

So she'd gone to the right college, earned the right degree, married the right kind of man. Which was why she wasn't prepared for Frank to secretly gamble away their house, their savings, even the family bread business. The last part was the straw that broke their marriage.

Broke her heart.

"I thought you were taking the swing down?" she said, measuring out exactly three cups of flour.

"It's a chair, not a guillotine." The girls' laughter faded into the background until Teagan had to admit, for the first time that morning, it was actually quiet. "Aren't you glad I didn't?"

No, she was not. Having a moment of quiet was nice. Having her sister judge her parenting was the exact opposite of nice. In fact, the only thing that would make Teagan truly happy was for her unwelcome guest to pack up and move out. At that thought a whispered *Liar, liar* flitted around her head.

"It's a trip to the ER waiting to happen," Teagan explained. She didn't have arbitrary rules. Each and every rule in her PAR-ENTS GET PARENTING binder was there for a reason.

Teagan pulled a tray of Brioche col Tuppo from the oven and Harley snagged not one—but two—Italian sweet rolls before Teagan set the tray on the wood cutting board. She watched as Harley pulled the cute little top off a roll and popped it into her mouth.

Breathing steam out of her mouth, she panted, "Hot. Hot."

"Then maybe you should wait until they're on the cooling

rack before stealing one. Or hey, how about leaving my rolls alone? Or cleaning up after yourself. I had to clean the kitchen this morning before I could start breakfast."

Harley ignored her. "Oh my God, these taste exactly like Nonna's."

The compliment warmed her heart. She worked hard to uphold her family's legacy and do her nonna proud. Teagan had dropped the ball once, allowing Frank full control of the back end of the business, and the results were devastating. It was a mistake she wouldn't make again.

"It's her recipe but it's all in the touch."

Harley hopped up on the counter and reached, once again, for Teagan's coffee mug. This time succeeding and taking two sips before Teagan caught on.

"This is a counter. That is a chair. And each one of those buns took an hour and a half to rise. So, if you touch one more, I'll—"

"What? Shoot my eye out?"

Harley reached behind her and grabbed the coffee beans from the cupboard, then leaned over to fill the machine—all from her perch on the counter. When she reached for a third roll, Teagan smacked her hand with the spatula.

"Ow."

"Sorry, your hand was in my way," Teagan said tartly. "And since when do you get up before noon?"

"Since I turned five and learned how to cook my own breakfast," her sister said as if that were normal. Teagan never knew when she was joking, so she kept her mouth shut. "And I thought I'd help you get ready for the farmer's market before my yoga class." Which explained the yoga mat by the back door.

"You hate baking."

Harley shrugged. "I prefer my yeast from the tap and in a bar full of laughing and spirited people, but I don't mind pitching in. Think of it as my way of saying thanks for not kicking me to the curb." The *yet* was implied.

"The farmer's market opens at nine. I've already made twenty loaves of Coppia Ferrarese." An Italian sourdough whose double-twisted loaf was characterized by its golden color and distinctive malt undertones.

Brought over from Italy by her great-grandmother, the mother, or starter dough, had been in her family for over a hundred years. It was the most valuable thing Teagan owned. And the only thing left of Bread N Butter, the bread company Nonna Rose and her twin sister, Iris, had started in the sixties.

What began as a way for the ladies to keep the pantry stocked while their husbands were stationed in the South Pacific quickly grew from their two-bedroom house into a storefront downtown where they spent over fifty years making traditional Italian breads for the townspeople of Pacific Cove. Until Teagan convinced them to retire so she could open a second store in Seattle. Where she lost everything Rose and Iris had built.

Today's farmer's market marked the rebirth, the phoenix rising from the ashes. She would rebuild Rose's legacy in the same way that Nonna Rose and Zia Iris had begun. And nothing would make Rose happier than for her two granddaughters to share this moment.

And in Nonna Rose's memory, she'd make Harley feel welcome, at least until next week when she moved back to Los Angeles. She didn't want Rose to pay her an afterlife visit to talk about the importance of sisterhood.

"I made Nonna's basil focaccia yesterday." She'd stayed up all night finishing the loaves. "That was the last batch of brioche buns. All that's left are the Parmesan rolls. They are in three stages. Some in the oven, some ready for the oven, and some ready to be dusted with the cheese mix. Can you handle that?"

"You bet," Harley said with about as much confidence as a freshman at a senior party.

"Be sure because I need to be there at eight with enough product to look as if I'm an actual professional, and I don't have extras."

"I've totally got this."

Part of Teagan, the older sister part, wanted to give Harley a chance, maybe even rekindle some of the fun times they'd had in this very kitchen. But the part of Teagan that had been disappointed time and again by the people closest to her waved the red flag. The last time she'd let Harley crash at her place, her sister took Frank to a comedy show—at a casino. Frank cut out at intermission and blew enough money to sink the company.

First step in helping a recovering addict: Avoid tempting situations. Second step in helping a recovered addict: Refer to step one. Her sister literally drove Frank to a casino and vanished to the bathroom. Not that Teagan was blaming Harley. Frank was the only one responsible for his decisions and the subsequent disasters he left behind, but she was disappointed in the role Harley had played.

The last thing Teagan needed was Hurricane Harley blowing through her kitchen. Her car, her bedroom, her bathroom, pretty much any room Harley vacated always looked as if a natural disaster had struck. But Teagan was between a rock and a hurricane. The odds of her finishing in time to set up at the farmer's market were slim to none. Plus, she still had a batch of dough waiting to be kneaded and baked.

"Can you follow directions and a simple recipe?"

"I wiped and washed after I went. Does that count?"

"Don't make me regret this."

With a sarcastic salute, Harley pulled on an apron. Teagan wasn't trying to be a hard-ass, she just had a method—a tested, trusty, and foolproof method. She was a clean and orderly baker; Harley was the exact opposite.

"We clean as we go and no spontaneous additions to the recipe."

"Yes, boss."

She directed Harley to the mixing bowl, while Teagan started placing the filled rolls on trays. And for a while everything seemed to be going well. They worked around each other, moving in harmony. It was the first time in forever that Teagan and Harley had coexisted in the same universe without chaos. In fact, Harley had a fun and goodhearted personality that really drew the twins to her. And before long, the girls had abandoned the hanging deathtrap and all four Bianchi females were in the kitchen baking.

Teagan took in the precious moment and thought how Rose and Iris would have approved. It was reminiscent of the summers when Harley stayed with them, when three generations of Bianchi women would sing and dance around the kitchen.

The moment gave her a small bead of hope for this new generation.

The timer went off and she pulled out the first batch. Perfectly shaped, golden on the outside with a delicious mozzarella, tomato, and basil mixture on the inside, topped with sprinkled with Parmesan.

"You know, when I was little I used to think Nonna smelled like flour and summer," Harley said and Teagan laughed.

"Me too! Although once fall rolled in, and Nonna started baking her panettone bread, she smelled like lemon zest and honey."

"Huh," Harley said, and there was something in her voice that tugged at Teagan's heart. She thought back to those rainy mornings at the beach house and couldn't remember a single memory that included Harley.

"Um," Harley said and suddenly Teagan's heart tugged for an entirely different reason.

"Um, what?"

"Can you come look at this?"

"What did you do?" The little prerolled balls were now big and squishy. "The dough is gooey. How is that even possible?"

"I don't know. I swear, I followed Nonna's recipe, but they looked a little dry, so I spritzed them, like Mom used to do." Harley put her hands up in an *It wasn't me* gesture. "I have no idea what happened."

Teagan rested her palm against her forehead, closed her eyes, and reminded herself to breathe in and breathe out. By the fourth round her stomach had settled. "The ocean happened."

"What?"

"They looked dry because you forgot to factor in the closeness to the ocean. The more humidity, the faster they rise and now they're rising faster than the previous batch is baking. If I don't get these in the oven soon, this batch will be wasted."

"I am so sorry, Tee."

"I know you are. It's not your fault." It was Teagan's. "There are so many little unwritten tips in the recipes. They're almost impossible to execute correctly if you've never made them."

"Wait. I know. Go next door and use Colin's oven," Harley said. "His mom was quite the baker, so they have three."

"It's five in the morning. I don't want to wake them." Especially after the dreams she'd had about him over the past week.

"He's a doctor."

"A vet."

"Whatever, he wears scrubs and I happen to know he works all hours. Plus, he goes windsurfing on the beach every other morning."

Suspicion prickled down her neck. "I thought you said you've only been here a few weeks or so?"

"In the spirit of honesty, I'd lean more to the 'or so' part of that statement. And I happen to also know that he pulled up a half hour ago."

Chapter 5

One day I caught myself smiling and I
realized I was thinking of you.

—Unknown

Colin West had had a lot of surprises in the past few years but
the discovery of Teagan tapping on his back door at five a.m.
ranked in his top ten of WTF moments.

After a long day and even longer night, he'd taken a hot
shower, then crashed. He was three snores from dreamland
when there was a tap at the back door. Assuming it was his
older brother coming to raid his fridge, Colin tried to go back to
sleep. Ethan's wife had put him on a dairy-free, sugar-free, and
flavor-free diet, so Ethan kept a stash of doughnuts and beer at
Colin's.

Then came the second knock, a little louder, which woke the
cats, Purrsnickety and Purrito.

Over the years he'd become accustomed to their quirky
names, but when he said them aloud, he sometimes felt as if the
Man Card god would swoop down and stamp a big, red RELIN-
QUISHED across the front.

By the third knock, the Siamese sisters he'd rescued when
their owner dropped them off at the clinic for shots and never
came back sat on the bed staring at him. One perched on his
chest, the other on his pillow.

"*Purr, purr, yowl, trill,*" Purrsnickety said.

"*Chirp, trill, chirp,*" Purrito replied.

"*Purr, purr, yowl, trill.*"

And so the sisters went on, chatting back and forth like a bunch of old biddies, gossiping about the delusional man who thought his life was his own.

"Fuck," he grumbled. The ladies hopped down and snaked through his legs, nearly taking him out twice, as he padded downstairs toward the kitchen.

A fourth knock sounded, and he decided he was going to kill his brother. And take his time about it. "I fed your food to the cats, flushed your Frosted Flakes, and drank your beer, so go away."

And that was how he found himself looking at Teagan through the window while she looked back. Even with her light blond hair piled into a messy bun on top of her head and covered in flour, she was beautiful. He wasn't ready for beautiful at this hour—especially when there was a ninety-nine-percent chance Beautiful wasn't wearing a bra.

All day long he was confronted with pretty, single women looking to land the successful single dad. Colin wasn't looking to be landed. His marriage had been a mistake—one he would not make again. He'd known exactly who Amanda was when he'd proposed, so it wasn't a big shock when she bailed.

He'd spent three years with his ex, two of them shit, but he'd do it all over again. They had brought him his daughter, Maddison, and she was his world. Had been since the day she was born. Which was the reason he'd gone to exorbitant lengths to mollify his ex. He knew when Amanda walked, she never looked back. Not even for Maddie.

She'd left him behind with a fear of failing again when it came to love.

For a time, he'd loved his ex. Couldn't get enough of her. She was bold and captivating; being with her was like surfing in the middle of a lightning storm. Her unpredictability and worldly sophistication lured him in. Problem was that those traits weren't applicable to parenting.

Not that either of them had been looking to start a family. His dad had just passed when they'd met and they were barely six months into dating when she got pregnant. The second those double pink lines appeared, Colin was committed. After hearing her heartbeat for the first time, he was in love—his little girl had him wrapped around her tiny finger.

Now he had less than five months left before Maddison set off for college. Distractions weren't an option. With prom, graduation, college tours, dorm selection, and registration, his plate was overflowing. He didn't have the capacity to deal with the box Teagan had slapped shut all those years back. He'd put a lock on it with a giant DO NOT OPEN seal. Her moving back home didn't change that. While Teagan had once been the best thing that ever happened to him, she had also, up until his parents died, been the worst.

When he didn't move to open the door, she stepped back. "I'm sorry," she said through the glass. "I shouldn't have bothered you."

She turned to leave, and war waged inside him: Let her go and head back to bed—the odds of his falling back to sleep were one in never-going-to-happen—or find out why she was there.

Curiosity won out.

He opened the door. "I thought you were Ethan."

"I thought you'd be awake."

"It's five in the morning."

"Right. I knew you'd gotten home just a little while ago, so I thought . . ."

"You're keeping tabs on me, Bianchi?" he asked, clueless as to why he'd used her nickname or, more concerning, why his heart raced with anticipation over her answer.

It was likely heartburn from the breakfast burrito he'd picked up on his way home.

"No. I just need to ask a favor."

In a snap of the fingers, his heartburn vanished. "Is something wrong?"

"Yes, everything's wrong. I'd like to borrow your ovens. Actually, I need to borrow your oven and—" She looked down and her eyes squeezed shut. "You're in your underwear."

Like she was one to talk. She had a killer body, her feet were bare, her toes painted a bright blue. And that wasn't the only thing that was bare. She was in a pair of teeny-tiny, silky, patriotic-themed pajama shorts and a faded NSYNC T-shirt, with JUSTIN scrawled across her chest. The bottom curve of the J and N were stretched so tightly, there could be no question about her current bra of choice.

God bless America, the answer was a resounding none.

She must have gotten in a good peek too because she was blushing. A reaction that was as fascinating as her asking him for a favor. She had other neighbors she could have bothered— but she'd chosen to bother him. Why?

"I repeat, it's five a.m."

She let out a long breath. "I know. I told Harley it was too early, but she assured me you'd be awake." Her voice became a whisper. "Sorry, did I wake Amanda?"

Her eyes were still firmly closed tight, as if she hadn't seen everything before. Normally he'd think it was funny, and a little sexy, but Amanda's name threw ice water over the moment. She was not a topic he liked to discuss on a good day, and today was definitely not that.

He'd received an emergency call at two a.m. from a client, Jack, whose horse got spooked and ran through a barbed wire fence. When he'd arrived home, Maddison was crawling through her bedroom window, coming back in from, hell if he knew. She said she was at Shay's, as if A) visiting her cousin in the middle of the night was normal, B) Ethan would have ever allowed Maddie to walk home in the dark, and C) she wasn't wearing a headband for a skirt.

He called bullshit, said they'd talk about it later, then sent her straight to bed. Now his first heartbreak was inquiring about his last heartbreak, as if this was an episode of *Dr. Phil*.

"She split."

Her eyes opened and met his. "I'm so sorry." There was so much earnestness in those big brown pools, he almost invited her in for a cup of tea.

Jesus. He rubbed a hand down his face. He was losing it. It was too damn early for this conservation. And he was too damn tired to play Sherlock.

"I'm not." There. Two words followed by a period. A few years ago, it would have been followed with a few four-letter words, each accompanied by its own exclamation mark.

"Was it recent?" she whispered gently.

"No." One word. Much better than two. It implied "End of conversation."

"Divorce is awful." Clearly, she'd lost her ability to read his mind, not that he was complaining.

"Yup."

They stared at each other, but he didn't invite her in. No way. He'd let Teagan in once before and she'd slammed the metaphorical door shut without any notice, then hung a *Dear John* letter to let him know they were out of business. And he'd rather punch himself in the face than have a therapy session with the first woman to obliterate his life plan. Hard pass.

"You can say no, Colin. I wouldn't blame you." And, well shit, he felt like a prick. He could slam the door in her face, and she'd accept it. Teagan didn't have a vindictive or judgy bone in her body—unless it came to Harley. Those two were like a fork and a power outlet.

"I'm not an ass. It's just early and you caught me off guard." She opened her mouth to say something compassionate and understanding, but since he wasn't feeling nearly as mature, he turned and walked back into the kitchen, leaving the door open behind him. If she wanted to follow, fine, but he wasn't going to encourage anything more than the pleasantries exchanged between one neighbor helping another.

"Be nice," he whispered to the biddies, who took one sniff and, with their noses in the air, walked away as if Teagan wasn't worthy. "Oven is over there. Pretty standard. The bottom one runs hot."

"How hot?"

He turned to see if she was flirting with him, but she was opening each of his ovens, checking the insides as if she was under the hood of a Formula 1 car. She must have liked what she uncovered because she shut each door and began fiddling with the temperature gauges. When she went to turn the bottom gauge, those pajama bottoms fiddled their way up her thighs—way up—and his gauge appreciated just how athletic and mouthwatering her body still was.

"About twenty degrees."

"Thanks again for letting me . . . Oh." She'd caught him staring at her ass.

Then they were staring at each other, but he wasn't going to admit to anything. Neither spoke and the silence grew, thickened with sexual tension until the air crackled between them.

Oh, was right.

She cleared her throat and waved a hand over his body. "Could you, uh . . ."

"I will if you will," was all he said, and he moved to the laundry room, where he pulled on a pair of jeans. When he returned, he found the door open but no Teagan.

She was gone. Only a footprint of flour marked the spot where she'd been. He padded to the door and looked out . . . she'd vanished.

With a sigh, he was about to close it when she hollered, "Hold it. I'm coming!"

Dressed in a new outfit consisting of leggings, a blue tank that read LIFE'S A BEACH, and, sadly, a bra, Teagan crossed the sandy path between their houses. Barefoot and balancing a cookie sheet in each hand, she pushed past him into the kitchen.

He relieved her of one of the trays and opened all three preheated ovens. "Tell me how I can help."

"Maybe put on a shirt."

"Or you could just take off yours and we'd be even," he said. While the jury was still out on whether her "How hot" comment had been flirty, Colin's was unmistakable.

He had spent most of his teen years fantasizing about Teagan Bianchi naked. All it took, though, was one kiss for him to fall so hard, the landing wrecked him.

He was older now, wiser. Attuned to his weakness for commitment-phobes hiding in girl-next-door clothing, which was why he followed a strict regimen when it came to women. It did not include complicated entanglements. Then what the heck was he doing flirting with fire?

She swallowed nervously, followed by an uncertain smile, which made his chest pinch. And that right there was the problem. He had a habit of letting his guard down around Teagan. A dangerous habit he thought he'd broken.

He hadn't always been a cynic. BA—Before Amanda—he was an open guy who laughed and took pleasure in the small things. AD—After Divorce—he'd become closed off and distant, even with his brother. Then after his mom passed a few years ago, he'd been lost. Now Teagan was back on his radar, and it was the first time AD that he'd smiled at a woman with returned interest.

A clear sign to steer clear of anything other than a neighborly wave or asking for a cup of sugar, which was why his flirting had caught him off guard. She looked as spooked as he should have felt because she said, "Be right back," and burned rubber out his kitchen.

In the laundry room, he grabbed a T-shirt that smelled clean enough. *"Then we'll be even?"* he mumbled to himself. "You're an idiot."

An idiot who'd clearly been out of the dating pool too long. Good thing he wasn't planning on diving in anytime soon. His brother would tell him he needed to get laid. Maybe he should. As long as it was a single woman with no complications from his past, he'd consider it.

He found the kitchen empty again. Ovens empty. No bread, no Teagan, just sandy footprints from the door to the far counter. He also found Purrsnickety and Purrito sitting in front of their food bowls, glaring at him for daring to talk to another human before their morning feeding. He put a scoop of kibble in each bowl and gave them fresh water.

His kitchen was still short one baker. He was about to chalk the entire exchange up to sleep deprivation when she walked through the door, holding three additional trays, stacked in her hands, one on top of the other, with none of them touching.

Another baking skill her grandma had passed down. During the summer, when his family stayed at their beach house, Colin worked part-time at Bread N Butter. He'd claimed he was saving up for a car, but really it was all about the beautiful blond girl-next-door. By the time his family returned to the city, he'd fallen hard. But with a hundred-ish miles between them, they'd agreed to leave the relationship undefined. But every summer, they picked up where they'd left off. Until the last summer, when she'd picked up and moved on without even saying goodbye.

"Thanks again and . . ." She put the new trays in and was about to finish that thought when her phone pinged. She checked the screen and let out a long breath.

"Do you need to get that?"

"Yes," she said, but her tone said the exact opposite. He knew that voice, had used it for the first few years after his divorce. She quickly responded, three words by his guesstimation, then set her cell on the counter—screen down. "Sorry, it was the girls' dad."

He didn't think she understood how she distanced herself from her ex by using the impersonal title, but he did. It had taken him a hell of a lot longer to extinguish hope that Amanda would come around—if not for him, for Maddie.

Good on you, Teagan.

"Not a problem." And then, because he would have wanted someone to get the awkwardness out in the open if the situation were reversed, he said, "And sorry about Frank."

Horror and humiliation flashed over her face. "How did you hear about Frank?"

"Harley." Screw getting it out in the open—his answer seemed to piss her off. "I didn't think—"

Only Teagan was gone again. Lips pursed, eyes narrowed into two slits, she marched out the door. He waited for a long minute, and when she didn't return, he set the timer for twenty minutes, started the coffee, and kicked the door shut.

He'd just pulled up a stool to the counter and was sipping his coffee, with an extra mug for her, when the door reopened. No knock. No apology. She was all business.

"Harley apologizes for sharing my personal information." She picked up the extra mug and took a sip. "It won't happen again."

"Noted and understood." He wasn't the only one who didn't like to talk about exes. Nobody understood the need for privacy better than Colin.

If she wanted to keep her own counsel, that was fine with him. Because then he didn't have to talk about Amanda.

"She also apologized for ruining two batches of dough." She sat across the counter from him. "Oh, and to let you know that if you want to join her beach yoga class, she'll give you a ten percent discount."

"That's very neighborly of her."

She took another sip, then stopped. Embarrassment tinting her cheeks, she held up the mug. "*This* is very neighborly. I should have thanked you for the coffee as soon as I walked through the door." She dropped her head to the counter. "I also should have knocked before barging in. I'm having a morning."

"That seems to be happening a lot."

"It's just that I wanted today to go perfectly, and my rolls are—" She leapt up. "My rolls!"

"I set the timer. You have eleven minutes left."

"How did you know the bake time?"

"Just because I don't like to bake, that doesn't mean I can't."

"Frank didn't know his way around the kitchen. Are you a unicorn?"

He wasn't going to touch that one. "Didn't you guys run a bakery?"

"I baked. He ran our business. Right into the ground."

Something twinged inside him. He knew what Bread N Butter meant to Teagan and how much pressure she put on herself to do right by her family. That someone had taken the business from her pissed him off.

"I had no idea. I'm sorry." He'd always known Frank was a prick and never trusted him. Especially with Teagan's heart, which she pretty much wore on her sleeve. Even now, after Colin had only grudgingly invited her in, her body language was open, her eyes cautious but willing to trust.

"Me too." She was silent for a long moment. "Do you still miss her?" she asked, then held up a silencing hand. "I'm sorry, I promised no more personal information. Maybe we should change the topic."

"Definitely," he said, not wanting to talk about either of their exes. "How long are you back for?"

So much for not sharing personal information.

"Ready to get rid of me?" she teased, but she looked as if his answer would shift reality, crack the space-time continuum, and magically erase the past twenty years.

A few minutes ago, he could have cared less about reconnecting, wishing she'd just leave. Now he wasn't sure what he was wishing for. Maybe a little part of him was wishing her move to Pacific Cove was more than a temporary stopover.

The timer buzzed and they were back to the silent staring thing. It was as if they were each waiting for the other to talk first. For one of them to say, "Hey, let's keep talking."

Four words that would never come out of his mouth. He was safer sticking with two. "You're buzzing."

She blinked and the openness vanished a little. "That's the bread at my house." She slipped off her barstool. "I have to put in the next batch."

Chapter 6

Whoever said negotiating with terrorists is a bad
tactical move has clearly never raised twins.

—Unknown

The frosty relationship after Parmesangate had been weighing heavily on Harley. Another transgression she needed to atone for was showing up uninvited. But she didn't really have anyplace else to go. After Bryan had suggested they move in together, Harley did what any cornered chicken would do.

She ran like hell.

She packed her bags, her fear of commitments and rejection, and every other insecurity left over from a lifetime of emotional neglect. Oh, Harley had never gone hungry or been left wanting, but to Dale, love was a noun instead of a verb. He was the first man in her life who had trouble expressing emotion. There followed a string of men who expressed those eight letters, then quickly retracted their proclamation when things became difficult. And Harley always managed to make things difficult.

As far as she was concerned, love was a fiction. Like Santa and the Tooth Fairy, it was something parents told kids to make life a little magical. But magic was another fiction, especially the magic of marriage. Not that Bryan would lie. There wasn't a disingenuous bone in his body, but the second he realized how difficult she was to love, he'd call it quits.

So Harley was just saving them both heartache, because the last thing she'd ever want to do was hurt Bryan. After losing his fiancée to breast cancer, he'd had enough heartbreak for a lifetime.

Her What's Best for Bryan plan had been going swimmingly, until Teagan turned up and activated a countdown clock on Harley's peace and tranquility. She needed at least another month to get her head on straight, but her sister had made it clear she wanted her gone yesterday.

When it came to her sister there was a large, complicated knot of emotions, history, and disappointment always at war in Harley's stomach. Today, the disappointment was winning. Not about coming to Nonna's house—she'd never feel bad about that—but about how Teagan had responded. Her sister might hold the deed but that didn't make the house hers. Regardless, the mature thing to do would have been to give Teagan a heads-up about Operation Goldilocks—or at least apologize.

Then again, if Harley made mature decisions, she wouldn't be hiding out in Pacific Cove because some cute boy said he liked her. But when it came to Bryan, like and love were closely related.

With a heavy sigh, she slid her laptop into her yoga bag and headed downstairs.

Even before she hit the landing, any thoughts of apologizing went right out the window. Because there, on the entry table, stuffed into a garbage bag, sat Harley's prized possession— her macramé hammock-style chair. It was Teagan's passive-aggressive way of saying, *Don't let the door hit you in the ass on the way out.*

Hurt and pissed, she shoved Teagan's "shoes off and no eating on the furniture" white linen, modern wingback chair under the ceiling hook. Slipping her shoes on—her sandy beach yoga shoes—Harley climbed up and rehung her swinging deathtrap.

Too Short Teagan would have to drag the ladder out of the garage, through the house, down the long hallway, and into the family room. Her sister was a perfectionist, so a bohemian hammock violating her "showroom inspired" decor would drive her crazy. Just as Harley's presence did.

To Harley, that macramé hammock wasn't just a hammock. It was the first thing she hung up and the last thing she took down as she bounced around the country. It made any space feel like her space, an important quality because she moved so often. That chair had been with her through some of the most difficult times of her life, and some of the best. It was her creative space—a hand-me-down from Zia Iris.

Sitting in Iris's hammock, Harley felt not so lost. And Teagan wanted it gone. She wanted Harley gone. Which was too damn bad because Harley wasn't ready to leave. Not until she knew how to handle the whole Bryan situation.

Bryan, who'd called her twice last night. Bryan, whom she'd sent to voice mail. Bryan, who would have the best advice on how to tackle the Teagan situation.

Good thing Harley had been handling her own business since she could walk. She lived by a strict kick-ass-and-get-shit-done attitude on life and, while she didn't particularly enjoy confrontation, it was a playing field she knew how to navigate.

"Tee," Harley called out. "We need to talk."

"Take a number."

Normally, Harley would have told her where to shove that number, if not for the sound of nuclear annihilation erupting from the second floor. Curious, Harley peeked her head into the girls' room and experienced a small prickle of guilt.

Teagan sat on the edge of Poppy's bed. Her lipstick was smudged, her blouse wrinkled, and she was still in the Lamaste pajama bottoms Harley had sent her for Christmas. Which looked as if someone had bumped into her with a bouquet of strawberries. Based on Poppy's red moustache, Harley had a good guess as to the culprit.

The Red Bandit was also on the bed, wiggling and wailing for escape, while her mom tried to wrangle her into a shirt.

"You need to sit still."

"Buts I don't wike pink!" Poppy yelled.

"You *loved* pink last night when we picked out your outfit," Teagan said.

"I don't like nights!"

God, Harley couldn't wait to see Teagan try to rein *that* in.

She'd put ten-to-one odds that Poppy was going to emerge the victor but hadn't written off Teagan just yet. Mother of Twins looked crazed enough to pull out a win.

"Where's my cape, Mama?"

"It's in the dirty clothes and you need to wear your pink class shirt. Today is field trip day, and the pink shirt is standard school field trip uniform. It's the rules," Teagan explained as if Poppy gave a shit about the rules. "Plus, Mommy has a big meeting today so there isn't time to find your cape. Now, hands up."

Poppy did the opposite, her arms super-glued to her sides.

Looking a little frazzled and a whole lot determined, Teagan lowered the shirt as if waving the flag and, the moment Poppy lost focus, Teagan faked right then yanked the shirt over Poppy's head.

One arm in, the other flapping in a fit, Poppy arched her back in an upward-facing dog pose, wailing at a pitch that only bats could hear.

Harley had opened her mouth to tell Teagan this was the universe's way of punishing her for all her shenanigans with Harley's hammock, when she heard someone say, "You need help with that?"

Harley looked around the room to see who was offering, surprised to discover it was her. Teagan went stock still, the girls halted, everyone frozen in time. Teagan looked over Poppy's head and leveled Harley with a long, disbelieving look. "What did you say?"

"You just look like you could use some help. Gah!" She slapped a hand over her mouth before she offered to be a surrogate for Teagan's next batch of twins. "With the girls." She covered her mouth with her other hand, but it was too late. Both girls were jumping up and down, Poppy chanting, "Auntie Har-ley! Aun-tie Har-ley!"

Teagan looked at her with both wariness and hope. "I thought you were leaving?"

"I can stay."

"What about that job you had to get back to?"

"Eh, my boss can wait."

"Is the job even real?"

Like an arrow through the heart.

"Why do you always do that? Make me sound like a flighty idiot. And a liar."

"You are the furthest thing from an idiot," Teagan said quietly. "You're the more intelligent one of us but you waste it. Jumping from job to job, running every time things get complicated. If you stuck it out, you might build some roots and decide you like it."

"I noticed you didn't take back the liar part."

"I noticed you didn't defend the running part."

Touché. "I'm not the one running this time. I'm offering to stay and help out. And just because I don't like complicated situations doesn't mean I'm a flake."

"We'll have to agree to disagree."

Harley rolled her eyes. "What happened to 'Families stick together and embrace each other's differences'? What happened to 'Ohana.'" It was what Teagan had promised Harley when their parents split up the sisters after their divorce. It was the first of many forgotten promises.

"Ohana." Poppy stopped struggling. "Lilo said that to Stitch when he was being bad. It means nobody gets left behind."

"Out of the mouth of babes," Harley deadpanned, and stepped away from the doorjamb. "And you know, just because Nonna left you the house doesn't mean I can't come for a visit now and then. This was my home too."

"For a couple weeks a year."

And the hits keep coming. "Six weeks. I spent the spring break and a month every summer here. Even after you got married and moved to Seattle, I came every few months to visit Nonna."

Teagan paused, as if Nonna's image had just appeared to her in a loaf of sourdough. "I didn't know that."

"News flash. You don't know everything. Look at my room.

Nonna left it exactly the same for a reason. And after she died, I sometimes came here for long weekends with Mom. This house is as much mine as it is yours."

That stopped Teagan in her tracks. "You came here with Mom?" she asked, making a tactical error. Poppy took advantage of her shift in focus to break free.

Teagan reached out, but it was too late. The kid squirmed out of her mom's lap like a fish out of water. "Poppy. Come here and sit on the bed," she commanded, but there was no conviction behind the order so Poppy ignored her.

"Every Fourth of July and the two weeks leading up to Christmas," Harley pointed out. Not wanting to make waves, Harley still obeyed the divorce decree that said she belonged to her dad on Christmas, New Year's, and the rest of the 323 days of the year. "So you aren't the only one who made memories here. Just because mine were later in life doesn't make them less important. Not that it matters, because I'm leaving in a couple weeks, anyway."

"You said that a couple of weeks ago."

She had, hadn't she? *Huh.* She'd meant it when she'd said it but then Mrs. Sims, who lived down the street and ran the senior center, asked her for a favor. She'd been a close friend of Nonna's and a regular at the bread shop. With a homemade gooseberry pie, she'd sweet-talked Harley into crafting an inclusive mission statement for the senior center that would appeal to baby boomers and recent retirees alike.

"What does a couple weeks matter when you desperately need my help?" she asked.

"Yes, I need help but not *your* help. Things are stressful enough without Hurricane Harley blowing through." Teagan had the decency to grimace. Not that it made a dent in the pain her words caused. "Harley, I—"

Harley waved her off. "Here's how Hurricane Harley sees it. The girls love me, I need a place to crash until I figure some things out, and you're drowning."

Teagan perked up. "What things?"

"Private things."

"You tell everyone about my private things."

"Which is why I promised never to discuss private things again," she said. "You need a nanny. You're going under and I'm offering you a branch. Take it or not, your choice. Just remember, if you go under, I get the house."

Teagan studied her seriously. "Do you promise to take that swing down?"

"Can't promise, but we can negotiate." When Teagan took forever to answer, Harley turned to the girls. "Want my help?"

"Yay!" Poppy shouted and both girls immediately rushed to Harley.

"It's not even summer. Do you really want me to leave?"

Teagan watched Poppy mount Garbage Disposal like a pony and sighed. Her sister realized she was losing the battle. She needed backup.

"What are you proposing?"

What *was* she proposing?

Harley had survived being a family of one by keeping her heart locked up tightly. Which had been a lot easier before her nieces. When the Wonder Twins were born, maintaining emotional distance became impossible. Then Casino Night from Hell happened, when Frank not only fell off the path of recovery but gambled away nine months' rent on the bakery. Even though it was the fuckup to end all fuckups, she'd never imagined Teagan would kick her out.

But she had.

Lesson learned. As Harley had pulled out of that Seattle driveway, she'd decided it was for the best. Watching Teagan with her family, something Harley had never had and likely never would have, hurt. That was the day Harley decided that if she got too close to the fire, she was bound to get burned.

So then why was she working so hard to stay here? Sure, Bryan was part of it, but there was something else. A little whisper in the back of her head saying, *Maybe this is the time.* The time she'd finally have a full-time family.

"You let me stay through the summer and I'll help out with the kids."

"Why?"

If she were being honest, she wasn't ready to leave. Suddenly, being the cool Aun-tie Har-ley who blew into town on random holidays wasn't enough. She wanted to be a reliable presence in their life, who not only showed up for all the milestones but took part in the little things. Collecting shells at the beach, eating caramel apples at the wharf, weekend waffle breakfasts.

If she wanted to stay, she'd need to be invited—or at least prove to Teagan she wasn't like Dale. That she wouldn't win the girls over only to bail.

"Because you need me. And you've been there when I needed you." Maybe not as adults, but Teagan had been Harley's rock when she was little.

On nights when her parents' arguing grew so loud the neighbors could hear, Teagan would crawl into Harley's bed and snuggle up. She'd read *Bear and Rabbit's Great Adventures* as many times as it took for Harley to fall asleep. Her sister taught her that, no matter how bad things got, or how loud and long their parents yelled, life would still go on. And if they could just make it until morning, there would be a new day filled with new possibilities.

Behind that bedroom door all they had was each other. Just like Bear and Rabbit in the children's book.

Teagan let out a long-suffering sigh. "Okay, but there are some rules."

"Shocker."

"You have to take that swing back down and learn to clean up after yourself. No more plates on the counter and no more using the shower to air-dry your P. A. N. T. I. E. S." She mouthed the last part.

"If you're calling them P. A. N. T. I. E. S., then you clearly need a thong of your own."

Lily whispered something to Poppy. "Lily wants to know, what's a thong?"

Teagan sent Harley a pointed look. "Fair enough. But the swing stays."

"You said it was negotiable."

"That was before you considered too long. It's like on *Shark Tank*. If you hesitate, you lose your bargaining power. You hesitated. No deal for you."

"Fine. But you babysit the twins whenever I need."

"Most of my classes are early morning, and I'm working with a few places in town." She purposely left out the fact that the places were not studios or gyms, but rather shops on Main Street, which Harley thought might be good outlets for Bread N Butter. She'd approached management, explained what their bread company could provide, then scheduled follow-up appointments.

In the kitchen, she was more of a bother than a bread baker, so she decided to help Teagan by applying her strengths—branding and sales, two things Bread N Butter were in desperate need of. But she was keeping her efforts a secret until something panned out.

She'd already met with Delores, who owned the largest boutique hotel in town. The older woman had agreed to visit the farmer's market and taste their products. In passing, Harley explained how she could use social media to get the word out about the hot spots in town, by posting videos and photos highlighting the unique shops and scenic views the area had to offer. And how to position her hotel to appeal to millennials.

Delores hired her on the spot, and they had a follow-up meeting scheduled for Tuesday after next.

What started as Harley helping a few people had taken on a life of its own. She might as well pad her résumé while she was here. More than that, this freelance work allowed her the creative freedom she lacked back in LA.

It felt good to help the people who had known Nonna and supported her in her last years. Harley didn't have many roots back in LA. It was hard to make deep connections when you had one foot out the door. Plus, casual connections made it easier on everyone when Harley got that itch to explore.

But her mind kept circling back to Bryan and the realization she didn't get that itch when she was with him. Which brought her back to the reason she was here. To make things right with

Teagan, earn a place in her nieces' lives, and give Bryan the space he needed to move on.

"So we have a deal?" she asked.

"Fair enough," Teagan all but groaned. "We'll work out a schedule."

"See. No hesitation. I got my deal."

Teagan rolled her eyes. "The deal is, we make a family calendar, and you promise to abide by the schedule."

"Why is nothing ever easy with you?"

"Adulting is never easy."

"Is that rule one in the official Adulting Handbook? 'Adulting is never easy'? Sign me up."

"See why this arrangement will never work?"

"Why, because there isn't room for me on your schedule?" Harley thought back to the giant, detailed, minute-to-minute schedule on the fridge. "I'm surprised you don't have potty time scheduled on the calendar."

"Kids need structure. A schedule makes them feel safe."

"Let me get a pen." She licked the tip of her pretend pen and scribbled on her pretend paper. "Rule two. Structure is security."

"It is."

"I disagree." Harley had a disregard for schedules.

Her one semester at Catholic school proved that schedules made Harley break out in hives. Although that hadn't always been the case. Summers at the beach house, knowing dinner would be at six, eaten around the table, and that they'd always play hi-low, where everyone had to say what the lowest part of the day was and then the highest.

In those days, Harley had so many highs she could ramble on forever about sandcastles, collecting beach glass, baking bread from scratch, wearing her mom's heels and pearls, family game night, trips to the library, visiting the sea lions. Her nonna and mom listened to every word, while Teagan sat patiently waiting for her turn.

Huh, they were kind of like the twins. Only the kiddos

seemed to use their differences to complement each other rather than antagonize each other. She wondered if by the end of the summer she and Teagan would learn to live with each other's differences. And Harley wondered how she'd change with some structure and the security that came with consistency.

People were always fascinated by her childhood as the kid of a roadie, but the truth was she hadn't really had a childhood, except for her time in Pacific Cove.

"Really?" Teagan said, and it was a challenge. This was the *give in or give up the chance to experience the kind of life she'd never had* moment.

She took a deep breath and smiled, big and full of bullshit. "Any other rules?"

"Yes. No sugar before noon, no snacks after four p.m., naptimes are mandatory regardless of what Poppy will have you believe, and at no time is Poppy allowed to change, renegotiate, or make addenda to the rules. And don't underestimate Lily."

"I thought Lily didn't talk."

"She might be quiet, but she's the brains behind the operation."

"Should I write this down?"

"No, I will show you where the PARENTS GET PARENTING binder is."

Teagan led Harley downstairs and into the kitchen. She pulled a two-inch-wide, three-ring binder from the cupboard and dropped it on the counter. It landed with a thud. Harley flipped through the color-coded sections. "You have an entire chapter dedicated to bath time routines?" Talk about a way to suck the fun out of bath time. "Wow, was this what it was like living with Mom?"

Maybe she'd completely romanticized her summers.

"It wasn't Mom; it was Nonna. And it's also common sense."

Harley blinked. "Nonna wasn't like that with me."

Teagan shrugged. "I know. When you were here, it was like every day was a vacation."

Harley wondered if that was the case or if Nonna, in all her wisdom, had raised them differently because each girl had different needs. Nonna had a way about her, an open-minded and unconditional love that she adapted to match each person. Especially both of her granddaughters.

Harley knew she was better at adapting than Teagan. A result of going where the wind blew for the past twenty-plus years. Meeting so many different people, all from different walks of life made her appreciate that everyone had a unique story and a unique place in the world.

Hell, her theme song was Pink's "Raise Your Glass," which she'd sung live onstage with the artist at Coachella. Not that she'd ever mentioned it. Sure, she liked to brag about playing Xbox with Steven Tyler or trying on Dolly Parton's wig, but one of her favorite memories was at Nonna's house, jumping on Teagan's bed, both of them screaming Pink at the top of their lungs.

She liked to think of it as their song.

"How about I get the girls dressed, fed, and take them to school. Would that help?"

Teagan sighed. "That would be amazing. But why?"

Harley looked at her sister, and suddenly all the history and past hurts faded away, along with the uncertainty about Bryan, and a warm sense of nostalgia washed over her. Her grandma's love filled her heart. And she made the only response that felt right.

"Ohana."

Chapter 7

Big sisters are the crab grass in the lawn of life.

—Charles M. Schulz

Feeling like she'd earned a gold star, Harley corralled the girls back into their room. Getting them focused on the tasks required to deliver them to class on time was like trying to grab hold of two greased piglets at the state fair. But deep down inside she loved the chaos, the hell-on-wheels attitude of Poppy and the sweet hugs from Lily. Though she loved her nieces equally, she found it harder to connect with Lily.

Lily was focused, quiet, introverted, a sweet and gentle spirit. All the qualities Teagan possessed, and all the traits Harley had tried to adopt over the years, unsuccessfully. On the other hand, Poppy was a hellion, and Harley understood her need to flip society the bird from time to time.

"Lily, how fast can you get the capes out of the laundry basket?"

She looked at Poppy. "She said one-two-fwee."

"No, you said that." She turned back to Lily. "Next time you want your cape, you're going to have to ask. Because big girls tell the universe what form they want to take. Got me?"

Lily nodded and raced downstairs. Or at least Harley thought she did. The girl moved like a cat burglar. Huh, maybe she *was* the brains of the operation.

"You," she said to Poppy. "You want to wear that cape? You have until the count of one-two-three to get dressed. Shirt first, the rest you decide."

"I don'ts want to. It's itchy."

Well, that made complete sense. Who was Harley to force uncomfortable fashion on a kid?

"Then you double-layer, got me? Whatever shirt you want on bottom, then pink on top. Now, get ready to race the clock. On go . . . Go!"

Poppy pulled a pajama shirt over her head, struggling to get the right arm in. "One." Poppy yanked the pink top down. "Don't forget pants."

"Pants." She raced to her dresser and pulled out her purple pajama bottoms. "Two." One foot in. "Two and a half." Then the other. When she was finished, Poppy grabbed a matching tutu from the dress-up box and stepped into it. "And . . ." Poppy yanked the elastic-waisted mesh around her belly. "Three."

Poppy lifted her hands and stepped back as if she was a contestant on *Cupcake Wars*. Harley lifted her hand, and Poppy jumped as high she could, her tongue peeking out as she did a one-two high five followed by an impressive mic drop.

"Good form."

"Up," Poppy said and Harley complied, not expecting her niece to wrap her arms around Harley's neck and give her a kiss on the lips. As the little girl rested her head on Harley's shoulder, she added a new rule to the Adulting Handbook:

Rule Three: Being cool isn't the same thing as being loved.

And Harley realized she wanted to be loved and to give love. She just wasn't sure how to go about it.

"Down," Poppy said. Harley set her down just as Lily burst into the room holding the two cherished capes in hand. Harley secured them to both girls' shoulders and walked to the door. She didn't hear anything from the kitchen.

She wondered if Teagan had already left or if she'd taken the vodka from the freezer and was working her way toward a serious hangover.

"You two pick up your room and put things where they belong. As fast as you can."

"Like a race?"

"Like a race." Poppy looked even more excited than before,

if that was even possible. "You clean and I'll go pack some lunches. Winner gets a Pop-Tart for lunch."

The girls jumped into action, cleaning their room at lightning speed. Harley walked to the kitchen and found Teagan surprisingly absent. The binder was open on the kitchen table, turned to APPROPRIATE LUNCHBOX FOODS. Nowhere on the list did it say Pop-Tarts. In fact, Pop-Tarts were nowhere to be found in the kitchen.

Shit.

She'd have to swing by the mini-mart on their way to the drop-off location. Directions were also on the counter, written in perfect writing, sitting right next to the binder, with a sticky note stuck to the paper.

I owe you . . .
Bear

Harley's eyes filled with tears and her nose tingled with emotion. It was the first sign that Teagan still remembered the good moments together, and for now it was enough.

"Are you sad?" Poppy asked.

She turned to find the girls in the doorway and a laugh escaped. "No, I'm happy."

Lily was looking like a Gap ad in white capris, white sandals, and a white cardigan with a pink KIDDIE COVE PRE-K shirt. Poppy looked like she'd fallen out of a 1980s music video—her hair was still matted in the back, and she was sporting a pair of battered red high tops with dog-sized bite marks in the toe, purple dinosaur–printed pajama bottoms, matching tutu and cape, with a unicorn headband and—of course—the school appropriate T-shirt.

They were proud of their fashion choices. And wasn't that what mattered?

"Dressed, fed, and ten minutes to spare," Harley called into the inner depths of the house, hoping Teagan heard wherever she was hiding. "You can come out now—we're leaving."

She had the girls out the door, into the back of Nonna Rose's

Ford Fairlane, and strapped in their car seats before Teagan had a chance to emerge and steal kids' dreams everywhere by explaining that fruit snacks weren't real fruit.

Nonetheless, Teagan appeared out of nowhere.

"Did you pack the sun lotion?" she called from the porch. "They have a field trip to the tidepools today and the weather calls for full sun."

"Lotioned up and ready to roll," Harley shouted.

"Ready to roll, Mommy," Poppy repeated. "With the ragtop down so our hair can blow?"

Harley pulled out of the driveway and Lily, eyes big and smile even bigger, raised her hands in the air as if she were on a roller coaster.

"The speed limit is twenty-five, texting and driving is illegal in California, and remember, no sugar before noon."

Harley just waved. With her middle finger.

Chapter 8

There are so many other things I should be
doing with my life right now but instead, I am stuck
here crushing on you.

—Unknown

Teagan sat at the kitchen table, sipping her morning coffee, watching the sunrise, and thinking back on how the past week had gone. Pacific Cove had cornered the market on breathtaking mornings. The sky was painted in the colors of late spring, pinks and yellows casting a warm glow over the Pacific. Waves crashed against the rocky shore, sandhill cranes glided gracefully overhead, and in the distance a raft of otters bobbed up and down with the incoming tide.

Teagan breathed in the sweet, caffeinated silence. Harley was gone, the girls were upstairs watching a cartoon on Teagan's tablet, and she had an entire twenty minutes to herself. The time between sunrise and breakfast was coveted.

It was just her, the rising sun, and the dog fast asleep at her feet. Harley had done Teagan a solid, making the girls their lunch for school. The brown bags sat on the counter, each one with the girl's name in superhero font, with a sketch of the respective Wonder Twin. Harley had always been so artistic, the creative sister. It was a talent and passion she'd shared with Zia Iris.

There was even a bag for Teagan. It read TEE and the T was a Red Rider BB gun. She rolled her eyes but could not stop herself from laughing.

Teagan decided that maybe having Harley around wouldn't be so bad. The girls loved her, Teagan had the time she needed to bake and catch up on some much-needed sleep. More importantly, she had the space to come to terms with the past year and organize her emotions.

She pulled the button top off her brioche bun and leaned down to give Garbage Disposal a nice treat. He loved her breakfast brioche. Well, he loved everything, but her brioche ranked somewhere between a T-bone and flip-flops.

"What the hell?"

Teagan checked under the table, in the kitchen area, where sometimes the dog licked the floor, and in the living room. No four-legged companion.

"GD," she called out. "I've got a cookie for you."

Cookie, treats, yum-yums were all at the very top of his list. But Teagan heard nothing. No skidding of nails on wood, no rhinos pounding down the stairs, not even a single bark.

Panic grabbed her by the throat as she turned toward the back kitchen door—the same door through which Harley had departed. Which was cracked open.

"Nonono." In one fluid motion, Teagan was out of the chair and—in slipper-clad feet—racing down the steps of the deck.

She looked right then left. No sign of her dog. She cupped her hands around her mouth. "GD, come here, buddy. GD."

Still nothing. She started south, knowing that three doors down, Mr. Jessup, who liked to fish early, sometimes left his smoker open when he was making salmon jerky. Last week, Garbage Disposal chewed through a double layer, leak-proof, break-proof plastic cooler and scarfed down five pounds of salmon jerky, then threw it all up on Teagan's bed.

"GD," she called out, her voice getting lost in the sound of the surf. "GD!"

That's when she saw him, at the base of Mr. Jessup's deck, nose deep in the sand, inhaling whatever smoked scraps he could find. She put her fingers between her teeth and blew. "You get over here, Mr. Man!"

Garbage Disposal's head popped up and, with a smile that said he found the whole moment thrilling, loped over.

"Stop!" She put her hand out like Colin.

Garbage Disposal did not stop. In fact, he picked up speed. Teagan considered rushing him, the way one was supposed to do when confronted by a bear, but since her dog was a brick wall with elephant feet, she braced herself for impact.

The force was like a wrecking ball, knocking her over, thankfully, in the sand. Garbage Disposal licked her face as if it had been an eternity since he'd seen her. And for once, she didn't mind the slobbery kisses.

"I missed you, too."

Garbage Disposal made a *cacking* sound followed by exactly three dry heaves. Teagan tried to roll out of the way. Too late. He gave one final heave and yacked up everything he'd eaten. On her top.

"Come. On," she groaned, standing and snapping the hem of her shirt, watching the majority of the regurgitated breakfast fling onto the sand. Salmon jerky, doggie kibble, sand, and—"Is that my thong?"

He looked up at her, all innocent puppy face. A feeling of urgency she couldn't explain hammered against her chest.

"Sand!" She'd read an article explaining that, like grapes and chocolate, sand could be deadly for dogs, depending on how much they ate. "Come here, buddy."

Garbage Disposal looked as if he were having a crisis of faith as he had to choose between obeying the keeper of the treats and heading for the hills. He was reacting to her panic, so she took a calming breath to lower her heart rate.

Calm used to be her old stomping ground. Back before becoming a mom, she'd relied on her cool-as-a-cucumber levelheadedness to keep her world spinning. Nowadays, calm was such a rarity, she'd come to rely on order.

"I need to look in your mouth."

The dopey dog disguise vanished, leaving a calculating creature who'd clearly had her bamboozled. Locking his gaze with hers, Garbage Disposal zigged right then zagged left, shifting the weight between his front legs, and Teagan recognized the scent of rebellion.

"Don't you dare."

Oh, he dared, barking three times, then taking off past her up the beach. Slippers forgotten, Teagan set off after him, her feet sinking into the soft sand while little seashells were pushed into her soles. It took her six houses to realize she was outmaneuvered and outmatched.

Harley had been the athlete of the family, Teagan the strategist. It was the battle between right brain and left brain. Teagan played to her strengths and tapped into those mom skills that had pulled her through the past year.

She stopped and waited, then let out another ear-piercing whistle. Two houses later, Garbage Disposal glanced over his shoulder, panting with sheer abandon, his tongue lolling out the side of his mouth—her thong dangling from his lower teeth. He leapt in the air, doing a one-eighty on the landing. He repeated his earlier the zigzag move, but Teagan held her ground. The next bark was a question: *What happened to* Catch Me If You Can, *doggie edition?*

"Who wants a cookie?" she sang. "Mommy's got cookies."

Garbage Disposal barked so happily his body left the ground; then he raced straight toward her. Right as he was about to shoot past her toward the treat jar in the pantry, she grabbed his collar and dug her heels into the sand.

He pulled her a good foot before they came to a slow stop. Not wanting to give him the upper hand, she mounted him the way Poppy had, holding him down. "Drop the thong, you panty raider, and show me your mouth!"

When he did no such thing, she pried it open. Other than deathly breath, she couldn't tell if he was in danger of sand poisoning.

He gagged and hacked, and a blob of sand-crusted jerky popped out. He might be a disaster of a dog, but he was her disaster dog. All those fierce mama bear feelings she reserved for her girls erupted. She wouldn't rest until she knew he was going to be okay.

The article had suggested consulting a veterinarian if it was unclear how much sand had been consumed. Her local veterinarian lived five decks back and was going to be really irritated if she woke him this early again for no good reason. But she had to be sure.

"You'd better be really sick, because this is going to be humiliating," she said, maintaining a tight hold on his collar and dragging him to Colin's. They barely made it up the back deck when Garbage Disposal gagged and hacked and eventually yacked.

"Hang in there." She didn't bother to tap lightly, she rapped on Colin's back door hard enough to rattle the window. She waited a whole count of ten and rapped again. On the third rap the door opened.

Colin appeared in what had become his uniform—boxers, bedhead, and bare, breathtaking abs. Not to mention some other key muscles, which were covered—but barely.

He rubbed his eyes. "Maybe I should leave a key under the mat."

"Maybe you should sleep in something more than boxers."

"You woke me, at"—he looked at his watch—"five a.m. You're punctual. And boxers *are* more."

Oh my. The sexy vet next door slept in the nude. That was news to her. Then again, while they might have slept together, they'd never actually *slept* together. Had they been caught, his dad would have killed him, and that was only if Nonna Rose hadn't gotten to him first.

"It's GD. He snuck out and I found him eating sand." She looked down at her yack-stained shirt. "And possibly a bologna sandwich. When I knew we were moving home, I read up on the dangers of dogs on the beach. And I distinctly remember that some dogs eat sand, and it can become lodged in their belly and become dangerous if not treated. I'm not sure if this ranks as dangerous—he was only out there for three minutes tops—but he's been known to chew through a chair leg in less."

Instead of reminding her that he already knew this because he'd gone to the top vet school in the world—he was that smart—he took Garbage Disposal by the collar and led him inside. He grabbed a pair of board shorts off the mudroom hanger and pulled them on.

Teagan had to force her attention on the ceiling. She could have sworn he chuckled but when she looked back, he was in serious animal doctor mode.

"How much sand did he eat?" Colin asked.

"I don't know. He snuck out. Someone left the back door open."

Someone being Hurricane Harley, whom Teagan had stupidly believed when she said she'd changed. Grown up. Maybe she had, but she still clearly had a long way to go.

"Is he going to be okay?"

"Not to toot my own horn, but you do know I'm the best vet in town. People come from five towns over and trust me with their pets."

She believed him. Even as a teenager, Colin had a way with animals. He worked weekends at a local farm, doing everything from cleaning the stalls to helping deliver a baby calf. He knew what he wanted and where he wanted his life to take him. Which was a big reason she'd left without saying goodbye. They both had big dreams pulling them in opposite directions. Just look at what he'd accomplished with his life. Had she stayed home that last summer, she would have taken his future from him—and she'd loved him too much for that.

He'd been the first love of her life and she hadn't been strong enough to walk away from one last kiss, so she'd applied for early enrollment and began college a semester early—a safe three thousand miles away.

"I thought it was because you were the sexy animal doctor." She sobered. "Is he going to die?"

"No. Some fluids and he should be fine."

She shivered. "Does that bag of saline include an IV needle?"

"He won't feel even a pinch."

She would. "I hate needles."

"I remember."

She wondered what else he remembered. Like maybe the way she loved it when he kissed the back of her neck.

"He's going to be okay," Colin added.

"You sure? Because I already broke my kids' family apart. I can't break their dog." Her voice was strangled.

"Whoa, hey, I've got you." That's when she realized she was crying. "You didn't break anything."

He wiped her tears with the pad of his thumb and pulled her to him, yack and all, giving her a reassuring hug. She closed her eyes to enjoy the feeling of a man's arms around her. Scratch that: the feeling of this man's arms. It was as good as she remembered. With him still lacking upper body clothing, maybe even better.

Hell, it was the closest she'd come to intimacy in years.

"You put your kids first—that takes guts."

"Or cowardice, since I broke up the family."

He dipped his head to look at her. "Who called you a coward?"

"You did," she whispered. When he looked as if he were ready to argue his innocence in front of a jury, she explained, "You implied it when you said, 'Noted,' like we were still eighteen and stupid."

His lips twitched. "Are you admitting that your *Dear Colin* decision was stupid?"

"It was responsible," she said primly. "Painful but responsible. There's a difference."

"Not to a stupid, head-over-heels-in-love eighteen-year-old." His hands dropped indecently low on her back as he nudged her closer.

"I didn't know how to say goodbye and actually leave for college after spending another summer with you. Maybe I *was* a coward, but you were the one who cut me out. I called, left messages with your mom, tried to explain."

"I was so confused, I just went into protection mode," he admitted.

"Confusion went both ways," she whispered. "My letter was meant to be a 'time to move on to the next chapter.' You chose to take it as a goodbye."

"I was wrecked."

"So was I." She was surprised how much emotion talking about those last few months brought up. "Maybe I did take the easy way out, but you ghosted me."

She watched him consider her viewpoint and knew when he'd let the leftover resentment go. "I took the easy way out. You took the hard way," he assured her. "And I'm glad you did because I'm not sure I wouldn't have changed my life plan to follow you to Boston."

She knew how important his plans were to him. She'd known it then and she knew it now, which was why she had so much empathy for his need to keep everything nice and tidy.

Teagan's childhood wasn't all bad but a lot of the parts, the uncertain parts before her parents' divorce, had left some lasting marks. One of the reasons she led with her head instead of her heart.

Society had rules for a reason. She followed those rules out of necessity. Which was why it was dangerous to be this close to him.

They were at different phases in their lives. He was about to be an empty nester and, including GD, her house was a dysfunctional Party of Five. Plus, she was still gun-shy when it came to relationships. She gave herself one last moment to absorb his strength and reassurance, then stepped back—out of his arms and away from temptation.

She grabbed a wad of paper towels from the counter and wiped at the stain on her shirt. It only smeared the mess around. She felt his gaze still on her, so she asked the question she'd been holding in her heart for twenty years. "Do you still hate me?"

"I never hated you." His eyes dropped to her lips. "That was the problem."

It was still a gigantic problem. He knew it, she knew it, and when their gazes locked, the air practically crackled. His hazel-green eyes flickered with surprise before carefully going blank.

"Let's get inside and see what we're dealing with. Plus, you must be cold."

She knew her shirt showed him just how "cold" she'd become.

He took Garbage Disposal, who wore a suspicious *all's good* smile—as if this had been his plan all along—by the collar and led him into the house.

"Grab a towel from the cupboard above the washer and I'll go get my medical bag." He looked at Garbage Disposal. "You stay."

She started to tell him that the dog wasn't big on following commands when she noticed Garbage Disposal sitting, back straight as if holding the line until his commander in chief returned.

"You and I are going to have a talk," she said.

Garbage Disposal farted, releasing a stink bomb powerful enough to fill the kitchen with the scent of death and decay.

She located the towels in the laundry room, which was neat and orderly. The counters were clean of clutter, the floor free of piles in different stages of dirty. It even appeared that he separated clothes by colors and care instructions.

What a turn-on.

Impressed, and a little curious about the laid-back boy turned meticulous man, she casually snooped through his cupboards, and thumbed through the basket of clean shirts. Men's shirts.

She lifted one and held it to her nose, breathed in, and groaned. The faded University of California, Davis shirt smelled like laundry soap, sea air, and testosterone. Waves of testosterone with a hint of cologne that called to her nipples like a sexy male siren luring her in for another sniff.

"You need a moment?"

She whirled around to find Colin standing in the doorway. He'd found a pair of jeans, but still no shirt, making his current position, hands gripping the trim above the door, all the more problematic. She now had a visual to match the feel and scent.

"Yes, I mean, no. I was just . . ."

"Smelling my shirt like it was porn?"

"Mine's wet." She closed her eyes and groaned again, this time from embarrassment. "My shirt is wet."

He headed toward her, not stopping until they were sharing the same space and she was forced to take a step back—bumping up against the counter. Colin rested his palms on the cabinets next to her head, his arms caging her in, his lips . . .

Oh my, this is bad. Incredibly, wonderfully bad.

"What else would you be referring to?"

"I don't want to talk about it." She had always been a tactile kind of person, so she quickly shoved the shirt between them like a shield so as not to climb him like a tree—a big, built tree than smelled like the hot summer nights of her teenage past.

"Talk about this?" He traced a finger along her jaw and the air went *snap-crackle-pop.*

Teagan swallowed and was a nanosecond away from agreeing when, from the kitchen, came an impatient, *"Arf! Arf! Yack."*

Gaze locked and loaded, Colin stepped back and came away with a fresh shirt. The big jerk winked. "Remember those towels. Second door to the right."

Colin West was in survival mode.

Hell, he'd blown right past survival mode.

That little run-in with Teagan yesterday had his fight-or-flight response sounding the alarm. He wasn't hardwired for flight, never had been, which was why it was imperative he fight the urge to follow through on any fireworks—past or future.

Each unexpected encounter threw him more off-kilter. Despite being a creature of habit, Teagan had become a master of the unexpected. There were a few times growing up that she'd shocked the hell out of him. Some of them good.

One of them not. And, going forward, that was the memory he needed to remember.

He'd been honest when he said he didn't hate her. But that didn't mean he trusted her. With neither one of them leaving Pacific Cove for the foreseeable future, navigating this situation was about as simple as navigating an abandoned minefield.

Good thing Colin knew better than to show weakness in the face of danger. After treating an injured and scared bear in the field, not much threw Colin off his game. He was levelheaded, calm under pressure, and knew how to take charge in even the most life-threatening of situations. It was what made him such a great vet. But it was his years of single parenthood that made his game face impenetrable.

Colin's phone pinged with a text. It was his daughter and,

Lord help him, she wanted to know if she could stay home from school. Apparently, she was having a pimple crisis.

Setting his internal response to cool, calm, and in control, he texted back.

> USE THE EXPENSIVE COVERUP YOU JUST HAD TO HAVE AND CHARGED TO THE "FOR EMERGENCIES ONLY" CARD.

> IT WAS AN EMERGENCY. I'M ON MY PERIOD & HAVE CRAMPS.

A few years ago, that tactic would have worked. But he'd since learned that, while he wasn't a woman and would never know what it felt like to have cramps, high school girls tended to use them as a go-to excuse for skirting responsibilities, skipping chores and school and—

> IT'S SWIM WEEK IN PE.

PE. Maddie's least favorite class of the day. She could toss a teammate twenty feet in the air, flip and fly across a cheer mat, but she couldn't run a mile without her asthma acting up or go in the shallow end without triggering swim-induced cramps. That was her story, and she was sticking to it.

> THERE ARE TAMPONS IN THE BATHROOM. IBUPROFEN'S IN THE MEDICINE CABINET.

> CAN YOU CALL THE SCHOOL & TELL THEM I CAN'T DO PE.

> YOU CAN ARGUE YOUR
> CASE WHEN YOU GET THERE.
> I'M AT WORK.

Colin put his phone on silent and grabbed the chart outside the exam room. The first patient of the morning was Ulysses, a seventy-pound bullmastiff puppy. Colin loved puppies. Their slobbery licks and wagging tails reminded him why he'd become a vet in the first place. And some days he needed that reminder. With his newly appointed boss, he needed those reminders more than ever.

He was reaching for the exam room door when his phone buzzed. Three separate times in rapid succession. Boom. Boom. Boom.

With a tired groan, he pulled the phone back out.

> IT'S MONDAY SO I HAVE MR. MILLER.

> HE DOESN'T KNOW HOW IT FEELS TO
> BE A WOMAN.

> AND HE'S A TOTAL DICK.

> LANGUAGE.

> IT'S TRUE. MAYBE I'LL ARGUE
> MY CASE BY KICKING HIM IN THE
> NUTS AND TELLING HIM THAT'S
> HOW CRAMPS FEEL.

OR MAYBE JUST SWIM

THE DAMN LAP.

LANGUAGE

The three blinking dots vanished, and he took a moment to enjoy the rare but refreshing drama-free silence as he slipped the phone into his lab coat pocket and entered the room.

"Good morning," he said, walking over to his patient and ruffling his ears, which led to Ulysses's entire body wagging. "It looks like Ulysses is in for a well-puppy checkup to get his last round of shots and a pre-neuter exam."

"About that," said Ulysses's dad, Gary. "I want his testicles in a jar."

Chapter 9

Mess with me and I'll fight back, mess with my
daughter and they'll never find your body.

—Unknown

"That's not a service we really provide," Colin said, wondering which one of the gods he'd pissed off. He wasn't a Greek scholar but whichever one liked to cause chaos was clearly behind the fuckery of the past few days.

"I'll pay extra. Whatever you want because this isn't a normal problem," Gary said.

"Why don't you take a seat, Mr. Kent, and tell me what's going on." Because it must be dire. Gary's hair was standing on end, his scruff was three days old, and his bloodshot eyes said he hadn't slept in a week.

Instead of sitting, Gary paced back and forth in the ten-by-twelve exam room, which only took three steps. At six-four and two-twenty pounds, with a dozen different tattoos on his arms, Gary didn't seem like an easily frazzled person. But the man was good and gone.

"I've got a daughter. Vivi. She plays varsity volleyball for Monterey High."

"Congratulations?"

Vet visits were about as much fun as going to the dentist. But this guy's response was different, almost as if Gary were borderline hysterical—a word he'd never ever use around Maddie.

Wanting to get back on track, Colin asked, "Is Ulysses showing any unusual behavior?" Colin ran his hands down the dog's sides and flanks, gently pushing on the kidneys and stomach. "What has you concerned?"

"Oh, she's good. That's what has me concerned."

"Ulysses?"

"No, Vivi." Gary ran a hand down his face. "She's better than good. Too good. So good that she's one of a handful of high school volleyball players picked to play on the premiere division's beach volleyball team."

Colin was used to wearing a therapist's hat. Between clients losing pets and the stress that accompanies procedures on beloved fur-babies, that one psychology class he'd taken during pre-med had more than paid off. But this was the first time he'd been asked to weigh in on family matters. After the last few weeks of drama with his own kid, he wasn't sure he was qualified.

Out of solidarity, Colin extended a bro-branch. "How does Vivi feel about the summer program?"

"She's over the moon. But the uniforms. God, those uniforms. They're going to give me an aneurism." Gary was back to pacing. "Overnight, she went from playing dress-up to dressing like she's in training to be on the cover of *Sports Illustrated*. Which is why I need Ulysses's . . . you know?"

Colin didn't know what Ulysses's *you know* had to do with it, but he felt Gary's pain.

Lately, Maddie had been testing the limits—on everything. It started after her birthday, when her mom reneged on her promise to fly Maddie to New York for spring break. Seemed Amanda's stepson was taking the semester off and was living with her, and she didn't want the added stress of trying, after all these years, to "blend" the families. That's when Maddie's 'tude went supersonic.

For a while, Colin let it slide. Gave her a pass. Until last Friday when she lied about sleeping at her cousin's to go to a party. His brother, Ethan, thought the girls were at Colin's, Colin thought the opposite, and the little sneaks thought they'd get away with it.

They failed to see the hole in their scheme. Colin had practically written the Successful Sneak Handbook. Doors, windows, trellises, trees, he knew all the tricks. Including when to trust his intuition.

That night, his Spidey senses tingled. Kind of the way they'd reacted when he'd spied the grape juice stain on Teagan's shirt—the cleavage part.

"And what does Ulysses have to do with this?"

"His testicles. After you castrate him, of course."

At the word, Ulysses whimpered, then put his butt firmly on the concrete floor, guarding his testicles from any jars that might be present.

"We call it neutering." Colin gave the dog a reassuring pet, then rolled his chair over and took a seat, leaning in, making sure his posture conveyed openness to reassure Gary.

"Call it what you like, but I want to keep them. I mean, I don't want to hold them—I want them in a jar. Preserved in liquid so I can place it on my desk. That way when some punk from school decides to hit on my Vivi, I can bring him into my office and explain what happened to the last punk who hit on her."

Colin's pocket vibrated. Speaking of testicles, he'd give his left one to be at a poker game with the guys, a good hand, a cold beer, and his phone on the bottom of the Pacific.

"Do you need to get that, Doc?"

Colin paused. "You heard that? It's in my pocket on silence."

"Dad hearing. It comes with having five daughters."

"Is Vivi the—?"

"Oldest." Gary rubbed his chest as if trying to relieve heartburn. "I have four more to go. My blood pressure is through the roof. I have to keep myself from punching little pricks in the throat who look at her. And my hair. I've got premature balding. I'll have a comb-over by forty."

Colin could relate. While he could still run a marathon in under four hours, some days he felt eighty.

"Wow, just saying it out loud . . . well, I guess I've lost my mind." He shook his head. "It's bad enough that Ulysses is losing his manhood. What kind of dog dad would I be to display evidence of the most traumatic day of his life?"

"I assure you that the procedure is quick, and the pain will be minimal. Ulysses might be a little sore and slow the first couple days but we'll send him home with some painkillers and a cone, so he doesn't nip at the stitches. But he'll be just fine. I'll send in my vet tech, Barb, to schedule the appointment."

"Thanks, Doc," Gary said, sticking out his hand. "For hearing me out. It really helped."

Colin didn't know about that, but he left Ulysses and Gary in the capable hands of his vet tech, Barb, who specialized in husbandry—the human and animal kind—and headed to the breakroom, where he turned on the Keurig. He was checking his schedule for the day when the percolating stopped, leaving him a steaming cup of joe. He breathed in the heavenly scent of caffeine and took a sip as his phone vibrated.

He set down the mug and, sure as shit, it was Maddison.

> CAN I BORROW THE CAR AFTER SCHOOL?

> SHOULDN'T YOU BE IN CLASS?

> I AM. SO CAN I?

> WHY? AND DON'T THEY HAVE A STRICT NO PHONE IN CLASS POLICY?

> I HAVE PLANS.

> AND NO ONE CALLS THEM PHONES, DAD. THEY'RE DEVICES.

I DIDN'T GET THAT MEMO.
WHAT KIND OF PLANS?

HANGING OUT.

WITH WHO?

SHAY.

AND?

FRIENDS.

MALE FRIENDS?

...

The dots disappeared. His gut told him the two girls were getting her story straight. Never ones to make the same mistake twice, they would concoct a smarter plan for next time. Today being next time.

But there wouldn't be a next time. Not with him on notice until they both left for college.

MALE FRIENDS I KNOW?

SO THERE MIGHT BE A GUY
AND NO YOU DON'T KNOW HIM.

> WHERE DID YOU MEET?

> ...

Colin watched his "device" as a long, conspiring silence ensued. The three dots made a fast and furious disappearing act, which worked for him since his patient load was double-booked and they were short one vet.

His hot coffee a lost cause, Colin walked to the front desk, where Barb was effortlessly juggling the phone, printer, and receiving incoming patients. She looked up and smiled. "Your brother wants to get together for lunch."

Colin had planned on scarfing down a sub sandwich at his desk so the backlog of patients didn't get any worse. "Can you call him back and tell him I'm busy today?"

"Can't. He's in your office."

"And you're just telling me now?"

"Kim called first," she said, referring to Ethan's wife. "She told me not to tell you until Ethan was here."

His phone pinged again. And again.

"Shit." Colin pinched the bridge of his nose and let out a breath. He was overworked, over dependable, and over being over. "Tell Ethan he can wait." He looked at his screen. Maddie broke her earlier record with four rapid-fire texts.

> CAN I HAVE THE CAR THEN?

> OKAY. WHAT ABOUT NEXT WEEK?

> HELLO?

> DAD!?! WHY ARE YOU IGNORING ME?

> I'M NOT IGNORING YOU.
> I'M AT WORK.

> OH. RIGHT. SORRY.

> SO ABOUT THE CAR?

> WHAT PART OF AT WORK DID YOU MISS?

He'd just lowered his cell when the reception phone rang.

"If that's Maddie, tell her, one more question about the car, and she's grounded for the rest of the foreseeable future."

"And have her stink-eyeing me? Pass." Barb answered the phone. "Jackson and Son Pacific Cove Animal Clinic. How can I help you?"

Every time he heard the "and Son" part, he felt a fiery ball of rage over what Ronald Senior's son had done to the practice. It made Colin question his decision to pass up the chance to buy the practice from his mentor.

Barb covered the mouthpiece. "Not Maddie."

"Thank God."

"It's Nancy from the Coffeekat. She has a litter of kittens that need to be vaccinated."

"Tell her to come by Saturday after ten."

Colin ran FurGet Me Not, a pro-bono, nonprofit animal out-reach every weekend. It was a *pay what you can* kind of arrangement. Besides time with Maddie, it was the best part of his week.

"Ronnie said I had to run every pro-bono case through him first," Barb explained. "Even threatened to take the expenses out of my paycheck if I went behind his back again. The little peckerhead."

Ronnie was a weasel in a cheap suit.

When Colin had taken a job with Ronald instead of opening up his own practice, his mentor promised to sell Colin the practice. Only he'd retired earlier than anticipated. Maddison had just started middle school and Colin didn't have the time to run the business end of the clinic. Colin had passed on the opportunity and Ronald Senior had passed everything down to his son, Ronnie, who was all about the bottom line with no interest in patient care.

"Tell Nancy to be here Saturday at ten. I'll handle Ronnie."

He'd do more than handle him. All Colin wanted was one day when he arrived home before midnight and woke after the sun. Although if Teagan showed up in those itty-bitty silky pajama bottoms, he'd crawl out of bed at five.

"What if he goes after my paycheck?"

"Anything the clinic won't absorb, I'll cover."

Barb shook her head. "You're going to wind up broke, sinking all your money into this place."

"I'm not homeless yet." In fact, in addition to the beach house, his parents had left their two sons a nice-sized inheritance.

"Your mom, God bless her soul, left you all that money so you could open your own practice."

"And I will, when the time is right." When Maddison was in LA, settled and starting her own life. Until then, she was his first concern.

He reached exam room three and took out his phone when it pinged. With a sigh he read the text.

BACK TO THE CAR

BACK TO WHERE YOU MET THIS FRIEND.

...

...

...

TINDER?

GOD! YOU NEVER LISTEN TO ME!

He'd hit the nail on the head. His fingers flew over the screen, responding in full caps so that there wouldn't be any misunderstandings. Even used her favorite punctuation.

HARD NOPE!

BUT YOU DON'T EVEN KNOW HIM

HE'S ON TINDER, THAT'S ALL I NEED TO KNOW.

SO, IS THAT A NO TO NEXT WEEK?

IT WILL BE A NO NEXT WEEK.
NO NEXT MONTH. AND A NO
NEXT YEAR. PLUS, YOU'RE
STILL GROUNDED FROM THAT
LITTLE STUNT YOU AND SHAY
PULLED.

WHATEVER!

Another ping . . .

YOU'RE RUINING MY
LIFE!

Another ping . . .

FYI. WHEN I'M IN
COLLEGE YOU WON'T
HAVE A SAY!

His heart dropped. Why did she keep reminding him he was about to be an empty nester? He'd already lost so much in the past few years—his dad, followed closely by his mom. Didn't she know his heart was breaking over the day she'd leave him too?

THEN WE'LL REVISIT
THIS WHEN YOU'RE
IN COLLEGE.

Between Maddie's texts and Ethan's unexpected visit, he was strongly considering divorcing his family. He was still thinking about the talk with his daughter when he spotted Ethan with a casserole dish of lasagna. Maybe lunch with Ethan was the exact lifeline Colin needed. Because as any smart doctor knew, when out of one's area of expertise, consult peers. Who better to find solidarity in than his big brother?

Ethan was four years older, married to the love of his life, with whom he had two teen daughters. Double hormonal trouble. His older daughter, Shay, was closer in age to Maddie, and they'd been inseparable since they were in diapers.

"Maddie wants to date some prick off Tinder."

"This is why I wanted to send the girls to Catholic school," Ethan pointed out. "You do know that this is all your fault. And why did you let her download Tinder?"

"Let? When was the last time either of us *let* them do anything?"

"It's getting out of hand." As if his appetite was gone, Ethan shoved his plate away and sat back on the office couch. "Kim keeps telling me it's time to cut the umbilical cord. Saying that if we gave the girls a little space, they might surprise us."

"Of course Kim said that. She went to Catholic school."

"She also went through puberty and grew boobs. We aren't exactly armed with the right equipment to empathize."

And there was the difference. Colin didn't have the luxury of empathy when it came to keeping Maddie safe. He didn't have a wife or partner to troubleshoot with or rely on as his brother did. Ethan and Kim were a united front when it came to their family. They had each other's back.

Maddie had Colin and he wasn't about to get distracted by things like dating apps or sexy neighbors. It was his job, and his job alone, to keep his kid safe and happy.

Not for the first time since the divorce, Colin wanted to strangle his ex for the way she'd handled things . . . still handled things. Present tense. If Amanda only knew how her bailing had shaped Maddie's world, shaken her daughter's confidence and self-worth. Not that Amanda ever would know, because that would require showing up.

A skill that was not in his ex's wheelhouse. Leaving Maddie's heart shattered.

Ethan let out a long breath. "I don't know, bro. Maybe she's right."

"Are you suggesting I should have said yes?" Colin asked. "With makeup and a push-up bra, Maddie could pass for twenty-five."

"Fuck no. You can quote me on that." Ethan went quiet, a clue that he was turning something over in his mind.

"Just say it."

"Kim thinks the girls have been sneaking out for a while. Going to the mall, hanging at the beach, cutting cheer practice."

"What?" Colin sat up. "No way. Maddie might have tried to sneak out to go to that party, but she promised me it was a first-time thing. Plus, I'd know if she skipped practice."

"Did you know about the guy on Tinder?"

"This is your fault."

"My fault?" Ethan argued. "You're the genius who let Maddie get her license. Kim and I are making Shay wait until graduation. It will eliminate unchaperoned trips to the mall that result in the getup my kid wore to school yesterday. Oh, and before you go laughing your ass off, Maddie's was worse."

Colin went stock still. "Describe worse?"

"She's my niece, I can't." Ethan closed his eyes as if trying to scrub the image from his database. "Just go through her closet."

"I wouldn't have to if you hadn't convinced me to put Maddie in kindergarten at four. She's a winter baby. I should have waited until she was five, but you went on and on about how the girls would do better together."

"And they have," Ethan said. "But we can't be with them twenty-four/seven."

"You're just saying this shit because Kim has control of your nuts," Colin said. "And Shay will be what? Almost nineteen when she goes off to college? Maddie won't even be eighteen."

"Which is why I've come up with a plan, since I know how you like your plans." Ethan sat forward, looking as if he were about to sell Colin on some multilevel marketing business. "GPS tracker."

"On the girls?"

"No, on your car so we can see where they're going."

"That 'we' sounds suspiciously like a 'me,' which means I get to be the bad guy. No way. Equal risk for equal reward."

"Well, tracing their phones doesn't work when they can hack them to say they're one place when they're someplace else. Like the mall." Ethan sat back, arms crossed over his chest, as if he was having a temper tantrum. "If you don't like it, then come up with a better idea, because I don't want to hear you crying when we discover our girls have a better dating life than you, Grandpa."

"Maddie isn't dating right now. And you're the grandpa."

"Are you getting laid on the regular?"

"No." Last year, he'd started seeing a single mom in town, who was looking for the same thing as Colin, a little fun. They'd met up a couple of times. The first time, they met at her place when her kids were at their dad's. She'd made it clear that this was a benefits-only situation. Which had been a-okay with him.

No promises, no drama, and absolutely no strings or expectations beyond the night. He'd never stayed over, always keeping it casual. The plan had been working until a couple months back, when she'd admitted she was looking for more than benefits and they'd parted ways.

Again, he was fine with that.

The whole situation made him gun-shy about women. A name flickered in his head, but he quickly banished it. Blamed it on nostalgia and the need to get laid.

"Then you're a grandpa." Ethan chuckled, like he was soooo funny. "You know, Amanda would be laughing her ass off if she heard that you're not getting any. Hell, when was the last time you even talked to a woman who wasn't asking you to castrate her poor dog?"

"It hasn't been that long, and who says I'm not dating? In fact, I saw Teagan three times this week."

"Wow, Teagan." Ethan studied him long and hard. "Define 'saw.'"

How did he describe what had transpired? They'd flirted, the air had crackled, he'd seen her thong, and she'd worn his sweatshirt home. And all of that happened without a single touch.

Ethan held up a hand. "You know what? I don't want to know. But Teagan?" He made a low whistle. "Talk about a blast from the past. I thought that ship had long since sailed."

"It never sailed. I mean it did."

"You don't sound so confident there, bro. It either has or hasn't."

"Hell." Colin ran a hand down his face, realizing he hadn't shaved in two days. Hadn't had time. "Between work, Maddie's schedule, and the time I spend at the free clinic, I can't remember when I had an entire day to myself. A day to relax and just be. Let alone date."

"That's all on you, man. Tell that little prick Ronnie Junior to go fuck himself when he comes to you to save the day after he fired three of the last hires."

"Soon he won't be my problem."

"Soon, soon, soon. Open your practice or stop flapping your lips," Ethan said. "Because we're tired of hearing you bitch about Ronnie."

"Waiting for the right time."

"And here I thought it was because Amanda took you to the bank."

"It was part of our divorce plan. I got full custody and the house. And why are you coming at me?" Colin asked.

"I'm tired of watching you bend over backward for the assholes of the world." Ethan shrugged. "You're always going to be my kid brother, so sue me if I get pissed on your behalf."

"I didn't give her anything I didn't want to." And that was the God's honest truth. "She got the cars and 401(k). I got Maddie. Which is why I'm waiting until she's settled in college to get my finances in order. Then I'll find the right location."

"Settled or retired? You and your plans. Mom is probably wagging her finger at you from heaven. Telling you to stop talking and do."

"Great advice. I'm done talking—now leave me so I can eat my lasagna in peace."

"Think about the tracker," Ethan said as Colin pushed him out the door. And he did think about it. Five minutes later, he decided Ethan didn't seem so crazy.

He walked to the reception desk. "Barb, is Mr. Kent still interested in saving, Ulysses's, uh—"

"Stallion-sized beanbags?"

"You heard?"

"Everyone heard. Mr. Kent was bellowing about it before I took him into the exam room. I actually moved him ahead of six patients."

Colin grimaced. "Thanks for that. And beanbags? Really?"

"Okay, how about meat clackers? Bojangles? Wrecking balls?"

"I get it. Is he on the books?"

"Yup, booked him an appointment for next week. Why?"

He closed his eyes. "Can you call him back and tell him the special request"—he whispered as if he were explaining sex positions to a librarian—"is on the house. I'll even provide the glass jar."

Chapter 10

Raising multiples is a walk in the park.

Jurassic Park.

— Unknown

Whoever said, "After having twins you get organized," clearly forgot the big "NOT" at the end.

Teagan, who used to be the Queen of Organized, had been dethroned so many times her crown no longer stood upright. The girls had awoken their usual squirmy selves, Garbage Disposal got into the trash and then immediately threw up the trash—plastic and all—and Teagan's wavy blond hair resembled a Q-tip. Then there was the schedule that had flipped her a resounding bird.

She was expected at Seaside Sandwiches in thirty minutes to pitch her rolls, Poppy was refusing to wear anything but pajama bottoms, and Lily was still refusing to talk to anyone except Poppy. *And* . . . bringing her super-fun morning full circle, Teagan was so tired from baking cupcakes for the entire preschool class, she'd accidently miscounted her sandwich rolls, leaving her short product for her big meeting. Seaside Sandwiches would be her first commercial account if she landed it.

She'd sell her best push-up bra for another adult to help her get through the morning. Sadly, her push-up bra was in the dirty clothes hamper and Harley wasn't well versed in adulting. After volunteering to drive the girls to school, Harley had pulled a Houdini, flaking on her promise, and leaving Teagan to keep their little world spinning—alone.

To that point, she was finishing up the girls' lunches when a piece of waffle hit her square in the chest.

"Whoa, hey. We don't throw," she scolded. Lily proved her wrong by throwing another piece of her precut, Mickey-shaped waffle onto the floor, where Garbage Disposal inhaled it in one breath. "What is going on?"

Lily tapped her sister on the arm. Her sister looked over and they did that silent communicate-through-the-ether thing.

"We don't like waffles," Poppy explained, and Lily crossed her arms in defiance.

"You love waffles."

"Nots your waffles. We likes Daddy's waffles." As if she weren't having a bad enough morning. Being compared to the most irresponsible person in her life and coming up short was more than a little upsetting.

It was gutting.

She looked at the ceiling and did some rapid blinking. She didn't have time for a breakdown, not to mention processing how, even though Frank was absent, he still managed to be the good cop. Today, she needed to appear personable and professional, sell herself as a baking goddess who made deals happen. At this point, she'd settle for anything that didn't resemble a frazzled, overworked, single mom who couldn't even count to ten.

"Everyone tackles things differently. For example, waffles," she said, reminding herself of her vow never, ever to talk trash about Frank—even when he made it so easy. "Just because I make them differently from your dad doesn't mean mine aren't good. Or that his are better. We're just different waffle makers who both love you with all of our hearts."

Lily whispered into Poppy's ear. Poppy said, "We want cheesy poofs!"

Teagan took in a deep, calming, recentering breath. Oh, to live in a world where the balance hung on one's ability to secure cheesy poofs. "They are not a breakfast food. Cheesy poofs are a snack food. And snacks are eaten after—"

"Then Pop-Tarts."

"Again, a snack not a meal." They weren't even on the approved snack list.

"Auntie Harley lets us have Pop-Tarts for breakfast," Poppy informed her. Lily's stare went all *Tell her* and Poppy added, "With Kool-Aid."

"Well, I'm not Harley and—"

Lily threw another waffle bomb which, had Garbage Disposal not intercepted it in mid-flight, would have splattered syrup on Teagan's new dark jeans.

"Young lady. One more move like that and you're going into time-out. Do you understand me?" Lily looked as if time-out were for sissies but Poppy, overwrought at the idea of being separated from her sister, began to wail, working her way up to an epic meltdown.

Lily, not so much. She crossed her little arms and dug in.

Most people thought that Poppy was the rabble-rouser because Lily was so soft-spoken. But Lily was the strategist and instigator, while Poppy was the executer. In the current clash between Teagan's healthy breakfast and Harley's Pop-Tarts and Kool-Aid combo, Lily had initiated a standoff.

Luckily for Lily, they were out of time. If Teagan didn't get them on the road ASAP, they'd all be late. Harley's irresponsible forgetfulness forced Teagan into a corner, with only two choices: eating in the car or no breakfast.

She hated breaking her *no eating in the car* rule, but if they were late, she'd have to go into the office to sign the girls in to school and she might miss her meeting.

Meeting first, bring down the hammer later.

"Okay, breakfast to-go."

"Yay!" Poppy cheered as if the tears had been a front.

"Get your shoes on and grab your backpacks. Your ride leaves in five minutes."

"Put her up high, Lily Cakes," Poppy said, in a voice resembling Harley. They did a high-five followed by a five-part secret handshake, which would have been adorable had Teagan been let in on the secret.

"Did Auntie teach you that?" she asked, irritated by how tiffed she sounded. So what if Harley was in on a secret handshake? Teagan had four years of memorable moments—like being pegged with a defiant piece of waffle.

Poppy was already slipping out of her booster and heading for the stairs with Lily on her heels. Teagan quickly loaded her bread into the car and was headed back into the kitchen when she saw it—the crocheted eyesore hanging from the living room ceiling, swinging in the morning breeze.

"Not today," Teagan murmured.

Too short to get it down by herself and too short on time to drag in the ladder, she grabbed The Slugger. Leaping in the air, she swung and missed. She swung and missed so many times that Garbage Disposal began to think it was a game.

Teagan would jump. He'd jump. Over and over the game went until Teagan made contact and hit the ceiling hook so hard it was ripped out of the ceiling. Sheetrock dust and pieces of plaster rained down on her blue blouse, but it was worth it. She gathered up the swing, wrapped the crocheted rope around the seat until there was just enough left to tie a pretty little bow, and placed it in the middle of Harley's bed, then decided to text her own personal hurricane.

WTF

YOU NEED TO BE MORE SPECIFIC THAN THAT.

THERE ARE MANY OPTIONS.

> 1) WERE THE HELL ARE YOU?
> 2) YOU WERE SUPPOSED TO
> DRIVE THEM TO SCHOOL TODAY
> 3) WHAT HAPPENED TO
> "NO SUGAR UNTIL AFTER LUNCH"?

> IT WAS THE ONLY THING THEY'D
> EAT.

> YOU'RE THE ADULT. AND WHY
> WOULD THEY EAT WHOLE
> WHEAT WAFFLES WHEN POP-TARTS ARE AN OPTION?

> I WAS RAISED ON POP-TARTS
> AND I TURNED OUT JUST FINE.

> NO COMMENT.

Teagan felt a tiny bit bad for that last crack.

Harley's upbringing had been unconventional. Teagan could only imagine, after the few summers she'd spent with their dad, how unstructured and unpredictable it must have been. But sins of the father, and all that, would not touch her girls. She'd refused to let Frank's bad decisions affect them; there was no way she'd let her own dad's bad influence on Harley creep into the girls' life.

> I THOUGHT I WAS SUPPOSED
> TO TAKE THEM ON THURSDAY.

TODAY IS THURSDAY.
ALL DAY.

YOU SURE?

Teagan didn't bother to respond. She barely had the energy to get her kids out the front door, let alone reunite with her estranged sister, when they were about as compatible as clown shoes and a minefield.

As hard as her situation was, Teagan always behaved like an adult. Harley, on the other hand, had zero concept of personal space, zero filter, and zero adulting skills to speak of.

She also had zero money in her bank, leaving Teagan with a freeloader of a tenant, who had a problem showing up.

"How are you girls coming?" she called upstairs, quickly sliding into a silky white tank, which complemented her light blue fitted blazer and stylish lapis necklace.

Both girls blew down the steps past her. Poppy was still in her purple pajama bottoms, and both girls were wearing their pink shirts. Today was white shirt day because it was an in-class day.

"Only white shirts get cheesy poofs for snack," she called after Poppy, who pretended she couldn't hear as she burst out the front door. The *You have to catch me first* was implied—and very Harley-esque. Lily took off after her sister with Garbage Disposal on their heels.

"Oh, no, you don't." She snagged Garbage Disposal by the collar. "No leash, no go." She snapped the leash on but, suffering from a severe case of FOMO, the dog kept yanking on her arm.

Teagan had to make a fast decision: a dislocated shoulder or go with a less conventional but still nutritious breakfast. She dropped extra cheese sticks and apple slices into their bags.

#MomOfTheYear.

She grabbed two white school tees from the dirty clothes

hamper, a two-tiered tray of cupcakes, which could hold their own in *The Great British Bakeoff,* and the dog walked her to the door.

The cupcakes were loaded in the front. The dog in the back where a new Houdini-proof gate had been installed. And the two girls, reminding Teagan that she was no longer needed, loaded themselves into their respective boosters.

Teagan double-checked the doggie lock, double-checked the girls' boosters, and climbed into the SUV.

"Here." She handed each girl a lunch sack and tee. "Inside is an extra cheese stick and apple slices. You can eat them on the way to school, but the cheesy poofs don't leave that sack bag until lunchtime. Understood?"

They both nodded as if waffle-gate was nothing more than a conspiracy.

"Good. And I expect you to be in these white shirts by the time I pull into the drop-off queue."

There. Take control, line in the sand, large and in-charge mom.

"Then we're off." She pushed the key fob and the engine came to life. She let it idle for a moment while she rearranged the passenger seat. Not wanting the cupcakes to slide off, she picked up the boxes and was shifting them to the floorboard when all hell broke loose.

Garbage Disposal and his super sniffer managed to magically steal Poppy's cheese right out of her hot little hands from behind his all-wheel drive confines. Poppy turned to take it back, her legs jerking as she reached backward.

Fire-red converse high-tops hit a grand slam, the top cupcake box flying over the console to land on the driver's-side floorboard. Cupcakes, which she had made as her first Snack Mom showing, ricocheted around the plastic container, icing painting the lid and sides. Then there was the smaller container, holding only two cupcakes to make an even twenty-six, one for every pre-K kiddo in the class. It didn't clear the console but landed instead on the cup holder.

The lid and container parted ways, two generously frosted

cupcakes nailing her in the right boob, before tumbling down her front to rest on her dark jeans.

"No." She picked the cupcake up and tried to right the frosting. It was no use—the frosting and cake were about as likely to reconcile as Teagan and Frank.

"*No, no, no.*" She rubbed at the frosting, only making things worse. "*No! No, no, no!*" As if denying it over and over would make the cupcakes climb back into the containers and the morning spin back to daybreak, giving her a redo on the whole ordeal. She deserved a redo.

Today was supposed to be her redo. The day she proved her abilities, reaffirmed that she was capable of delivering on her promises. To her nonna, her girls, and to herself.

If not, then what was the point of it all? She'd uprooted her family to come home and revive her family's business. To reclaim her life, use her fresh new start to change the trajectory, seize new possibilities—and undo all the heartbreaking wrongs.

Picking up on Teagan's emotions and stress, Poppy started crying and Lily joined in, sending Garbage Disposal into a howling fit that made wolves look like sissies.

"It's okay," she said quietly, reaching out to take each girl's hand and creating that physical bond between mother and daughter, before channeling the calm, in-control woman she'd been before kids.

She might not be in the running for #MomOfTheYear but she knew how to pull her shit together #LikeAMom.

"We're okay. It wasn't anyone's fault. Mommy just needs a quiet moment to reboot." And a new shirt. She turned back around to assess the damage, and that's when she realized the gravity of the situation. She had hot, sticky, melting frosting on her blouse, her pants, and even her black heels.

More importantly, the girls were looking to her for reassurance. Not to Harley or Frank, but the most dependable, constant—if somewhat boring—person in their little worlds.

The outcome of this moment is yours to decide. It could be a game ender or a game changer. Whatever actions and letdowns had led her to this moment, the outcome was up to her.

You hear that, Universe? Screw you! Had she said that out loud?

"Screw you," a tiny voice echoed from the back seat.

Teagan could have sworn it was Lily, but when she turned around, Lily had a hand over her mouth and Poppy was smiling as if she'd just exploded a piñata.

"While I commend the sentiment, other mommies might not. So, here's how it's going to go down. Neither of you repeat that word outside of this car and it's cheesy poofs for breakfast for the rest of the week."

"Yay!" Poppy cheered, and Teagan heard the sound of cheesy poof bags opening. Then the most wonderfully, amazingly beautiful thing happened. Lily cheered along. It wasn't a word, it was more of a sound, but it was enough to reassure Teagan that things were going to work out. Right there, in that moment, she was the kind of mom she wanted to be.

Their family might be little but they were fierce.

Bianchi fierce.

Teagan wasn't good at going with the flow but, as a baker, she knew when the formula failed, it was time to go by feel. This morning's fiasco was nothing more than a problem to be solved. And she loved solving problems.

First Problem: how to change clothes without leaving the girls alone in the car.

"Mommy needs your help. Lily, can you hand me the gym bag at your feet?"

She'd already slid off her blazer, which was miraculously frosting-free, and had carefully inched her silky tank off without getting more frosting on herself, when her gym bag slid through the two front seats. She rummaged through the bag— the nearly empty bag.

Crap. Her gym clothes were in the laundry room with the other piles of clean clothes ready to be put away. Time for Mac-Gyver mode.

"Poppy, I need the white shirt next to you."

"I can see that," a very amused, very sexy voice said from outside the window. She looked up and groaned because there stood Colin, dressed in blue scrubs like a responsible, professional adult. As if his world was in complete control.

He looked down at her bra and grinned.

She challenged that grin with one of her own. "May I help you?"

He looked at her daughters with cheesy poof powder all over their lips, and matching handprints on every piece of clothing, then back to her bra—which was cheesy poof powder–free.

He chuckled but wisely chose not to mention her current state of undress—or the frosting in her hair.

She decided he'd live to tease her another day. Plus, she might need his oven again, and dead he'd be no use to her.

"With the kids or my shirt?"

He casually leaned his forearms against the upper door. "It is hump day, so why don't we say, ladies' choice." Their gazes locked and there went that *snapcracklepop.*

Oh boy. Teagan slid her arms into the shirt. He may have gotten a peek, but she wasn't ready to give him a full eyeful, so she quickly yanked the micronized shirt over her head, tugging down on the hem. It was like trying to shove her respectable Bs into a training bra.

She was about to put her blazer back on when his comment sank to the pit of her stomach. "Wait. It's Wednesday?"

"Yes."

Man, she'd really screwed up. Teagan had been the one responsible for the mix-up, not Harley. Her sister had been in the right and yet, she didn't gloat. Teagan had just assumed Harley had screwed up again.

"I owe Harley an apology." Not wanting to exchange small talk with her ex sex-on-a-stick neighbor while busting out of her KIDDIE COVE PRE-K sausage casing, she folded her arms over her chest.

He shrugged. "It's Harley—she'll get over it."

"But she shouldn't have to." She owed her sister more than an apology. As well as the girls. It was pink day because today was a field trip to the Monterey Bay Aquarium. Which also meant that tomorrow was cupcake day.

"Hey, Mommy got it wrong," she said, looking at her daughters in the rearview mirror. "It *is* pink shirt day."

"We know," Poppy said.

"I really blew it," she said, quietly trying to pull herself together. To not let the simple mistake rock her newfound confidence. "If today is Wednesday, the bus already left for the aquarium, which means I have to drive the girls to their field trip to meet their class, and I'm dressed like I'm entering a wet T-shirt contest."

"If they're looking for a judge, sign me up." He glanced in the back seat, where the girls were entertaining themselves by feeding cheesy poofs to Garbage Disposal, oblivious to the world around them.

"Did I mention I'm a chaperone?"

"Would it make you feel better if I told you I've been there."

She snorted. "You are the most organized, together parent I've ever met. And from a former control queen, that is high praise."

"The first time I chaperoned a field trip, I lost a kid. Not my kid either."

"Oh no." She covered her mouth.

"Oh yes. Because I was the only dad there, they stuck me with a group of boys. They failed to mention I had a wanderer. One minute the kid was there, the next he'd vanished into thin air. I looked everywhere and eventually found him at the lost and found with the entire class and principal. Let's just say, I didn't get asked to chaperone for the rest of the year."

"At least you didn't look like you exploded out of the cake at a bachelor party."

"Slip on your workout leggings and the blazer over the top and no one will notice." He put a hand over his eyes, then parted two fingers. "I promise I won't look."

She reached out to give him a playful shove and he caught her hand and held it to his chest. They stayed like that for a frozen moment and that *snapcracklepop* became a *sizzlesizzlesnap*, sending tingles her way—tingles that went a little farther south than expected.

He stepped back. "I should probably go. . . ."

"You probably should." But neither moved.

"Bianchi."

"Yeah," she said again.

His expression softened with empathy and his voice gentled. "Don't be so hard on yourself. It doesn't matter what the other moms think. As long as you love your kids, you can't go wrong."

"Anything else I should know about, Dr. West?"

"I've found that the best way to keep it all straight is a good plan. I'd be more than happy to help you with that. Oh, as for the shirt. I say skip the blazer, you look incredible."

"Are you flirting with me?" she asked, because this felt different from a moment ago. This felt genuine and even a bit vulnerable.

He grinned, the double-barreled dimpled kind of smile that reminded her of the boy she'd fallen for. "I guess I am."

"I guess I am too," she said, surprised at her answer.

It was as if the past had fallen away and he was the same sweet boy who had stolen her heart.

Chapter 11

I'm sorry, were you talking? Because all I
heard was, "Lie, lie, lie, lie, lie, lie, lie," coming
from your mouth.

—Unknown

Colin was screwed. The kind of screwed that had nothing to
do with sex and everything to do with the sexy girl-next-door
whose life was set to permanent crisis mode. Even if he hadn't
been adamant about waiting for the right time to start dating,
Teagan was hands down the wrong woman. When he got back
out in the dating pool, it would be with someone who was at a
similar stage in life as he.

He'd spent the last seventeen years being someone's dad; he
wasn't looking to add anyone to the list of people who depended
on him. And while deep down Teagan wasn't someone who
needed saving, she definitely had that crazy cutie thing going on.

Colin had done crazy. Married her, divorced her, not looking
for a replacement. Plus, he already had one drama queen in his
life, and Teagan was drama personified.

But even as he rejected the idea, he couldn't deny a small
flicker of curiosity about what might happen. Colin was used to
pushing aside his own needs for others. Being a dad, he'd always
strived to do the right thing, even though it was rarely the easy
thing.

When it came to Teagan, he wasn't sure what he wanted to
do, but he had a good idea it bordered on trouble. For both of
them.

He sat on the back porch, sipping his morning espresso and

watching the waves crash against the shoreline. The early morning sun struggled to shine through the blanket of thick marine layer overhead. This was Colin's favorite time of day. The world was still asleep, the air was crisp, and he could feel the gentle sea spray in his face.

Hell, the whole reason he'd set his alarm was that he'd secretly been hoping Teagan would need to borrow his ovens again. Why he'd been disappointed when she didn't show up was beyond him. He had more offers from women than he had days in the week. So why then was he so caught up on the comings and goings of a woman he should be avoiding?

One month was all it took for Teagan to draw him into her crazy, chaotic, sexy vortex. He found it humorous that she was always pointing the finger at her sister for being a hurricane when Teagan herself could be a category five. It appeared Colin was drawn to hurricanes. Which explained why he was sitting in the one place that provided a clear view into her kitchen.

For the most part it was nothing but dirty bowls and cluttered counters. But every once in a while, he'd catch a glimpse of a knockout in an apron, flour, and, of course, her barely-there pajamas. It reminded him of that barely-there bra. It had been peach, lacy, and the inspiration for recent cold morning showers.

He hadn't been this giddy to see a girl since high school. Same girl, vastly different circumstances. Didn't mean he wasn't going to visit the farmer's market later. The way she glided around the kitchen, shaking her bum as if listening to an upbeat song, had him grinning.

His original plans had been an early morning surf, then heading to the clinic to start his patient load. He'd decided to skip the surf and instead go to the farmer's market.

Ethan's family was coming over for dinner and Colin had been thinking about barbecuing some salmon and maybe steamed clams, in his mom's garlic and white wine recipe. All ingredients he could get at the farmer's market. Maybe he'd pick up a loaf or two of fresh sourdough to soak up the clam broth.

He didn't know why he kept putting himself in the way of

the woman he was trying to avoid. Maybe it was because he felt bad for her. Divorce was hard. Being a single parent was overwhelming. Not that there weren't amazing moments. In fact, most of his time as a parent had been incredible. But it was the difficult times that really tested a person. And Teagan seemed to be tested at every turn.

At least Colin had Ethan and Kim, and when Maddison had been little, his parents had been a huge help. Teagan had Harley, but it was clear she wasn't confident she could rely on her sister. Colin understood that fear—he'd lived it. It was better to have no help than someone who would disappoint your kid.

The doorbell rang and a small ripple of anticipation zinged through his body. He walked through the house, took in a deep breath, went for casual, and opened the door. "You come to show me your cupcakes?"

"Uh, no, sir, but I'd be happy to go get you some if you'd like." Dressed in a pair of board shorts, a hooded sweatshirt, and a blink-and-you'll-miss-it beard, his beanpole of a lawn boy shifted nervously from side to side.

"You okay?" Colin asked.

Kade just nodded, took off his PACIFIC COLLEGE SURFING TEAM ballcap to wipe his forehead, put it back on, and nodded again.

"Oh man, did I forget to pay you this month?" Colin asked, rifling through the catch-all bowl on the entry table for his money clip. "How much do I owe you?"

It appeared Teagan wasn't the only one letting things slip through the cracks. Skipping a payment to Kade wasn't like being late on the cable bill. The kid was a hard worker and most of his money went to help his mom.

"Yes, well . . . no, sir." The kid nervously shuffled his feet. "I mean, yes, sir. You owe me for two weeks, but I'm not here on business."

Colin barely suppressed a grin. He liked this kid. Punctual, respectful, a hard worker. All traits that made him a good minientrepreneur. Even if he did look as if he were about to puke.

"All right, what can I do for you?"

"I was hoping you'd tell Maddie I'm here."

"Not going to happen." Colin slammed the door, then re-opened it, right as Kade was getting ready to knock again. "And you're fired."

"You didn't hire me, sir. Maddie did."

"For what?"

"Surfing lessons."

Colin thought back to the bathing suit he'd discovered in her closet. Not that he'd been snooping around—even he had his boundaries—but he'd been looking for her laundry hamper and there it was, two red triangles held together with fishing line. He hadn't seen the bottoms. Didn't need to. He knew exactly what went with that top.

His worst nightmare.

Surfing lesson, his ass. Maddie had hired a twenty-year-old college sophomore as an instructor, a boy who was studying marine biology and How to Seduce Girls at the local junior college. If she needed surfing lessons, Colin could teach her. When he was younger, he could have gone pro if vet school hadn't been calling.

"Yeah, that's a hard no." And he slammed the door—for a final time.

This was how he'd survived single parenthood, using skills left over from medical school to analyze and categorize information at lightning speed, then taking quick and decisive action. Sure, he'd made some mistakes over the years, but keeping his family in the forefront of his priorities was key. So it surprised him that he was waffling somewhere between Ethan and Barb's advice.

He didn't want Maddie to sneak behind his back. Then again, he didn't want her losing sight of the next chapter of her life—her life away from Pacific Cove. No matter how much he griped about her leaving for college, or how much the idea made his heart ache. He was proud of Maddie for working hard and getting into one of the most competitive public universities in the country. But, damn, he was going to miss her. He also wasn't going to be there.

So while he wanted to tell the kid to fuck off, he was no longer confident about what the right call was. He opened the door. "Come back after three and you and I will have a talk. Just you and me, man to man, and we'll see how I feel then."

Kade actually smiled as if he'd just won the lottery.

And that's how Colin found himself, eight hours later, after a particularly long and frustrating day when he'd been up to his eyeballs in patients because of understaffing issues, in a cramped position under his car, securing a GPS tracker to the underside of the back right wheel well.

He'd identified the in-between: He would give Maddison the benefit of the doubt while maintaining his own peace of mind. Plus, Kade was about as dangerous as a milkshake.

"What are you doing?"

He looked up to find his daughter. "I could ask you the same. Doesn't really look like surfing attire to me."

It didn't look like attire at all. Even though the fog had burned off, the temperature was still below seventy, yet she was wearing a flowy skirt whose hemline was an inch above the danger zone and a pair of thigh-high boots that reminded him of the one time a pharmaceutical rep took him to a strip club.

"Aren't you forgetting something?" Colin asked, because there was no way Maddie was wearing a bra under that crop top.

"Hashtag Free The Nip, Dad. Look it up."

Oh, he knew exactly what she was talking about. But it was clear she didn't fully understand the movement. Thank God.

Her eyes narrowed. "Wait. What are *you* doing?"

"Checking the tires." He stood, kicking the device box under the car and out of sight. Only not fast enough.

"No, that's a tracking device. Are you spying on me in my own car?"

"No, I was spying on you in *my* car. And I don't remember you asking to sign up for surfing lessons."

"Because I knew you'd say no. And I want to feel safe surfing this summer."

She had him there. Maddie has been wanting to get better at surfing since she'd picked up the hobby a few summers back.

Granted, she'd picked it up in hopes of getting picked up by some age-inappropriate punk but maybe, this time, he'd been too quick to jump to conclusions.

And if it had to be any guy, Kade was a good entry point.

"Fine, but you're not wearing that swimsuit I most definitely did not buy." Relationships were about compromise. Relationships that involved a teenage daughter were about picking which battles to fight.

"Mom bought it."

Of course she did. "You went behind my back, Mads."

"I asked her because—"

"You knew I'd say no?"

"Because I don't want to be the only girl on senior cut day to wear a razorback one-piece," she said, her voice catching and breaking his heart a little.

He didn't know what a razorback was, but it sounded a whole lot better than bikini.

His daughter sounded distraught. Maddie had a huge heart, which tended to make her a people pleaser. And sometimes, that caused her to give more weight to other people's opinions than her own.

Colin stood and opened his arms. "Come here."

When she didn't roll her eyes or scoff, but instead walked into his arms, Colin felt his world go right. Boys, hormones, and crop tops couldn't hide the fact that she'd always be his little girl. Although when he pulled her into a bear hug and she tucked her head under his chin, he registered that she didn't fit the way she used to. Also, her arms were draped by her sides and she felt as if she were enduring the hug rather than participating—but he'd take what he could get.

"Maybe we can work something out," he offered.

She pulled back, those big, daddy's girl eyes staring up at him, the tip of her nose dotted pink from tears. "Like what?"

His heart rolled over. "Why don't we start with surf lessons."

"Really?"

Colin took a deep breath and had to clench his jaw when he said, "Yeah. Kade seems like a stand-up guy."

"Ohmigod! Thank you so much." And she hugged him. Initiated and participated—it almost made agreeing to the date worth it. Colin knew Kade wouldn't push his luck because the kid was already scared shitless; he'd never risk life and limb by lying to Colin. But Maddie. *Oh, sweet Maddie.* She was born pushing—the rules, the limits, and every other thing that kept Colin sane.

She'd wear the poor kid down in an hour, tops, which was why Colin was going to have that sit-down before their lesson. He might even call Gary to borrow his jar.

Maddison had gone boy crazy around the same time she'd grown boobs. Two things for which he blamed her mother. Maddie was a West through and through. From her hazel-green eyes to her stubborn, do-or-die attitude. But she had her mother's freckles and red hair—and the fire that went with it. He wondered if Amanda recognized their daughter's tenacity. Her walk-on role in Maddie's life made it unlikely.

She'd have to put her daughter's needs ahead of her "full-time family" and that wasn't going to happen anytime soon. Sadly, Amanda had run out of time when it came to raising her amazing daughter.

"I'm going to text Kade about the lesson." Maddison pulled out her phone, and he didn't say a word. He and the kid had an understanding, so he let her little fingers swipe away. "Okay, he's going to meet me at Shay's in twenty minutes."

"You want to try that again?"

"What?" Maddie asked, sweet as honey. "You said I could take surf lessons. I already missed my first lesson this morning."

Something wasn't right, and there went those Spidey senses.

"Your first lesson with Kade?"

"Uh-huh." Despite everything she'd tried to get away with of late, Maddison was a terrible liar and an even worse keeper of secrets.

"Why is he meeting you at Shay's?" He was giving his daughter one last chance to roll back her lie of omission.

"The break is better there."

"The break is shit there. Third strike, Maddie. I talked with

Kade, and we had an agreement, which included a sit-down between the two of us." He held out his hand. "Privileges revoked. Hand over the keys."

"How do you know *he* wasn't lying?" Her tone was accusing, as if she were the offended party. "You're going to trust some guy over me?"

"Fair enough." He held out his hand. "Let me see the text thread."

She held the phone to her chest. "I don't have to prove myself to you."

"No, you don't, but if you want to leave the house anytime between now and your first day of college, you might want to give me Kade's number so I can set up a payment system with him." Her eyes began to tear up. "Were you even going to take lessons with him or was he just a patsy?" This time she had the decency to look ashamed. "Phone now."

"But . . ." she said.

He brought on the Dad look, and she folded like a deck of cards in Vegas. With a begrudging sigh, she handed him her cell. He checked that last text thread and, *yup*, a goddamned guy other than Kade. "Who the fuck names a kid Oak?"

"His parents are naturopaths."

"Is this the Tinder guy?" he asked and her face told him everything he needed to know. "So, what? You were going to lie to me, then ditch Kade to meet up with some guy you met on a dating app?"

"You say that like he's some serial killer."

"That's not what I'm worried about." There were so many other evils in the world that came from lying about your plans to meet up with a virtual stranger. "You have no idea who he is, and you were willing to meet him alone?"

"Shay knows him from work, and she knew where I was going."

"I'm sure her parents would like to hear about that."

"This isn't Shay's fault! And I just got off being grounded. This is so unfair."

"You say that as if you've never dated. You were with what's-his-name all junior year."

"That's what I mean! You never even called Liam by his name or trusted him."

"No. I didn't. But I trusted you. Enough to let you go to the after-prom party and stay at the hotel with your friends. I know he was there." She studied the tops of her shoes. "I never said no to postgame fun, even when I knew there'd be alcohol, because I trusted you enough to know you'd call me if you'd been drinking."

And she had called. Twice. He'd never punished her, instead praising her for making the right call. He was more interested in keeping an open line of communication than doling out punishment. And what was there to punish? Colin had done some pretty stupid shit as a teen. Partying, sneaking out, sweet-talking the prim girl-next-door into skinny-dipping—and more. But he'd snuck around because his parents were over-the-top strict.

He'd promised himself he wouldn't be that kind of parent. Then he'd become a dad and his perspective shifted. Parenting was hard—parenting a teen was terrifying. It was finding that right balance between giving them the freedom to make good choices and being there when they misstepped.

He wasn't some out-of-touch dad. He'd known that Maddie and Liam were fooling around, and even though that had been an awkward conversation, they'd worked through it. But this? It was as if he was using the wrong playbook.

Dating guys who were age-appropriate? He didn't like it but he accepted it.

Colin might hold the line a little closer than other parents, but for the most part he'd encouraged Maddie to explore her independence. Lately though, it was as if she was lying for the sake of lying. Sneaking around to get a rise out of him. Pushing him further and further away, which made decisions like this all the harder.

"Kade's almost twenty, you're a minor, but he was so up front and respectful about the whole thing, I was working my way up to a yes." Then she'd blown right past lying into using someone, and if there was one thing Colin hated worse than a liar it was a user. "I raised you better than that."

"You've raised me to be my own person and go after what I want. I want to date guys who aren't from my high school."

"Then date some guy from Monterey or Carmel High. Not some predator off a dating app. Does he know that you're a minor?"

"He knows I'm almost eighteen."

"State of California says that doesn't come for another ten months." He shook his head. "So you and this Oak guy are not going to happen." He handed her back the phone. "You blew it, kid. Until I can trust you, no car, no friends, and no phone unless you're on the home Wi-Fi."

"But Shay's eighteenth birthday is next weekend."

"You might want to call her and unRSVP."

Kim was going to chew his ass out for making Shay celebrate a milestone without her cousin, but Ethan would understand. If he didn't, Colin might call Gary for some father-to-father support. Hell, maybe Colin and Gary could start a Daddies of Teen Daughters support group.

"What about school? How will I get to and from practice?"

"Better invest some of that birthday money in a bus pass."

This time real tears ensued. A lot of them. Colin almost tried to convince himself that her tears no longer affected him—but then he'd be the liar.

"You just wait until I turn eighteen," she threatened, her voice so loud, Ms. Jessup's head poked out from between the blinds. "I'll get a job like Shay and buy my own car. Then you can't stop me from going wherever I want."

"While you're saving money for that car, remember that you'll also need insurance and gas money," he said calmly.

She fisted her hands and dramatically yelled, "You're ruining my life."

"I thought I did that last week."

"Mom wouldn't have been such a hard-ass."

She was angry and ashamed for being caught in a lie, and she'd lashed out. Even though he knew the whys, understanding didn't take away the sledgehammer to the chest.

"Maybe, but she's not here. I am," he said and, *ouch,* maybe she wasn't the only one angry. Sure, Amanda hadn't hesitated to take the money and run, then use her own daughter as a bargaining chip to clean Colin out. But his comment wasn't cool.

Maddison's tears spilled down her face and she took a small step back. He felt like an ass for using Amanda to get his point across. His heart ached whenever Maddison talked about her mom. He knew there was still a part of her that wanted her mommy to come home and come through on her promises.

Amanda might like holiday calls and school photos to show her friends what a beautiful daughter she had, but she was predictable when it came to her kid's needs. Amanda would always be a no-show.

Something he refused to be. But that didn't give him the right to act holier than thou. So even though Maddie had lashed out, that didn't give him an excuse to bite back. He was the parent, and she was a cornered and emotional teen.

"That wasn't my best moment," he admitted quietly. "And I'm sorry."

"It doesn't matter." Maddison wiped angrily at her tears. "This is just another reason why I'm going to New York after graduation."

His heart stilled right there in his chest. "You mean UCLA."

"Nope." She popped that P so loud, Ethan probably heard it across town. "NYU."

He shook his head even as she was nodding hers. "What about the plan? UCLA then Berkeley."

"Your plan sucks."

What sucked was that everyone kept changing *their* plans. He had a life plan too, which was continuously getting jacked up by everyone else in his life. But this was the most important plan and he needed it to work. Needed Maddie to stay close to home, because when Amanda became tired of playing Mom of the Year, and she would, Maddie's heart would be shattered and Colin wouldn't be nearby to put it back together again.

"It was your plan," he reminded her. "You came home from cheer camp and told me you wanted to go to UCLA, so we both made plans around your moving to Los Angeles."

"Well, I want different things now."

"Your different things aren't covered in your college fund. UCLA is in-state." Five hours away. Far enough for independence but close enough to come home on the weekends—or if she got homesick. New York had no homesick emergency button. "NYU is not only private, it's triple the cost."

"Hudson is loaded—did you know that?" Yes, he did. Amanda made a point of bragging about her husband's worth on every call. "Mom said he'd cover half."

Colin would believe it when the bank transfer came through. But even if Amanda did cover half, neither Maddie's college fund nor his retirement plan included an expensive private university in Manhattan.

"Your mom and I will talk about it."

"Too late," Maddie spat. "I've already declined all the California schools. NYU is our only option. Unless I take a gap year."

"Not happening and this decision required a conversation between you and me. I'll cover the cost I promised, but anything after that is up to you."

"Why does everything revolve around your stupid plans?" Maddie screamed, then ran into the house crying as if her world had truly ended. He heard her march up the steps, down the hall, and slam the bedroom door.

Colin pinched the spot between his eyes, which did nothing to ward off his impending headache, then pulled out his phone. "You slam it one more time and you lose it."

He calmly disconnected. The door opened and slammed once again with enough pent-up teenage drama to rattle the foundation. The focused anger was like a gunshot right through his chest.

Chapter 12

Being a single parent is like being tossed into
an MMA match with a toy lightsaber.

—Marina Adair

Teagan hadn't meant to eavesdrop. She was unloading groceries when she overheard arguing. She should have gone inside and minded her own business, but curiosity won out. Watching the calm, cool-as-a-cumber, in-control Colin sweat was worth the melting chocolate-chocolate-chunk ice cream in her truck.

She'd stopped at the bottom of her driveway, out of sight, so she didn't get a good look at the prosecution or the defendant, but she could hear every word. Mostly because Maddison was shouting at a level that reminded her of Garbage Disposal's squeaky toys.

Teagan couldn't help herself, nor could she look away. Partly because she wanted to make mental notes for when one—or both—of the girls hit puberty and aliens overtook their bodies, but mostly because she wanted to watch Colin in dad mode. Which was incredibly hot.

She was about to leave when he exited the house holding a pink bedroom door.

The sexy neighbor and arbitrator was dressed in street clothes today. Flip-flops, cargo shorts with a million-and-one different pockets, holding a million-and-one different secrets, and just tight enough in the rear to showcase a butt for the ages. Up top he had on a light green T-shirt advertising the FURGET ME NOT ANIMAL FOUNDATION, which clung to his biceps and that jaw-dropping chest that had been made for cuddling.

Naked cuddling.

But right now he didn't look as if he were thinking about cuddling, his posture was more frustrated man, brought on, no doubt, by a pissy teen. But it was the tired expression beneath it all that tugged at her strings. Colin had sounded casual, but his stance told a different story. Maddison's words had cut deep.

She turned to make a stealth escape but the Colin-induced emotions she still hadn't admitted to prompted her to step out from her hidey-hole and onto his driveway.

Colin stopped dead in his tracks—*was he blushing?*—and expelled a breath. He leaned the door against a sidewall in the garage, then grabbed two beers by the necks from an ice cooler. Based on the empty bottles on top, she assumed the door debate had been the most recent in a long line of disappointments that day.

"How long have you been standing there?" he asked.

"Long enough to hear how you were ruining her life."

He shrugged as he walked toward her. "I do it daily."

"I'm so sorry. I didn't mean to snoop."

"Look, my boss short-staffed the clinic today and lied about it. He also canceled a pro bono contract with a local shelter and lied about it. My kid went behind my back to try to go surfing with a guy who's probably old enough to buy beer and lied about it," he said, sounding bone tired. "I can't take any more lies, white or door-slamming levels."

"I listened in on your argument and I'm sorry." That was a hard truth. "I was emptying the trunk when I heard that she's going to NYU."

"That's still up in the air." He looked up at the sky as if asking for divine intervention. "On a scale of 'silent treatment for a week' to 'finishing high school in New York with her mom,' how bad did I blow it?"

"Kind of like walking through a balloon factory dressed as a porcupine."

"Before you go there," he warned, twisting off the bottle caps and handing her a beer, "just remember, you'll have two of them."

"Take that back."

"Can't." He tapped her bottle with his, then took a long pull. "So, prepare yourself now. Soak up these moments, because it only gets harder."

"Said the man who didn't raise multiples. If it gets harder, I might rent them out to the high school as birth control."

He laughed, but the lines around his eyes didn't crinkle.

"I'm sorry about your boss," she said.

"Me too. I had to reroute eight foster pups to county services. In order to get them added to the shelter's already overflowing calendar, I had to agree to take on sixteen volunteer hours."

She reached out and brushed her hand against his, their knuckles barely touching. "I wish I could help you somehow."

"You can," he said and a thrill took flight in her chest. "How about you help me polish off these beers on my back deck?'

Spending time with him would be anything but a hardship, but . . . "Is that such a good idea?"

"Probably not."

She sighed. "I just pulled my girls out of their old school, away from their friends. This probably isn't the right time for me to be making bad decisions."

"Then let's make a good decision. You, me, those beers, and nothing more than two friends throwing back a few."

"Now who's lying?" she said and he chuckled—a real, *you can make my day* kind of chuckle that always made her chest go warm and fluttery. "Lead the way, friend."

She followed him through his garage and out the back, taking a seat next to him on his deck steps. They sat side by side, drinking beer and quietly watching the waves kiss the shoreline as the sun faded into the horizon. That golden hour right before sunset had always been her favorite time of day.

"This whole thing about surf lessons has me thinking," he said, his gaze still on the water. "The offer still stands."

She looked at him. "You made that offer when we were teenagers."

"Back then, I made it because I'd do anything to get my hands on you, especially in that barely-there white bathing suit."

Full-body tingles exploded. "And now?"

He slid her a sexy, heated sidelong look. "Do you still have that bathing suit?"

"I don't even remember what suit you're talking about."

His gaze finally met hers and, *whoa baby,* it nearly made her panties wet. "I can describe it for you . . . in great detail."

She swallowed. "Even if I had it, I doubt it would fit."

His gaze slid down her body and back. "Is that a challenge?"

She didn't know how to handle that curveball. Over the past month, he'd gone from stone cold to lukewarm with a few heat bubbles added to the mix. Now, he was at a solid ten on the seduction scale—and she didn't know how she felt about that. Her body knew, but her mind was warning that she should step away and remember there was no room in her life for a man.

Even a sexy, *make her heart skip a beat* man whom she might or might not have had a sex dream about last night—and the night before.

"I didn't mean it as one, but now I don't know," she admitted.

His gaze held hers until she had to look away. He chuckled, then went back to staring out at the ocean. "When you figure it out, let me know. As for the surfing lessons, the offer stands."

Her palms went damp at the thought of being in the open water. "Honestly, that offer scares me worse than the first."

"I know," he simply said. "Just remember that I'd be with you the whole time."

He knew why water more than ankle-deep sent her into a panic attack. Used to tell her how a father should be and how, when it came to kids, they'd do better. Even though they never had kids together, Colin had kept up his end of that promise.

"I know you're wondering if you made the right call, but you're an outstanding father, Colin. Don't lose sight of that."

She looked at his profile and it brought her back to those summer nights long ago when they'd share their deepest secrets and dreams on that same deck, holding hands and watching the tide roll in.

His thoughts must have tapped into a similar memory because, eyes still on the ocean, he reached out and took her hand.

She scooted close enough to rest her head on his shoulder and they both released an exhausted breath.

"When did everything become so complicated?" she asked quietly, not wanting to disturb the sounds of the ocean coming in to wash away the footsteps and lines in the sand.

"I wish I knew because I'd go back to that moment and appreciate it." He didn't have to remind her that those struggles had begun that last summer before college. She wondered how differently things would have turned out had she stayed.

"I'm sorry I left without saying goodbye."

He gave her hand a gentle squeeze. "You already apologized."

"For not saying goodbye. But I never told you how many times I regretted robbing us of those last few months."

He bent his head to meet her gaze. "We started out as friends, and though I was hurt for a long time, I knew deep down that you didn't do it to hurt me—you did it to protect yourself. And how could I be mad at you for that?"

She'd been with Frank for over a decade, but she'd never felt so understood or seen as she did with Colin. Their connection hadn't diminished with time, and she hoped it never would because he was the only person who knew the adventurous and fun-loving dreamer she'd been before the suffocating responsibility and heartache that came with adulthood.

Marriage, divorce, losing loved ones—it was enough to disillusion a person.

"Thank you." She had to look away to tame her emotions. "And thank you for still being that patient and forgiving guy I spent the best summers of my life with."

"Best summers of your life? Wow." He nudged her shoulder with his. "I might use that as an endorsement."

The last comment pricked a little, which was completely ridiculous. Who cared if he used it to pick up another woman. She wasn't looking to date and she certainly wasn't ready to date the guy who'd once owned her heart. No, tonight's walk down memory lane was enough.

She casually nudged him back, feeling anything but casual. She had not a single idea as to how he was feeling. That was one thing that had changed. Colin kept his feelings locked up tight these days. Not surprising, since his divorce sounded as turbulent as Teagan's parents' split. Betrayal did permanent damage, especially when you were the betrayed.

"Have you considered giving Maddison another chance?" she asked, hoping to turn the conversation away from them and onto common ground—kids.

"Clearly, you weren't there for the 'three strikes and you're out' part of the conversation." He straightened and let go of her hand.

"I have no idea what it's like to have a teen in the house but maybe she'll surprise you. If Harley turned it around maybe Maddison can too."

He looked at her as if she were crazy. "Do you remember how many times you snuck out of your house to meet me at the beach?"

"This is different. And if I hadn't snuck out, *we* never would have been."

He turned to face her, his gaze flicking to her lips, long enough to let her know she wasn't the only one having some unwanted feels. "Do you remember what we did those nights we snuck out?"

"Yes," she said, breathless.

He traced his thumb along her jawline, and the feels spread to encompass all the great continent of You Know You Want Him. "Yeah, so I know exactly what those guys are thinking. And I'm not ready for that."

"You mean the white bathing suit line of thinking?"

My word! Sizzle, sizzle, pop indeed. "That bathing suit consumed my every thought."

He pulled away and even though she knew it was for the best, she really wanted to see what would have happened if he let the pops and crackles take the lead.

"I know how much you love Maddison and worry about her." She was reminded of how, earlier at the grocer's, Poppy had pulled one of her famous disappearing acts, letting go of the cart to sniff out the Pop-Tarts. "The worry is justified. I fully understand parent worry. But don't forget that you raised her. You're a great dad, which means, lies aside, she's a smart, responsible kid."

"Most of the time. But lately?" He shook his head. "I've seriously considered putting in a babycam that activates whenever it detects a body climbing in, or out, her bedroom window. I may have raised her, but she has her mom's tenacity. When she wants something, she makes it happen."

"Isn't that a good thing?"

"When used for good instead of evil. She not only figured out how to apply to NYU on her own, but she managed to write some pretty amazing essays."

"Is that such a bad thing?" she asked. "Showing initiative? Lily is relentless too."

He laughed. "Lily?"

"Oh yeah. Poppy always manages to find trouble, but Lily is the one who nods '*yes, mama*,' while concocting a plan to take over the world."

"So just like you and Harley."

"Basically. But I turned out fine." Hadn't Harley said the exact same thing? Maybe her sister wasn't the only one who needed to do some reflecting.

"Parenting takes trust, and it's hard to give her much freedom when she lies."

Teagan understood that on a cellular level. Ever since discovering Frank had lost everything they'd been building toward, trust was difficult. She needed to forgive him for the girls' sake, but bridging the gap between needing and doing was like crossing the Mariana Trench without sinking to the bottom.

The hardest pill to swallow was that Frank hadn't come to her when things started getting bad. His lack of trust in her ability to handle a difficult situation played a big factor in her decision to file for divorce.

She turned toward Colin and suddenly they were face-to-face, so close she could see the green flecks in his eyes and the fact that he hadn't shaved, leaving him deliciously scruffy. Professional Colin was heart stopping; rough around the edges Colin made her nipples stand up and take notice.

"Are you upset that she lied or that she did something huge without talking to you?"

He slid her a guilty look. "Kids lie, teenagers lie a lot, but I hate that she didn't come to me. We've always talked to each other about everything. If I can handle the sex or period talk, I'm equipped to have the college talk. Now, when she leaves the house, I don't even know if she's going behind my back or making smart decisions."

Teagan covered her mouth and laughed. "I know this is not funny and you're really disappointed, and probably worried, but she's almost eighteen and will be leaving for college soon. When we were that age, we pretty much had complete and absolute freedom and anonymity."

"She's barely seventeen and according to California Penal Code 261.5, a minor is any person under the age of eighteen. So even when she goes off to New York, she'll still be a minor and therefore has to listen to me."

She chuckled again. Colin didn't seem to see the humor. "Didn't sound like she was listening a minute ago."

He raised a single brow. "You want to throw stones, Bianchi?"

She put her palms up in surrender. "Nope, just making an observation and, trust me, I am the last person to give parenting advice. I've spent the past year feeling like a complete failure in the mommy department. Between work, finalizing the divorce, and reinventing Bread N Butter, I feel like I'm missing all the good stuff."

His expression softened, warmed. "I remember those days, right after Amanda left, and I was a single parent to a toddler overnight. Thankfully, my parents were still around. I don't know if I could have managed without them."

"I didn't realize she was so young when you divorced."

"More like Amanda bailed. And not just on me, but Maddison too."

Her heart ached for Maddison, who had woken up one morning to find her family shattered and a parent MIA. Divorce had been enough to steal Lily's voice; Teagan could only imagine the lasting scars Maddison still carried.

"That's awful. It's also my fear with Frank," she admitted. "That he'll relapse, and the girls will suffer. Even worse, that he'll decide parenting from a distance is too hard. When things get rough, Frank's MO is to disappear. He always has a justification, but the devastation is the same."

"There isn't any problem big enough to keep a good parent from their kid."

"Remind me of that when he comes around and I act as if everything is fine." Teagan always liked to appear as though she had it all together. She felt that if she hid the fact that she was afraid her life was falling apart, the fear wouldn't become reality. It was how she'd made it through her childhood, and then her failed marriage.

As if reading her mind, he said, "Being a single parent is like being tossed into an MMA match with a toy lightsaber."

She laughed. "When do we get to the part where you make me feel better?"

"Right now." He leaned in and he gave her cheek a sweet kiss, then whispered, "You're doing a great job. Your kids are clearly happy and feel secure and, most importantly, they're surrounded with love. Cut yourself some slack, Bianchi. You're doing the best you can right now."

"Then why does it feel like my best isn't good enough?"

He crooked a finger under her chin and lifted her head so he could look her square in the eye. "Because good parents are always the hardest on themselves. Look at me—I just ripped the door off my daughter's room."

"It seemed justifiable. I'm actually impressed that you didn't run it through a wood chipper."

He grinned. "Impressed, huh?"

"I can't believe I'm going to go through this, times two," she said. "And I can't believe I'm saying this, but Harley is really coming through."

"I guess we are both learning that people can change, and sometimes for the better."

Chapter 13

Being sisters means you always have backup.

—Unknown

Harley was stuck between adulting and a huge promise. Two things that gave her hives.

She didn't do the first because it meant being reliable. And she didn't do the second because it meant being reliable. Growing up, Harley hadn't been shown many examples of what that even looked like.

She'd been a lot of things in her lifetime: crony, colleague, sister, wing-girl, alibi, backup driver. But she'd never been the backup plan. The person who held down the fort while the parents were away. She was large and in charge but not when it came to anything that really mattered.

Like family.

It was Saturday, which was farmer's market day. Harley had been assistant baker, brander, marketer, packager, and that was all before sunrise.

Knowing that Bread N Butter's branding was thirty years outdated, she'd spent the better part of the week designing a new logo, even making pamphlets for tourists and small businesses. Then there were the new BREAD N BUTTER ME BEAUTIFUL stickers, which she'd stuck on every package of bread before it went out the door. And when that door had closed, Harley switched gears.

Nannying had become one of her favorite parts of the day. She loved every moment of it because it brought her and her nieces closer—and carved out a small place in their day-to-day lives where Auntie Harley belonged.

But right then, Harley belonged across town for an appointment with a prospective client. She was meeting with Ian, the owner of the Soup Stop, a waterfront café that was famous for its clam chowder and chili bowls. Ian had agreed to meet her for coffee to discuss serving his soups in Bread N Butter's sourdough bowls. Which would be a huge win for the business—and it was too late to cancel. Especially since Harley had rescheduled with him twice already due to family calendar mishaps.

And now, Teagan had called a couple of hours ago, saying she'd be a little late. Delores, from Lighthouse Hotel, had finally swung by the farmer's market to taste their bread. It sounded as if it was going well and Harley didn't want to rush things, but even when both she and Teagan were home, they were clearly outmatched by the twins.

Sure, there were times over the past month when Harley had screwed up and let Teagan down. Hell, they were both screwed up, thanks to their crazy childhood, but this was her time to right some of those wrongs. So, last week, Harley had made an executive decision that would make her sister's life so much easier. She'd put out feelers for a when-needed nanny and found the perfect one. The sitter was mature, reliable, and lived nearby. Providing Teagan and Harley with a solution for the occasional cross-booking on the family calendar.

Which was how Harley made it to the historic downtown with time to spare.

Downtown Pacific Cove was over a century old and spanned five blocks, which were lined with gas lamps and double-storied storefronts, made of hand-laid brick with brightly painted trim. Retailers and cafés occupied the ground-floor spaces, while the upper floors were mostly residential.

With its cobblestoned sidewalks and upcycled water basins, which were originally used for tired horses and now overflowed with white tulips and bright lavender ornamental cabbage, Pacific Cove looked like the set of a Hallmark movie. To Harley, it was starting to feel like home.

Laptop and branding package in hand, stride dialed to a full strut, she headed up Lighthouse Way, reaching the Soup Stop right as her phone pinged.

Nervous that it might be the sitter texting to tell her that the twins were anarchists, she quickly pulled her cell out of her purse. And that strut turned into a stumble.

It was Bryan. Sending the latest text in a never-ending and ongoing thread which consisted of him asking how she was doing, and her promising herself she'd answer as soon as she got up the courage. But courage or not—and it was definitely a not situation—she knew she had to respond now.

Besides the sporadic *I'm good* and *How are you*s, she'd been putting him off for weeks, and that wasn't the mature or right thing to do. And Harley was on a new path.

Rule Four: Adulting is doing the right thing even when it's the hard thing.

She read his text.

> WHEN YOU'RE NOT DEAD YOU RETURN A TEXT.

> I'M NOT DEAD & I'M SORRY FOR WORRYING YOU. I'M JUST TRYING TO FIGURE THINGS OUT.

She hit Send, surprised at the emotions barreling through her as she waited for a response. Her feelings were in direct conflict with her decision to move on.

Harley didn't know how to do long-term. She couldn't even commit to a to-go order. Who knew what they wanted before standing at the cash register? Sadly, she knew she wanted Bryan the moment they met. Only he wanted things she couldn't give him. Things she didn't even know how to give—commitment, permanence, and the kind of relationship that went the distance.

All those things conflicted with her *take life as it comes* philosophy. Fear and uncertainty consumed her. She didn't want to let go of Bryan. Yet no matter how many times her head told her it was "time's up," her heart kept delaying the inevitable.

> PEOPLE PAY ME A LOT OF MONEY TO FIGURE THINGS OUT.

> I'LL GIVE YOU THE FAMILY DISCOUNT.

Something deep inside twisted painfully at the word *family*. She was barely managing to be a part of her own family; there was zero chance she could handle being a part of his family. No matter how much she wanted to. Three brothers, two sisters, and parents who'd been married for forty years. Nowhere in that equation was there room for a frequent flyer of a girlfriend who had unlimited miles and a rule against round-trip relationships.

> I TOLD YOU WHEN I LEFT, DON'T WAIT FOR ME. YOU DO YOU WHILE I DO ME.

> CAN YOU AT LEAST TELL ME WHERE YOU ARE?

> I'M AT HOME.

FUNNY, YOU NEVER MENTIONED WHERE HOME WAS. JUST THAT YOU GREW UP ON THE ROAD WITH YOUR DAD. I ALSO DIDN'T KNOW YOU HAD A NONNA. OR A HOME WITHIN DRIVING DISTANCE.

She had grown up on the road. Zero permanence. Zero commitments. Zero heartache. But her heart was aching now. Which was the only reason she could come up with for why she was throwing out mixed signals.

I NEED A LITTLE MORE TIME.

TIME I CAN GIVE YOU AS LONG AS YOU ANSWER MY TEXTS AND LET ME KNOW YOU'RE OKAY.

. . .

. . .

HAR?

OKAY

Who knew that one word—four little letters—could be such a boldface, cowardly lie.

Bok, Bok, Harley Ashford. *Bok, bok.*

By the time Teagan pulled into the driveway, it was nearly three and she was dead on her feet. Her excitement, though, that was at a giddy grin. Not only had she sold out, she'd run into Delores, who owned the Lighthouse Hotel and wanted to give Bread N Butter a trial run as her sole bread supplier.

It was one of those right place right time situations. Serendipity at its best.

She walked through the front door and headed straight for the family room. She needed to see her girls, put her feet up, and maybe even have a celebratory glass of wine. Teagan hadn't treated herself to an afternoon glass in years. But she was bursting with pride and excitement.

She totally had this mommy-preneur thing down. Successfully balancing work and parenthood and excelling at both. A harmonious split she hadn't been sure she'd ever achieve. And a huge part of that achievement was due to Harley really stepping up.

"Har?" she called out. "You're never going to believe what happened."

She reached the entry and stopped. The house was a complete disaster. Toys were strewn across the floor; plates with sandwich crusts and neglected carrot sticks sat on the no-food-allowed coffee table.

The house had been spotless when Teagan had left and now it looked as if a toy bomb had detonated. Hard proof of a hurricane blowing through.

Teagan moved to pick up an abandoned tutu and nearly tripped over a stranger, sitting in Harley's re-hung hammock, her well-worn tennies violating Teagan's treasured coffee table.

Her first thought was that one of Harley's tumbleweed friends had decided to crash. Or maybe she'd forgotten to lock the door on her way out. She was tired as hell and three days ago she didn't know what day of the week it was.

None of that mattered now. Maybe it was all the true crime shows she'd been marathoning, but for all she knew, she could possibly be facing down a serial killer.

Her heart pounding, knee pits sweating, she grabbed The Slugger from the umbrella stand and choked up on it as if she were Babe Ruth and this was the World Series.

"Who are you and what the hell are you doing in my house?" Teagan demanded. "You have thirty seconds to leave or I'm calling the cops."

"Please don't call the cops—my dad will freak." The woman slowly turned and Teagan gasped, because it wasn't a woman—it was a teenager.

"Maddison?" she asked because, with her wavy hair and green eyes, she was a dead ringer for her father. "What are you doing here?"

She tried to come up with a good answer to that question, or why the teen was watching her television and eating her Pop-Tarts in her front room. Nothing came to mind.

Hands in the air, Maddison said, "I'm the new PA."

"PA?"

The girl looked ready to cry. "Yeah, like Harley's personal assistant? Your wife hired me to help out around the house and stuff? And there's two kids who I sometimes watch?" she said, putting a question mark on every statement.

"She's my sister."

Her irresponsible, hammock-hanging sister! Teagan should have known the honeymoon phase was too good to last. It wasn't just that her sister had hired a sitter without consulting her; she was mad at herself because she knew better than to put her trust in someone who hadn't earned long-term trust in, well, ever.

Teagan had been taken in by Harley's playful way with the girls and confused her connection to them with actually being reliable and responsible. And to think, just the other day, she'd laughed at Colin for not trusting his daughter. But there was a big difference between a high school student and a responsible adult. At least there should be.

Her sister was as reliable as a snowstorm in Vegas. Had Teagan gotten more than five hours' sleep in any one stretch she would have remembered that. It was times like this she missed having a husband—or her co-parent—close by.

"Wait." What exactly did "sometimes" mean?" Because she was pretty sure that Maddison, who was denied phone use and anything outside of her doorless bedroom, wasn't a Colin-approved PA. "Does your dad know you're here?"

She shrugged a big N. O. "He's at work and Harley was desperate. Her word not mine. She lets me join her beach yoga for free. She's so cool."

"She's something," Teagan mumbled. "Where is my sister?"

"Um, she's with some guy named Ian."

Of course she was. Like the seventeen-year-old across from her, Harley was, and always had been, boy crazy. She went through guys the way most people went through ice cream.

"But today's my first day. So I haven't seen him, and it really isn't a big deal. Harley had me fold some pamphlets, then left me in charge so she could go to the Coffeekat."

"She's having coffee and left you here? In charge?" Teagan closed her eyes. "Please tell me are you first-aid certified?"

"It's not current, but I was a junior lifeguard three summers in a row if that counts. Looks good on a college application, you know?" At least there was that. "Can I let my hands down?"

"Oh, of course." Teagan realized she was still holding the bat. "I'm sorry, I didn't mean to scare you."

"Are you still going to call the cops?"

"No. I just didn't expect to find a stranger in my house." Her heart was still pounding. "You startled me is all."

The teen let out a whoosh of relieved air. "You okay?" Teagan asked.

"Yeah," she said, but had the same woozy look Lily got when she was about to puke. "Can I go home now?"

"We're not done talking about your dad."

To Teagan's surprise, the teen actually met her gaze. "Do we have to? I mean, it's not like I'm out with a boy. I'm showing initiative by earning money."

"How would your dad feel about you showing initiative?"

"If he found out, he'd ground me for life. Luckily, that's an *if*, right?" Maddison gave a bright smile. Teagan's reply was a long, serious mom expression that resulted in more kiddo confessions than a Supreme Court judge. "Please. You can't tell him."

"Oh, I'm not telling him, you are."

"I can't." The girl sat down in the chair, her feet keeping it from swinging. "He'll just freak, like he always does."

"He doesn't seem like the freak-out type to me," Teagan said. "And you don't want to spend your last few months fighting with him, do you?"

Maddison shrugged. "I want my door back."

"And?"

"And maybe I should come clean."

"You mean, 'And I'm going to come clean, over dinner tonight.'"

Maddison rolled her eyes, but Teagan had gotten through to her. "Can I go home now?"

"Absolutely. And thanks for watching the kids." She looked around the house, groaning because, after a long, tiring day, it would take two hours to clean up the mess. "Speaking of my kids, where are they?"

"They're napping?"

"You got them to go down?" Teagan looked at her watch. "And they're still sleeping?"

Maddison looked confused. "Yeah, it was on the calendar."

"Wait. Why aren't they at Katie's birthday party?" Because that was on the calendar too, which meant Harley hadn't even needed a sitter. All she'd needed to do was to drop the girls off at Katie's.

"I guess it was canceled. Something about a lice outbreak. Ew. Harley asked me to cover since she had a coffee date."

Teagan paused. "No, you must have the wrong day because her 'date' isn't on the family calendar."

"Oh, Harley sent me a screenshot of the calendar, and I could have sworn I saw it."

Teagan was convinced there had been no coffee date on the

calendar, but when she looked at the girl's phone, there it was. Once again, guilt weighed heavily on her shoulders. "Oh, I forgot about that."

Second time in a week.

"How much do I owe you?"

Maddison grabbed her backpack. "Harley already paid me. A lot. See ya, Ms. Ashford."

"Bianchi," she corrected, but Maddison was already gone.

Chapter 14

They act like they fuck with me but I just act
like I believe them.

—Anonymous

"You've got Kitty Poppins waiting in exam room three," Barb said, handing Colin the file.

He flipped through it, got up to speed on his patient, and ignored the six texts that vibrated in his pocket. "This is the third time this month Gloria has brought Kitty Poppins in."

"Don't I know it," Barb said. "She's still not sleeping well."

"Is Gloria still sharing her morning cup of coffee with the cat?"

"Apparently, it's not the coffee." Barb bit back a smile and Colin wanted to walk away right then and there. "Kitty Poppins is urinating on mothballs and the urine combined with the mothballs is making meth."

"Gloria is claiming . . . ?"

Barb leveled him with a look that said she was about to ask for a vacation any moment. "That Kitty Poppins is high."

His vet-tech-slash-office-manager-slash-gatekeeper extraordinaire looked over her shoulder and leaned in conspiratorially. "Nancy called. She has an elderly cat who needs some dental work."

"Why are you whispering?"

"Because that little shit Ronnie told me that if I booked her, I'm fired."

"Tell her to drop the cat off and I'll slide him into the schedule."

Barb lowered her voice even more. "He cleared your pro bono schedule and now it's booked solid with paying customers."

Colin was done with having someone who didn't work at the clinic decide how the clinic would work.

"Schedule the cat," he said. "Where is he?"

"His office."

The "office" was where Ronnie watched the Golf Channel and twiddled his thumbs, which were lodged so far up his ass, Colin was surprised the idiot could sit.

He didn't bother knocking. "You want to explain what happened to my Saturday schedule?"

Eyes glued to the flat-screen, Ronnie said, "Saturdays are for paying customers."

"Your dad and I had a deal. Weekend mornings are for Fur-Get Me Not clients." It was part of the reason Colin had signed on with the practice. "Which your dad always supported. He believed in it and so do I."

Ronnie finally looked at Colin. "I'm not my dad and I'm not in the business of giving handouts. I'm in the business of making money."

"Actually, you're in the business of saving animals."

Arms folded behind his head, Ronnie leaned back in his chair. "That's why my dad left the business to me."

"Actually, he offered it to me first, but it wasn't the right time." A decision Colin was regretting at the moment.

"Still isn't. And if you want to continue to run the free clinic, you need to get outside funding to cover any and all expenses. Plus find a time other than work hours."

"The only reason your dad's clinic is so successful is because he understood the importance of giving back to the community. This isn't a business for someone looking to get rich. If so, your dad would have been a doctor."

"Lucky for all of us, that not's what happened. This isn't personal; it's about the bottom line."

Colin rested his palms flat on the desk and leaned in—real close. "This is personal as hell to me. I've dedicated nearly ten years to this practice, and I was operating on animals while you were still in grade school."

"If you want to make this personal, I can open Sunday mornings for paying customers as well."

Colin wanted like hell to argue but his phone rang. It was Maddison, who never called him. It was as if her entire generation was allergic to verbal communication. So his heart lurched.

"If I start working Sundays, I might just have to take off Mondays."

Ronnie's face paled. If Colin took off Mondays, there would be no one to do surgeries or run the back of the clinic. The threat was empty—he'd never do that to his patients—but it did scare Ronnie shitless.

With Ronnie still blabbering on about contracts and schedules, Colin walked out of the office and took the call. One look at Maddison's face on the screen and his stomach hollowed out with worry. Her nose was red and her cheeks were blotchy. She'd been crying and crying pretty hard.

"Baby, are you okay?" he asked even as he was grabbing his keys off his desk and heading down the hall, with Ronnie yelling that he didn't have another surgeon to cover Mondays.

"It's not personal, man, it's about the bottom line." And at that moment, Maddison was his bottom line.

"Yes," Maddie said. "I mean no. I mean, I'm okay but I'm totally freaking out."

"Slow down, tell me what's going on."

"I think I broke her."

"Cancel all my non-emergency patients, and call Dr. Lim in. He's on call," he said to Barb, not stopping as he rounded the registration desk and started out the front door.

"Broke who, Maddie?" he asked.

"Her." Maddison turned the phone's camera around to show a little girl holding a towel to another child's head. A bloody towel. Even worse, it was Teagan's little girl.

"Where's Teagan?"

"Who?"

"Her mom?"

"Oh, I think she's at work."

"Think?" *What the hell is going on?*

"Uh-huh. And I also think I'm going to pass out."

"Sit down and start with what happened," he said, running through the parking lot and climbing into his car. He didn't even have the door shut before he pushed the ignition button, the engine firing up as he snapped his cell into the holder.

"She fell and she's bleeding. And there's so much blood. And you know how I get with blood." Maddison gagged.

"I know, honey," he said, pulling out of the parking lot. He hit a red light and looked at his screen. "Turn the phone back and show me what we're dealing with."

Maddison turned the phone. After a quick glance he sighed, relieved that it was just a split chin. "She's going to be okay. It's just a cut."

"But there's so much blood." *Gak!*

"Head wounds always look worse than they are." He tapped his fingers on the steering wheel, agitated. "It's probably just a little cut."

"Don't say wounds." *Gak. Gak.*

Shit! Colin knew exactly what that sound meant and what would follow. Last time Maddison got a cut knee, she passed out and still managed to throw up all over his shirt.

"Take a deep breath."

Sitting on the porch steps, Maddie put her head between her knees and took a few deep breaths. "What do I do?" she asked, her voice muffled from her need-a-paper-bag position.

"Grab an adult." At the green light, he tore through the intersection, turning into his neighborhood.

"I'm the only adult here."

"Teagan left her kids alone?"

"Kind of. Harley hired me to be her PA."

Great, a child leading children. "We'll circle back to that later."

Maddie lifted her head and looked directly into the camera.

"Fantastic, looking forward to that. Since our talks work out so great for me."

"Did you call her mom?"

"I'm afraid to call. Cuz I'm also supposed to be the nanny and I don't want to lose this job."

When the hell had she started nannying?

On the one hand, he was relieved that Maddison was safe and that this crisis wasn't over a boy, but his gut told him that there was a part to this story he was missing. A big part.

"Hold tight, I'll call her mom." Damn, he didn't have Teagan's number. "Actually, do you have an emergency number?"

"I'm not a total idiot." She sniffled. "But can you call her?"

"This is your responsibility. The second you took the job, you agreed to be the responsible party. How are you going to move across country if you can't handle a little blood?"

"It isn't a little." *Gak. Gak.* "It's a lot because head wounds look worse than they are."

He rolled his eyes. "This is part of babysitting, so text her mom about what's going on."

"Okay, but don't hang up."

"I won't. I'm almost there." He made a hard right.

"I don't want you to leave work. I can handle it. Just tell me how to . . ." *Gak! Gak!*

"I'm just around the corner. Have the other twin grab a clean towel."

"Other twin, can you go grab a towel?" When he heard a loud reply, he guessed Lily was the bleeder. "Okay, got one."

"Now cover the wound and look away."

"Daddy, I'm really sorry." She was back to head-in-a-bag position.

"We'll talk about that later."

"I hate later as much as I hate blood."

"I'm just glad you called." She'd called him. It was the first time in months she'd initiated a conversation. She was mad at him, but she'd still called. Which meant she still needed him. He'd loved his old man, who was the best father, but Colin never would have called his dad in an emergency. Yet Maddie had called him.

"I'm glad you're my dad. Oh God, it's coming through the towel."

"I'm here." He pulled into Teagan's driveway and hopped out. "Did you hear back from Teagan?"

Maddison checked the phone. "No. I texted."

"Then you need to text her again, and if she doesn't respond, you'll have to call her." Because small cut or not, Teagan needed to know what had happened.

He turned to the injured party while Maddie texted again. "Hey there, which one are you?"

"That's Lily and she only talks to me," Poppy said.

He couldn't help but grin. Lily might not talk, but she was trouper. Not a single tear. "Want to tell me what happened?"

"We were going to find Miss Maddison to see if she could push us on Auntie's swing. But she was in da driveway, so I pushed and Lily slid off and felled."

He looked at Maddison. "Why were you in the driveway?"

Maddison looked away, so Poppy answered. "She was talking to a boy."

"We were talking about homework!" Maddison said with a hint of attitude. Colin shot her a look and she started crying. Again. "I know that's going to go in the *later* pile too."

And here he'd thought they were getting somewhere. He'd bragged to Ethan that he had things under control, but he didn't have shit under control. In fact, his entire life was out of control. All because he had to adjust his plan. And it would take a lot of adjustments to get back on track. Because of other people: like Amanda, like Ronnie and, even though he loved her more than life, like Maddison, who had been the latest sideswipe to his life.

At this point, the smart thing would be to steer into the skid. It was time to take back the reins. In fact, he was adopting a new plan.

He was tired of waiting. He was going to get his mojo back.

Chapter 15

Go ahead and act like Mom of the Year, but
don't forget some of us know you in real life.

–Unknown

It was dark by the time Teagan arrived home. The porch light
was on, the house looked intact, but the high from her meeting with Bread N Butter's first potential corporate client was
crushed under the uncertainty souring her stomach.

She'd been so caught up in work she'd failed her kids. The
eight texts and three missed calls confirmed it. The first two
calls were from Maddison, the last a voice mail from Colin,
saying he had the girls, and that Lily was okay, nothing a few
Steri-Strips and an ice pack couldn't fix.

Even so, the ride home was, unquestionably, the worst twenty
minutes of her life.

Not wanting to seem unprofessional to Delores, Teagan had
put her phone on silent for the duration of the meeting. What
kind of mom does that? If anything had happened to one of her
girls, she'd never forgive herself.

Maddison assured her that everything was okay, Lily was
fine, but Teagan needed to see her babies with her own eyes before her mind could stop envisioning every worst-case scenario.

When she pulled up at her house, her heart rate kicked into
overdrive, bordering on hypertension when she saw Colin's car
parked crooked in her driveway, as if he'd been in too much of a
rush to park—the kind of rush that implied more than a little cut.

She pulled in behind him. Grabbing her purse and sample bags, she ran up the walkway and burst into the house.

"Colin?" she called out. "Girls?"

She heard noise coming from the back of the house and followed it to the kitchen. This time her heart rate raced for a different reason all together.

Colin stood in her kitchen, in scrubs and socks, looking sexy and capable, like some modern-day knight in the pink IS IT READY YET? IS IT READY YET? IS IT READY YET? apron that the girls had gifted her last Christmas.

Lily stood on her flower-shaped kiddie stool with a bandage on her chin, nibbling on her lower lip as she did when in deep concentration. Poppy was thrown over Colin's shoulder in a fireman's hold, squealing with delight. They were happy, content—and safe.

Remarkable, considering everything that had happened. Even more remarkable was Colin, handling her world in a way that she'd never achieved on even her best days. He was calm and capable, his lighthearted energy setting the tone for the others.

When she'd left earlier, her house, the kids, even the kitchen had been a disaster. Now, the floor was toy-free, the kitchen relatively clean, considering it was occupied by just-under-four-feet twins. As Teagan caught a glimpse of her reflection in the window, she couldn't help but notice that she was the disaster in the room.

Her hair was frizzy, her top speckled with bread crumbs from clutching the sample bag to her chest. In fact, she was a hot mess. Then there was Colin, the prince of cool, keeping everything afloat in the middle of a shitstorm.

What was she doing wrong? Today only added to her greatest fear: that the amazing maternal genes possessed by her mom and Nonna had skipped a generation. Even her tumbleweed of a sister had a better connection with her kids. In a fun, carefree way that Teagan didn't have the luxury of adopting.

They hadn't noticed her yet, so she stood silently, watching as Colin set Poppy on the counter, something she'd never allow. But the girls' excitement at assisting with dinner made her rethink her rules.

She blinked her eyes and tried to connect this precious picture to her PARENTS GET PARENTING binder and couldn't. There was no room for this scene between those rigid, plastic covers.

Colin was handling the heavy lifting, Maddison was running the kitchen, and her kids were enlisted as sous-chefs.

This picture would forever be imprinted on her heart, but she wasn't a part of it. Watching them work as a whole family unit, the girls happy and content, pulled at the core of her insecurities. She was out doing what she needed to do to pay the bills while someone else was living the best moments of her life.

"Drizzle the sauce over each one until they're all moist," Maddison instructed Lily, who carefully spooned enchilada sauce over the tortillas. "Good job. Can you do that for the rest of them?"

Lily nodded, an actual form of communication with someone other than family, and Teagan's throat tightened with emotion and pride. Her little girl was coming back out of the safety shell she'd adopted during the divorce.

Lily, her gold-star student in the art of following instructions, methodically took care to ensure each dollop was the same size, while keeping her white-and-lavender-flowered sundress impeccably clean. Lily's matching bows held back her baby-fine blond hair.

Next to her, kneeling on the counter was Poppy, the quality control expert. "Do I gets a 'good jobs' too?" Poppy asked, her sweet voice filled with giddy anticipation.

"You bet you do," Colin said. "Good job for being so patient with your sister."

Patience wasn't a quality she'd usually attribute to Poppy, yet there she was, spoon in one hand, the other in a bag of cheese. She'd wait for Lily to finish with an enchilada, then dump a handful of shredded cheese on top of each one. Cheese spilled all over the counter and floor, but Colin praised her for being patient and doing a good job.

Teagan realized that, while she praised the girls all the time, she mainly praised them for their strengths.

As the working parent and responsible party in her marriage, she'd had to find a balance between establishing order, being the clean-up police, and savoring those tender moments and milestones most moms experience in spades.

But there Poppy knelt, her feet bare, her hair waging war with her bows, covered in a shirt-to-toe enchilada sauce stain— proud of her patience and hard work. What had Teagan's heart rolling over was how the two girls worked together. Completely different approaches but somehow complementing each other. Her four-year-old daughters had figured out what Teagan and Harley still struggled to find.

Sisterhood.

The floor creaked under her feet and Garbage Disposal, who was passed out in his doggie bed, came alert and clambered to his feet. A "hello" bark echoed in the kitchen. Rearing up like a stallion, he galloped toward her as if going in for a tackle.

Colin put out one hand and simply said, "Sit." Garbage Disposal sat.

His tail was still wagging, and he had that dopy grin that Teagan was coming to love, but he didn't move from his spot, instead waiting for her to approach him. She gave him a pet just as the girls looked up.

"Mommy," Poppy yelled, but it was Lily who ran around the island and hugged Teagan's legs. Poppy couldn't be bothered, too fascinated with her mountain of cheese.

Lily went arms up and Teagan lifted her into a huge hug. Her daughter hugged her back, long and fiercely, as if finally allowed to be scared.

"I got you," she whispered, and Lily rested her cheek on Teagan's shoulder. "You were so brave today."

And stoic. Always holding things close to her chest. Like mother like daughter—a comparison that made Teagan's heart break. She knew how taxing it was to always put on a brave face. She didn't want that for her daughter—it wasn't the behavior she wanted to model. She wanted her girls to express themselves fully and completely, without apology.

An image of Harley flashed in her mind. Bold and fearless

seven-year-old Harley, taking on Dale when, at the last minute, he canceled Teagan's birthday trip to Disney World. Teagan never wanted to see him again but had been too afraid to hurt his feelings or make things harder on her mom after the ugly divorce.

So she'd remained silent.

Not her sister. It had been little Harley who'd given him hell for disappointing her sister, while Teagan sat silently, reassuring everyone she was okay when she so wasn't.

It hadn't been the first time he'd bailed at the eleventh hour, but it was the last summer Teagan had spent her court-appointed month with him and the last time she'd considered him her dad. She'd decided she'd do whatever it took to never feel insignificant again or like she wasn't a priority.

"I'm so sorry I wasn't here," she whispered. "Mommy missed you."

She kissed Lily's head and breathed in the scent of crayons and all things little girl. Lily pulled back for some butterfly kisses before squirming out of Teagan's embrace. Once her little feet made contact with the floor, she was off, racing back to her sister's side.

"Thank you for coming over," she said to Colin gratefully. Then to Maddison, she said, "Thanks for babysitting again today and for calling your dad when you needed help."

"Again?" he asked and Maddison's gaze skittered to the enchiladas, guilt written in the way she held her body, hunched over as if trying to become small enough to disappear.

Oh boy, Colin had no idea about Maddison's afterschool activities, and Teagan hadn't told him. Granted, she hadn't really seen him since the other day, but that was no excuse.

She'd left her girls with a sitter who had no permission to be there in the first place. What if her conscience hadn't won out and Maddison had been more scared of getting in trouble than worried about protecting the girls? She knew Maddison hadn't been honest with Colin before, yet Teagan hadn't bothered to find out if she'd come clean.

That was on her. Not Harley. Not Maddison. Her. And wasn't that a bitter pill to swallow?

"What happened to your over dinner chat?" she asked Maddison.

Maddison gave one of her trademark shrugs. "Dad worked late so we didn't have dinner that night."

Colin didn't like that answer, but Teagan couldn't tell whether it was because of Maddison's cover-up or that he'd come home late on a night his daughter wanted to talk to him.

He slipped the apron over his head, tying it around Lily. "You're in charge, capisce?" Then he turned to Teagan, pointing to the back door. "Can I have a word with you?"

His expression was hard to read, but his body language spoke volumes. It reminded her of the way strangers looked at her when one of her kids acted up in the grocery store.

"He never uses one word when he's mad," Maddison warned. "And be careful that he doesn't say 'later.' 'Later' sucks even worse than 'words.'"

"Get used to it because you're next, kiddo," he said to Maddison, then led Teagan to the deck.

Teagan had to agree. She was pretty sure she was in trouble, and it was going to suck. Not that she blamed him. Based on his scrubs, he'd likely left work early to deal with an emergency Teagan should have handled.

Hand on the small of her back, and not in a nurturing way, he guided her through the back door and onto the deck.

He ran his fingers through his hair, making it stand on end. And up close she could see how tired he was, how the creases around his eyes were deep with exhaustion.

"I'm not the only one delirious with fatigue?" she asked.

"It's been a day." He crossed his arms, testing the seams of his shirt. "Hell, it's been a week."

"I'm sorry if I made it worse," she said.

"You didn't." He paused, and she placed a silencing hand on his chest, which she may or may not have slid up and over his pec—and back again. But he had an amazing chest, and abs and all the muscles in between, which tempted smart women into doing stupid.

"You're playing with fire, Bianchi."

She didn't move her hand. "What if I'm not afraid of a little heat?"

He placed his hand over hers. "How hot are we talking?"

They both looked through the window to see her kids waving back. He chuckled. "I think we've just been downgraded from Cinemax to Disney."

"That's probably good, since I need to tell you something before you distract me."

"I'm distracting you?" he asked, amused. "You're the one feeling me up. If I did that to you, people would call me a perv."

She wanted to join in his lighthearted banter, but she couldn't relax until she told him how much his being there for her kids meant to her. "I'm sorry about today. Actually, first I need to thank you for today. I never should have put my phone on silent. I wasn't thinking and I don't know—"

"Bianchi," he said, taking her hand and tugging her deeper into the shadows. "Lily's fine. Nothing more than a few bandages. And you had the added benefit of your nanny's dad having a medical degree, even if his patients are of the four-legged variety. By the way, I use the term 'nanny' liberally."

"She likes to call herself Harley's PA who sometimes watches kids."

"Of course she does." He sighed. "Although I prefer the thought of her babysitting to whatever else Harley might dream up."

"From what I understand, it's just folding pamphlets and some paperwork."

"For what? I thought Harley taught yoga."

"She does. I guess she's trying to expand her classes, find new clients. Hey, if she can help out more with the bills, I'm game, but between our different meetings, I feel like the kids are getting lost in the mix."

"Same here. My whole goal was to spend as much time with Maddie as I could before college, but the clinic is short-staffed so I'm pulling long days and sometimes long nights when I'm on call."

She stepped closer. "Have I mentioned how sorry I am for not telling you about her babysitting?"

His expression was one of confusion. "I didn't come out here to yell at you."

She didn't know what to say to that. Had the tables been turned, she wasn't sure how she would have reacted. "You didn't?"

"Of course not," he said gently. "I came out to ask if Lily has said anything to you."

Her heart caught. "Is she talking to you?"

"I'm not sure. I asked Poppy if she could hand me an oven mitt and I heard a little, 'Uh-huh.' When I turned around, Poppy was smiling but I could have sworn it was Lily."

"She did the same thing to me. One of the girls said, 'Screw you.'"

Colin laughed. "'Screw you,' huh?"

"Not my best mom moment, but it sounded like Lily. Only when I turned around, Poppy took the blame." Bad word or not, a warm ball of relief swelled in her chest. "She stopped talking about a month after Frank moved out. Her pediatrician assured me that it's not all that uncommon for young kids to have behavioral shifts during a high-stress change. Frank and my divorce . . ." She trailed off. "We tried so hard to keep it from affecting the girls. Frank was the stay-at-home parent, so when he moved out, there was a lot of change for me. I can only imagine what it was like for them."

"Kids are more resilient than we give them credit for." He cupped her cheek, a gesture that was as thrilling as it was comforting. "She'll find her footing and so will you."

"After today I'm not so sure." She was exhausted and stretched thin. She couldn't afford to lose her sitter. "I'm sorry about how it went down today, especially with Maddison."

"You mean that I was the last to know she's your sitter or that today wasn't the first time?"

"It's been four times actually." Man, she'd screwed up royally. "She admitted that first time that you didn't know. I should have reached out to you about it the way you did today when you tried to get hold of me."

"You should have. I was in the dark. I thought she was at

home doing homework. When I checked her location, her cell pinged at the house."

"Because she was right next door." At Teagan's house hiding out and probably using Rose's landline to call friends or worse. "I can check the call log on the phone line if you want. See who she was talking to." She grimaced. "That sounded bad in my head, but hearing it aloud is horrifying."

"Horrifying might be a strong word. Let's go with problematic," he teased. "And I already know who she was talking to. A boy. Shocker. But she wouldn't have had to go behind my back if I hadn't been such a hard ass."

"I put you in a difficult situation that should have never happened. I should have given you the same consideration that you gave me today," she said. "Harley hired Maddison without consulting me, so I know how it feels."

"Since when did you start letting your sister make adult decisions?"

"When Frank screwed me over, and I became a single parent, and I lost a business that's been in my family for three generations, and I became a financially strapped single parent who can't afford a professional nanny. If I'd known that she still hadn't told you, I would have said something right away." She took a breath. "Actually, in the spirit of honesty, I knew she wasn't likely to tell you. I was just so desperate . . ." As difficult as it was, she met his gaze. "That's not an excuse. I messed up. And my mess-up affected your family."

She hadn't just left her kids high and dry, but she'd left Colin in a pinch. "I'm so sorry."

"How about we eliminate the phrase 'I'm sorry' from your vocabulary. You made a judgment call—it didn't work out. That's the definition of parenting." His smile conveyed sympathy, and a good dose of something else, something warm and sexy that made her stomach flip. "I have been there many, many times so I know how hard it can be," he said in that nonjudgy way of his, but this time she didn't believe him. Maybe it was from a stressful day, but she had a feeling that whatever had him so off-kilter was on a much larger scale than his daughter's secret personal assistant career.

"Again, thank you for today and next time I have Maddison babysit, I'll check in with you first."

"She wants to be an adult, so that's her responsibility." He sighed. "She's saving up to buy a car."

"I assumed she was saving up for her fancy East Coast school." His gaze narrowed. "Don't remind me."

He laced their fingers and tugged her closer, bringing her into his intimate zone. He smelled spicy and forbidden. When their gazes locked, the past and present collided.

"Thank you. If I couldn't be here, then I'm glad you were."

If he had an opinion on the subject, he didn't say, just took his sweet time studying her face, her jawline—and her lips. His eyes were more hazel than green, and when he finally spoke his voice was rough. "When we couldn't get ahold of you, Poppy showed me where Frank's number was on the emergency contact list. Maddison called him but the number was disconnected."

She blew out a nervous breath. She had hoped to go the rest of her life without having to explain to one more person about Frank's cycle of entering rehab then escaping into the night.

The men in her life had a bad habit of lying to her—lies that hurt.

Although she'd learned a lot about addictions, and understood more about what Frank was going through, there were times where she couldn't shake off the resentment. It would creep up on her late at night, when the girls were in bed, the house had settled, and the quiet became suffocating.

A complicated knot of guilt, disappointment, and embarrassment tightened in her stomach until she was afraid she'd be sick. "It's part of the rules in rehab. No access to technology. He gets to call the girls twice a week from a pay phone."

"Twice a week. That must be hard," he said quietly.

"In the beginning, the girls used to ask about him all the time. Now, they rarely bring him up. I think they just got tired of hearing 'Soon.'"

He moved closer, his voice dropping lower. "I meant you. It must be hard to be thrown into the deep end without anyone to hand you a safety vest." She had opened her mouth to say she was fine, when he said, "Don't do that. Don't downplay how you feel. You have the right to feel sad, angry, frustrated."

"How about surface-of-the-sun pissed off."

He laughed. "That too."

How was it that no one else in her life really understood what she was going through? Not her mom, not her friends, not Harley, and certainly not Frank. To him, the only thing that mattered was working on himself.

But Colin understood. Maybe it was because he'd gone through a similar situation or maybe it was because they knew each other inside and out—regardless of how much time had passed. Either way, she felt validated, and that was equally refreshing and touching.

"For the family of an addict, recovery is about forgiveness. For the addict, recovery is about introspection, putting their needs above all else," she began. "And sometimes I feel awful for even thinking it but, every once in a while, I just want something to be about me. Not Teagan the mom or the spouse or Teagan the sister, not even Teagan the responsible party, but just plain old Teagan."

"You could never be plain old anything. You are smart and determined and impressive as hell."

Tears pricked her eyes. "I used to be back when I was Girl on Fire Teagan, who knew what she wanted and who she was. Now, I'm lucky if I get to watch *The Great British Bake-Off* before bed. I guess I just want to be seen as more than my situation."

"I see you." He moved even closer, his voice dropping lower. "I always have. From the first 'hello' you had me. It was your understated boldness and quiet confidence that drew me in."

She rolled her eyes. "I was a shy bookworm who had zero game."

"You were the most incredible thing I'd ever seen." He tugged her hands. "You still are."

And wasn't that the most romantic thing she'd ever heard. It left her speechless, her heart beating wildly. "I had a crush on you that first night when you caught me on the roof and asked me to go skinny-dipping."

He groaned. "Not my best line, but I had been working up the courage to talk to you for weeks. I'm surprised anything I said was intelligible. The day we moved in for the summer, I started formulating a plan to convince you I was worth your time."

"You in a wetsuit was enough."

"Lately, I've been thinking about hitting the waves." He let go of her hands to cup her hips, his big palms sprawling around to her lower back. "But every morning, around five, when your bread goes in the oven, I get so distracted I lose track of time."

"You miss your window?" she asked softly.

"For a glimpse of a better, more beautiful window."

"I guess I'll have to move my coffee break up a little."

"I'd like that." His expression went serious. "Promise me when it gets hard, you'll just remind yourself that divorce sucks. It scrambles you brain and makes you think you're losing your mind."

True fact, since she was staring at his lips.

"A couple months back, Amanda called me to renege on her birthday promise to Maddison. I got so worked up I accidently used Maddie's shampoo. I smelled like Ariana Grande, and the guys at poker let me know it." She laughed. "See, divorce sucks."

"Divorce sucks," she agreed.

"If you ever forget that cold hard fact, just ask me and I'll remind you," he said. "I have no doubt that you'll land on your feet. Give yourself time. You've been a single parent for, what, six months?"

"A year."

"Okay, so a year. That means you parented as part of a couple for three quarters of the girls' lives."

He slid his hands around her back and pulled her into his strong arms.

She should have backed away. She didn't need to ruin her

fresh start by relying on a man to save her. But, because she was a complete idiot, she leaned into him, allowed herself to be saved. If only for a minute.

Releasing a deep breath, she buried her head in his chest and locked her arms behind him. He rested his chin on her head, so when he spoke she could feel the rumble of every murmured word—right down to her toes.

"I used to feel that if I'd done one thing different maybe Amanda would have stayed," he admitted. "But after some time, I figured out that although I might be partially at fault, it was her choice to leave. It was Frank's choice to keep his gambling from you."

She tightened her hold. "Thank you," she whispered. "One, for understanding. Two, for taking care of my girls." She paused and looked up into his eyes. "And three, for making me feel as if everything will be okay."

"Because it will be."

Right then, she believed him. She hadn't felt safe or secure in so long, she almost didn't recognize the feeling. "So can I assume that the other Unknown Phone Number is yours?"

His hands slipped a little lower and his gaze heated. "Why, Bianchi? You angling to get my number?"

"I orchestrated this entire day for the sole purpose of getting your number," she teased.

"I'm flattered, but you could have just asked."

"Yeah?" she whispered.

"Hell, yeah." His voice was gruff, his hands moving slowly up and down her spine. And as they softened, molding to the contours of her hips, she felt a tingle start in her stomach.

Correction, the tingles spread south, and the air crackled with awareness. She tried really hard not to nibble her way up his neck, until that soft and skilled mouth—which always knew how to drive her out of her mind—was on hers.

Oh boy, she knew there was still something between them, but his something was front and center, pressed against her, playing an adult game of Get to Know You Again where his king was on a direct course for her queen.

She looked up and her belly quivered. So did other parts known and unknown, because he was looking back, his gaze hooded. Sex-drunk was the only word she could find to describe it.

"Why do you look so surprised?" he asked. "Chemistry like that doesn't just go away."

A fact that her body could attest to. "It's not that—I'm just not sure this is a smart idea."

"Oh, I can tell you with absolute certainty that it is a completely idiotic idea."

"Then why don't I feel scared?"

"Lust is a good scrambler," came his low voice.

"Which is why we should probably think through the pitfalls."

"We do that, and we might as well go back to avoiding each other."

"I don't want that." She wanted him in her life somehow, but she didn't know what that might entail. They were neighbors, his daughter was her babysitter and, based on tonight, her daughters loved the entire West family. And in a way—a very distant and nostalgic way—she loved Colin too.

When wanting overshadowed reason, people got hurt. In her experience, nothing good came from going on pure emotion.

"Maybe we should wait until we don't have our hands all over each other before we make a decision."

"I think you're forgetting how this works."

She remembered exactly how this worked, especially with Colin. And she didn't want anyone to get hurt.

"Maybe we should take things slow. See how we feel tomorrow."

"That sounds like the responsible thing to do."

"Then why are you pulling me closer?" she whispered.

He grinned, that sexy boyish grin that made her clothes want to melt right off. "Sweetheart, you're the one doing the pulling."

Teagan looked down to find her hands fisted in his shirt. "Whoops." But she didn't let go. "I guess I'm a little confused on what I want."

"You said as much the other day."

Responsible Teagan told her to abort while Girl on Fire Teagan told her to be bold and go after what she wanted without apology. And right then she wanted Colin.

He started to back away, but she held on, even pulling him closer. "I know." She ran her hands up his chest to the back of his neck. "I have something to tell you."

"I'm all ears."

"It's the fourth thank-you."

His grin was sleepy and sexy. "I have a feeling four is going to be my new favorite number."

So did she. She liked her men tall, dark, and kind, with a gentle soul. She liked a man who fiercely protected and cared for those in his world. Once upon a time, she'd been one of those people and, right then, she wanted to go back to being his person.

She pulled his head down so she could reach his lips and then went after what she wanted.

Colin.

"Thank you for being you," she said against his mouth, then brushed her lips against his, back and forth, back and forth. A slow, gentle repetition that quickly became anything but. His hands tightened on her hips, his thumbs on the move until they were millimeters from her breasts. Then with a rough groan he took over.

His mouth opened on hers, proving that, after all these years, the chemistry was still explosive. The only thing different was that they were both more experienced.

She had a hard time breathing, let alone thinking, because it was a kiss to end all kisses. It was no teenage kiss. Just like the man himself, he'd only gotten better.

After a long, luscious moment he pulled back. "I guess that answers that question."

Oh yeah, it was still there.

Chapter 16

In the cookies of life, sisters are the chocolate chips.

—Unknown

Harley returned from her morning goat yoga class early. The goats had gotten into a crate of oranges, the equivalent of a carton of ice cream for the lactose intolerant. To avoid potential digestive distress, Harley limited class to two-legged paying patrons, so things had wrapped up earlier than expected.

She left her shoes and mat on the deck—the Teagan-approved location—and entered through the back door, heading straight for the coffeepot.

After a sunrise run and teaching three classes before the fog had lifted, green tea wasn't going to cut it.

"Hey," Teagan said. She was sitting at the table, her laptop open and a spreadsheet by her right hand. Given the messy bun, crumb-dusted apron, and spicy smell of cooking anise, her sister was baking one of Harley's favorite desserts—an Italian spiced Bundt cake.

"Are you making Nonna's Buccellato di Lucca?"

"Yes," Teagan said, and Harley opened the oven. "Can you not? You're letting the heat out."

"I don't barge into your room when I hear the telltale buzzing, so don't deny me my morning food porn."

"There's one on the counter. Have your way with it."

Harley spotted the delicious goodness on a cooling rack. She picked off a little bite, which was a million degrees, so she had to bounce it between her palms, blowing on it before she popped it in her mouth.

Huh, food porn was a lot like people porn, only without the distraction of a man.

Harley felt her sister's stare burning into her back. "What?"

"The other one." Teagan pointed to a cooling rack on the other side of the island. "The one that's not cooling and can deflate when poked and prodded."

"My bad." Harley sliced off a big hunk, dropped it on a paper towel.

"A plate?"

"Too much work. Maybe on my second helping."

"I made that for the girls."

"Who come up to my kneecaps and eat like birds." She reconsidered that. "Actually, they can both throw back a serious number of cheesy poofs."

She poured a cup of coffee, then—remembering that she was practicing being a considerate adult—checked her sister's cup. It was empty so she filled it up, then sat down.

"Thanks." Teagan sounded surprised. Harley had to work on that.

"What'cha doing?" she asked Teagan.

"I was trying to ignore the death trap I took down that's once again suspiciously hanging in the front room."

Harley pretended to look surprised. "I wonder how that got up there? It sure looks great though. Very bohemian modern. Plus, it's our thing."

"It's your thing," Teagan said but Harley could tell she was lying. The *blink and you'll miss it* quirk of the lip was a dead giveaway.

It reminded her of when they were little, before the divorce, the way they were constantly pulling pranks. Sometimes on each other, but mostly it was the two of them against the world. No one had been safe. Their mom, Nonna, Zia Iris, even the West brothers next door. Although pranking the latter had more to do with Teagan's hormones than her inner trickster. Still did.

She wasn't sure if her sister had acknowledged that little truth yet, but Harley had a feeling from the constant grin on her sister's face, the most stubborn not-a-couple couple had gotten together at last.

"Not to mention the swing is dangerous," Teagan went on. "You do remember that Lily nearly went to the emergency room after sitting in it."

"Actually, Poppy was hanging from the top like a little Tarzan and lost her grip. Lily, who was lying underneath, tried to break her fall and banged her chin on the coffee table. So, technically, it was user error."

Teagan went still. "That's not the story I heard. Did they tell you that?"

"Not directly," she said around a bite of cake. "Poppy confessed to the Forgiveness Fairy the other night while I was putting them to bed. I kind of learned it by eavesdropping."

Harley paused, wondering if she should even mention the other fairy Poppy confessed to. In the end, she decided Teagan had a right to know. Plus, things always seemed to go sideways when she kept things from the people she loved.

Which brough her to the next rule of adulting:

Rule Five: Secrets are for sorority girls.

Since the only sorority Harley had ever belonged to involved Cher, Alanis Morissette, and a parade of motorcycles, she had no excuse.

"The Birthday Fairy was also invited to Poppy's little clambake." Harley used a gentle tone to signal that she had Teagan's back. "She said that she and Lily would forgo birthday presents in exchange for Frank's early homecoming. It sounded like a Frank-jumping-out-of-a-cake wish."

"Poppy said as much to me too," Teagan admitted, suddenly looking very tired. The kind of tired that stemmed from long-term exposure to rat bastard exes. "And while I'd love to give them their wish, Frank is nowhere near ready to leave rehab or his support group."

Harley put her hand over Teagan's. "Then I guess you and I will have to throw them a Birthday Fairy Fabulous party."

Teagan swallowed hard. "Thanks, Rabbit."

"Anytime, Bear." And before Harley started crying over that reminder of how close they used to be, she said, "What are you looking at?"

"I just got off the phone with Ian from Soup Stop. He wants Bread N Butter to be his exclusive sourdough bread bowls and bread supplier. We're meeting next week to sign the papers and make it official."

"That's fantastic. Better than fantastic." She waved her hands. "This is amazing!"

"Yeah, pretty amazing since I never called him."

"He must have heard about you via word of mouth." Harley shrugged and tried to maintain eye contact but looked to the right, a tell cops used to put liars behind bars. "Isn't that what you always say? Natural, sustainable growth comes from word of mouth."

"I do. As it turns out, he heard about Bread N Butter from your mouth."

"I may have given him your number, but your bread earned its way into his shop." She grabbed her sister's hands and shook them vigorously with excitement. "Your bread is amazing. Ian would be an idiot not to use it."

"Ian, huh? I thought you just gave him my number?"

"So I may have had coffee with the guy."

"Wait, is that why you were at the Coffeekat? Talking to Ian about Nonna's breads?"

"Yes, but I was talking to him about your breads. *Your* breads, Tee."

Teagan gently nodded her head as if overcome with emotion. "I needed to hear that. But this couldn't have happened without you. I can't believe you did that for me."

"Why are you so surprised?"

"As grown-ups, we haven't really had the best relationship."

The words cut Harley all the way to the core. Maybe they bickered, and had their differences, huge differences, like Grand Canyon–depth differences, but she'd never say they had a bad relationship. She'd always liked to think it was a sisters-to-the-end kind of situation.

Maybe that was another rule of adulting.

Rule Six: Tell the people in your life that you love them.

"I know you have a lot of people who love you, but for me, you're it," Harley said. "I love you and I love Nonna's business. I want Bread N Butter to succeed as much as you do."

Teagan pressed a hand to her chest as if she'd been waiting for this moment. "I never thought you were all that interested."

"Just because I react to things differently than you, that doesn't mean I don't love Nonna's house or business."

"I know. I just never knew you wanted . . . well, I guess I don't know what you want. What do you want?"

That was a good question. Harley wasn't sure what she wanted either, only that it was more than what she'd wanted when she'd first arrived from LA to hide from her feelings.

She wanted to be a real part of this family, to have a place in the Bianchi legacy, and she wanted to go back to before, when they were so close that they were like the twins. She wanted to know that she'd be chosen to be in Teagan's lifeboat, because for Harley, her boat was reserved for the people in this house.

And Bryan, her heart said before she could shut it down.

"I want to know that I matter to you as you matter to me. That we can go back to being Bear and Rabbit in our cave brewing tea and eating popcorn while the rest of the world rages around us."

"You're right." This time it was Teagan who reached out. "We are vastly different and react differently, but that doesn't mean I should disrespect your feelings. What you add to this house, the girls' lives, and Mom and Nonna's business is uniquely you. And I never stopped being the Bear to your Rabbit."

Harley felt tears burn in the pit of her stomach and start to radiate out to her chest. "It was just coffee."

"It was so much more. We landed our second official account. *You* landed it. In order to sell the bread into restaurants, we have to cook out of a commercial kitchen. Which is what I was looking at when you came in." She turned the screen so they could both see. "I've narrowed it down to five, but I need a dreamer's perspective."

"Well, not only am I a born-and-bred dreamer but I am a master at picking out real estate online." A skill that came from spending the past decade moving from one city to the next, chasing a dream she wasn't sure she wanted anymore.

"How about that one?"

Teagan's face lit up. "I know, it's my favorite too. But it's bigger than what I need right now."

"You don't know what you need. Not until you reach out to every restaurant and café in town." Not to mention the other clients Harley had solicited for Bread N Butter, which had recently become a family partnership.

Teagan let out a sigh. "I don't have enough money for the down payment, and I don't want to grow too fast and blow what savings I do have."

"Why not think big? You sell out at every farmer's market. You already have a trial period arranged with the hotel. Now you signed with a big client this week. And that's just from handing out flyers. Imagine what we can do if we go at this hard."

"What are you not telling me?" Teagan asked.

"We may be hearing from the Coffeekat about your sandwich rolls and scones. I convinced them that they are open to a change in suppliers."

Teagan leaned over and kissed Harley on the cheek. "I never would have thought about approaching those people. I know I can be rigid and off-putting, but you, you rock this."

"Targeted messaging is my jam. Baking is your expertise. Which is why you shouldn't limit yourself. You got this."

"I don't want to bite off more than I can chew. The divorce really cleaned me out."

"Correction. Frank cleaned you out. But don't underestimate yourself. Don't overthink this, just do it. For once, do something for you."

"That's exactly what I was telling Colin the other night. I want something that's just for me."

"Teagan and Colin sitting in a tree, F. U. C.—"

Teagan put her hand over Harley's mouth. "It's not like that."

"Not yet, but it will be."

"You don't know that."

Harley pointed to Teagan's face. "Now I do. You totally went beet red when you said his name."

"Maybe it will." *Oh, it will.* Her sister's expression said everything.

"Are you okay with that?"

"I'm not sure. It's a huge risk but surprisingly I'm not scared."

"Then don't be afraid to take risks in your professional life. Throw out your playbook, Bear. For once, Rabbit is the expert. It's time to make your dreams happen."

"Wow, did we just have an adult conversation without being reduced to acting like toddlers?"

They both turned to look at the twins, who were playing quietly, helping each other put together a wooden puzzle.

"You know, we can learn a lot from them."

Teagan took Harley's hand. "Maybe we already have."

Chapter 17

A kiss is a lovely trick designed by nature to
stop speech when words become superfluous.

—Ingrid Bergman

Colin walked into Lover's Point Bistro, wondering why the hell he was there. After work, he'd found a note stuck to his front windshield. Written on an electricity bill envelope and scribbled in crayon, it was from Teagan, asking him to meet her after work.

Yes, they'd shared a fuck-tastic kiss—that she'd initiated. But since that night on her back deck, she'd gone radio silent and Colin wasn't sure how he felt about that. Oh, he knew how he felt about the kiss and his new lease on life. He could already feel his confidence surging. And he hoped like hell Teagan wanted to be a part of his Get Your Mojo Back plan.

The fact that this wasn't some order-at-the-window kind of establishment and more of a fine dining restaurant gave him hope.

Perched atop a thirty-foot cliff overlooking whitecapped waters, the restaurant offered panoramic views of the Pacific. It was also the kind of place people came for a romantic evening. A date, even.

If memory served, when a woman asked a man to show up to a candlelit restaurant with a wine cellar, it usually implied a date with a capital D. But it had been so long since he'd actually had dinner with a woman, he wasn't sure if he'd gotten his signals crossed. To be safe, he'd settled on dark jeans and a blue button-up. It looked causal but the shoes made it date appropriate.

If that's what this was.

Damn, he really hoped it was. It had been a week, and he couldn't stop thinking about her lips and the way her body fit so perfectly against his. Then there were her eyes—he could look into those amber pools forever.

Colin had no clue as to where Teagan stood. She'd been upset and a little off balance after Lily's fall. She'd said she wanted to take things slow, then *she'd* kissed *him*. And, damn, what a kiss it was. First, she'd been tentative, as if judging where he stood on the topic of locking lips. So he'd shown her his exact stance on the subject.

He wanted her.

Badly. Hard stop.

And not just a benefit kind of situation like he'd had with other women. Oh, no. He wanted to wake up next to her, something they'd never experienced.

Back in the day, they'd had to sneak around, get creative. He could still remember every moment of those days, but he'd always wanted more. He wasn't talking about sex—they were compatible as hell in that department—but the kind of intimacy that came from late-night talks and early morning kisses. That really wasn't under the umbrella of mojo, but he'd come up with the plan, so he got to make the rules.

Nerves prickled the back of his neck as he scanned the restaurant. She'd said she was sitting on the outdoor terrace, and there she was, exactly where she promised she'd be, waiting in case he could make it. As if he'd miss this. The whole setup felt a little like one of those Cary Grant movies his mom used to make him watch.

She was at the far end of the patio, at a table beside the railing, staring out on the ocean. She looked beautiful. The sinking sun cast a golden glow on her face and highlighted the paler strands of her blond hair. The rhythmic sounds of the waves crashing on the cliffs below set a more-than-friends tone. Then there were the cocktails, two to be exact. Martini glasses, not his usual go-to—he was more of a beer guy—but he'd take it since cocktails at five were the universal, grand-slam sign that he was walking into an impending date.

Except for her outfit choice. Faded jean skirt, a teal tank, which had I POSSESS NICE BUNS with the company logo printed on it, and tennies. To top off the absolutely, positively not-a-date ensemble, she had a smudge of flour on her cheek and a sprinkle of crumbs in her hair as if she'd just come from the kitchen.

Well hell, that was a hit and a miss. Maybe he was more out of practice than he thought. It had been more than a hot minute since he'd been in the game. Then again, he'd never been all that skilled at games. He liked it honest and real, with consistent follow-through.

"Hey," he said, approaching the table, thankful he'd left the flowers he'd brought in the car in case of this exact scenario.

"I wasn't sure if you'd come," she said, looking relieved.

Oh, he wouldn't miss this for the world. Teagan was more complicated than a nuclear reactor, holding everything so close to her chest it was nearly impossible to read her. Which made her all the more interesting.

"Sorry I'm late. The clinic was understaffed so I had to work a little overtime." He'd made it home thirty minutes before the time specified in her dinner invitation. Had Ronnie cost him tonight, he'd have pummeled the guy. Luckily, Colin had been relieved by one of the other vets on call.

"That's okay," she said, standing to give him a closer-than-friends hug, then a gentle kiss—on the lips. "I'm just happy you made it."

If he'd been happy before, now he was giddy as hell.

"Drinks before five? Better be careful, Bianchi, or you'll have every single guy in town lining up to buy you a second round."

She rested her arms on the table and leaned forward. "It wouldn't be so bad, if it were the right guy."

He nearly raised his hand. Crumbs or not, she was stunning. And smart and sexy and a whole lot of other things that made him stupid. Then there was her tank with a neckline made to drive a man crazy in that sophisticated flirty way, a scoop neck low enough to give him an inspiring view of mouthwatering cleavage.

Then she rested her elbows on the table and leaned in, the movement tugging her tank just enough to officially fry his brain.

He pulled his chair out and took a seat. Pushing the menu and wine list aside, he leaned forward until—

Damn if she didn't smell amazing. For the rest of eternity, cinnamon would give him a hard-on.

"What kind of guy are we talking?" he asked.

"I'll let you know." But her gaze flickered to his mouth, long enough for him to know that he might be that kind of guy. That, in itself, was intriguing. Then there was the fact that she was flirting with him.

His gaze paid it forward, only doing more of a lingering sweep, and this time she caught him taking in the gap at her neckline. Righting her tank, she sat back.

What a shame.

Before she looked away, a flash of sexual awareness flickered in her whisky eyes. "So, what are we drinking?"

"Lemonade with something a little stronger. I know martini glasses aren't your thing, but I figured since we're celebrating, it was fitting." She lifted her glass. He touched the rim, noticing that hers was untouched. Either this was round two, or she'd waited for him.

"What's the occasion?" He hoped they were celebrating with another kiss. Blond, curvy and gorgeous, she was his type to a T. But it was that girl-next-door sweetness that slayed him.

"Me time," she said. "Maddison has the kids, I have a night off, and you're the person I want to spend it with." Her face was lit with so much excitement it was contagious. "Harley landed us another cooperate client."

"Harley, huh?"

"Yeah. She's been going around town lining up clients for regular orders. Restaurants, cafés, even the Lighthouse Hotel."

He couldn't help but smile. "That's amazing."

"She did it all on her own and she didn't even tell me. She

didn't even want credit. I only found out because Delores spilled the beans. She's really come through for me. Not just with the business but with the kids. I've been so busy focusing on how much she drives me crazy that I forgot how great she is with people. She's charismatic and her playfulness draws people in and puts them at ease. She's always been that way."

"Sounds like you're a good team."

Her smile was a little surprised and a whole lot warm. "I guess we are. She's terrible in the kitchen and I need a lot of work in the people department. When it comes to people skills, public perception, and targeting customers, she runs circles around me. Although she still drives me crazy at times."

"Siblings are supposed to drive each other crazy. Ethan is always trying to tell me how to run my life, and don't even get me started on his wife. The two of them treat me like I'm still a troublemaking seventeen-year-old kid."

She shifted closer until they were eye to eye. "I thought you were a pretty amazing seventeen-year-old, and I like the trouble we got into."

"Were?" he asked, his voice gruff. He studied her face, caught between his memories and the present, knowing that this was the do-or-die moment, when they either bridged the gap between them or remained merely neighbors.

"Are," she whispered.

"Go on," he teased, and she laughed.

"You mean about my big celebratory moment?"

He sat back with a chuckle. "That too."

This time when she laughed, he found himself smiling like an idiot.

She caught him up-to-date on the whole story of how she and her sister were finally working as a team, and how she'd forgotten just how much she loved her sister—and how they'd been torn apart at a young age but managed to find their way back to each other.

"I can't believe anyone would tear siblings apart."

"When I was a kid, I never questioned it. But now that I have the twins . . ." She shook her head. "I'd rather live next door to

Frank than sever that bond. Sisterhood is a sacred thing that my parents broke, but I think ours is strong enough to eventually heal."

"I've watched you two together these past few months."

She gave an uncertain laugh. "You've watched us fight?"

"No, I've watched you care for each other. Fighting aside, it's easy to see that you love each other."

It gave him hope that his and Maddie's bond was strong enough to withstand her move to New York and finding her own path. He needed to let her know that no matter what, she always had a place to come home to, and a father who loved her and was proud of her. Even when she started her own life, a life separate from his, she'd always have his heart.

"Neither of you are running away from a difficult and probably painful situation. You're meeting in the middle and showing up for each other." He held up his glass again. "And that's inspiring."

Her open and honest smile and shy vulnerability made his chest thump.

"The longer she's with us, the more I want her to stay."

"Have you told her that?"

She shook her head. "I think I need to. She's even taken over our search for a commercial kitchen. Calling round, getting quotes, negotiation terms, all while doing her yoga classes."

"Commercial kitchen?"

"Delores doesn't mind where I cook the bread but in order to sell to the Soup Stop, I have to find a commercial kitchen, or the owner won't sign on the dotted line. And I have a feeling that if Harley starts bringing in more clients, I'll need a big kitchen just to keep up with demand. She showed me a few that I want to look at in person. I'm going this Saturday. Harley was going to go with me, but I asked her if she'd take the girls to the beach so I can go with you." Her cheeks went pink. "That is, if you're not busy. And if you're interested."

He was so interested he almost leaned across the table to seal that date with a kiss.

"Count me in. In fact, one of my longtime clients owns a

bunch of retail property. I bet he could show us some this weekend. Do you want me to give him a call?"

"Is this the one with the meth-head cat or the one who wanted to keep his dog's family jewels?"

"The one who has a quarter horse, Sugar. Chestnut, black tail and mane. Eighteen, and has a crush on the donkey next door. The fencing around the corral acts as a bundling board."

"Bundling board, huh?" she said. "Thank you and yes." She leaned across the table again, this time shifting closer. He smelled the cool evening air on her skin. Her lashes fluttered closed and—surprise of fucking surprises—she kissed him. On the lips. In public. With a hundred or so witnesses. And her barely-there lip gloss with the little sparkles as proof on his mouth.

Oh, it wasn't quite a *Nightcap, anyone?* kiss but more than a *trip down memory lane* brush of the mouth, leading him to believe that this was, indeed, a date.

If there was one thing he'd learned about females, assuming you were both on the same page was an astronomically bad idea. When in doubt, clarify, clarify, and absolutely, positively— throw out everything you thought you knew because there a ninety-nine percent chance it's wrong—clarify.

"Is this a date, Bianchi?"

Colin held his breath waiting for her answer. How she responded would influence the next few hours and impact the course of their relationship. She was right. One misstep and life would get really complicated really fast.

He was in deep trouble. He'd already had a taste and, watching her watch him, he knew he wanted another. Needed another. Then he'd be so gone there was no coming back. Was it wise to let himself be caught, hook, line, and sinker, by a woman who, in the past, had proved to be a catch-and-release kind of lover?

His brain was giving him a clear sign to keep his distance. But he'd tried distance and he was tired of fighting the inevitable. Which was the only reason he could come up with for the intense anticipation that had his heart pounding out of his chest.

She bit her lip and looked up at him through her lashes. God, he loved it when she got shy. "I had hoped so."

"Me too. So, are we taking this slow?"

"That's what we agreed."

"Actually, that's what you said. I never agreed. I was too interested in the fact that your mouth was on me, proving that our chemistry is off the fucking charts."

"There is that."

It was like trying to decipher code with the wrong key. "Correct me if I'm jumping the lead, but usually taking it slow means waiting until we're under the porch light."

"We came in separate cars."

"We live next door."

"Private moments under porch light become common knowledge in this town."

"I have a fix for that."

"One of your plans?"

"Tonight, I'm going by instinct."

She seemed to like that answer, because she switched seats so that they were next to each other. Her hand was as gentle as her voice, when she cupped his cheek. "For us, this is slow."

Chapter 18

I lost my teddy, will you sleep with me?

—Unknown

By the time Teagan arrived home, her body was humming with anticipation—and something a little more dangerous. A lot more dangerous. Her brain might want to take things slow, but the rest of her was ready for a little game of naked Twister.

They'd spent three hours at the bistro talking and flirting while the sun set. On the way to the car, he'd placed his hand on the small of her back, slipping his thumb just under the hem of her top, rubbing it back and forth along her bare skin. Which, in public, felt almost erotic. Then there was the fact that he'd led her to his car—where there was a beautiful bouquet of blush-colored dogwood, her favorite—and insisted he drive her home since this was a date.

Cue their current situation: sitting in Colin's driveway, with sexual tension pulling them together like two big hormone magnets.

Even though they'd barely said "Boo" to each other over the past twenty years, it was as if they'd never lost touch—as if every cell in her body still recognized his.

So when he pulled into his driveway and turned off the engine, she didn't move for the door handle. Neither did he. They just stared at each other until the dome light slowly dimmed, plunging them into darkness. Instead of making things better, the darkness created a sense of intimacy that brought her back to a time and place where she'd been free to be herself—explore whatever direction felt right.

Right then, any direction that led to more time with Colin was the one she wanted to explore. She also wanted a replay of that kiss. By the way he'd stared at her lips all night, so did he.

"Thank you for tonight," she said, enjoying the fact that she was in a confined space with a yummy-smelling, sexy man. "And the flowers. They're my favorite."

"I know."

"I haven't received flowers in a really long time." Flowers that were for no special occasion, but just because. They made her feel appreciated, adored.

Even though she heard him shift closer, she was still surprised when his steady, masculine hand rested on her knee, his thumb making slow circular sweeps.

"I had a great time." His voice was as gentle as his touch. "I wasn't sure what I was walking into tonight, but I'm glad I went."

"For a minute there, I was preparing myself for a party-of-one kind of celebration."

"That would never have happened," he assured her with an unwavering tone that reminded her of just how protective he was to those he cared for. She really hoped that circle had come to include her. "The only reason I would have been a no-show was if I'd gotten the note too late, which almost happened. But I would have called you to explain."

"I knew you'd gone in early, but I had no idea when you'd get home. Maddison mentioned you usually get home around six, so I was counting on your impressive punctuality."

"My punctuality isn't the most impressive thing about me," he teased, and her nipples brought out their cocktail shakers.

"Our kiss the other night proved that."

His hand moved a little higher, his fingers continuing to drive her right out of her mind. He had her at a nine and there was a console between them. "I loved that you invited me and that I was able to share in your special night. You were fascinating back then. You're more so now."

An unmistakable thrill raced through her. It had been a long time since someone found her fascinating. "I should be thanking you for making me laugh. For making me forget how awful the past year has been. For making me . . . feel like me again." She looked at her house and back to him. "I don't want to open the door. I'm afraid when I do, real life will suck me back in."

"I know what you mean."

"Then let's stay here a little while longer?"

"And do what?" he asked, his voice rough and sexy—his hands now sliding up and down her thigh, getting higher with every pass.

She moved closer to the console. "When I saw you walk up to the table, a few things came to mind."

"Like this?" he asked, his eyes dark with lust and focused on hers. He leaned over, across the console, moving in slow, giving her a chance to back out.

She moved closer.

Their gaze held until they were a breath away from touchdown. She wasn't sure who kissed who first, but suddenly they were a tangle of arms and legs, their lips gliding and searching. Her hands fisted in his hair and then, one minute she was in her seat, the next she was in his lap, straddling him, his hands on her ass.

They kissed, and kissed, and kissed some more. His lips were amazing, purposeful and skilled, but unlike the patient and controlled Colin of the night on her back deck, he was all testosterone and raw hunger, as if kissing her were his God-given right.

Being kissed like this, and by him, was a game changer. In his arms she felt safe and desired, as if he saw her and embraced her truth. So she embraced him back, locking her arms around his head and holding him to her, letting him know that she needed him like she needed her next breath.

With a groan he met her halfway, touching and devouring until it looked as if a blanket of tule fog had settled inside the car, creating whiteout conditions with zero visibility.

"We fogged up the windows," she said.

"I promised you a private moment."

"You always deliver on your promises." She said it flirty, but he turned serious.

"I do. Always. Do you, Bianchi?"

Her heart went out to him. It was clear that deep down, beneath his controlled confidence, was the shadow of a man who needed clarification of his worth—the man who still carried the scars that came with abandonment.

"Colin, you are the kind of man who deserves loyalty," she whispered with a gentle kiss.

He didn't move, just studied her face. His usually calm and assured eyes looked a bit wild and uncertain, telegraphing how nervous he was about getting played again. How terrified he was of being left behind to put his world back together.

He was as scared of being a disappointment as he was of being disappointed.

"All I care about is your loyalty."

"You have it."

This time when he kissed her, it was tender, reverent, as if he were savoring the moment. A hand slid up her back, cradling her head as he continued to melt her heart. His other hand spanned her lower back, moving down, down, down until he reached the curve. With her sitting on his lap, he couldn't go any further, so she lifted up, rising on her knees and pressing all the way against him as his hand reached all the way below her ass to hold her in place.

Soon the kissing turned hungrier until they couldn't keep their hands off each other.

"Hell, Teagan," he moaned. "You want to tell me what you're thinking? Because you get to set the pace, but I hope this is leading to more than some fogged-up windows."

Body revved up and ready to blow through to the finish line, she said, "Fogged windows are a good start, but suddenly slow doesn't work for me."

"I'm aiming a little higher than good." His voice sounded thrillingly rough against her neck. She leaned back, giving him better access. "And, if we're being honest, my body is pushing for a whole lot more than slow tonight."

"Well, I have a babysitter until midnight."

He pulled back. "Her curfew is eleven."

"She said midnight." She slid down his chest until she was back on his lap. His gaze dropped to her lips, and she knew she had him.

"She didn't know you were out with me. It's eleven." He didn't sound as if he were going to enforce that particular rule tonight.

"Well, then that gives us"—she looked at her phone—"sixty-nine minutes."

"Please tell me you're wearing that sexy peach lace bra you wore the first day you came home?"

"You were paying attention."

"I always pay attention to you." His hands moved up her thighs, over her hips, around her waist, paying attention to every inch as he slowly slid up the tank top, stopping a scant inch from her bra.

"I was covered in grape juice."

"And you were damn sexy." Back and forth, back and forth his thumbs went.

"Tick, tock, West. Sixty-five minutes and counting. And remember, I do love me some good foreplay."

"Oh, I remember everything you like, and even the things you love." He gave her a quick kiss. "As for the countdown clock, I can make it worth your while."

"That's a big statement."

"I'm a big guy," he said, giving her a drugging kiss and leaving her with no question of just how big he was. "What do you say, Bianchi?"

That this was an epically bad decision. Kissing in the car was one thing, going into his house would lead to a whole lot of other freaking fantastic things—like him making it worth her while. Between the girls crawling into bed with her and Harley's habit of entering while knocking, Teagan hadn't had any "while" in a long while.

But mixed in with the fantastic things were a few scary

things—like feelings. Real, deep, and rapidly growing feelings. Feelings that would be disastrous to admit, even to herself.

Past Teagan and Colin had been simple. There was nothing simple about what would happen if they took this to the next step.

Not only did they both have families depending on them—families that needed their time and attention and needed to come first—but there was the whole next-door-neighbor thing, which wouldn't be changing anytime soon. He was headed toward empty nester and, for the foreseeable future, she was the grown-up in her family of four.

She could get out of the car and walk home or get out of the car and go to Colin's home. Either choice came with upsides and pitfalls, just as they'd both—

"I know you're in your head right now, wondering what the right move is. Just know, the next move is all yours." Leaning in, he put his mouth to her ear. "I dare you to go for it, Bianchi."

Teagan was transported back to the summer before freshman year of high school. Her dad had just canceled their Disney World trip and, not wanting anyone to see her cry, she'd climbed out on the rooftop, right in time to watch Colin sneak out his bedroom window. Instead of going off into the night, he'd walked over to her back deck and dared her to sneak down to the beach with him. At first, she'd said no. But by summer's end, she'd said yes.

And she'd never stopped saying yes, all the way up to that last summer.

She was fairly certain, given the right situation, he could still sweet-talk her into doing something reckless, like take the tempting offer he'd just presented. Her Bad Idea alarm was blaring and refused to be snoozed.

She'd never been a fan of alarms.

She kissed him long and languidly. "Will it be better than a lemon drop?"

"It will be the best damn cocktail you've ever had."

They both reached for the door handle.

*   *   *

Too many cocktails led to lapses in judgment. And while Teagan was alcohol sober, she was stumbling drunk on the promise of sex.

Pressed with her back against the front door and Colin's mouth on hers, stoking the fire, she'd never felt so nervous or alive. She grabbed the front of his shirt and tugged him closer. "We should move inside."

"No can do. I promised you a damn fine cocktail and that starts with the right ingredients."

"And what would they be?"

"For starters, a kiss under the porch light."

"How about a kiss on the wall behind the porch light, just in case the kids heard us drive up."

One strong hand rested at the small of her back, the other reached up and twisted the porch light, plunging them into darkness. "Just in case."

He threaded her fingers between his and pressed them against the door above her head. This time when his mouth moved against hers, it was tender and unhurried, as if this was their first date. As if, for him, tonight was about more than chemistry and hormones and, even though they were in a time crunch, he wouldn't be rushed.

He nibbled and kissed, gently sucking on her lower lip. With only their linked hands and mouths touching, he had her melting against the door. Kissing him, like this, was about the sexiest thing she'd ever experienced, until eventually she was so wrapped up in everything that was Colin, the stress, the responsibility, and all the problems that came with her daily life vanished. She forgot that this thing between them would likely blow up in their faces, that they were on his front porch in clear view of the entire block and gave in to the moment, matching his languid pace.

"That's what I was waiting for," he whispered, his mouth never leaving hers. Her brain was so befuddled that she was caught off guard when the door clicked open. She braced herself for a fall only to find herself in Colin's arms. "I got you."

Taking that promise as word, she tugged him toward the staircase, but he pulled her to a stop.

"Second thoughts?"

Before he could answer, two furry felines wove themselves between her and Colin's ankles. They looked at her with bored disregard.

"*Chirp, trill, chirp,*" the smaller one said.

"*Purr, purr, yowl, trill,*" the other let out.

Colin rested his head against hers. "I either press the Hold button here and feed them now, leaving us sixtyish minutes of uninterrupted time, or I don't and they scream at the door until I do."

"According to the clock above your television, fifty-eight minutes," she teased.

"Fuck it, they can eat kibble."

"Or you feed them, and I make sure we're still shaken." She linked her hands behind his back. "Catch me."

His palms were cupping her ass in record time and lifting her. Her skirt was too short to cover much, so his hands gripped bare skin.

"Jesus, Bianchi," he groaned. "We talking a thong or commando?"

"I guess that depends on how well you multitask."

"I'm a grand master of multitasking." As soon as her ankles locked around his back, turning her skirt into a Hula-Hoop around her waist, he was on the move, carrying her through the kitchen and into the laundry room. She kept her end of the bargain, nipping his earlobe, nuzzling the curve of his neck, and whispering exactly what she wanted him to do once this time-out was over. Only she got impatient.

She unbuttoned his shirt, running her fingers over his abs, fully appreciating the effects of habitual windsurfing. Next up, his jeans. First the button—*pop*—then his zipper—*oh so slowly.*

"Fuck," he groaned. "That's not playing fair."

"I didn't realize there were rules." It was a little tricky, but she managed to slip a hand between them. "Maybe you can tell me about them later."

"Later," he agreed. "Much later."

He set her ass on the tile. "It's cold."

"I didn't realize there were rules," he parroted, then gave her thighs a little squeeze. "Don't move."

He pulled two bowls from the pantry, poured enough kibble for three days, slid them across the hardwood and outside the door, then slammed it. He turned back around and froze.

"I might have moved a little." Oh, she'd moved a lot. She dumped everything but her bra and thong, which he couldn't stop staring at.

He ran a hand over his jaw, erasing every ounce of surprise and replacing it with swagger—panty-melting swagger. "I think I can overlook the transgression."

Leaning back on her palms, she primly crossed one leg over the other. "It isn't peach. Today felt more like a daffodil yellow day. I hope you don't mind."

He stalked toward her, resting his palms on the edge of the counter. "Did you know daffodil yellow is my favorite color? I'm thinking of painting it all over the counters and maybe up against the door."

Suddenly, her confidence dwindled as she realized that her body wasn't what it used to be. She was a mom, had more curves, and no longer possessed that seventeen-year-old figure. On the other hand, Colin looked even better than ever.

Self-conscious, she wrapped her arms around her tummy. His expression softened.

"Don't," he said, taking her hands in his. "You're beautiful."

"I've carried twins."

"Did I mention I'm into hot moms?" he teased, then went serious. "Don't ever feel the need to hide from me, Teagan." The use of her full name sent butterflies spinning in her chest. "You are sexy and smart and you have this shy way about you that turns me on."

He held her hands out to her sides, his gaze taking a slow journey down her body. When he met her eyes and she saw the hunger there, that uncertainty vanished and was replaced with the same raw need.

"You know, I hear that washing machines, when properly loaded, make some nice vibrations. Maybe even take it from stirred to shaken." She uncrossed her legs. "So I guess the only question is: Do you prefer thong or commando?"

"I prefer you." He stepped between her legs, taking her mouth in another searing kiss. "You know what I like about choices? You can try out one, then switch to another."

She loosely wrapped her legs around him again. "You want to try with my thong on first?"

"I'm going to try you on," he said. Placing his hands on her inner thighs, he slid them apart, making room for him to step in between. "You know what I love about this counter?" He gave it a little pat. "How sturdy it is."

Teagan bounced, giving a little test of her own, and Colin's hand went right to her chest. His smile indicated that her decision to go yellow lace with no underwire received a resounding thumbs-up.

"Sturdy indeed." She gave the counter a mischievous pat. "Seems like the perfect place for a taste of that cocktail you promised."

"You in a shaken or stirred mood?" he asked.

"Do I have to decide right now?"

"Take your time," he said, his mouth on the move, kissing her neck, her collarbone, then her lace, which—with a single tug—came undone. The scrap of fabric fell down her arms to the floor, baring her breasts. "No rush."

Oh no, he wasn't rushed at all. Teagan watched breathlessly as he pulled her into his mouth, paying extra attention to her nipple. First one breast, then the other. Back and forth he went, blowing lightly on her wet skin in between passes.

A small vibration nestled itself in the epicenter of the holy land, aftershocks spreading until she was certain Colin could hear her body shaking.

"Shaken," she realized. "I want shaken."

"The lady wants shaken," he said, but didn't give in to her want.

Nope, the ultimate tease took his time, made her wait, kissing his way down her stomach to the top of her southern lace, pulling it back with his teeth, letting it snap. And because Colin was never one to be rushed, he knelt, settling in for the long haul.

He trailed his lips down her right inner thigh, placing open-mouthed kisses as he went. On the return, he got closer and closer until, *finally*, he was right there, so close, that Teagan shifted her hips slightly, trying to line up his mouth with where she craved him most.

He gave her one, solitary, barely-there lick up the center of her lace, ripping a moan from her. Wrapping his fingers around her ankle, he lifted and placed it on the counter, leaving her thrillingly on display.

There was something incredibly empowering about being completely laid out for his viewing pleasure. And he took a few moments to appreciate the view before he went back to her pleasure, making his way down the other thigh and back up.

"Shaken," she groaned. "I need shaken. Now."

"Then lean back."

Before she could prepare herself, he scooted her forward until she was teetering on the edge of the counter, bracing her bent leg against his shoulder.

His eyes met hers through his thick lashes and he smiled—with so much wicked promise her mouth went dry. "Shaken it is."

This time it was more than a passing kiss; he took his time. Using his tongue, his lips, and even his teeth, he drove her higher and higher, until she was about to burst. And then he tugged the lace aside and—*oh, sweet, sweet relief*—she was there, launching into the sky like a rocket, exploding at the top and raining down little flickers of fire.

Colin held on, watching her as she came and guiding her as she floated back to earth. Her heart was pounding and her vision was a little fuzzy, but when she opened her eyes, he was right there, kissing her softly as her breathing returned to normal.

"Six minutes," she said. "That must be a record."

"Honey, if you're counting the time, I'm doing this wrong."

"You're doing it perfect. I just want to make it to the shaken *and* stirred parts." She shimmied off the counter and, slipping her fingers under the lace waist of her thong, gave it a little push past her hips. With a little wiggle it hit the floor.

Gripping his belt loops, she tugged him forward until her back was up against the door. With a flick of her wrist, his pants joined the pile. "I think we painted the counters. Now onto the door."

"I love decorating with you."

Teagan's heart flipped at the four-letter word; then she quickly squashed the feeling. "Just think, we have three thousand square feet to decorate."

"Thirty-one hundred," he corrected.

"Then you'd better get a move on." He lost the rest of his clothes and was lifting her up until she was pressed between the door and him.

"You ready?"

"As long as I get to watch this time," she said, surprised at her request. She'd never watched in her entire life, but right then, with this man, she wanted it as badly as she wanted him inside her.

His grin was slow and full of trouble. If her request stumped him, he didn't show it, instead lacing their fingers and guiding their linked hands down and inside. Both their fingers moving in a rhythm.

She gasped at the intimacy, the way it felt, like an equal partnership.

"Like this?" he asked, moving their fingers in and out. His thumb teased her pleasure button, while he guided their hands in a series of practiced and precise movements, giving her a sneak peek at what was to come—her, to be specific.

His fingers must have picked up on her desperate SOS because he added another finger, picking up the pace. Her breathing became ragged, her brain cells firing so fast she was afraid she'd pass out. She dropped her head to his shoulder and the movements immediately halted.

"Open your eyes, Bianchi." Lifting her chin, his fingers positioned her head so that he could run his tongue along her lower lip. "You're not going to want to miss this."

It took everything she had but she opened her eyes and, before she could think, he was covered and inside her, sliding home. And he was right, she watched him disappear, then pull back out, and what a sight to behold.

She couldn't take her eyes off him. Think of anything besides him. It felt better than before. *They* felt better than before. Sure, they were older and far more experienced, but it was something about the way the fit that felt so natural—so ridiculously right.

"Colin," she breathed, taking every ounce of oxygen she had left.

"I know." His voice held a low rasp that ignited a hum of anticipation under her skin, because he wasn't looking at her mouth. He too was watching as their bodies moved together, as if they'd never fallen out of sync.

The pace picked up, the door clicking shut over and over with every slow release and deep thrust. The give of the door made it hard to get traction, and the faster they moved, the more she slipped down his body.

"More," she begged.

"Hell yeah, more." Never stopping, never hesitating, he turned and pressed her against the wall, which gave him exactly the leverage he needed.

No longer wanting to watch and desperately needing to feel every moment, she said, "Kiss me."

And kiss her he did, hungry and sensual. His lips were amazing, full and skilled, all patience and finesse. He kissed her as though he couldn't get enough, which worked for her, since she was pretty sure that this was the best kiss of her life.

In fact, kissing Colin was like being reborn, like she was being kissed for the first time. It was needy and desperate. A kiss that belonged to dreamers.

She fought the urge to squeeze her thighs, fought the urge to scream, not wanting to miss a single second of what was about to happen. She was rewarded, because he added his hand to the equation. Finding the perfect location and using the exact right amount of pressure, he drove her right to the edge and kept her there. Nuclear-powered tingles exploded through her body.

He kept the pace slow, purposeful, taking her higher and higher without rushing her. But there was something genuine, reverent about the way he held the back of her head, the way his thumb slid back and forth over her jawline, offering her comfort and connection.

"Now," she moaned.

"Thank God." His arms came around her, tight and unyielding, plastering her to him, as he kissed her, hard. She felt him let go. Actually felt the moment Colin West went all in.

A piece of her that she kept locked away peeked out, leaving her vulnerable and a little scared. But he looked a little off-kilter too, as if maybe she wasn't the only one in the danger zone.

With a groan, Colin kissed her as though she was his, held her as though he would never let go, as though he would never *want* to let go. And Teagan allowed herself to believe, just for a moment, that he'd always have her.

Suddenly, all the history disappeared, and the trust that had been torn from her came rushing back, leaving just her and Colin. In the now. With a clean slate and a chance at a future.

Chapter 19

Sex with you is so good we should celebrate
by having sex.

—Unknown

After three delicious cocktails, they lay in Colin's bed with Teagan sprawled across him, both of them breathing as if they'd just finished a marathon. In a way they had. She now understood Cinderella's urgency—a time limit was one hell of a motivator. Which was fitting since their relationship had started with a timestamp and ended with one.

She wasn't sure what the outcome of their second chance would be; she was just grateful to have been given one. Not that she was getting ahead of herself. Teagan was planted firmly in the present with a healthy respect for the past.

Past and present, her ass. She was so far ahead she could see tomorrow morning. And the next. He felt like her safe place, the person who'd protect her as she fell. If she wasn't careful, that's exactly what would happen. And it would be fast and hard, with no chance of survival. Her only hope was that when she landed, he'd be right there to catch her.

"You're in your head again." His hands were doing a slow journey up her spine and back down, making that statement a near impossibility. "Care to share?"

Nope. She cared to keep her feelings close to her chest. "That if we had more time, I'd want another cocktail."

"Then let's give the lady what she wants." This time when his hands slid back down, they went all the way down, to her butt, then her thighs, which he parted so she was once again straddling him.

She sat up and the covers fell around them. "God, you're beautiful." His hands, large enough to span her waist, were slowly moving up, rib by rib. "What are you doing Saturday?"

She wasn't the only one who'd moved beyond the past, looking to the future. Maybe even some sort of future together.

She ran her hands up his chest until she was flush against him, close enough to kiss his chin. "Are you asking me on a date, Dr. West?"

"If it were a date, I'd be asking for a hell of a lot more than an afternoon."

Well, that was embarrassing.

She started to move off him but his hands dropped down to her butt, holding her still with a cheek-full in each palm. "For that proper date, I'd want a whole day—I was thinking of a morning out on the water, the afternoon strolling around town holding hands, and the evening in my hot tub." He scooched her up so he could kiss the hollow of her neck. "Skinny-dipping, of course."

"Of course." She moved against him, and he groaned. "Then what's Saturday?"

He grinned up at her as if he were about to tell her Santa had left her a big present downstairs. "Saturday is the next day Jack has off."

"Who's Jack? And I'm not sure I want him to come on our not-a-date date."

"Jack is the guy I was telling you about, who owns a handful of commercial spaces in town," he said, and her belly did an excited little flip.

"How did you manage to get that much information between dinner and now?"

"Master multitasker, remember?" he said. "I texted him while you were looking at the dessert menu. He doesn't have anything quite right for a bakery, but he's willing to do the renovations for the right renter."

She sat up. "I'm the right person."

"Of that I have no doubt," he said with a vulnerability that had her wondering if they were still talking about shops. "He offered to show us a few that are available."

"Us?" How could a tiny word like *us* send a tsunami of emotions rolling through her?

He shrugged. "If you want me to come along."

"Oh, I want you to come."

His hands, still cupping her backside, nudged her forward, so her palms rested on either side of his head. The teasing expression faded into something more serious, something warmer. "I think I like you, Bianchi," he whispered.

"I think I like you too." That was the understatement of the year. She liked him more than chocolate-chocolate-chunk ice cream with hot fudge and whipped cream.

"Glad we have that settled." He leaned up and snagged her mouth with his, taking his sweet old time, tenderly kissing her. His hold was gentle, his lips featherlight.

He cradled her the way he had that night they'd shared their first kiss, which had been her first ever kiss. It felt exactly like this and nothing like this. All the feels but now she had the maturity to know how special it was.

"What is this?" she whispered, needing to know she wasn't the only one feeling what she was feeling.

He met her gaze, then held it for an achingly long time. "I'm not sure, but I want to find out."

"Me too."

His eyes went dark—edgy—and he pulled her back to him for a kiss that was hot and panty-melting, a covers-on-the-floor, wild kiss that built and built until everything was in the martini shaker and all it needed was a little shake before the lid flew off.

"Colin," she groaned, and started moving her hips.

"Bianchi," he groaned back.

"Dad?"

They both froze. There was a knock, and just before Maddison entered, Teagan slid off Colin and threw the covers up over her head.

"Dad?" Maddison asked, clearly onto the fact that some mischief was afoot—or under the covers as it were. "What are you doing?"

"Ah." Colin sounded *caught red-handed* guilty. "Just catching up on some work."

"Really?" Maddison was no fool. "Because you're sweating a little. Since when does patient care make you sweat so much you lose your shirt?"

"It's a really hard case," he said, and Teagan snorted because his case was fully hard.

"Why am I not surprised?" Maddison sounded oddly calm and collected. As if she were the parent who'd walked in on two horny teens. "I guess this is the part where you tell me you can have sex but I can't."

"I'm an adult."

"So am I, but I'm the only one acting like it right now."

Teagan had to agree. Where Colin sounded defensive, Maddison sounded low-key. "Can you tell the other adult hiding under the covers she has a visitor at her own house, where her own bed and her own husband are waiting for her."

"Husband?" Panic flooded her, and that post-sex glow she'd been basking in vanished, turning to dread. There were only so many reasons Frank could be in Pacific Cove—none of them good. And all posing potential harm to her girls.

Blanket carefully tucked under her armpits, she popped her head out. Maddison was leaning against the doorjamb, arms crossed, expression dialed to bored. "Frank is here? Like next door?"

Maddison looked at her as if she was not only a hypocrite but a traitor. "He seemed *super* concerned when no one knew where you were."

"Of course he did." Like he was the one put out.

Reaching with a single arm, she felt around for her bra, which was—shit, downstairs. Knowing that *that* wasn't going to work, she snagged her tank from the foot of the bed and dove back under the covers to put it on. Way harder than it looked in the movies.

"Seriously," Maddison said, sounding grossed out. "I'm right here." And that's when Teagan realized it looked as if she was giving Colin a blowie.

Tank in place, Teagan poked her head back out. "I'm getting dressed!"

"Whatever the kids are calling it these days," Maddison said.

Teagan slipped her hand out from under the covers to grab her skirt and, with her daffodil panties and bra MIA, stood and headed out the door. She heard Colin fumbling around behind her.

"Wait up! Let me walk you home," he called out.

Exactly the kind of chivalry she did not need at this particular moment. "Not necessary." She picked up the pace, hoping to outrun him.

"You can run," she heard from behind, "but I'm still walking you to your door, Bianchi."

"Great." *Just great.* Because having her past and present collide was exactly how she wanted to end this mind-blowing night.

When she'd walked through his front door, she'd known what she was agreeing to. When he'd sweetly and romantically asked her out on a date, she'd allowed herself to hope that he'd felt the shift toward something potentially amazing. But knowing what was awaiting her next door, and the father-daughter conversation awaiting Colin, Teagan worried that maybe they'd moved too fast without considering the repercussions.

If life was an adventure in forgiveness, then Teagan needed a new tour guide. Because there wasn't just one traitorous adult lounging on the couch sipping her expensive scotch in a tumbler like a character in a noir film, but two.

"What are you doing?" she asked Harley.

Her sister looked back and forth between Teagan and Frank before carefully answering, "Being a gracious host."

"You can practice being a gracious host when you have your own house, Martha Stewart."

Harley went quiet and Teagan turned to Frank, who had apparently escaped rehab, two months early, with a girl on each knee, sitting there like he hadn't missed a day. Like he hadn't turned her world upside town.

Like he hadn't completely fucked her over.

He looked up and smiled. "It's so good to see you. You look great."

She wanted to yell at him, to tell him to get the hell out, but she'd never do that in front of the girls. They were smiling up at her in their Wonder Twins pajamas, looking like a happy family Christmas card. And Frank knew that. He always knew how to make her feel guilty—as if she were responsible for the failure of their business, the failure of their marriage, and for every failure they'd encountered since they'd met.

"Why are you here?" Teagan asked.

"Why were you not?" Frank countered.

In the past, that question would have made her feel like a bad mom, but she knew that wasn't the truth. She was a good mom, and she was finally confident in that statement. Because of Harley and because of Colin, she was starting to realize that she did have that maternal Bianchi gene. Frank had just never allowed space for Teagan to explore that part of her personality. Their relationship had consisted of Teagan being the workhorse while Frank explored every whim and fancy that struck him.

He was a great dad, but he had an addiction that decimated everything in its path. So far, the girls didn't realize that, and Teagan would do whatever it took to make sure they never did.

Teagan's dad was a roadie who traveled three-hundred-plus days a year. For the most part, her mom had been okay with the arrangement. Minus the infidelity. Like Frank, Dale was an addict. But she didn't want Frank's problems to define his relationship with his kids, the way her parents' divorce had torn Teagan and Harley's security right out from under them.

"I was out." And it was none of his damn business where.

He took in her post-sex appearance. Teagan tried to right herself to the best of her ability, but she knew her hair was frizzy, her makeup nonexistent, her bra lost somewhere in Colin's house, and she had a glow that only three orgasms could create. "I can see that."

Teagan was one judgy stare away from telling him to *G-O. F-U-C-K. Y-O-U-R-S-E-L-F* when Poppy said, "Can Daddy stay?"

Teagan wanted to say hell no but the innocent hope in her daughter's sleepy eyes hurt her heart. She didn't want to be the one to disappoint the girls again. She wanted to be the mom who got to play hooky all day and read bedtime stories under blanket-forts at night.

"You know what, kiddo," Frank began, and Teagan almost whispered a "thank you" to her ex for taking the initiative. "It's up to your mom."

"Are you kidding me?" Why even give him the benefit of the doubt when he always disappointed? There he sat on the couch Teagan had bought herself after the divorce, bouncing a kid on each knee, sharing a glass of bourbon with her sister, in the home that had always been her safe place.

Poppy looked up at her with those big blue eyes, her dad's eyes, and said in her tiny girl voice, "But yous have to wet him stay. He gots eviscerated from his apartment and if he can't stay here, the birtf'day card won't find him. See."

Poppy held up a handmade birtf'day invitation and Lily smiled. Teagan sent her irritating, idiotic, and immature ex a pointed glare. *Fix this.*

"Sorry." He shrugged a *What are you going to do about it?* "It kind of slipped out when I was talking to Harley, and we were making plans for the girls' birthday. These two superheroes must have used their super hearing."

Teagan stared at Harley. "Really?"

Harley grimaced.

"Actually, Lily overheard and tolds me, so I tolds yous and why is your shirt inside out?"

Teagan ignored this question and looked at Frank. "For how long?"

"Good question," someone said from behind her—a very set-to-alpha-mode someone.

Frank studied Colin, long and hard, and Colin studied him back. Teagan knew the exact moment Frank registered exactly who was standing behind Teagan, with a supportive hand on her shoulder.

Nonna used to love to talk about Colin, partly because she hated Frank, but mostly because of how much she'd loved Colin. Frank always got pissy whenever Colin was brought up. Now, Colin wasn't just a footnote in her past, he was standing in Nonna's living room, emitting a protective vibe that was a complete turn-on.

"We've got this," Frank said, but possessive wasn't a good look on him—it came off like Winnie-the-Pooh staring down a grizzly.

"You just tell me how I can help," Colin said quietly enough for only her ears.

"Thank you," was all she got out before Poppy was talking again.

"Just till he gets a new place. Right, Daddy? He's moving close to be near us," Poppy proclaimed as if it were the truth. She started clapping. Then Lily joined. "Can he stay, pwease, pwease, pretty pwease? It's all we wants for our birf'hday. Daddy and a unicorn and Wonder Twins cupcakes and dat's all, just Daddy and a unicorn and Wonder Twins cupcakes."

There was no way Teagan could say no. She could have said no to Frank, but she couldn't say no to Frank in front of her daughters with Frank egging them on.

Frank had left her only one choice. She turned to look at Colin, the man she'd just established an "us" with. He was staring at her silently, expressionless, giving her absolutely no clue as to what he was thinking.

And even though it killed her, she turned to her daughters and said, "We'll see," even as her whole mind and body were screaming no.

She turned to look at Colin, and he was gone.

Chapter 20

We may look old and wise to the outside world.
But to each other, we are still in junior school.

—Charlotte Gray

"**I** was suffering from an acute case of WWTD," Harley explained. "I know you would been mature and responsible." Instead of punching Frank in the throat.

But she was getting the distinct feeling Teagan didn't entirely disapprove of the throat punch. After that BS Frank had pulled, Harley was surprised her sister hadn't grabbed him by the nuts and dragged him to the door.

"Really? I know one thing I wouldn't do. I wouldn't let my ex-brother-in-law in and pour him a drink and wake the girls up at midnight," Teagan said, standing in the kitchen, lips pressed into a pissed-off line.

"You know, you might want to relax a little or your face might freeze that way." She tapped a finger to her sister's jowls and Teagan smacked her hands away. "Ow! And yes, that's exactly what you'd do. Literally, I was sitting there with Maddie trying to give you and lover boy some space when Frank knocked and I asked myself, 'Self, what would Teagan do?'"

"Cute." Her tone said she found not one iota of the comment cute.

"And do you know the answer? You'd lie down like a doormat and let Frank in. So I did WTWD and let him in. As for waking the girls? That was Frank."

"You could have told him it was past bedtime."

"First, not my place, Second, not my place. And third, he made that clear by pointing out I was just their aunt and had zero authority when it came to his girls."

"I'm sorry about that. He had no right to say that. You want to know WWT 2.0 do? She'd tell him waking the girls was a hard no." Teagan walked over to rest a hip on the opposite counter. Harley was on the island—literally and metaphorically—crisscross applesaucing while eating ice cream straight from the tub. "But you should have called me."

"I sent over Maddison, who was kind of like a carrier pigeon with a key to Colin's place."

"Yeah, that was kind of a shitshow. Since you were giving us space and all."

Harley grimaced. "I was a little freaked about not screwing up, and I guess I kind of screwed that part up. But you know what I didn't do, Sis? I didn't ignore the guy I just had sex with for my ex."

Dipping one finger in the ice cream, Teagan held another finger up, the middle one.

"Yeah, I imagine that's what you were doing. Either he was so bad you were running for the woods, or he was so good you were running because you're scared."

"That's not what happened."

Harley licked the scooper clean and pointed it at Teagan. "That is so what happened. You're talking to the queen of running."

"The only running I did was into my mooch of an ex. Thanks for that."

"Oh no, you don't get to blame this on me!"

"Why not? You're the sitter."

"You're the one who married Frank."

Teagan glared at her. "Only because I was too stupid to realize that, while a head-in-the-clouds dreamer seemed exciting, in reality he was a nightmare."

"Are we talking about him or me?" Harley asked and Teagan shrugged. "Just remember it's Harley 2.0 who's saved your ass more than once in the last couple of months. Have you been sitting around just waiting for me to flake?" Harley worked really hard to keep the hurt out of her voice. "I have been nothing but supportive."

"You supported me right into this disaster. You Hurricane Harleyed my life."

"I'm going to put that nasty attitude in the delete folder and pretend it never happened," Harley said. "Because how could your life possibly be screwed up? You have Nonna's house, mom's business, all those memories, and the perfect guy."

"You had the same golden ticket. You blew it."

"Money isn't the same as memories. Or a house full of them." She waved the scooper around and melted ice cream splattered Teagan's top. It was one of those sorry not sorry situations.

"Nonna left you the car because she knew how much you loved riding in it. How do the girls say it? 'With the rag top down so your hair can blow'?"

"Before you go air-quoting yourself into carpal tunnel, know that you are in possession of the world's smallest violin." Harley drew her pointer over her thumb for effect. "Did you ever think, maybe I wanted a home?"

"Then maybe, go back to LA, to your adult career, where you can save money and buy yourself one."

"I do have an adult job. I'm a branding expert. Without me, your little bread business would be a two-oven variety."

"Now, I'm going to be a commercial kitchen bread business, which will eat up my nest egg. Did you know that eighty percent of food industry businesses fail in the first year? And while I'm trying to turn a profit, I'll have to pay Frank alimony because he was never able to hold down a job."

"Forgive me if I roll my eyes. He might be a *flake,* but you've had ten years of love. A lifetime of love. Dad taught me zilch about love. Or, for that matter, family dynamics, money management," she ticked off, "running a business, making lasting relationships. You had daily support and strong role models. I have a shot glass collection from all fifty states. Nearly fifteen years and Dad and I made it to all fifty states. Do the math," she said. "Are you so self-absorbed that you can't see all I have is a car and a bunch of signatures from retired rock stars?"

Teagan's tone lost some of its bite. "You used to brag about your adventures with Dad."

"Do you ever wonder why I call him Dale? Because he was a pretty absent dad. I mean, he tried, but he was always so caught up in the next job. His hope to land his pass to fame. Women. 'The Life.'" She used her own air quotes. "I came second, Tee. Just like with Mom. Just like with you, but I came second every single day."

"I didn't know."

"You never asked." Harley pushed aside the carton, her heart too sad for comfort food. "God, all I wanted was to be you. To be a part of something permanent."

"When you came for visits, you couldn't sit still. You were always in motion and talking about the next big Dad Adventure."

"Because I knew my being here changed things, and I didn't want to impose or make you guys feel obligated to entertain me. The aquarium, beach days, trips to tourist locations."

It had been exhausting for Harley, always keeping up pretenses. She could only imagine how tiring it must be to make every day feel like a vacation for a longtime visitor. So Harley had done a lot of things on her own, feigned having friends, done whatever she could to make sure she wasn't in the way.

"Did I make you feel like that?" Teagan asked and Harley shrugged.

It wasn't just Dale who'd taught her that she wasn't enough. Harley had spent a lifetime coming in second to everyone in her family. Harley always though that somehow Nonna Rose, in all her wisdom, knew what a sad child Harley had been. How displaced and overlooked she'd felt growing up. Then Nonna passed. Left everything of meaning to Teagan and the twins, and Harley felt like that misunderstood kid all over again.

"You were a jerk," she said, looking away so Teagan wouldn't see just how difficult it was for her to talk about things she'd tried really hard to overcome. More like bury. She didn't like to think about those feelings much less talk about them. "And Mom would get super distant at the end of my stays."

Teagan moved closer, resting her arms on the island top. "It wasn't you. It was Dad. He made things hard."

"Who cared what it was? I was a kid. I didn't understand." She let out a wary breath. Her goal in coming here was to heal so that maybe, one day, she'd be whole enough to last more than six months in a single location. "Look, I didn't come back to argue. I screwed up in Seattle. Big time. But you have too, and I forgive you. Why is it so hard for you to forgive me?"

Teagan must have sensed the raw ache Harley was feeling because her expression softened. "I'm just mad. At myself about how I handled tonight."

"So you get to take it out on me?"

Teagan shook her head. "No. I don't."

"I don't want to fight. I just want a place in your life, wherever that might be."

"You are in my life. You and your dirty dishes and your death trap," she teased but Harley had a hard time seeing the humor through the hurt.

"See, that's what I'm talking about. I'm in your schedule. Not really in your life."

"What does that even mean?"

"You're so busy trying to fit me into some category to make our relationship nice and tidy, you don't even see how that makes me feel."

Rehashing old issues brought up things better left alone. They made Harley want to run. But if she ever wanted a healthy relationship with her big sister, this was the moment. She had to be brave and see it through, no matter how hard. "About that last night in Seattle, I left because I was ashamed that I didn't know how bad Frank's gambling problem had become. I'm your sister and I should have known. That's on me. Blaming me for everything wrong in your life, that's on you."

In the past, Harley would have internalized the blame. But Bryan had showed her how to be open, share the weight, trust that the people who loved you could shoulder it. Except that when he'd been open and shared his feelings, and it came time to handle his feelings, she'd bolted. Partly because she was scared. She'd rather walk away of her own accord than know what it would feel like if Bryan put her second. With his close-knit family, and her commitment issues, it was only a matter of time. Which was why she'd walked away.

"I realize I don't just get to make big promises. I have to earn your trust," Harley said. "But know I'm really trying because I want to fix whatever is broken between us. Mom and Dale made a decision based on anger that broke our sister bond. Now it's up to us." Scooper loaded with ice cream, Harley held it out like a Bianchi olive branch. "We can't change the past, but we can choose to make different decisions. And I'm going to need you to be a little patient, because I don't want to make the wrong one."

"When did you get so smart?"

"I have this cool older sister."

Teagan took a huge bite and handed it back to Harley. But when Harley reached for the scooper, Teagan hugged her. A real sisterly hug that Harley had waited her entire adult life to receive.

She held on fiercely, warm emotions bubbling up and pooling on her lashes. She closed her eyes to remember exactly what this moment felt like, not letting go until they were both sniffling. When she pulled back, she had ice cream on her boob.

"Is this where you tell me no tushies on the counter?"

"This is where I eat ice cream from the carton with my baby sister."

Teagan hopped up on the counter and did some crisscross applesaucing of her own until their knees touched. When they were little, and their parents were having one of their epic fights, they'd sneak downstairs, sit on the counter, and eat ice cream from the carton, just like this.

"I'm sorry," Teagan whispered.

"You already said that."

"No, I mean, I'm sorry about Bryan."

Harley froze, a cold blast of holy fuck hitting her square in the face. "How do you know about Bryan?"

"He called."

"Did you answer my phone?" Harley frantically scrolled through her cell. Not a single incoming call from LA since he'd promised to give her space.

"No, and apparently you don't either. So he called Nonna's house line. I guess he got worried when he didn't hear from you and looked up her number."

That was incredibly sweet. And incredibly irritating. If he wasn't so thoughtful, she might hate him. "This is bad, Tee. Really bad. Tell me exactly what you said."

Harley had a feeling Teagan's description of their living arrangement wouldn't line up with her own story about helping her sister settle her grandmother's estate in Pacific Cove. None of the facts were a lie, but they weren't the truth either.

"All I said was that you were out."

"You're the best." She hugged her sister again. "Thank you, thank you, thank you. You have no idea how grateful I am." She offered Teagan the next bite, which was loaded with chocolate chunks.

"You might want to hold off on the good scoop until I finish." Teagan swallowed. "I also might have told him that you'd call him back."

"You what? I'm here to avoid him. Not sit in Nonna's kitchen and have a high-school call with some cute boy while twirling the phone cord."

Teagan leaned in. "So he's cute, huh?"

"That's your takeaway?"

"It seems to explain a lot of things, which is why I gave him Nonna's address."

"What! Why?" Harley hopped off the counter, ready to pack up her things and head north for the summer. Teagan grabbed her by the elbow and patted the vacant counter spot. Harley hopped back up but held the scooper hostage until her sister fully explained herself.

"Maybe because I wanted to see if you'd actually hold a funeral for our poor nonna, God bless her soul." Teagan made the sign of the cross. "Seriously? Who lies about their grandma dying to avoid a breakup?"

"Well, she is dead. Plus, I figured Nonna would get a kick out of being my alibi."

Teagan ignored this. "Did you hit your six-month limit?"

"How do you know about my six-month limit?"

"Har, the Pope knows about your six-month limit."

"I'll have you know, I lasted ten months." Harley ate the good bite.

"Wow, 'lasted.' Past tense. Does he know that?"

"Not exactly. But don't you dare tell him."

"Oh, I won't. Already cleaning up one person's mess. Don't have time for another."

"I might handle things differently from you, but don't mistake my differences for ineptitude. I'll tell Bryan when I'm ready." She wasn't sure when that time would come, but she knew it had to be sooner rather than later.

"I never would, and I didn't mean to imply that." It was Harley's turn to lift a brow. "Okay, maybe I did a little, but only because you're right. I do micromanage because structure makes me feel safe. Without it, I feel like that scared kid I used to be, who knew that everything was one mistake from falling apart. That I'll fall apart." She buried her face in her hands. "God, I'm the inept one."

"Stick up your ass? Sometimes. Inept? Never. And in the times you feel like you're drowning, always remember, 'You are braver than you believe, stronger than you seem, and smarter than you think.'"

"Nonna used to say that."

"Actually, Christopher Robin said it first, but Nonna sounded better."

Teagan licked the scooper, leaving a chocolate mustache in the process. "Tell me about Bryan. He sounds special."

"He's more than special, which is why I left."

"That makes no sense."

"Mom and Dale didn't exactly model healthy love, and Dale didn't model anything remotely healthy when it came to relationships."

"Someone once told me that we can't change the past, but we can choose to make different decisions."

"She sounds wise," Harley said, snagging the scooper from Teagan. "Did you give him the home address or the PO box in town?"

"The box in town. Of course."

They hugged, making it the most hugs shared in a single hour since they were little.

"I'll text him and give him the house address," Harley promised.

That was something she could give him. As well as the truth about why she'd left and how she felt around him. She felt the sprouting of a seed of hope that he'd want her anyway. Broken parts and all.

Chapter 21

Well, my dear Sister, no wonder we are looking
like an old teabag, we have been in lots of
hot water together!

—Catherine Pulsifer

Teagan sat on the back deck watching the moonlight flicker off the ocean, the steam from her hot mint tea turning to mist in the heavy marine fog. The tide was higher than normal, the tail of the waves rolling as far as the sand dunes. The events of the evening had pushed her right into an emotional riptide.

She replayed the order of the night's happenings. From drinks with Colin, to an unexpected first date. Every time she saw him seemed to build naturally to the next, until the beginnings of a bond had begun to form—a bond she desperately wanted to explore. Then she was faced with another unexpected first, which overshadowed a wonderful evening.

Not that her decisions would have been different, but she could have handled them differently.

For one, she never should have allowed Frank to put her on the spot in front of the girls. She should have told him they'd table the discussion until a better time. Also, the moment she felt Colin behind her, she should have told Frank to put a cork in it and given Colin a proper goodbye. A date like that deserved a proper goodbye kiss, under a bright porch light.

She glanced at her cell. It was three in the morning. It was too early to knock on his door and bring him a makeup brioche; it was also too late for his back door to suddenly open.

Heart ricocheting off her ribs, Teagan watched as someone

stepped onto the deck. She strained her eyes, telling herself that this was her chance to set things right. To apologize and promise that Frank had been handled and he had zero effect on where this thing between them stood.

Her grip on her tea mug tightened as the shadow stepped into the moonlight. Teagan's heart gave a little sad trombone. Instead of a devilishly addictive sex-god sneaking out the back door, a redheaded teenager wearing platform heels, a micro mini sundress, and enough apprehension to advertise she was up to no good cautiously unscrewed the motion sensor light and shut the door behind her.

The cocky swing of her hips said this was about a boy, whom Colin would kill if he ever learned of their middle-of-the-night rendezvous. Maddison tiptoed across the back deck, her shoes sounding like a stampede of elephants attempting ballet.

"Pro tip," Teagan said, just loud enough to carry to the neighboring deck. "You might want to put your shoes on after you're down the street. Heels on wood planks are a dead giveaway."

Maddison froze and slowly spun around. Even in the darkness, Teagan could make out two *deer in the headlight* eyes. "I'm meeting my cousin. She's super upset? And needs to vent?"

Teagan made a foul-play buzzer sound. "Sorry, try again."

"Fine, maybe I'm the one who needs to vent. I'm super scarred over catching my dad and my boss, postcoital, if you know what I mean."

Oh, she knew. And if Maddison was feeling even a tenth as awkward at Teagan was right then, maybe they needed to have a girl-to-girl talk. Not that she doubted Colin's ability to handle tough conversations, but Teagan was the interloper in this equation. "Scarring? I don't know about that, but for sure embarrassing and super awkward. Maybe if we talked about—"

It was Maddison's turn to make the buzzer sound.

Teagan shrugged and went back to sipping her tea. "Maybe you want to talk about how scarred your dad would be if something happened to you?"

"I know what I'm doing. It's not like I'm meeting a stranger or anything."

"Good to know, that eases my worry." Teagan grabbed her cell off the patio table and dialed.

"Let me guess, you're calling my dad, not to tell him about this, but to force me to tell him."

"Wrong again. Played that game once before. It didn't work out so well for me. I'm going to camp on your deck and tell him as soon as the sun comes up." But right now, she had a window of opportunity to help his daughter get through some of her anger. Maybe she'd aim it all Teagan's way so it would be one less thing Colin had to deal with. After all, the girl wasn't mad at her dad. She was as scared as Teagan was that tonight would somehow change everything.

"Of course you are." She could practically see Maddison roll her eyes. "Then who are you calling?"

"The cops."

"Why?"

"There was a guy in a suspicious black truck parked down the block earlier."

Maddison took off her heels and padded to the edge of the deck. She glanced right and left, going on her toes to make sure Teagan wasn't lying. "Where is he?" she accused.

"Oh, your cousin? *He* waited about ten minutes, then took off."

"So you didn't call the cops on him?" Maddison asked, sounding a little relieved that the truck was gone. "Why do I not believe you?"

"You don't have to. But if I'd known he was here to pick up you, I would have."

"Because I'm too young?"

"Because he's too old."

"You don't know anything about him."

"I know that he was drinking while waiting."

"Maybe it was a soda."

"Your lack of conviction makes me believe he's driven drunk before. Hopefully, not with you in the car."

"I've never been in his car."

That was a relief. "Hey, I'm going to go grab you a cup of

tea. If you're here when I get back, you can ask me anything you want."

"And if I'm not?"

"Then we'll both have a long night waiting for your dad to wake up." Teagan headed for the teapot in the kitchen, praying to God that when she returned, Maddison would be there. She didn't know what she'd tell Colin if Maddison slipped right through Teagan's fingers to find Black Truck Guy.

To her utter relief, Maddison was sitting in the lounger when Teagan returned. She looked at Teagan as if she were about to say something parent-y, then took the mug.

They were quiet for a long moment, listening to the distant bell on a buoy.

"Do you like my dad?" Maddison finally asked.

"Yes."

"Do you love him?"

Sweat broke out on Teagan's forehead. Of course she didn't love him, not like the in-love kind of love. They'd had one date followed by fifty-three minutes of amazing sex. "That's not how this works. A question for a question."

"I knew you weren't that cool."

Teagan realized that if she was going to earn the trust of a secretive teen, she'd have to sweeten the pot. Kind of like the girls when they wanted to watch one more cartoon before bed. If the tablets went away without a fuss, they could get two bedtime stories.

"Okay, two to one. But you have to answer honestly."

The teen considered this. "Deal." She felt Maddison turn to look at her. "So do you?"

"Not in the way you're asking," she said honestly. "He was my first love, and I will always have a place in my heart for him, but if you're asking if I'm in love with him, then the answer is no."

This seemed to please Maddison. Now, it was Teagan's turn, but she wasn't sure what to ask. She wanted to create a safe environment for the girl to talk, but she didn't want to step on Colin's toes.

"Why are you so set on Black Truck Guy?" she asked.

"He thinks I'm pretty."

Teagan had been prepared for a million different answers but not one that would break her heart. "You are pretty. Stunning, actually."

"You have to say that."

Teagan snorted. "Why, because I'm a parent?"

"Because you're dating my parent."

She turned to look Maddison in the eye so the girl would see her honesty. "I'm saying this as a fellow woman. You are, without a doubt, beautiful. Just because Truck Guy is the first guy brave enough to tell you, that doesn't mean other, better guys aren't thinking it."

"You mean like Kade?"

"I have no idea who Kade is, but I can tell by the way you said his name that he thinks you're pretty and you know it. Okay, two to one. My turn," she said, and Maddison didn't argue, just sipped her tea.

"Do you miss your mom?" she asked and from the way Maddison's gaze went misty, she had her answer. "I'm only asking because I wonder how my girls are feeling without their dad around. They don't say much about him, but I know they miss him, and I don't know how to make it better."

"I used to miss my mom a lot," Maddison admitted. "And I still want to be with her, even though I know she'll flake on me. I guess it's a parent-kid kind of situation that makes me want to give her more chances."

"My dad was kind of absent too. I remember wanting so badly for him to follow through on his promises, but after a while I just stopped hoping."

"Did it help? With the pain?"

Teagan took a sip of tea and really contemplated her answer. She wanted to be truthful without influencing Maddison's relationship with her mom. "After all these years, the pain is still there. Not as bad, but it's always lingering in the background."

"Do you wish you'd stayed in touch?"

"That was question three," she teased. "But I'll let it slide."

Maddison laughed, a tiny, barely audible laugh but her entire demeanor went from brooding to brokenhearted.

"Sometimes, like when I graduated from college or got married. Now, I think about the kind of grandpa he'd be. He's funny and loud and even gentlehearted in a gregarious kind of way. His Peter Pan lifestyle wasn't conducive to parenting but he would have made one hell of a granddad."

And that gave Teagan pause. Was she robbing her girls of the things that came with having a grandpa, all because she couldn't put her own hurt aside?

Maddison opened her mouth, then snapped it shut. "Your turn."

"Did you choose NYU over UCLA because you want to give your mom another chance?"

"Kind of. I want her in my life, and I guess I wonder if she might be around more if I lived closer," she admitted. Teagan was surprised at how candid Maddison was being. "I mean, I get it. She's super busy with work. She works for a fashion magazine, which is cool since I get free samples. But my stepbrother is taking a gap year from college and moved back home with her, so there's that."

"Are you guys close?" she asked.

Maddison just shrugged. Teagan might not know what it was like to have an absent mom, but she knew the pain that came with abandonment. Colin said that Amanda had remarried ten years ago and yet Maddison didn't have a relationship with her mom's new family. That must hurt more than being the child left behind.

"You know, you might want to tell your dad why you're going so he doesn't think you're leaving to get away from him."

"He knows."

Teagan looked over at the girl. "You know, I made the same mistake years back when I mistook your dad's generous heart, compassion, and understanding."

"What happened?"

"I hurt him badly, and I would give anything to go back and

change the way things went down. He looks tough, but he's not invincible."

Maddison seemed to consider this for a long moment, so long Teagan was convinced she was going to hand back the mug and say, "It's been real." But instead she said, "How do you know Gabriel, I mean Truck Guy, isn't good for me?" While it wasn't *conversation over*, it clarified that questions about her parents were off-limits.

"I know that he asked you to sneak out and I'm guessing he also asked you to keep your time together on the DL."

"Only old people say DL," Maddison explained as if she were the keeper of all things old and all things older. "Did my dad know you're married?"

"Divorced." She looked at Maddison. "Do you really think I'd bring your dad into something so wrong?" Maddison shrugged. Teagan clearly had a long road to prove herself to Colin's family. "For the record, I'm not a cheater. I would never date someone while I was with someone else. And I'm not a fan of keeping my family in the dark."

"You mean, like me?"

"From my experience, secrets can tear families apart."

"So honesty's the best policy? Kind of ironic since you and my dad were sleeping together behind everyone's back."

And . . . Maddison was back to being angry. Not at Teagan, but at the fact that she'd snuck out, and now she had to admit it to her dad.

"It wasn't everyone's business," Teagan said, sidestepping a question that Colin should answer. "And awkward discovery or not, we're two consenting adults who had—"

"Gross." Maddison covered her ears. "Can we not."

"I'm good with that." She laughed and Maddison laughed with her, sounding more like a teenager than a girl about to sneak into a car with a virtual stranger. "So how do you want to play this?"

"Any way that doesn't end in me being grounded more."

"The way I see it, you have two choices. Wake your dad now

and spill or join me for breakfast on the deck and we come clean together?"

"Do you think he'd come clean with me? About tonight." Maddison didn't have to say she wanted clarity on the whole naked woman in her dad's bed situation.

"Maybe if you give him a chance."

Maddison snorted. "He barely even told me what went down with my mom. He isn't going to talk about you."

Teagan thought back on how her mom had sheltered Teagan from so much disappointment, which reminded her of what Harley had said earlier. What her sister's life must have been like with a parent who had zero filter. "Sometimes parents forget that their desire to protect their kids from harm might be misconstrued as being controlling."

A statement Teagan would have to thoroughly explore later. Perhaps in her desire to keep her girls safe, she was denying them the chance to experience some of the best parts of childhood. Like playing in the front yard without an onlooking adult, riding bikes around town, walking to school with their friends. Not that Poppy and Lily were old enough for some of those things. But when they were age-appropriate, how would Teagan react?

"I'm not misconstruing anything. His helicopter ways are real," Maddison said. "I'm leaving for college soon, and he still treats me like I'm a kid."

"Then stop acting like a kid."

"I'm trying, but my dad works, like all the time. So I guess I'm living my life by Dr. West's handbook. I'm showing initiative by earning my own money."

Teagan's chest pinched painfully for the girl who was acting out to get her dad's attention. She was in such a rush to grow up but didn't want to face the separation that came with it. "How would he feel about your showing that initiative?" Teagan sat on the lounger next to her. "If you started being honest with him, he might loosen his grip a little."

"He's never loosened anything no matter what I do."

"He never let you stay out after curfew or go somewhere

he'd rather you didn't?" she asked, and Maddison studied her purple-painted toes.

That's what I thought. Because while Colin had sounded like a crazed dad the other day and never bothered to sugarcoat things—things like his unresolved feelings about that *Dear Colin* letter—Teagan knew he was a fair man.

"I guess. Sometimes. But not lately."

"What happened lately?"

"I lied to him."

"About a guy?" Maddison gave another of her little shrugs. "Don't start lying for a guy now or you might end up my age and still lying for them."

"I didn't lie *for* a guy, I lied *about* a guy."

"A lie is a lie," Teagan said. "Take it from me, lies lead to mistrust."

"You sound like my dad."

Teagan shrugged. "Your dad's a smart guy. And he loves you."

Teagan didn't know what she'd said, but she'd stepped on a landmine because Maddison shot to her feet and stalked to the end of the porch. "He'll never love you, if that's what you're after."

The comment was meant to hurt and it did. But Teagan wasn't angry. Maddison was scared of being replaced. But she was failing to see that Colin was equally sacred. Parents had one job. To prepare their kids for adulthood, make sure their wings were ready for flight before they left the nest. But no one talked about what happened to the mama bird left behind. Or, in this case, the papa bird.

Colin was about to go from a house full of life and laughter to weekly video chats with the daughter who, for the past seventeen years, had been his everything.

"You know your dad's going to miss you when you go off to college," she explained. "He'll miss you every moment of the day."

"I know," she said quietly, leaving Teagan to wonder if she really did know. After being left by one parent, it was hard not to wait for the second shoe to drop—no matter how devoted that parent might be.

"He's probably going to be a little lost after you leave."

Maddison snorted. "He has my uncle and aunt. And he has work."

"Your uncle has your aunt. His patients all have owners. Your dad has you. That's how it's been since the day you were born."

"And he'll still have me."

"Of course, but—"

"Look." Maddison stood. "I hate to break it to you, but he doesn't do long-term," she said, and Teagan worked hard to school her features. "He lives for his work and family; there isn't any room for anyone else. I'm not trying to be mean, just telling you how it is."

With that, Maddison walked back across the sand and, shoes off, slipped through the back door.

Chapter 22

No relationship is all sunshine, but two
people can share one umbrella and survive the
storm together.

—Unknown

Saturday couldn't come soon enough. Colin's mental count-down clock activated the second Teagan said yes to property shopping—and their day-long date—then sealed it with a kiss. They'd agreed to meet at ten, but he'd been ready by nine thirty and, instead of pacing the length of his house another million times, he headed next door.

Smoothing his hair and doing a quick breath check, he knocked on the door. And waited.

And waited.

And was about to knock again when the door swung open.

Between searching for lost treasure to pay for the NYU money and dealing with his boss, Colin couldn't afford any more de-railments. So he wasn't about to get sideswiped now. Not by some mooch who cornered his ex-wife to get what he wanted.

Frank stood in the doorway, looking cozy—bare feet, pajama bottoms, no shirt, with the girls climbing all over him. Lily was wrapped around his right foot, Poppy around his left, looking like two baby opossums clinging to their daddy.

"Hey girls," he said because they were the most important factors in this equation. He squatted down on his haunches and held out his arms.

"Cowin," Poppy squealed, and both girls ran to him. He

swung Poppy over his shoulder in a fireman's hold and picked Lily up, making a bench seat with his forearm.

Frank sized him up, and Colin just smiled. *Take that, jackass.* "Can I help you?"

"I thought you were in rebab," Colin said.

"I thought you were married."

"Are you really moving to town?"

"Thinking about it." Frank puffed his chest out. Colin would puff his back except the kids were still crawling all over him like he was a toddler whisperer. "Man's got to be near his family."

"Man should have thought about that before he lost the family home."

"Not all of us were born with a silver spoon."

That grated on Colin because, even though his parents were successful, he never once took a handout. Getting through college on scholarships and loans, paying them off only three years after graduation. He'd worked his ass off to get where he was. Yes, he'd been willed some money, but that was only a few years ago. And he hadn't touched a penny. In fact, Colin never took anything from anyone, unlike the freeloader standing in front of him.

He set the girls down and waited until they chased each other into the house before speaking. "You already destroyed her once. What are you doing?"

"Trying to right my wrongs." He looked so self-righteous and smug, Colin almost punched him but he didn't want to make any more waves for Teagan.

Every move from here forward was with Teagan in mind.

"You trying to right things for you or for her?" Colin asked, and Frank shut the door on his face.

Teagan heard part of the conversation, and the knot in her gut told her she should probably put some hustle in her bustle to get downstairs before round two began.

With only a swipe of mascara and lip gloss—War of the Exes didn't allow for more—she rushed down the stairs. Taking a moment outside the kitchen entry, she checked herself in the mirror.

Lord, she looked frazzled. And breathless.

She closed her eyes, pictured a sandy beach with gentle waves rippling along the shoreline. When that didn't work, she told herself to breathe.

Breathe in. Breathe out. Breathe in.

She checked herself again. A bit tousled but she'd take it. Smoothing down her sundress—which she'd bought specifically for today—she gave a big, welcoming smile and entered the kitchen.

"I hope I didn't keep you wait—" She glanced around the kitchen for a tall, dark, and delicious man, only to find Frank with a big, braggart's smile in place.

"Not at all," Frank replied with a wink. "Just about to serve up some waffles. Your favorite. Why don't you take a seat at the bar and—"

She held up a silencing hand. "Where's Colin?"

"I don't keep tabs on your boyfriend." His voice had a distinct *neener-neener-neener* tone.

"Don't try me, Frank. Not today. And he's not my boy—" She stopped before even finishing that statement and reflected on the past month. Colin sure felt like her boyfriend.

Being with him was amazing. He was amazing. And the other night she should have shown him that.

"Girls, enjoy the waffles. Frank, put a shirt on. You are a guest here, no more, so before you speak or act, I want you to imagine Rose is here."

Frank paled. Teagan smiled, then walked to the door and opened it to find Colin still standing there, leaning against the porch railing, arms crossed, looking at her from behind his dark glasses.

Even after Frank's cold welcome, he'd waited for her.

Seizing her second chance, she walked right up to him, slid her arms around his neck, and gave him a kiss. A long, deep, lingering, this-is-a-proper-date kiss. He leaned into it and—*oh my*—talk about leaving her breathless.

"I missed you," she whispered against his lips.

"Good to hear."

"After that shitty welcome, I wouldn't have blamed you if you'd left."

"It was a damn fine welcome from the person who mattered." She kissed him again. "And I wouldn't have blamed you for taking your time. I know how much you like your waffles."

"I like you more." She didn't want to ruin the moment, but she had some apologizing to do. "About the other night, I should have let you walk me home and I should have told you what an amazing time I had."

"If I remember correctly, it was amazing times three." He palmed her butt. "And I should have trusted you enough to handle your business. I'm learning. How to trust that is. I just didn't know where I stood or if there was room for me."

"I was in the middle of an emotional storm and you stood exactly where I needed you, even making room for me under your umbrella."

"There's always room for you under my umbrella," he whispered. "Even when the storm seems too much, know I'll be right there, waiting."

Her heart sank, nervous about what his comment might mean. "Do you want to wait?"

He took her hands in his and kissed them. "No, but I imagine the other night was a lot. The whole situation must be overwhelming. I'd understand if you needed time to figure things out."

"We're parents, Colin. Both of our lives are overwhelming and crazy. If we wait for the perfect time, I think we'll be waiting another twenty years."

"Crazy, like you catching my kid sneaking out in the middle of the night?"

"Crazy, like maybe if she knew what you were dealing with, she might back off on the sneaking. And before you look at me like that, this is coming from someone who has yet to raise a teenager. But I'd like to point out that Harley and Maddison have a lot in common, and when I told her I needed her to step up, she did. *And* Maddison wasn't doing anything both of us haven't done."

Maddison had been so distraught by the end of their conversation, Teagan wondered if, maybe, her sneaking out had ended up being a good thing.

"Thank you for not telling her that last part," he said, brushing a hair off her temple and trailing his finger down her cheek to her lips.

"Thank you for showing up here today, after that disaster of a night."

"It could have been a disaster, but being part of an 'us' made it manageable." Nerves had her hands sweating. "Do you still want to be an 'us'?" An invitation he was well within his rights to retract. "I'd understand if you're having seconds thoughts."

"Bianchi, there was you, then us, then a night full of one hell of an us. The rest is kind of a blur. My only regret is that I didn't get to wake up with you in my arms and share waffles in bed."

"Speaking of waffles, how about we grab some on the way to our first appointment?"

"I can think of some better ways to spend time before our first appointment," he said. "But since both houses are full and my moves need more than a reclining seat, waffles will do just fine."

With Teagan gone and Frank taking the girls to the beach, Harley performed Zia Iris's sage cleanse to help with some of the tension in the house but felt about as useful as a junior lifeguard at the X Games.

No matter how complicated, her sister was handling things with her ex, while Harley was still dodging her own. Not that Bryan was an ex, at least not yet. It actually required someone to say the words before they were officially broken up.

She either needed to be bold enough to let him go or bold enough to keep him for herself. And she really wanted to keep him no matter how romantically inept she was. All her life, she'd run from commitment, heading toward a lonely future. Being raised by Peter Pan had created a self-fulfilling prophesy that always ended with Harley being alone.

She didn't have to be one of Dale's Lost Tomboys; she just

had to learn how to be an adult. Spring was coming to a close and she was still in Pacific Cove. Only this time it wasn't just a place to hide out; it had become so much more, and though she often felt like a fraud, there were days she almost forgot she was a poser playing a role in somebody else's life.

"Hold that pose," she said. "Make sure your hips are up high, bending at the waist."

When Harley had first come to Pacific Cove, she knew she needed to get a temporary job or go hungry, so she'd chosen something that made her happy. She loved the ocean, animals, and yoga.

Today's class involved all three. "Now pull back into Downward Dog," Harley instructed. "Remember to breathe, take in the smells of the ocean, the earth beneath us, and—poop," she said and everyone giggled.

Butt Head, a pygmy goat and the star of her yoga class, ran up Harley's back as if she was a bale of hay and dropped pellets. A measuring cup full. They rolled down her back and onto her mat.

Today Harley was teaching goat yoga at Nature's Namaste, a working farm that ran chicken and goat yoga classes in their hilltop pasture. Classes were taught overlooking downtown, with breathtaking views of the ocean. She was filling in for a friend and, even though she had Butt Head pellets in her hair, she felt at peace. Being around goats made her happy, made all the problems in her life seem resolvable.

"Inhale, not too deeply if Butt Head left some good luck pee on your mat or your person, and exhale, going back down into Cobra Position. Hold."

A phone pinged in the background. "Remember, phones on silent, please. This is a time to disconnect and become one with the earth."

A follow-up ping broke through the calm but she ignored it.

"Exhale and arch your back, feeling your muscles relax as you lean into the stretch. Really listen to what your body is telling you."

Ping.

Ping.

At the sound, Ramsey, who was a fainting goat, fell over, his legs in the air like roadkill.

"Before we invoke a mass fainting, please silence your phones."

"Um, Harley, I think that's you," one of her students said.

Harley was about to explain that she always turned her phone to silent, when she wisely chose to double-check. It was indeed her phone. She glanced at the screen. It was her phone and her man.

She froze at that crazy thought but as she listened to her body, her heart to be precise, it didn't seem so crazy after all.

"Let's inhale and go to our knees, then exhale and push back into Child's Pose."

Harley finished her class a little more quickly than normal, then let the students take selfies with Butt Head and his gang of goat yogis. She walked far enough away from the group for some privacy and read the texts. There were two.

> THINKING OF YOU.
> MISSING YOU.

She hadn't stopped thinking about him or missing him. But she didn't know what to do with that realization.

With Bryan, she'd learned that relationships required both give and take. But Harley had had her moment and lost it because she was too afraid to trust. She'd left him hanging. Which was worse than letting him go because "hanging" implied hope—an emotion Harley feared even more than trust.

Being vulnerable was hard. It opened one up to heartache. Ironic, since her heart was already aching.

"You're in the driver's seat—take the wheel," she said, exhaling. For once, instead of reacting out of fear, she found herself in a place of peace and acceptance. A soul-deep peace that came from acknowledging her feelings. She might not be right for Bryan, but he was right for her.

She had to accept her vulnerability and trust that he'd listen to her, *really* listen. Something few people in her life had taken the time to do. This was a moment for honesty.

THINKING OF YOU TOO.
MISSING YOU TOO.

Her heart thumped in her throat as she waited for his answer. She still wasn't sure what came next, but for once she wasn't looking for an exit so much as a solution.

Then the three dots disappeared, and her panic turned to appreciation. He'd promised her space and he was following through on that promise. She wasn't sure if space was what she needed anymore. She was certain that they both deserved to have an honest conversation.

She just didn't know how to do that without blowing things up.

Chapter 23

I want someone to look at me the same way I
look at chocolate-chocolate-chunk ice cream.

—Unknown

"It's a little more expensive than the others I showed you," Jack, the property owner, explained.

Distracted by the opportunity in front of her, Teagan had a hard time focusing on what he was saying. She did a slow three-sixty of the former pizzeria, and her heart pounded with excitement.

"But it has four ovens, gas stove tops, and a woodfire oven in the kitchen."

Teagan tilted her head back and admired the antique tin ceilings and redwood beams. "Is the roof original?"

"Almost a hundred years old," Jack said.

"It's beautiful."

"That's why I showed you this one. It checks nearly all the boxes on your list."

"Everything and more." The last time something had felt this right had been when she'd graduated from college and her nonna let her open a second location of the family bread shop in Seattle. A lot had happened since then, and she'd taken more than a few detours along the way—some unexpected, others forced, but all of them had brought her to this moment.

It was kismet. The way everything lined up. If you'd asked her a couple months ago if she'd make different life decisions she would have said, "Hell yes." But now, standing in what could become her dream, with her dream man, she decided she wouldn't do one single thing different.

She had her kids, her sister, now Colin, and she was standing in the space she'd always dreamed of. They'd have to repaint, build a wall separating the kitchen from the shop area, completely reconfigure the back counters and island, redesign the retail space into a traditional *forno*—Italian bread shop.

Nothing too elaborate, six to eight tabletops, an espresso machine, hand pressed like Nonna used. She'd spotted it while going through Nonna's things in Iris's apartment above the garage. An Italian-style menu of cheese platters, charcuterie boards, and warm olives, with the star being her Coppia Ferrarese—Nonna's famous sourdough recipe.

Of course, she'd have to purchase tables, chairs, display cases, proofing cabinets, and cooling racks. When she'd walked out her front door earlier, her plan had been to start small and grow slowly. But from the moment she walked into that shop, the bell jingling in greeting, she felt as if she were home.

It was the way the sun shone through the leaded glass windows, the look of the original hundred-year-old Dutch delft tile flooring. And this property was just a block from the original Bread N Butter shop.

"It's perfect." She looked at Colin. "What to do you think?"

"Perfection," he said but when she glanced over her shoulder, he was staring at her. A shy blush crept to her cheeks.

"I mean the shop," she clarified.

"I can see you standing in the kitchen making your bread." He leaned in to whisper, "In nothing but a daffodil thong and heels."

She gave his shoulder a playful shove, then focused on Jake. It was time to negotiate. She'd pulled up a list of tips to successfully negotiate a car sale. She wasn't buying a car, but the basic principles had to apply. Right?

1. DON'T FOCUS ON THE MONTHLY, FOCUS ON THE OVERALL PRICE.

"What is the bottom line?" she asked. "All in, what are we talking?"

"With the work it will take to get you to pass inspection and open, we're looking at . . ." Jack dropped a number, and she nearly choked because it was in direct violation of rule two:

2. KNOW YOUR BUDGET.

She knew her budget and that number wasn't anywhere close. Not if she wanted to get the equipment needed to run a bread shop.

"I'm not sure I can swing it, but, God, I want to." And maybe she still could. One of the most interesting pieces of advice Harley had read aloud to her last night over dinner was:

3. IF POSSIBLE, DRAW UP SEPARATE CONTRACTS FOR THE RENT AND THE OVERALL PRICE.

"I'd like to separate the renovation price from the overall number. I know a few contractors who might give me a more competitive quote," she said as if she had a contractor on speed dial. She did not.

Jack shook his head. "I don't trust other crews in my buildings. My son does all my work."

"Your son's prices have always seemed high," Colin pointed out, giving her a sly wink. She bit her lip and winked back—not so slyly because Jack chuckled.

"Like I told you," he said to Colin, "six people have already looked at it. I promised you I'd wait until she could see it."

"I've seen it," she said, taking control of the conversation. "I'm interested, but I can't commit at that price."

Jack rocked back on his heels, his expression one of pure contemplation. "Your grandma was a fierce businesswoman. I once saw her trying to barter a better price on fava beans at the market. I can see that you inherited some of her tenacity. If you want the place, I'll give you first dibs."

"First dibs?" she said, trying not to sound too eager. There were still negotiations to be made. "How long do I have to think about it?"

"It won't last the day."

Locations like this didn't come up for lease all that often in Pacific Cove. Most of the shops on Lighthouse Way had been family owned and run for generations, like Nonna's shop. She wanted to leave that kind of legacy for her girls.

Tucking them into bed last night, she couldn't help but picture them in her bakery, like she used to help Nonna Rose and Zia Iris. She wanted that for her girls. It was right here for the taking if she had the courage. She remembered the fourth tip.

4. KNOWLEDGE IS KEY.

She didn't know Jack all that well, but she did know he'd had three tenants in five years. And that represented a lot of lost revenue between tenants.

"You might have six other people interested, but how many of them are locals with ties to the community? I'm here for the long haul. So I'm willing to sign a longer lease if you're willing to lower the price."

Jack groaned but looked impressed. "Five-year lease and we can take another look at the price."

5. DON'T BE AFRAID TO NEGOTIATE.

"Three and your son matches my contractor's bid." Which depended on Colin helping her find a reasonable contractor. She might have grown up here, but she'd lived in Seattle since leaving for college.

"This is a prime location. A place like this will allow you to take on more corporate clients, grow faster," Jack said.

She thought back to Harley's advice to dream big, do something for herself. Her sister. Maybe this was her time to go for it. Which took her to that last tip:

6. THINK ABOUT FINANCING EARLY.

If she ran low on funds, she could always take out a small business loan. People did it all the time.

"I can make it work. I'll find a way. It really is everything I asked for. Where do I sign?"

"Can you give us a moment?" Colin touched her shoulder gently and pulled her into a corner so they could talk privately. "Aren't you rushing things a bit?"

"I don't want to lose this place. Why should I let something perfect slip by so that someone else can grab it?"

"It's twice your budget, and I promise you there will be other places."

"We saw other places, and I promise you none of them were as perfect as this."

"We saw two places. There are three more coming on the market in just a few weeks," Colin said and she started to wonder why he was throwing cold water on her excitement.

"I'm tired of waiting for all the good things in life. Possibilities, opportunities, happiness. I want this one. I can do this."

"Maybe you should start slow, like with a business plan, and then see if you can afford this right now."

"I realize I'm talking to Dr. Always Has a Plan Colin. I'd really rather be talking to my Boyfriend Colin."

"Boyfriend Colin likes that title, but let's put a pin in that and circle back later."

"I'm done with later, and if I start overthinking this place like you would, then I'll lose it."

She saw the look on his face, knew she'd hurt him. She touched his arm. "I didn't mean it like that."

"Then how did you mean it?"

"That maybe Harley isn't so crazy. Maybe acting without thinking, following where my heart leads me and counting on instinct and emotions isn't all wrong. I'm tired of watching the world pass me by. And following my heart can't be so bad. It led me back to you."

He looked at her for a long moment and said, "I get it."

"Yeah?" she whispered.

"Yeah."

She kissed him and went back to Jack. "I'll take it."

"I'm going to be honest," Jack said. "Your credit score is lacking." Great, Frank, the gift that keeps on giving. "I'd be more comfortable if you had a cosigner."

"Would you be willing to accept six months' rent up front?"

Colin whispered, "Where are you going to get that kind of money?"

"I can take an equity loan out on my house."

"I don't want you to risk your family's future. Plus, the rates will be outrageous."

Colin picked up the pen. "I'll be your cosigner."

She snatched the pen from his overly generous fingers before he could finish signing. "I can't ask you to do that."

"You didn't ask." He slowly slipped the pen out of her hand. "If you say you have this, then you have this. That's part of becoming an 'Us.' Trusting each other. I trust you, Bianchi."

Jack grinned. "If Colin vouches for you, I'm good."

Chapter 24

I hope you step on a Lego (nothing personal).

—Unknown

As Colin stood in the animal clinic's reception area, getting angrier and angrier by the second, he knew there weren't enough words in the dictionary to express how sorry he was.

Every good vet knew that clients took emotional cues from the practitioner to guide them through even the most devastating of situations, which was why Colin worked hard to keep his emotions in check. But this was no ordinary patient and no ordinary situation.

Oliver, a twelve-year-old boy with cerebral palsy, whose mobility and freedom lay in the paws of his service dog, had been delivered a devastating blow. A blow that could have been prevented had Colin been notified of the emergency sooner.

Harbor, a certified retrieval dog, acted as the boy's hands and means of independence. He wasn't just a four-legged companion; Harbor was the kid's best friend. But because of the clinic's new policy, an entire family was grieving. The dog had pushed Oliver out of the way of a car that ran a stop sign. Oliver made it out unscathed, but Harbor hadn't. He'd been hit, then brought into the clinic in critical condition.

As a service dog, Harbor qualified for a reduced rate on visits, but Ronnie, fucking Ronnie, had put a new protocol in place, giving priority to full-price patients. Colin was the only qualified vet on duty to perform the surgery but because he was performing a procedure for a full-price patient, a procedure any first-year intern could have handled, he hadn't had a clue as to what was happening at the front of the clinic. Sadly, Ronnie was too much of a tight-ass to notify the vet on call, so he'd turned the family away, rerouting them to an emergency animal hospital in Monterey.

The twenty-minute delay caused by an unnecessary drive cost Harbor his back leg, leaving him unable to perform his job. Once a service dog was unable to perform its duties, it loses its classification, and is often rehomed to a family looking for a well-trained pet. Oliver had been on the national service dog wait list for over three years before he received Harbor.

After consoling the understandably distraught family, Colin hunted down Ronnie. He went straight to Ronnie's office, which was more of a man cave than a workspace, with a virtual golf simulator and foosball table. Colin stormed in without knocking, not surprised to find Ronnie, dressed in tasseled loafers, white dress shirt, and loosened tie, with a golf club in hand.

Without looking up, Ronnie held a single finger in the air, signaling Colin to give him a moment of silence so he could tee off.

"What the actual fuck?" Colin asked, his voice calm, the kind of calm that would send a smart man running.

Ronnie wasn't only stupid; he was so arrogant he didn't bother to look up. He took the shot, watched the ball fly, even leaning to the right when it went off course.

"Is this about the dog?"

"Oh, it's about a lot of things." Unacceptable things that had Colin seeing red.

"What did you want me to do?" Ronnie walked behind his desk and sat down. "It was a four-thousand-dollar procedure, half of which we'd absorb. So I sent them to Southside Clinic. They're better set up for that kind of thing."

"I'm better equipped for 'that kind of thing,' since I've been his vet for six years."

Ronnie gave an unconcerned shrug. "You were in with another animal, so I made a judgment call."

"It was the wrong call. And your judgment led to an amputation. If I'd been notified the moment they came in, I could have saved his leg."

"How is this my fault? If she'd called ahead of time, I would have had Barb explain that we were booked solid."

"It was an emergency visit which should have had priority. And we're booked solid because you're too cheap to hire an additional veterinarian."

With only three full-time vets and a two part-time residents on the payroll, they had more clients than openings in the schedule. Clients who'd entrusted their pets to Pacific Cove Animal Clinic for more than thirty years. After the practice changed hands, Colin went from working a solid forty hours a week to nearly sixty, just so he could keep up with their regulars. That wasn't including the new clients brought in by all the ads Ronnie was placing.

He wanted a full roster of paying customers with an understaffed office. Colin was surprised a travesty of this magnitude hadn't happened sooner. That it'd happened on his watch made it all the more devastating.

"You could have brought in the on-call vet. That's what the term means."

"Time and a half, buddy. We might as well start paying clients for services rendered. Sorry about the dog, but what was I to do?"

"Have Barb call Thuy, who lives two blocks away. Jesus, man, Harbor was a service dog who, because of you, lost his back leg and won't be able to do his duty. You essentially robbed a disabled kid of his only means of independence. Do you have any idea how this is going to affect the hospital's standing in the community?"

For the first time Ronnie looked scared. "Shit, had I known this would hurt our reputation, I'd have called you in immediately."

"You know this will end up in the newspaper." Because Colin was going to call the editor and explain what a little weasel Ronnie was. "No matter how you spin it, this is a huge lawsuit in the offing. This hospital's reputation is dead. That family deserved so much better and oh, by the way, I quit." Because Colin deserved better as well.

Plan Get Your Mojo Back now entailed a complete life overhaul—personal and professional.

Friday night game night at the Bianchis' was a tradition going back as far as the seventies, when Rose and Iris would invite the other neighborhood military wives over for a game of high-stakes bunco. Each week, the ladies would bring a dish to share and each week a different player would provide a bottle of hootch. The women would gossip and laugh, forming a special bond that helped them through some of the toughest times.

In keeping with tradition, Harley had taken the initiative and planned this week's family game night. Teagan had been working hard all week and Harley wanted to surprise her with a no-stress, come as you are, fun and relaxing evening with the kids.

She and the girls made popcorn balls—a preapproved late-night snack—and homemade pizza on cauliflower crust. Frank made himself comfortable on the couch watching basketball.

By the time her sister walked through the front door, Harley had cleaned the house, bathed the girls, and—after a conversation about house safety rules—rehung the hammock. She was exhausted.

She'd never realized how much work went into being the mom of twins—cleaning, entertaining, disciplining, and getting dinner on the table, all at the same time. Then there were the special nights, like movie-a-thon or tonight, which Harley had assumed would be easy-peasy.

It made her respect her sister even more.

The front door opened and closed and moments later, Teagan walked into the kitchen.

Garbage Disposal, who'd been sound asleep in his doggie bed, sprang into action, his tail moving like the rear propeller on a helicopter as he catapulted himself straight at Teagan. Her sister prepared herself for impact.

Harley stuck a foot out, boxing him in.

"Down," Harley commanded. To her utter surprise, Garbage

Disposal dropped to all fours, then rolled over to expose his doggie bits, looking for a belly rub.

She gave him a few pats. "It's a work in progress," she said to her sister, who was looking around the kitchen.

"What is this?" Teagan asked.

"Finger food Friday," Frank said as if he'd been the mastermind.

Teagan looked at Harley. "You set this up?"

Harley felt emotion burn the back of her eyes. A month ago, Teagan would have assumed Frank was the responsible party, but she was looking at Harley as if she knew. Knew how hard Harley had worked to prove herself. For once, being the responsible party was a good thing.

"The girls helped."

"I'm . . . wow, I . . ." Teagan walked over and gave Harley a warm hug. "I'm so tired I was going to just order pizza. But you made pizza."

"With cauliflower crust."

Teagan smiled like a proud mama. "With cauliflower crust."

"A vegetable posing as junk food."

"Thank you."

Harley shook her head. "Thank *you*. For letting me stay, for being patient with me, and for being the kind of sister who forgives me when I screw up."

"Don't talk that way about my sister."

They both laughed, and when they sat down for dinner, Harley felt like she'd found home.

After dinner, they reconvened around the coffee table, sipping sparkling apple juice and playing their third round of Disney Princess Uno, which Lily was winning. Harley was ninety-nine percent sure that the girls were stacking the deck and playing the long con. Teagan didn't seem to care that her kids were adorable little cheats, so Harley suppressed her need to send the girls to cheater jail. A place Dale had sent her whenever she tried to pull one out of her sleeve—ironic since Dale himself was a notorious cheat. He'd once been banned from Gene Simmons's weekly poker game for counting cards.

Dale might be a flake, but he was a brilliant flake.

Since coming to Pacific Cove, Harley was realizing that her upbringing had left more scars than she'd like to acknowledge. Marks that were just starting to heal. She had issues about trust and love and all the things Harley was coming to understand being around her sister and nieces. Her new understanding made her want to reassess the possibility of life with Bryan. When he'd brought her to meet his family, the stark difference between their upbringings had been intimidating. Being around her nieces, watching unconditional love at its purest, spoke to a part of Harley that was desperate for a sense of permanence, and made her question what kind of mother she wanted to be.

Harley froze. Since when had she ever thought of her life in terms of motherhood? She'd made a decision years ago that there wasn't room in her life for marriage or the baby carriage. But watching her sister's courage as she'd morphed into Teagan 2.0 made Harley wonder if, maybe, she too could choose a new path.

"Uno!" Poppy said, even though she still had more cards than her little hands could hold.

"Uno means one," Harley explained. "You've got to be down to one card to call Uno."

"We are." She pointed to Lily, who had a single, solitary card—a miracle since she'd had to draw nine on the last round.

Harley looked at Frank, who said, "It's a game. It's about fun."

"It's about rules," Harley said.

Teagan bit back a smile and lifted a brow. "Freaky Friday much? When did you become me?"

"When your kids started swapping cards back and forth like a couple of casino con artists."

"We wons," Poppy proclaimed, and Lily held up her hands in a *voilà* gesture.

"It wasn't even Lily's turn." Harley looked at Frank. "This is your fault."

Chapter 25

You're my favorite place to go when my
mind searches for peace.

—Unknown

Teagan looked at Frank on the couch, a kid tucked under each arm as they watched *Frozen*. The precious picture almost made the headache of having him here worth it. Almost.

"Can I help with the dishes?" she asked Harley.

"Nope. I've got it. Why don't you go rest or drink a bottle of wine."

Teagan laughed. "The whole bottle?"

"Three weeks under the same roof as Frank and I want to strangle him. You spent a decade with that guy—you deserve the whole bottle," Harley said. "I'll even take the early shift and make the kids breakfast so you can sleep off the hangover."

"I might take you up on that," Teagan said when her phone rang. "It's Maddison."

"I didn't know the girl understood how to initiate a call."

"I didn't know if she'd ever talk to me again after I ratted her out for sneaking around with Truck Guy." She swiped to answer. "Hey, Maddison."

"My dad just got home, and he went straight to his office," she said. "I'm kind of freaking out."

Teagan could hear the panic and fear in Maddison's voice. Though the girl had a knack for the dramatic, this sounded different. "Maybe he just had some work to finish up."

"No, it's daddy-daughter dinner night. We always cook together but when I asked him what we were making, he said he needed a rain check. He never asks for a rain check. Like ever."

Teagan couldn't imagine Colin missing a dinner date with his daughter unless it was unavoidable. "Have you tried talking to him?"

There was a long pause. "I don't know what to say. Can you come over?"

Teagan was touched that Maddison had called her. After that disastrous night when Maddison had walked in on Teagan and Colin, she didn't know if the girl would ever talk to her again. And that was before Teagan stopped Maddison from going out with Truck Guy.

She turned to Harley. "Could you watch the girls?"

"Done."

"Why don't you come over and hang with the girls," Teagan said to Maddison. "They're just watching a movie." She was suddenly worried about Colin. He hadn't returned any of her earlier texts either. "You know what, bring your pajamas and just plan on staying the night."

Teagan kissed each of her girls good night.

"Where are you going?" Frank asked just as Maddison walked in the front door.

"I wasn't sure if I should knock." Maddison's eyes were red-rimmed and puffy.

"It's okay," Teagan said, and the teen walked right into her arms for a hug. "You're okay."

Maddison sniffled and, while still holding on to Teagan as if she was her lifeline, said, "Promise you won't leave him alone."

Teagan pulled back and took her by the shoulders. "Don't worry, I've got your dad."

Maddison wiped her nose on the back of her hand. "I was wrong before. When I said he doesn't have room for anyone else. I'm glad he has you."

"He's lucky he has a daughter like you."

Over the teen's head, Teagan met Harley's questioning gaze. Teagan shrugged her shoulders and Harley waved her off. "Go, I've got this."

Ignoring Frank's thousand-and-one questions, Teagan grabbed her cell and headed next door. She didn't bother to knock, but let herself in.

The minute she stepped inside, she knew something was wrong. Colin's coat was on the entry table, his shoes kicked haphazardly by the door. The cats eyeballed her as if they had been denied their dinner.

"Colin," she called out. "It's me."

When he didn't answer, she followed the light, which led her to his office. And Colin. Hunched over his deck, frantically working at his computer. He was still in his scrubs, and his hair was a little crazy, as if he'd run his fingers through it over and over again. *He* looked a bit crazed. And a whole lot sad.

There was such intensity to his posture, as if he was about to break under the weight of the world. He was so engrossed in what he was doing, he didn't even notice her at the door.

She gave a light tap with her knuckle. "Colin?"

Eyes locked on the screen, he held up a finger. "I need a minute."

She got the distinct impression that he needed all the minutes, months and months of minutes, and things still wouldn't be right. Putting her worry on the back burner, she clung to patience as best she could. One minute bled into another, until five minutes had passed, and he still hadn't looked up. His fingers only moved slightly, as if his mode were set to deep thought rather than actual work.

Starting to freak out a little and wondering if maybe Maddison hadn't been overly dramatic earlier, she became more and more concerned with each passing moment. Unable to wait any longer, she walked over and put a hand on his shoulder. "Colin?"

"Almost there," he said absently.

"How can I help?"

He shut his laptop and pushed his chair back, then swiveled to face her. He didn't look like his usual calm and confident self, and her heart rolled over. He was closed off, distant. Devastation and self-torment rolled off him in waves.

He opened his mouth a couple of times before he actually formed words. "I don't have a plan to make any of this better."

Standing in front of him, she took both of his hands. "What happened?"

"Ronnie's business model is to make money—I knew this. I knew it when he took over and knew it when he cut our free clinic hours. I knew he was a greedy fucker, but I never thought he'd do this much damage." He finally met her gaze, and what she saw there shook her. The soul-deep exhaustion of someone who'd been set adrift. "A dog lost his leg today for no reason other than money."

She brought his hands to her lips. "That's awful."

"He was a service dog to a twelve-year-old." He quietly told her the story, and the more he spoke, the rougher his voice became until he was at a near whisper. "I quit."

"Good for you," she whispered, and he looked surprised.

"I didn't fight hard enough."

Her heart ached for the man who had lost the two so many people he loved. "People can't always stay, Colin. Losing people and letting go are parts of life, awful and painful but still parts."

"Maybe, but some of the time they choose to go, even knowing how hard it is on those left behind."

Colin had a huge heart and he'd been dealt a lot of blows over the years by the women in his life. Once upon a time, she'd been one of those women. Quickly followed by Amber, and now Maddison had one foot out the door—a realization that must be terrifying for him.

A big part of his identity was wrapped up in being a dad and a veterinarian. Which explained the lost look in his gaze.

"None of this is your fault," she said. "No matter how hard you wish you'd challenged Ronnie's changes."

"Maybe, but it doesn't change the outcome."

She cupped his face with both hands. "You are changing future outcomes. Tonight, you quit. You said, this is not the life I want." She ran a hand through his hair. She loved his hair. Thick and soft and a little too long to be considered stylish. "If there's one thing I learned from my divorce, it's that you need to choose your own direction in life and not let anyone derail you. Okay, I didn't learn that from my divorce. Nonna Rose told me that. It just took a decade for her wisdom to sink in."

"After the last few months, I'm so turned around I don't have a clue as to which direction is mine."

"Then let me remind you," she said, repeating his promise to her. "You have been dreaming about your own practice since I met you. A scrawny fifteen-year-old who already knew what he wanted in life and how he was going to get it."

"I wanted you and I lost you."

Guilt smacked her between the ribs, making a crack in those walls she'd so carefully built and hidden behind. If she wasn't careful, he'd slide right past them and into her heart.

"I'm here now."

As if realizing this for the first time, he slipped his arms around her waist and tugged her closer. And since she was standing, he rested his forehead against her stomach and hugged her to him.

She ran her hands through his hair, showing that she had him. That no matter how bad things were, she'd always have him.

He needed a lifeboat right now and she was going to pull him aboard. Remind him of that long-ago dream he'd back-burnered because of his family, his clients, even his own fears.

"What do you want now? You have the time and opportunity to make FurGet Me Not a full-time thing."

"It's not the right time. With Maddison switching to NYU, tripling tuitions costs, and a gap in animal care for the people who can't afford it. Jesus, it's all spiraling down and I don't have a plan to fix it."

She tilted his head up. "Yes, you do. You told me about it the summer before senior year. College, vet school, five years under your mentor, then open your own practice. Maybe this is the universe's way of saying it's your time."

"My life is a little different from yours. Maddison's bags are practically packed to move on to the next stage of her life. I don't have the luxury of time, which means things that don't matter will have to wait."

She started to step back at his comment and the tone in which he'd made it, but stopped. Though his comment stung, she knew he'd made it out of frustration. His plans were his coping mechanism. So while her pride might have taken a small hit, he needed her right now, not her hurt feelings.

Colin was a man who loved deeply and was fiercely protective of those around him. He had so much responsibility, terrifying responsibility, on his shoulders. She wanted to take some of the weight for him.

She leaned down and held him tightly. She didn't know how long they stood there, but she allowed him the time he needed to process everything. Then she felt a shift. The warm energy around them crackled, and his hand hold was no longer about comfort.

"Shouldn't you be next door enjoying movie night?" he asked even as he slowly kissed her stomach.

"Harley's babysitting and it's *Frozen*," she said. "Spoiler, it ends in a snowy musical number."

He kissed her neck, lifting her shirt as his lips moved over her bare skin. "Where's Maddison?"

"Babysitting Harley."

"I figured out how you can help," he said.

"Yeah?"

"Oh yeah." He tugged her into his lap. He kissed her cheek, her chin, working down to the curve of her neck—a gentle brush of the lips that had butterflies taking flight in her belly.

"Far be it from me to decide what kind of help you need."

He looked up, his hooded gaze heated with desire. "I need you, Bianchi. I just need you."

Just as she wasn't great at reaching out for help, he was an island. But he was letting her ashore.

"Then I'm yours."

He didn't speak and neither did she, letting him set the pace. Reaching out, he stroked her hair behind her ears, then slowly trailed his finger down her jaw to her lips. Lowering his head, he replaced his finger with his mouth, nibbling her lower lips between his. He kissed her gently, then not so gently. His moan reverberated deep inside her chest, making her panties go damp.

His hand slid down her thigh and back up, under the hem of her dress. Higher and higher until he hit pay dirt and smiled. "Thong. Daffodil yellow?"

"Red and white striped."

"Like a lifeguard?" The fingers that had been tracing the lace edge of her panties stilled. "Are you here to save me, Bianchi?"

"Do you need to be saved?"

"By you, always." His hand was on the move again, gliding down the lace edging to her core, dipping his finger under. She let him drive her a little crazy.

"I thought I got to take care of you."

He didn't comment, rubbing up and down, his mouth on her neck. He pushed a little harder, just enough to have her quivering. Someone moaned. That someone being her of course.

"You are," he said. "But I have one request."

"I think we can do better than one, Dr. West."

"Then how about the first request." He reached into his pocket and pulled out a thong—a daffodil-yellow thong.

"Where did you get that?"

"Someone left it in my laundry room. Sexiest damn calling card I've ever seen."

"I've been looking for that."

"Then I guess I'm in possession of stolen property." He kissed her bare shoulder. "And there won't be any rushing tonight. Tonight's going to be slow and tender."

"I like slow and tender," she breathed.

"I know you do," he said.

She snatched back the thong, but he held tight. "Did you go on a panty hunt?" she asked.

"I did. Then I found this and kept it in my pocket for the past week, picturing you in nothing but this and that sweatshirt you stole."

"You gave it to me," she said primly.

"Only because I could see right through your shirt." She

wondered if his X-ray vision was kind of like his body heat, which she could feel going right through her dress.

"You were looking?"

He popped the first button on her sundress. "I couldn't not. Then I dreamed about you in nothing but my clothes and these."

He dangled the thong from his finger. "Only problem is, it doesn't smell like you anymore."

"I think we can rectify that." She stood and hiked her dress up, just enough to bare her thighs. Gaze locked on his, she did a little shimmy and slid the red and white stripes down her legs. When she came up, her thong was dangling from her fingers. "Is this better?"

He released a groan that was a thousand percent unadulterated, male appreciation. "You make everything better. Come here." He held the panties out for her.

She put one foot in, then the other, watching him as he slid the yellow lace up her legs and around her hips.

"You're usually taking those off."

"I want to see this on you first—then we'll decide if it comes off."

Sometime later, Teagan came awake. It was well past midnight, and the house was quiet. Except for Colin's steady, rhythmic breathing. They were on his office couch, no blankets, with only each other's body heat for warmth.

Not that there was a heat problem. She was wrapped in a big, hot, Colin burrito, locked in a game of big spoon, little spoon, where her bum was pressed against his erection, and his hand was cupping her breast like he owned it.

Oh, and they were naked. Well, he was naked; she still had on the thong, which he said he wanted back in the morning. She was interested to know how he planned on taking it off.

His phone buzzed again so she tried to quietly slip out of his vise-like hold. But his arm tightened, locking her tightly against him.

"Ignore it," he said, his voice sleep-roughened.

"It might be Maddison or one of the girls."

"Who are all next door with your sister." He nuzzled her hair, placing open-mouthed kisses down the back of her neck. While his lips caused her eyes to slide shut, his thumb traced the sliver of skin under her breast, teasing her wide awake. She arched into him, which caused her backside to press firmly against his front side.

"Teagan," he groaned. "Much more of that and this will be a one-sided game of naked Tetris."

Teagan froze as Maddison's statement crashed around in her head. *"He doesn't do long-term."*

His hands came to a stop. "You disappeared on me."

She looked over her shoulder at him through her lashes. "Is that what this is?" she asked quietly. "A game?"

He studied her for a long moment, then kissed the tip of her nose. "Nothing about this is a game. Not to me."

His expression softened, showing her just how seriously he was taking their interaction. Just as it was clear that deep down, beneath the confidence and swagger, was the shadow of a man who'd been on the losing end of life in the past.

"It's not for me either," she assured him.

"This can be whatever we want it to be," he said quietly, his gaze quickly flickering away. "What do you want?"

He was asking a person who still had no idea who she was or what she wanted. On the outside it was easy: raise her kids, grow her business. Both very tangible and actionable goals. But when it came to her emotions, her identity, she felt about as lost as Colin.

What did she want? Who was she outside of being a mom, a daughter, a baker, and someone's ex-wife? She didn't have the answer, but she imagined it would feel a lot like this. "Tonight, I want to stay here as long as we can."

"Done." He leaned down to kiss her, long and drugging, but with a tender reverence. "And tomorrow?"

Before she answered, the phone buzzed with an incoming text. This time it was Teagan's cell. Colin reached up, grabbed it from the end table, and handed it to her. "It's Harley, telling us not to worry. Poppy got hold of my phone and was learning how to butt-dial. Frank had her butt-dial me, then you. Harley took his phone away, too, and locked it in the toy-timeout box."

"Who do you think is babysitting who?" she asked, and felt him smile against her ear, which he was currently teasing with his teeth.

"Lily."

A few moments passed, without either phone activating, and she felt herself relax.

"See." His fingers skated down her arm and back up, leaving goose bumps in their wake. "If it's important, Harley will call us."

"We're only right next door," she agreed. His touch gave her a full-bodied shiver, which had nothing to do with the lack of clothes and everything to do with him. "They'd send someone if it was an emergency."

"I think *we* have an emergency." He pressed up against her from behind and she had to agree, they had an emergency of the best kind.

"How can I be of assistance, Dr. West?" This time his fingers danced down her knee, lifting it so he could slide his thigh between her legs.

"Just like that."

His hands started their descent again, tracing the hollow of her neck, her collarbone, her breasts—he spent a lot of time there. He had her body writhing by the time he reached her belly button.

"Now, stay still." His hand slid between her legs, his palm pressed firmly against her pleasure button, his fingers working on stirring her up.

Teagan rubbed back and forth against the knee between her thighs, pressing harder so his fingers went deeper. "What happened to staying still?"

"Based on last time, moving works out more to my benefit."

"I'd have to agree."

Little dots appeared and her vision went blurry as she entered the shaken phase of his delicious cocktail. She was quickly learning that, with him, no cocktail was the same. Each one was an erotic creation invented to drive her out of her mind.

Which he was doing for a third time. "Colin, I'm almost . . ."

"Teagan, turn over," he whispered.

"I can't move." Although she was moving just fine. Back and forth, creating a magical friction that made her believe in fairies and unicorns and, maybe even, ever-afters.

"Look at me," he said, but didn't stop his torture, teasing her halfway to an orgasm. "This time I want to watch."

Before she knew what was happening, she was under him while he rolled on top of her. With a heated, hooded gaze locked on hers, he leaned down and gave her a searing kiss, which had her rubbing against him. Her nipples brushed against his chest, her good parts against his good parts.

And if she thought he was going for a double the pleasure, she was wrong. Colin made this moment about her. In his dark office, only lit by the soft glow of the moonlight streaming in, he looked like a Greek god, leaning over her, driving her right up to the edge and over. Her entire body tensed like a tightly wound spring ready to snap when her orgasm hit and hit hard. She rode out one aftershock followed by another, with Colin gently guiding her back.

When she finally caught her breath, she lifted her lashes and found him looking down on her.

"You're the most beautiful thing I've ever seen," he said.

"You make me feel beautiful." She kissed his jaw. "And sexy." His cheek. "You, Colin West"—she kissed him square on the mouth—"make me feel seen." She studied every emotion that flashed through his eyes: surprise, nervous excitement, and a little flicker of fear. She held his jaw. "You're not responsible for me and you're not responsible to me. To me, you are special," she said. "Happy, heartbroken, weathering one of life's storms, you are my favorite place to go."

He swallowed hard, as if unsure what to do with her honest assessment of his invaluable worth. She wondered when was the last time someone had reminded him of just how special he was.

"About tonight—"

"If you're going to apologize, I don't want to hear it."

He delivered a searing kiss that had her toes curling and her heart melting. "I was going to thank you. I needed an umbrella. I needed you."

"You have me," she returned, slipping her ankles around him. Gently crossing them right under his butt.

"I think I need to have you again." His arms went under her and he stood, taking her with him. She squeaked and held on for dear life. Not that it was a hardship. Being wrapped around Colin, with his *I tackle riptide daily* biceps, and *I also windsurf* abs, while he walked unabashedly naked through his house was a turn-on.

"Where are we going?"

"Someone once told me that washing machines, when properly loaded, can make some nice vibrations." He entered the laundry room and gave her a playful smack on the ass before plopping her on top of the washer. "All that's left to decide, Bianchi, is regular or extra-large."

"I think you've already answered that question. There's nothing regular about you."

Chapter 26

Silly me. Expecting too much from people again.

—Unknown

Colin stood in the kitchen helping prepare dinner and she couldn't help but smile.

The last two weeks had been amazing. In one house or the other, they'd been together every day. Even successfully dodging Maddison, two toddlers, and a mooching douchebag of an ex. It forced them to be creative. And he loved it when Teagan got creative. His hot tub, her patio, the beach, the bathroom at the Lover's Point, her car, his car, and even Ethan's truck when he realized his car was too small to really bring it home.

Tonight was special. Maddison and Harley had organized a barbecue as a way to bring both families together. He wasn't thrilled about sharing the night with Frank, but even they'd made strides. They'd downgraded from the OK Corral to the occasional pissing contest. Not that Frank wasn't still inserting himself in their relationship at every turn. The coward even used his kids when necessary.

Colin wasn't thrilled about Frank setting up house at Teagan's, since the guy was clearly still in love with her and trying to work his way back into her life. He knew how stressed she was about keeping the birthday promise to the girls. Colin had asked her again if she needed space to figure things out, even offered to take a step back. All while assuring her that, no matter her answer, he was just a driveway away and not going anywhere.

The end of any relationship was messy.

Every day, in one way or another, his divorce from Amanda still affected his family. Maddie's heartbreaking need to be validated, Colin's instinct to guard himself from potential pain, even the way he'd handled his time at the clinic—staying far too long in hopes of salvaging the situation. But he'd suppressed all doubt, instead trusting Teagan that, in spite of all the crazy, there was room for him in her life.

Grabbing two beers from the fridge, he cracked them open and walked up behind her. Setting the bottles on the counter, he placed his palms flat, moving forward until he boxed her in with his body. She didn't seem to mind because she pushed back up against him, her backside in an advantageous position.

She'd been a knockout in high school. Now, she had this sexy sophistication, which only came with age—and *Lord Almighty,* she'd aged well. She smelled like a snickerdoodle that had collided with a lingerie shop. And she looked like sex. A no-holds-barred, from-morning-to-night and straight-through-the-weekend sexcapade that had his body giving her a hometown parade and good old-fashioned flag raising.

"I don't know if I can wait till midnight," he admitted roughly.

Another thing he didn't know? Why he thought he could stand here with her in that sundress and not undress her. He was doing a pretty good job, just with his eyes, but his hands called a false start penalty since they were sidelined until later tonight.

"What do you have planned?" she asked, her voice hushed.

He leaned in to whisper in her ear. "No can do, Bianchi. The first rule about secret sex-dezvous is that you don't talk about secret sex-dezvous."

She glanced over her shoulder, her eyes twinkling with humor. "Not even if you are a member of said sex-dezvous?"

"Especially then." Over the past few weeks they'd taken turns planning their late-night activities, and tonight was Colin's turn. He already had a bag packed: wine, two glasses, two towels, and a plan to revisit their first kiss. "All you need to know is that at midnight sharp, I'll be waiting below your bedroom window."

"Maybe you should meet me on the porch, because unlike last night, I'll be using the back door."

"But I loved watching you shimmy down the trellis in those silky pajama bottoms," he whispered, his lips grazing the rim of her ear and making her shiver.

"Is that why you almost let me fall?"

"I'd never let you fall."

"Too late, I'm already falling." This time when she looked over her shoulder, her eyes were warm and full of something a hell of a lot like love. If not, then it was damn near close. They hadn't said those words, but he was pretty sure he was half in love with her.

Hell, he'd fallen hard and fast. He couldn't wait to be with her, and when he wasn't with her, he was thinking about being with her. So there was something in *his* chest that felt a lot like love too.

"I know the feeling."

She turned in his arms and looped her fingers in the belt loops of his jeans. "That makes me remarkably happy."

"Remarkable, huh?"

"Which is why I'll let you live even though you won't give me a hint," she said. "But I'm still using the door. Last night, I woke Poppy when I snuck out my window. My body doesn't recover from that kind of jump like it used to."

"It reminded me of the first time you snuck out your window."

It had been a long time since that night, but he still remembered the barely there white bikini, the way the summer air smelled on her skin, and how she'd felt in his arms. It would take another two summers before they took the final step, but that kiss was enough to carry him through the school year until he was able to see her again.

Even now, it was one of his favorite memories. Hair slicked back with water, her smile full of life, her sea-wet lips on his.

"I had to help you back inside, remember? You almost woke Rose up with your giggling." He took the knife from her hands and diced the remaining tomatoes.

"It was also the first time I'd had alcohol."

He handed her a beer and she laughed. "You hoping for a reenactment?"

"Hell, yes," he whispered. "Only this time I don't have to worry about Rose. Man, when she chased me across the lawn, I thought I was done for."

"You had a foot and fifty pounds on her. I think you could have taken her." He thought back to how protective Rose had been and grinned. "Or at least outrun her."

"Trust me, I ran for my life but still came within an inch of being skinned alive."

Teagan's face softened with nostalgia. "She loved you, you know."

He did. Rose was the kind of person whose heart was so big, she had enough love for everyone in her life. She took pride in the way she cared for her family and friends and showed that love through food. Kind of like her granddaughter.

A gagging sound came from behind. Fucking Frank. They looked around, and he was playing innocent, sitting at the kitchen table with the girls on his lap, helping them fold the dinner napkins.

"Colin?" Harley called out, then walked in holding his cell, her hands over the mouthpiece and talking in a hushed voice. "I didn't mean to answer it, but your phone kept ringing and ringing and I wasn't sure if it was an emergency."

He didn't know if anything could be more dire than the last few weeks. He'd quit the practice he'd spent the past decade building up, argued with his ex about coming through on her promise to their daughter. Then, because he wasn't one to dole out advice and not take it, he heard Amanda out about the pros of Maddie going to NYU. Even mailed in the forms for a student loan, if Maddie decided it was still her college of choice.

Yet things with Teagan were damn near perfect.

"It's someone named Jack," Harley explained, handing Colin the phone. "He said he needs to talk to you. It's urgent."

Jack rarely used Colin's cell number unless it was an emergency. Colin took the phone. "Hey, is everything okay? How is Sugar?"

"Oh, she's fine. Nothing like that. I just heard back from Teagan's lender and, well . . ." Jack sounded genuinely regretful. "Her loan didn't go through. She was denied."

"I thought it was a done deal." He'd cosigned so it would be a done deal. He'd felt a strange prickle in his gut when they'd dropped off the loan papers. Something hadn't felt right then, and it sure as hell didn't feel right now.

"I thought so too, which is why I started the renovations. You and I have known each other for years now." He could almost hear Jack nervously scratching his bald head. "I went forward with the construction to meet the move-in date Teagan wanted."

"You didn't have to do that," Colin said, his gaze meeting Teagan's anxious one.

"I did it based on our long-standing relationship."

"I appreciate that. What happened?"

Teagan placed a supportive hand on his arm and whispered, "Is everything okay?"

He held up a finger because he had a feeling everything was so far from okay that she was about get her heart broken.

"Seems your lady friend's debt-to-income ratio is way off. At least that's how the bank explained it," Jack said. "She said she was going to call the bank and straighten things out but it sounds like things couldn't be straightened out. Her score is so low, I don't even think she would have qualified for one of my smaller rentals."

Colin ran a hand down his face. "I'm really sorry if I put you in a bad situation, and I understand you have to do what you have to do."

"I need you to understand this isn't personal, it's business," he said. "I'm just not a big company. Hell, I only bought that strip in downtown because my retirement guy told me to diversify. As much as I'd like to, I just can't absorb the renovation cost and the possibility of lost rent."

"And you shouldn't have to." Colin looked up and noticed Frank was nowhere to be seen. "How much are you in for?"

Jack told him a number that had Colin's head pounding. The man must be damn near done with all the renovations. "And this is where it gets a little uncomfortable. As her cosigner, you and I still have an agreement and I'm going to need to hold you to it." Jack sighed. "At least until I can find someone who's looking for a commercial kitchen to take the place off your hands. And you have my word, I'll start looking tomorrow."

That painful thump worked itself behind his eyes and down to his chest. "I gave you my word. I won't leave you high and dry."

Which meant Colin would be left high and dry. And the only way to make things right was to use the money his parents had left him. Which meant he was not going to be able to open his practice anytime soon. Cross FurGet Me Not off his plan. Hell, his whole plan needed to be scrapped.

He should have seen the writing on the wall the first time he caught Maddison sneaking out. Everyone in his life was so busy sneaking around, it was near impossible to lock down a plan.

He disconnected the call and looked at Teagan, who was looking nervously back.

"Is Jack reneging?" she asked. "Because I'll never find a place that perfect again."

"Actually, the problem is on your side. Seems your debt-to-income ratio is higher than expected."

"He needs to call the bank again," Teagan said. "After he called me, I reached out to Frank's finance guy, and he assured me it would be handled."

Frank's finance guy. "Do you think that when you learned there was a problem, you should have come to me, your cosigner?"

"You don't know our financial history, and I didn't want to worry you."

Frank? Our? What the hell was happening?

"The fact that you didn't come to me is what worries me. I hoped you would know that no matter what goes wrong, I'm your go-to."

"I do know. And you are."

"I don't know if I can say the same."

"It's not like that. When Bread N Butter went under, I paid off the debt so my mom wouldn't have to, and no one had to file bankruptcy. I may not be cash heavy, but I own my car and this beach house outright. Besides a few low-limit credit cards, I have no debt. So when Jack said there was a snafu with the credit check, I called Frank's guy."

Frank groaned and everyone turned his way. "I've been meaning to tell you about that. I kind of relapsed a few months back."

Teagan froze. "How? You were in rehab. How do you relapse in rehab?"

"It was a voluntary rehab and I kind of snuck out."

"How do you *kind of* sneak out?" Colin turned the full force of his anger toward Frank, who was drinking one of Colin's beers. "You either did and screwed Teagan over or you didn't, which would mean that call from Jack was a screw-up." Colin stalked toward him, and the coward actually brought his knees together, using his kids as a damn shield. "Which was it, Frank? Did the bank screw up or did you?"

"I wouldn't go as far as to say I 'screwed up' but there is a good learning lesson to the story here," he said as if the situation were an afterschool special and he was delivering the takeaway.

"What would you say? I really need you to clarify things right now," Teagan put in, and Colin could hear the quiver in her voice.

"Loans or liens can really be confusing," Frank chuckled.

Every adult in the room groaned, except Frank. He sat, with his daughters on his lap, looking for all the world like the victim. And those kids—damn, those kids—they were staring up at Colin as if he'd morphed into a big, scary monster.

"Poppy." He got down on a knee. "Why don't you take Lily to my office. I've got a tablet on my desk with that princess game you like on it."

Poppy leaned back into her dad's chest, arms crossed, shaking a big N.O. Lily followed suit. Teagan was busy staring at her ex, mouth gaping open, her eyes heartbreakingly glistening.

"Why did you leave rehab?" she asked. "We had a deal. I'd clean up the mess; you'd work on recovery."

"That's just it. I didn't want you to have to do it alone. I wanted to help. Which is why I went back to rehab, to work on myself," Frank said.

"Wait, how does your gambling still affect my sister's credit?" Harley looked at her sister. "I thought the divorce would sever your finances."

"It should have," Teagan said, her hands shaking. "So explain how this happened. And don't give me some line about The Man."

"It may have happened during that time between you signing the papers and me signing the papers."

Teagan sat as if her legs were about to buckle. "You promised. Never to bring me into your troubles again. Those were your exact words."

"That's why I kept going and went big, so that I'd come out even and wouldn't have to get you involved."

"I am involved!" And this time a single tear popped out.

"You son of a bitch, get out," Colin yelled.

Poppy started wailing. Lily hopped down and said, "Don't yell at my daddy."

The whole room went silent. Lily had placed herself between the two men in her life, her lips quivering. Making Colin feel like a class-A jerk. Her first words were to tell Colin to back away from the man she loved most.

Her father.

"Hey, why don't you come with Auntie Harley," Harley said, picking up Lily and taking Poppy's little hand. "I've got a box of Otter Pops behind the frozen broccoli that we can eat on the beach."

Even the promise of contraband frozen sugar and food coloring didn't keep Lily from staring back at Colin as she disappeared from the kitchen. When they were out of range, he stepped up to Frank, who had wisely stood.

"You need to get out and go," Colin said. "And not just from this house. You need to get your shit and get out of town."

"Sorry, bud. That's not your call."

They both look at Teagan, who hesitated. All Colin had left was this one last plan. His plan with Teagan. And she hesitated, leaving him plan negative. It was like taking a wrecking ball to the chest.

"I'm sorry," she began. "I promised Lily and Poppy he could stay until their birthday."

"That doesn't mean he has to stay with you. He can drive back from his hole for the party."

"I can't. I promised them their daddy could visit until their birthday," she repeated.

He stepped close and quietly said to the woman who had told him she'd be his safe harbor, "What about your promise to me?"

She took his hand and guided him to the seat beside her. "This has nothing do with us."

"But it does." He covered her hand with his. "You're defending him to me, after he made a massive mess that I'm going to have to clean up. This threatens everything I've already committed to."

"I'll fix it," she said.

"How? You have an extra thirty grand lying around to reimburse Jack for the renovations?"

"No, but . . ." Again, she hesitated.

"You said you had it. I trusted that you had it, and now I'm stuck holding the bag. How are you going to cover the four grand in rent every month? Rent that would have been double except Jack gave you a deal. Gave us a deal."

"I know that," she said quietly—wistfully. "I know what you put on the line for me, Colin. I know."

"Do you?" Because it was more than his signature on that lease. He didn't care about the signature; he cared about the fact that his chest felt as if it was crushing his heart. "I'm wondering how we went from 'us' to you totally failing to tell me what was going on." It was as if he was eighteen again, wondering what he'd done wrong as she left him in her rearview with a heartful of questions. "I have to reevaluate everything, move things around, important things. Not because of something I did or something I wanted, but because you didn't trust me."

"That's not it at all. I trust you."

"Then why did I have to find out from Jack and not you? Why did your ex and his 'finance guy' know before me?" He swallowed hard, a painful knot lodged in his throat. "When I needed an umbrella, you hesitated."

"I'm in an incredibly difficult situation. And I didn't tell you because it didn't seem like a big deal at the time." Her eyes filled with tears, and he wanted to promise her that everything would be okay, but he wasn't sure it would. "Plus, I didn't want to disappoint you. I was certain I could figure it out. I know I put you in a horrible situation."

"No, you don't know. This affects more than me and my plan. It reshapes the next few years. Unless Fucking Frank has an extra thirty grand in his pockets, that money will come out of my inheritance. Stop me from opening my own practice." He had to look away. She was crying. He knew the situation was painful, and what he was saying hurt her. But he was hurting too. In those three seconds when she froze, she'd broken his trust. His plan. His heart. "You know how much that meant to me."

She'd assured him that their relationship was a top priority, and he'd put his trust in her. Now he was left to question his current status in her life. Putting her kids first? He wouldn't expect any less. Making time for her sister? Family always came first. Allowing Frank to manipulate his way between her and Colin? Unacceptable.

It was like a spear straight through his chest, burning a hole through everything he'd been banking on. The future they'd talked about.

"Colin, look at me." Unlike her, he didn't hesitate. For her, he'd never been able to hesitate, which was part of the problem. "I don't know how, but I will come up with the money, even if I have to leverage my house."

"Why should you have do that?" He looked at Frank. "Why should she? This is your mess and, unlike you, I would never ask her to do something that would put the girls or their future at risk." He turned to Teagan. "And I'd never do anything to hurt you."

"I know, and that's why I'll come up with a plan to fix this myself."

"Funny, I thought we were becoming an 'us.'" He stood and rubbed his hand over his chest, trying to ease the raw ache that had started gnawing at him. It didn't help. He was starting to fear nothing would. "Jesus, I never wanted to feel this way again."

"What kind of asshole asks a woman to put her relationship ahead of her family?" said Frank.

Colin turned on him, going chest to chest. "You're not her family. That's what it meant when you signed those divorce papers. When are you going to get it in your fucking head?"

"We still share Poppy and Lily, which makes me more family than you. So maybe you should leave."

"You're staying in my house, Frank," she said, and a surge of hope filled him. He'd given her the space she needed to work out her relationship with Frank, but now he needed her to acknowledge that their relationship was important to her.

He wasn't being possessive or getting into a pissing contest with Frank. He was simply asking if he mattered. He needed to know that they were in this together—no matter who or what challenge they confronted.

"Are you asking me to leave?" Frank asked.

She paused and in the silence, Colin could hear his heart pounding in his ears.

"This shouldn't be a hard decision," Colin said quietly, holding his breath. "He's toxic. He leaves a wake of trouble in his path. For you, the girls, Harley, me, and now our relationship."

"It's more complicated than that," she said quietly. "I don't want my girls to go through what I went through after my parents divorced."

With a finger under her chin, Colin tilted her head up. "You aren't your parents. You are a strong, patient, and loving mother whose heart is so big, sometimes it gets in the way of your own happiness."

The first tear spilled over her lashes, and he caught it with his thumb. She was scared—he knew that—so he wanted to remind her of just how good they were together. "I don't want to make the same mistake."

"I'm not Frank. You aren't Amanda. We aren't who we were twenty years ago. I love you," he said roughly, and he heard her breath catch. He was pretty sure she loved him back, and before anything else happened, he wanted to put everything on the line. "I love you and I think you love me, but you're so busy living in the past you can't see the future."

"I'm over the past."

"If that were true, you wouldn't have hesitated, you would have already asked Frank to leave, and you wouldn't be using this situation to protect yourself."

"I'm trying," she said softly. "I just need time to figure things out."

"There isn't anything to figure out. Either you want this or you don't. I want to be with you so bad I don't care about the clinic because I know we'll figure it out together. Because I'm in. All the way in. I need to know if I'm alone."

"You're not alone."

"Then why haven't you answered his question?"

He watched her swallow, watched the struggle in her fathomless brown eyes. "This would be like me asking you to choose between your family and me."

"That's the difference between us—you are my family. And if you don't know that, then I don't know what we're doing here."

She was quiet for a long moment and that killed him. It fucking killed him.

"I love you," she whispered, although it didn't feel like a declaration so much as an albatross around her neck, weighing her down and taking her under.

"Love shouldn't be a burden, Bianchi." If it was, he was doing it wrong. Maybe the problem was he loved too much. Amanda had left because she felt suffocated, Maddison was moving across country to find freedom he couldn't give her, and Teagan, *God,* Teagan . . . She'd once left him because she'd said he would have kept her from the life she wanted.

He'd lost so many people he loved over the years, he didn't think he could handle one more.

"Do you love me?" he asked.

"This isn't about you and me, it's about giving the father of my kids another chance to make things right."

He could blame it on bad timing or wanting different things, but none of that mattered when someone was in love. Message received, loud and clear.

The dull emptiness in his chest was more painful than he'd imagined. It felt as if his lungs were filling with ice water and his heart was struggling to beat in the face of the piercing agony.

He stared at her, taking in the way she smelled, how soft her hands were in his, and how perfect she was. But unless she was willing to push past the fear, no amount of time and space would help.

"You're giving the wrong man a chance."

Chapter 27

Love is not determined by the one being
loved but rather by the one choosing to love.

—Stephen Kendrick

Harley's heart was breaking for her sister, and she didn't know how to help. She wanted to murder Frank.

But she had a pretty good idea Colin would tell her to get in line. So she'd done the only thing she could think of to help, distracted the girls with catching sand crabs.

Each of her nieces had her own pail filled with sand and a little seawater. A dozen burrowing crabs tickled the bottoms of their feet as the waves rushed back into the ocean and the little creatures dove into the soaked sand, leaving tiny air bubbles in their wake.

After they had a pailful, Harley held their hands as they waded knee-high into the ocean. They waited for the water to rise over the top of the pails and as the wave rolled back out, they tipped the pail out and watched the crabs skitter sideways across the wet sand.

A gentle wave rolled in, pushing the crabs back, but instead of fighting the force, they surfed the tail of the tide. Instead of running from an obstacle that was five times their size, they danced from side to side, finding a new perspective, then jumped right in again until they found their footing back on the sandy shoreline.

When it came to life, Harley was like the crab, more alive when she was surging into things head-on. In love she let the waves of emotion throw her off balance. Keep her from riding the surf. She was afraid that the tide would pull her under. Instead of riding the wave of feels, she'd gotten caught in the riptide—pulled out to sea, alone and scared.

Harley, the sister and aunt, was no longer scared of love. She'd faced more waves these past few months than in her entire life, and she'd learned to dive back in and find her balance.

With Bryan she was ready, for the first time, to dive back into the tide, back into Bryan's life. If he'd still have her.

With the girls settled on the blanket, eating their Otter Pops as the sun set, Harley pulled her phone out of her pocket.

> I DECIDED TIME IS OVERRATED.

> DEPENDS ON WHAT YOU DO WITH IT.

A strangled laugh escaped and the words became a little blurry. She quickly texted back.

> I DON'T KNOW WHAT I WANT TO DO BUT I WANT TO DO IT WITH YOU.

> UNLESS YOU HAVE OTHER PLANS.

She'd never considered he might have other plans. Other female-centric plans. She'd been gone for two months with only a handful of texts as communication. She wouldn't have waited for her.

> I'M SORRY I RAN.

THE GOOD THING ABOUT
RUNNING IS YOU USUALLY
END UP RIGHT BACK WHERE
YOU STARTED.

WHAT IF WHEN I GET
THERE NO ONE'S
WAITING.

Wasn't that her biggest fear? That when she found her way home, there'd be someone counting down the time until she left.

THERE'LL BE A PIECE OF
PAPER ON THE TABLE
WITH MY NUMBER ON IT
BEGGING YOU TO CALL ME.

I'D CALL. LIKE A REAL
CALL WHERE I COULD
HEAR YOUR VOICE.

YOU NAME THE TIME.

NOW.

I LIKE NOW.

ME TOO.
ACTUALLY I WANT TO SEE YOU.

She so liked now. She needed now. But she'd run so far from him, they were a good five hours distant from each other. And she couldn't just leave Teagan high and dry. She knew her sister would need her more now than ever.

> MY SISTER KIND OF NEEDS ME. HOW ABOUT MONDAY?

> MONDAY DOESN'T WORK FOR ME.

Right. Like other adults, he worked Monday and Tuesday and Wednesday, and all the weekdays.

> HOW ABOUT NEXT WEEKEND?

> I'M STILL STUCK ON NOW.

> I RAN TOO FAR FROM YOU FOR NOW.

> DID YOU KNOW THAT I WAS ALL-STATE IN CROSS-COUNTRY, THREE YEARS RUNNING?

> DID YOU SEE WHAT I DID THERE? RUNNING . . .

Harley laughed, a tear popping out all on its own. Her heart did some popping too. Right there in her chest, beating faster and louder as if, it too, was smiling.

> WELL, THIS TIME I'M
> RUNNING TO YOU.

> . . .
> . . .

Who knew her happiness could come down to three little dots.

> LET ME TEXT YOU THE
> FINISH LINE.

> PS. I'LL BE THAT GUY
> ON THE SIDELINES
> CHEERING YOU ON.

> LAST TIME I RAN A MARATHON
> I WOUND UP AT A DOUGHNUT
> SHOP.

> THEN I GUESS I'LL JUST
> HAVE TO SCOUT OUT
> EVERY DOUGHNUT SHOP
> ON THE COURSE.

Harley was done with letters and coded messages. She wanted to hear his voice, tell him the one thing she should have told him months ago.

She pressed the phone button and dialed him. It rang exactly once before he answered.

"Hi," she said the second the call connected.

"Hi back," he said and, God, his voice made her want to laugh and cry all at the same time. His low, gravelly voice reminded her of every happy memory they'd had together—which was mostly all their memories together.

She clutched the phone closer. "I miss you."

"I miss you so damn much it's hard to breathe," he said, his voice in stereo. She turned and there he was, standing at the top of a sand dune, looking like her very own prince, in flip-flops, a pair of low-slung jeans, and a dark gray T-shirt.

With phone to ear, he started toward her.

"What are you doing here?" she said into the phone, her legs moving toward him as the distance between grew closer and closer.

"You told me you missed me," he said, and then he was right there, in front of her, flashing that smile. The one that said, *Hi, hello and I'm yours*. It was so achingly familiar, her heart melted.

"But you're here." Still talking into the phone, she looked up at him. "At my nonna's house."

"Actually, we're on the beach." He took the phone from her and pocketed it along with his own. "I'm short doughnuts but I can get some if it would make you stop crying."

"I'm not crying." She felt her face to discover that she was, in fact, crying. "They're happy tears."

He stepped so close she could smell his familiar cologne and ten months of memories.

"Then they can stay." He reached out and cupped her face, the pad of his thumb wiping away her tears.

"Why are you here?" she repeated, because she needed to make sure this wasn't some Otter Pop–induced hallucination.

"There's this girl who drives me crazy."

"A good kind of crazy?"

"The best kind of crazy. Only she needed to be here for her family, so I decided someone needed to be her for her. Do you need me, Har?"

"So much, you have no idea," she admitted. "How did you know I'd need you tonight?"

"Your sister may or may not have called."

Harley didn't know what to say, but her tears were back. "Teagan?" Her loving, amazing, wonderful sister, who'd had the worst night of her life, had reached out to him. "Wait, when did she call you?"

"She texted. You Ashford sisters must have some big beef against calling."

"Bianchi sisters," she said. "My grandma was a Bianchi, my mom is a Bianchi, my sister is a Bianchi. And all along I was a Bianchi, but I was too scared to recognize it. See, I come from a long line of powerful women."

"Makes sense."

She looked up at him. "It does?"

"Honey, you are the strongest, smartest, and sexiest person I've ever met." His hands slid around her waist, tugging her snug up against him. "Did I mention sexy?"

She hugged him tightly. Her heart, which had been beating frantically, slowed to match his grounding rhythm. Why had she assumed he was the reason for her antsiness? He was her rock, the one person in her life who understood her, had her back no matter what. Well, she had Teagan now, but her sister was the rock for a family full of people. With Bryan, she was it.

He hadn't just told her, he'd shown her in the way he held her, listened to and respected her, and the way he kissed her. Speaking of kisses. He wasn't just all-state in cross-country.

"I'm so sorry I ran. I started missing you the moment I left, and every day it's gotten worse," she admitted.

"I love you."

She stilled, her hands breaking out in a sweat, her heart racing. He loved her. "How?"

"How can I not?"

She did too. The day she'd figured it out was the day she'd run. It terrified her because she wanted to stay.

"When did you know?" Suddenly, this was the most important conversation of her entire life, and she didn't want it to end.

"I think it was that time at O'Malley's bar when I asked to buy you a drink and you told me to fuck off."

"That was the first night we met."

"I've always been a little more advanced."

She laughed. "That's good because I'm a little slow on the uptake."

"Then we make a good team," he said, and this was when Harley had to lay it all on the table.

"I think I love you."

His smile was warm and gentle. "I know."

"How?" She wasn't even sure until right that second, when a million butterflies took flight in her belly and her heart told her head that this was the guy. This was her guy.

"For a card shark, you have a lot of tells."

"And one of my tells told you I love you?"

"Yup," he whispered. "The same one that's telling me you want to kiss me."

This time he didn't wait for her. His mouth came down on hers, and Harley actually felt her life begin. Felt the fear and the insecurities drift out with the tide, as their lips gently glided over one another, drinking each other in.

"Are you going to marry my auntie?" Poppy asked.

Harley pulled back and Bryan laughed. Standing right next to them, looking up with their big blue eyes, were her precious, adorable, snooping nieces.

Bryan hunched down to their level. "I have to get her to move in with me first."

Poppy looked up at Harley. "Do yous want to moves in with him?"

Her gaze met Bryan's. His was open and gentle, as he patiently awaited her reply. She decided that he'd been patient enough—he deserved the same kind of fierce loyalty he'd given her.

"Yes."

"She says yes," Poppy relayed, and as her little nieces grinned up at her, Harley realized that a life with Bryan meant a life away from being a constant in the girls' life. She didn't want to go back to being a drive-by aunt, but she didn't want to lose Bryan.

"Hey." He stood. "What did we say about crying?"

"I want to live with you, but I don't want to leave my family. I've just found them . . . I can't leave them."

"Good thing I rented us a house in town."

"You rented a house?" she croaked. "When?"

"Right after you told me you needed time."

"You've been here for a month?" That made her cry more. "How long were you planning on staying?"

"As long as it took," he said. "And I mean it, as long as it takes. You get to set the pace, the rules. You're running this rodeo. And before you ask me why again, it's because you're it for me, babe."

"You want to catch sand crabs wif us and Auntie Harley?" Lily asked, and now Harley was crying even harder. That was the first time Lily had ever said her name.

Everything in her world tilted back to right as she watched the man she loved take her nieces' hands. He looked up at her. "What do you say, Auntie Harley? You want to go catch sand crabs?"

Teagan rested her head against the kids' closed door. It took everything she had to keep it together while tucking them in. But the dam finally broke, and every tear felt like it had been torn from her soul.

She'd blown it. Big-time. Colin had reached out to her, asked to stand with her under the umbrella, and she closed it on him. Shut him out and stomped all over his love. He'd had the courage to speak those magical three words and, the first time their love had been tested, she'd thrown it back in his face. Just as she had all those years ago. Only this time, she was present to see the devastation and disappointment on his face—disappointment that he'd trusted her.

That he'd allowed himself to love her again.

She called Jack to figure out a plan, horrified when she burst into tears. He promised to give her a week to make things right. But first she had to make things right in her personal life.

She walked downstairs to find Frank sprawled out on the

couch as if he lived there, remote in hand, watching the base-ball highlights. As though he hadn't obliterated her world once again. Only this was worse than losing the bakery and her marriage—this was like losing a piece of herself.

One of the best pieces of herself.

"Go pack your bags and get yourself a hotel room."

He sat up, looking baffled. "What about the birthday party?"

"Talk to your lawyer."

"Since when do we need a lawyer?" He paused, clearly think-ing of a new strategy, then flashed the boyish smile that had once stolen her heart. Only, her heart wasn't available to be stolen. It was already taken. "This is me, TJ."

"It's Bianchi now. I changed it back."

He looked horrified and heartbroken. "When?"

"When you were supposed to be in rehab. I filed for a name change the same day as I filed for divorce."

"I need a drink."

She snatched an unopened beer—Colin's beer—away. "You need to listen. The girls and I need space to heal, to find our footing, and continue to grow as a new family."

"We're a family. You, me, and the girls."

"You and me, we are co-parents." She sat down next to him. "You and the girls are family." She softened her voice and placed a comforting hand on his knee. "You are always going to be my kids' father. Always. And I will always love you. But you're not good for any of us. Not like this. You need to get your shit together, get a job, your own place, and clean up your messes. I'm done taking care of you. It's long past time I took care of myself. I came to Pacific Cove for a fresh start, to tap into a part of myself I'd lost. I'm making a new life for myself and the girls, and you aren't a part of it."

"Is he?" Frank asked. His tone said he was close to crying.

"I hope so." God, she hoped so. "Colin makes me better, and I treated him horribly tonight. That's on me. The debt, that's on you and you're going to do whatever it takes to remove it from my name."

"Teagan Rose Bianchi," he clarified.

"Teagan Rose Bianchi," she agreed softly. "And so help me God, Frank, if you screw this up, you will never set foot in this town again. Understood?"

"Understood."

Her newfound backbone had him looking a little shell-shocked. Which was good. He needed his world to be shaken if he was going to change. And his kids deserved a father who put them first. She was no longer willing to meet him halfway. Oh no, he needed to rise to become the kind of co-parent she'd become.

The kind of dad she'd witnessed in Colin.

He covered her hand. "I never meant to ruin things between you and Dr. Dolittle."

She laughed. "Yes, you did."

"Okay, I did. But not if it means making you cry."

"I know. But you still need to go pack." When he didn't move, she gave him a little shove. "Now. And when you pick the girls up tomorrow and take them to their favorite place for waffles, you will explain the situation. And whatever you tell them it will be honest, age-appropriate, and reassuring. There will be no blame, no bad guy, just you reassuring them that no matter where you live, you will always be there for them and put them first."

Frank squeezed her hand. "I know I have a long way to go to earn back my place in their lives, and your trust, but I'm going to."

"I hope so, because we have amazing kids."

"They have an amazing mom." They stood and he brushed a sweet kiss on her cheek. "Who I hope will steer me right when my GPS goes wonky."

"I happen to have an excellent internal GPS." And it was pointing to the sweet, supportive, and sexy man next door whose love she had to earn back. Frank wasn't the only one who needed to right some wrongs.

"That's good because I'm blanking. Where's the girls' favorite waffle place?"

"Seriously? You've been here for weeks!" Wow, as she said it aloud she was shocked that Colin had stuck it out as long as he had.

"Kidding. It's Coastal Café," he said, heading toward the guestroom. He paused at the entry to the hallway. "Is that on Lighthouse or Coral?"

Teagan grabbed a throw pillow and made it earn its name. Frank ducked and it hit the wall. After he was gone, Teagan picked up the pillow, wondering if righting her wrongs with Colin would be as easy as a conversation.

It didn't matter. She was going to do whatever it took.

She set the pillow on the couch just as someone started to slow clap. She turned around to see Harley standing in the entry to the kitchen.

"Impressive," Harley said. "I'm inspired."

Chapter 28

If you don't annoy your big sister for no good
reason from time to time, she thinks you don't
love her anymore.

—Pearl Cleage

"You're inspired to kill Frank?" Teagan laughed and walked into the kitchen. On the counter sat a bottle of chilled champagne and two mason jars. "What's this?"

"A celebration."

"What are we celebrating?" she asked. "Me being a complete idiot and ruining everything with a pretty amazing guy?"

"Been there, know where you're going with this," Harley said.

"I have no idea what you're talking about."

"I'm talking about celebrating your divorce, for one." Harley poured a glass of champagne and handed it to Teagan. "Love." She poured herself a glass and held it up in toast. "And reclaiming lost parts."

Since that was something Teagan could get behind, she tinked jars.

"Where did you get this?"

"The store. I went when you were tucking in the girls."

Teagan hopped up on the island counter in an all-in, rules-be-damned, crisscross position, then patted the tile right next to her.

"This must be a new part, because even Tiny Teagan didn't break house rules."

"I guess I found some new parts along the way too."

Harley hopped up, and when they were facing each other she said, "So have I." Harley looked Teagan in the eye. "I heard what you were saying about needing space for you and the girls and I get it. Which is why"—she picked up the bottle—"I'm moving out." She took a big gulp straight from the bottle.

Teagan was doing some gulping of her own—on air.

"Where?" Teagan said as Harley offered her the bottle. "Why?"

"Hello? You've had one visitor too many for weeks. Since you sent Frank packing, I figured it was a good time for me to rehome my macramé hammock."

"I hate that thing." Teagan leaned close. "But I love you, and you're not a visitor. You're my sister."

"Exactly." She took another gulp. "You're my sister, not my mother. Say it with me. S. I. S. T. E. R. So we both need to start acting like it."

"But this is your house too."

"Actually, it's not. It was my home when I was a kid, but now it's yours."

"It can be ours." When Harley shook her head, Teagan grabbed the bottle and took a good, long swig, burping up the bubbles when she was done. "Nonna would want that."

"No, Nonna wanted us to heal our sistership. Don't you see? Nonna left you the house and me the car because it was her way of telling us that she loved us for our own unique qualities."

"But the girls love having you here. I love having you here. Don't go," Teagan begged.

"And I love being here, which is why we'll be staying in Pacific Cove for now."

Teagan stopped. "We?"

"Bryan and I."

Teagan felt a momentary dreamy smile take over her grief. "He came?"

"He came." Harley's eyes filled. "And we're moving in together. Well, more like moving around together."

"Oh my God." Teagan leaned over to hug her sister. "This is amazing news."

"I hope so because we want to stay in PC."

"When did it happen?"

"Don't play innocent. He told me you called."

"Yeah, like three hours ago."

Harley hugged herself, and Teagan realized she'd never seen her sister smile that way. She looked free and vulnerable and in love. If it weren't her sister's moment, Teagan would have burst into tears herself—not the good kind.

"When I was on the beach with the girls, he showed up and we had a long talk."

"The girls know?"

"I swore them to secrecy. I wanted to let you have the space you needed to process."

"I'm too upset at myself to even start processing." She was more than upset; she was crushed. She'd hurt someone she loved because she couldn't distance herself from her troubles; she wasn't about to make that mistake with her sister. "Distract me with your tales of happily ever after."

"We're not going there, yet. But you were right, he's special. I can't let go of special. And I guess he thinks that about me because he said he just wants to be with me. As I am. He knows that I don't sit still well so he told his boss he's going to work virtually. We can pick up and travel as much as my antsy pants desire."

Teagan choked up because she was so happy for her sister. And so incredibly sad over the disaster of her own making. She might not have left Colin a *Dear John* letter this time. What she'd done was worse. Just as she had with Harley, she'd taken his love and loyalty for granted.

She had a lot of making up to do with the special people in her life. Starting with Harley.

"I am so happy for you. But why rent when you can stay here?"

"Um, the offer is sweet, but Bryan and I are way too loud to live below my nieces' bedroom. Plus, did I ever mention that we do a lot of role-playing?"

Teagan shoved her fingers in her ears. "TMI."

Harley pulled her fingers out. "TMI can't penetrate the sacred bonds of Sistership."

"Gross. You said penetrate." They both laughed, and between the two of them made a serious dent in the champagne. "While I'm happy for you, selfishly I don't want to lose you. You're already going to be gone for months at a time. What about all the milestones? Our business?" An idea began taking shape. "Why waste money on rent when you can live in the apartment above the garage? Wow, that sounded way more appealing in my head."

"You mean Zia Iris's place?" There were two rooms with a bath and small kitchen—perfect size for world travelers. "I didn't even know it still existed. I thought it was storage."

"It is."

Harley studied her for a long moment. "Where will you put all of Grandma's stuff?"

"Renting a storage unit is a fraction of the cost of an apartment in PC. Especially since you'll be traveling."

Harley studied her cautiously for a long minute. "Are you sure?"

"Yes, but I can tell I'm going to have to earn your trust," Teagan said, and Harley smiled at her own words.

"Are you saying I have to pay for the storage unit?"

"S. I. S. T. E. R. Remember?" Teagan took a sip, then held up the bottle. "Plus, families stick together. Ohana."

"Drink on it." Harley held up the bottle. "Raise your glass if you are wrong."

"In all the right ways," Teagan added.

Together they sang the chorus—off-off-key. When they were giggling so hard the words were inaudible and the bottle was empty, Harley took Teagan's hand in the way only sisters hold hands and said, "Can I keep the swing down here?"

Teagan shoved her. "Don't push it."

"Okay, then let's talk about what went on with the sexy doctor next door."

And that's when the tears she'd been holding back spilled over. "I screwed up, Har. I screwed up so bad, and I don't know how to fix it."

"Lies. My older sister can do anything she sets her mind to. She once told me, 'In the times you feel like you're drowning, always remember, you are braver that you believe. Stronger than you seem, and smarter than you think.'"

Teagan rolled her eyes. "Christopher Robin said that."

"Actually, my sister—the smart one with the occasional stick up her ass—said the first half, and everyone knows you need two halves to make a whole."

"Like us?" Teagan asked.

"Like us." This time when they hugged neither of them let go for a long, long while.

"Now, where are the spare binders and color-coded tabs? We need to get organized."

And as she sat there crying over an empty bottle of champagne, formulating her next steps, Teagan remembered what it felt like to have a sister.

It felt like finding a best friend all over again.

Chapter 29

I want to be the reason you look down at
your phone and smile, then walk into a pole.

—Unknown

It was past seven in the morning when Teagan finally dragged herself into the kitchen, her eyes red and her heart raw, every cell aching from what felt like an endless night of crying.

Harley had stuck by her side through the worst of it, even crawling into bed with her the way they used to when they were kids. Teagan fluctuated between hope that Colin would forgive her and panic that he wouldn't.

She'd managed to shed her shirt—one of Colin's that she'd stolen last week—put on a sundress, and cover up some of the shadows under her eyes, but the grief she saw staring back at her was gutting. It took everything she had not to crawl back into bed.

With all she needed to do to prepare for her appointment with Jack, hiding in her house for a week and crying into a gallon of ice cream wasn't an option. Neither was not letting Colin know exactly how important he was to her. He owned her heart.

She and Harley had come up with a solid plan to settle up with Jack. It was the plan to win back Colin that had her heart pounding. God, she'd been so stupid. She was so busy trying to avoid another heartbreak, she'd betrayed Colin's trust in the same way Frank had shattered hers, letting her financial mistake ruin his dream.

She'd called Jack first thing, asking him to meet her at the shop. He'd sounded a little amused, which made her even more nervous. She was confident in her solution, but she'd clearly screwed up everything so far.

Like Colin. God, thinking about the look on his face last night made her want to cry all over again. But if she had any chance of winning back his trust, she first needed to make things right.

Taking a deep breath, telling herself there would be other shop locations, even though she knew there would never be another one like this, she opened the door.

"Mr. Kimble?" she called out, then noticed him sitting behind the counter. "Thank you for meeting me here so early. I can't even tell you how sorry I am about this mess, but I stayed up all night figuring out a solution. And I want you to know that Colin had nothing to do with the problem. It's all on me. Colin is an amazing man, and I hate that I burned a favor of his so please don't hold this against him. I reprinted the lease agreement and took Colin off as a cosigner. I have it signed."

On the way here, she'd stopped at the bank, where she'd started the process to take a home loan on the beach house. Since the house was paid off, it didn't matter that her credit was toast. Sure, she was given a ridiculously high rate, but she was confident that she could pay it off in three years.

The home loan broke her heart all over again. Rose had left her a house free and clear so that she and the kids would always have someplace to land. Her nonna had been so proud of the day she'd sent in her last payment. Nonna was just one more person she'd let down.

"Even if you don't want me as a tenant, I will pay you back for every penny you've sunk into the remodel. I'm also willing to pay you a year's rent up front. I'll do anything to make this right."

"Anything?" an unbearably familiar voice said. "That's a pretty broad offer. I think you need to define it for me."

Her breath caught as Colin walked out from behind the counter. He was in dark jeans and a dark green shirt that matched his eyes, which were impossible to read.

"What are you doing here?" she asked.

He headed for her. "I knew you'd come."

"You've been waiting for me?" she asked, emotion pushing up from her chest, stinging her eyes.

"Since five. I know how early you rise."

"I am so sorry—"

He cupped her hips, silencing her. "You already apologized. Now it's my turn."

"What do you have to apologize for?"

He looked her in the eye. "I was so focused on how I'd survive you walking away that I did before you could."

"I would never walk away."

"I know and that makes what I did even worse. I said I loved you but I didn't back it up. You can't walk away from love. Love is unconditional, and only works when you listen to your heart."

She swallowed. "And what does your heart say?"

"That, for me, you're it. You were my beginning and if you say yes, my end. I love you, Teagan. I hope to God you still love me back."

"My heart says yes, it has always said yes. I was just too busy listening to my brain."

"And now?"

"Here." She tapped a finger to his chest—right where his heart was rapidly beating.

"Thank Christ, because I finally found you again, and I never want to let go. So if you could still have this place, would you want it?"

She looked around. "So much, but I don't want to drag you into my financial disaster."

"But I have a really good plan. You know how I love a good plan. And this may be my best one ever."

A bead of hope flickered to life in her belly. "I'd like to hear it."

"You, Teagan Bianchi, are the smartest, most capable and amazing woman I've ever met. And you might not need me, but I need you. If you're open to sharing this space, with me, I'd love to be your office neighbor. I've decided to open my own practice, half vet office, half free animal clinic, where I can live my life listening to my heart and not some rigid formula."

"As long as I get the kitchen."

"As long as you promise that after hours is a thong optional time."

As Teagan went up on her toes and kissed the man of her dreams, she realized that Colin wasn't just her first or her last. He was her everything.

Epilogue

Some crushes just never went away. They built,
instead, into something permanent, obsessive
and all-consuming.

—Maya Banks

"That's right, Bianchi. Grip it tight," instructed Teagan's husband of just six days. Her body quivered when he wrapped his arms tightly around her, delivering a hot little kiss to her bare shoulder. "There you go. Let it slide though your fingers a little, *oh yeah*, just like that. Now lean back."

"Like this?" she asked.

"Lower," Colin said, and Teagan went lower.

"Lower?"

"Even lower," he whispered in her ear. And when she went lower still, she gave a little twist of the hips, which had Colin groaning in approval.

"What was that?" he asked.

"Me, leading with my hips." She pressed back farther into him, loving how his big body curled protectively around her. With him in nothing but low-slung board shorts and tanned skin, her body did some curling of its own. "The article I read about windsurfing suggested twisting the hips. The guy said it tells the board where to go with great authority."

"This guy says if you want to remain upright, then you might want to hold off on that twisting for now." Sliding his hands over hers, he leaned back. "You ready for this?"

"I'm not sure," she admitted.

"Do you trust me?"

Teagan looked over her shoulder at the man who'd reminded her that honest, deep love wasn't a gimmick sold by Hallmark. "With all my heart."

"Then hold on."

Teagan leaned all the way back into his body and watched as the wind caught the sail. It flapped, then pulled tight. For a brief moment, she thought they were going to tip over. Then Colin leaned all the way back and the board evened out and picked up speed—a lot of speed.

Teagan slammed her eyes tightly shut.

They were in the middle of the ocean—okay, maybe fifty yards from the shoreline, but it felt as if she were in the middle of the Gulf.

Knowing that she'd never made that trip to Disney World, Colin had booked them a two-week stay. One week on land at the parks with the girls and Maddison, who was heading off to NYU at the end of the summer, and the next week just the two of them on the water, where they were staying in a suite on the Disney cruise ship.

Right now, they were *on* the water, and she was pretty sure she was going to hyperventilate. Windsailing had been her idea, one of those face-your-fears efforts that had turned out to be the worst idea ever.

"Are we done yet?"

"Just rest against me," he said, his voice calm and reassuring. "I'm not going to let you fall."

"The article didn't mention that windsurfing is like a roller coaster on the open ocean."

"I think of it as foreplay," he whispered in her ear. "Open your eyes for me, Bianchi. I know how much you like to watch."

That had her laughing, and it was hard to be scared when laughing. It was impossible to be scared when wrapped in his arms.

Slowly she opened one eye, and when it wasn't so terrifying, she opened the other. And just like that, her world opened up. The board skimmed the clear waters of the Bahamas. Beneath them, purple coral and neon fish dotted the crystal-blue ocean. And the wind kissing her face felt exhilarating.

"I'm doing it!" she said, giving herself over to the moment and just letting go.

"And you're doing it in a white bikini," he said.

That had been her present to him—a teeny-tiny white bikini. It wasn't the one from high school, but it was pretty dang close. She'd worn it the first night of their honeymoon, and he didn't seem to care that she came to bed dressed in swimwear. Funnily enough, his present to her had been a bouquet of thongs, each with a coordinating IOU about all the things he was going to do to her in them.

They'd blown through four just that morning and she was excited to get back and see what kind of gift mango lace brought.

"Do you like it?" he asked.

"I love it." She looked over her shoulder and into the eyes of the man she was going to spend the rest of her life with. "And I love you."

Being the master multitasker, he was able to kiss her silly while still maintaining control of the board. Instead of turning back toward the shore, she gave a little twist and turned the sail toward the golden and fuchsia horizon—and a future filled with laughter and love.

If you enjoyed *Situationship*, you won't want to miss *RomeAntically Challenged* and *Hopelessly Romantic*.

ROMEANTICALLY CHALLENGED

"Fun, flirty and fresh!"
—*New York Times* bestselling author Jill Shalvis

"Marina Adair is a breath of fresh air. . . . Don't miss a word from this magnificent author!"
—*New York Times* bestselling author Darynda Jones

Growing up the lone Asian in a community of WASPs, Annie has always felt out of place. Her solution? Start a family of her own. Not easy when every man she's dated, including her ex-fiancé, finds "his person" right *after* breaking up with Annie. Even worse than canceling the wedding eight weeks beforehand? Learning the "other woman" plans to walk down the aisle wearing *her* wedding gown. New plan—find a fresh, man-free start. Too bad her exit strategy unexpectedly lands her working at a hospital in Rome, Rhode Island, rather than Rome, Italy, and sharing a cabin with a big, brooding, and annoyingly hot male roommate.

Home on medical leave after covering a literally explosive story in China, investigative photojournalist Emmitt embarks on his most important assignment—cementing his place in his daughter's life. Three men and a baby might work in the movies, but with a stepdad and devoted uncle competing for Paisley's attention, Emmitt has lost his place at the family table. Then there's the adorably sexy squatter in his cabin, who poses another problem, one he'd very much like to solve up close and personal. But he can't win—Annie has sworn off men, Paisley's gone boy crazy, and Emmitt's estranged father reappears with a secret that changes everything.

Annie and Emmitt are about to discover love comes in many forms, and sometimes the best families are the ones we make.

HOPELESS ROMANTIC

"Adair just keeps getting better!"
—*New York Times* bestselling author Jill Shalvis

Set against the breezy backdrop of coastal Rhode Island,
bestselling author Marina Adair's latest novel asks whether
two of a small town's biggest hearts can learn to put
themselves first—in the name of love . . .

As caregiver for her autistic brother, Beckett Hayes knows how
meaningful a little extra help can be when life happens. Which
is why she runs Consider It Done, a personal concierge service
in her small town. Her job also gives her the flexibility to follow her passion, being Rome, Rhode Island's unofficial special
needs advocate, training emotional support companions in her
spare time. There's not much of that, though, and certainly not
enough for serious dating. It's always been family first for Beck.
But one unquestionably gorgeous, good-natured man is suddenly a temptation that's getting tougher to resist . . .

Sixteen years ago, Levi Rhodes was ready to sail off into the
sunset—literally. But then his father's death and his sister's unexpected pregnancy postponed his sailing scholarship and the
adventures he had planned. Running the family marina and bar
was the least he could do for his grieving mother. Plus, his niece
needed a father-figure. But now that she's in high school and has
her bio-dad in her life, Levi's wondering if it's time to get his sea
legs under him again. Or he *was* wondering, until curvy, caring
Beck showed up in his bar, and then in his dreams . . .

Praise for Marina Adair

"Small town sweetness, endearing characters
and a unique quirky flair."
—Carly Phillips, *New York Times* bestselling author

Turn the page to check out Gage and Darcy's story,
Chasing I Do,
an Enemies to Lovers romance in stores now!

Chapter 1

Darcy Kincaid had dreamed about this day since she was six and uncovered her mother's stash of *Southern Wedding* magazines in the basement. After a lifetime of planning, handpicking two thousand of the palest of pink peonies, and her entire life savings, she was about to pull off, what she believed to be, the most romantic "I Do" in history. The sun was high, the sky was crystal blue, and a gentle June breeze carried the scent of the nearby primrose blooms and ever after.

Today was the perfect day to be married, and the rose garden at Belle Mont House was the ideal backdrop. And Darcy wasn't about to let a tail-chasing wedding crasher ruin her moment. No matter how charming.

Not this time.

"Nuzzling the bride's pillows before the wedding will only get you escorted out," Darcy said to the four-legged powderpuff in matching pink booties and hair bow.

The dog, who was more runway than runaway, dropped down low in the grass, eyes big black circles of excitement, tail wagging with delight—her jewel-encrusted collar winking in the sunlight.

Darcy squinted, but could only make out the first word. "Fancy." The little dog's ears perked up and her tail went wild.

"Such a pretty name," Darcy cooed, taking a cautious step

forward. "I'm Darcy; it's nice to meet you. I'm going to come a little closer so I can get a better look at your collar and find your mamma's number. Is that okay?"

With a playful snort, the animal's entire body was wiggling as if so excited by the idea of making a friend she couldn't hold in the glee. Darcy reached out to ruffle her ears, and Fancy, confusing Darcy's movement for time to play, snatched up the pillow and gave it a good shake.

"No!" Darcy cried, halting in her tracks while little bits of stuffing leached into the air, causing perspiration to bead on her forehead.

Fancy, on the other hand, wasn't worried in the slightest. Nope, she gave another rambunctious whip of the head before jumping up and down with the pillow as if this were all fun and games.

Sadly, this situation was about as close to fun and games as natural childbirth. Not only was the vintage silk pillow, a family heirloom passed down from the bride's great-grandmother, in danger of becoming a chew toy, but the bride's ring was swinging dangerously from the aged ribbon.

And this wasn't just any bride. Candice Covington was the former Miss Oregon, a Portland mover and shaker, and the first bride to be wed at the newly renovated Belle Mont House. Candice was already in the bridal suite, her beloved in the tower room, and two hundred of their closest friends and family were set to start arriving in just over an hour—and the dog looked content to nuzzle the pillow all afternoon.

With its teeth.

"Stop!" she said in her most authoritative tone, putting her hand out.

To Darcy's surprise, the dog stopped. Her snout going into hypersniffer mode, she dropped the pillow to the grass and rose up to smell the air. Seemed Fancy had caught the scent of the prosciutto-wrapped figs that Darcy had been tasting, and she stood up on her hind legs, then walked around in three perfect circles.

"Someone's got moves," she said. "Not bad, but mine are better."

A decade of planning events for Portland's pickiest clients and four years in the trenches as a single mother had taught Darcy the art of positive redirection. She'd lasted through potty training, teething, and chicken pox. This stubborn ball of fluff didn't stand a chance.

Eyeing the flower arrangement on the closest table, Darcy grabbed a decorative stick and gave it a little shake. "Want to play with the stick for a while?" The dog sat, eyes wide, head cocked to the side in an explosion of cuteness. "We can switch toys before you destroy the pillow, okay?"

"Yip!"

Tail up like a heat-seeking radar, the dog hit the fetch-and-retrieve position, pointing her nose toward one of the open fields.

"Ready?" Darcy wiggled the stick again for show. "Go get 'em!"

The stick flew through the air, going as far in the opposite direction as it could. Darcy released a sigh of relief when it cleared the fountain and landed in the middle of the field.

A low growl sounded, followed by a blur of white fur that bolted past.

Those little legs working for the prize. A position Darcy could relate to.

Located in the prestigious West Hills, Belle Mont House was three stories of Portland history with extensive manicured gardens, six bedrooms, a grand salon, and captivating views of the city and Mount Hood—all of which needed to be meticulously cared for. And Darcy was the sole caretaker.

She had driven by the old property a thousand times over the years. But she hadn't really recognized its potential until after her world had fallen apart and a heartbreaking betrayal had left her life in tatters—much like the foundation of this forgotten house. Unable to watch something so beautiful and full of history crumble, she'd saved it from demolition, then spent every penny and waking moment renovating it back to its original grandeur. In return, Belle Mont had given her something even more precious—a future for her and her daughter.

Today marked Belle Mont's first day in operation as the year's "Most Romantic" wedding destination in the Pacific Northwest and Darcy as its planner extraordinaire—according to the editor at *Wedding Magazine*, who'd left a message earlier about sending a high-profile couple to check out the location.

A couple so hush-hush, the editor refused to give the name for fear that the press would show. But if they decided that Belle Mont was their dream wedding venue, and Darcy could accommodate them with the last Sunday in July, the only date that worked around the couple's hectic schedule, then Belle Mont would land a huge spread in the August issue.

The endorsement alone was enough to make her say yes on the spot. Not to mention the profit for hosting such a lavish event would go a long way toward helping pay back all the money she'd invested into the renovation—and secure her future in Portland.

A future that now resided in the jaws of a dog that could fit in her pocket.

Fancy snatched the stick and darted across the lawn toward the twinkle-lit and peony-covered gazebo in record time—all with the pillow still in its jowls.

"Hey," she called out, "we had a deal!"

The dog's tail went up as if flipping the bird at their deal before she ran beneath a row of chairs and struck a different kind of pose altogether. A move that showed enough doggie bits to prove that under that pink bling, Fancy was all male. And about to shit all over Candice's perfect day.

A situation Darcy knew all too well.

"Had I known you had a stupid stick down there, I wouldn't have bothered trying to reason with you."

In Darcy's experience, men loved the forbidden almost as much as they loved their stick. So she fumbled with her skirt, pulling it above her thighs, and gave chase.

Fancy took off, and man, those toothpick legs could fly. Ears flapping behind him, butt moving like lightning bugs in a jar, the pooch headed straight for the rose garden, which lay directly across from the aisle runner that had CANDICE AND CARTER spelled out in the palest of pink peony petals.

"Not the runner!" she cried, only to watch in horror as Fancy raced up the center of the white pillowed Egyptian cotton, his legs pumping with the speed and grace of a cheetah in the wild, leaving a few dozen miniature muddy paw prints and a tornado of petals in his wake.

"No, no, no!" she called out. "Not the rose garden."

Terrified of the damage he could do to the roses and the pillow, she picked up the pace and rounded the white iron fencing, gravel sliding under her heels as she burst through the gate and snatched the pillow right before the Fancy dove his fancy-ass—and Candice's ring—into the fountain.

"Got it!" she yelled, but the celebration quickly faded as her momentum carried her forward—and right into the stone cherub boy's watering hole.

"Oh God, no!" Darcy yelped as water exploded around her.

Having landed ass first, she felt the cold wetness seep through her silk skirt and slosh into her shoes. Her brand-new designer shoes she'd found at a consignment store and purchased especially for today. "Please, no."

She clawed the edge of the fountain and pulled, mentally willing herself out of the fountain—but she couldn't gain any positive momentum.

No matter how hard she tried, she just couldn't pull herself out.

Refusing to give up, she looked around for Fancy, hoping to either send him to find help or pull him in with her. But he'd vanished, right before the wedding, leaving her waist-deep in his mess.

The situation was so painfully familiar, Darcy wanted to cry. Then devour the entire wedding cake in one sitting.

"Are you okay?" a husky voice asked from above.

"Thank God you're here," she said, pushing her hair out of her face and looking up, expecting to find one of her kitchen staff.

But instead of a clip-on tie with a comb-over, Darcy's unexpected hero looked like an underwear model in a dark blue button-up and a pair of slacks that fit him to perfection. And his arms—oh my, those arms—were impressive, perfect for helping a lady in need.

Although Darcy had worked hard to not be reliant on others—a lifetime of letdowns could do that to a girl—she knew that sometimes it was okay to take an offered hand. And those hands were big and solid and—whoa—reaching forward to wrap around her hips and easily lift her out. . . .

CPSIA information can be obtained
at www.ICGtesting.com
Printed in the USA
LVHW100036280522
719965LV00002B/34

9 781496 727688